OF BLOOD & SECRETS

FORSAKEN BY THE GODS
BOOK 2

T. B. WIESE

Cover design by GetCovers

Map by biblopolium on Fiverr

Keir hound chapter art by Jade Merien

Editor: Bookschecked

ISBN: 978-1-959657-04-0 ebook

ISBN: 978-1-959657-05-7 paperback

ISBN: 978-1-959657-06-4 hardcover

OTHER BOOKS IN THIS WORLD

- Of Spirit & Hope
- Of Blood & Secrets
- Of Power and Darkness

To Asta

You kept going, so I knew Thaeia could keep going too.

"Push past your limits."
- Captain Yami of the Black Bulls

AUTHOR'S NOTE

**Please take care of yourself and your mental health

Of Blood & Secrets is an ADULT fantasy that contains elements such as: abuse, anxiety, explosions, blood, torture, death, forced suicide, infanticide, emotional abuse, gore, violence, physical abuse, profanity, PTSD, light religion, sexually explicit scenes, and it ends on a cliffhanger

PRONUNCIATION GUIDE

Hello wonderful reader,

First off, I want to preface this with - if you find it easier or more natural to pronounce these names another way, go for it! This is your story now. Have fun.

But, if you're curious how I pronounced these names, here you go...

characters
    THAEIA: They-ah
    NOR: rhymes with four
    VALSAN: Val-san
    KEIR: rhymes with fear
    NEZERA: Nez-er-ah

places
    SODOLES : So-dough-leys
    KAPROS: Ka-prose
    ALOPSON: Al-op-son
    DRAKAM: Drah-kum
    KA CRUMMENS: Kah Crew-mens

AKARETH: Ah-car-eth
OXTARA: Ox-tar-a

creatures
PRAZAR: Pray-zar
HAGRAVEN: Hag-ra-ven
BASILISHOUND: Bas-ill-ish-ound

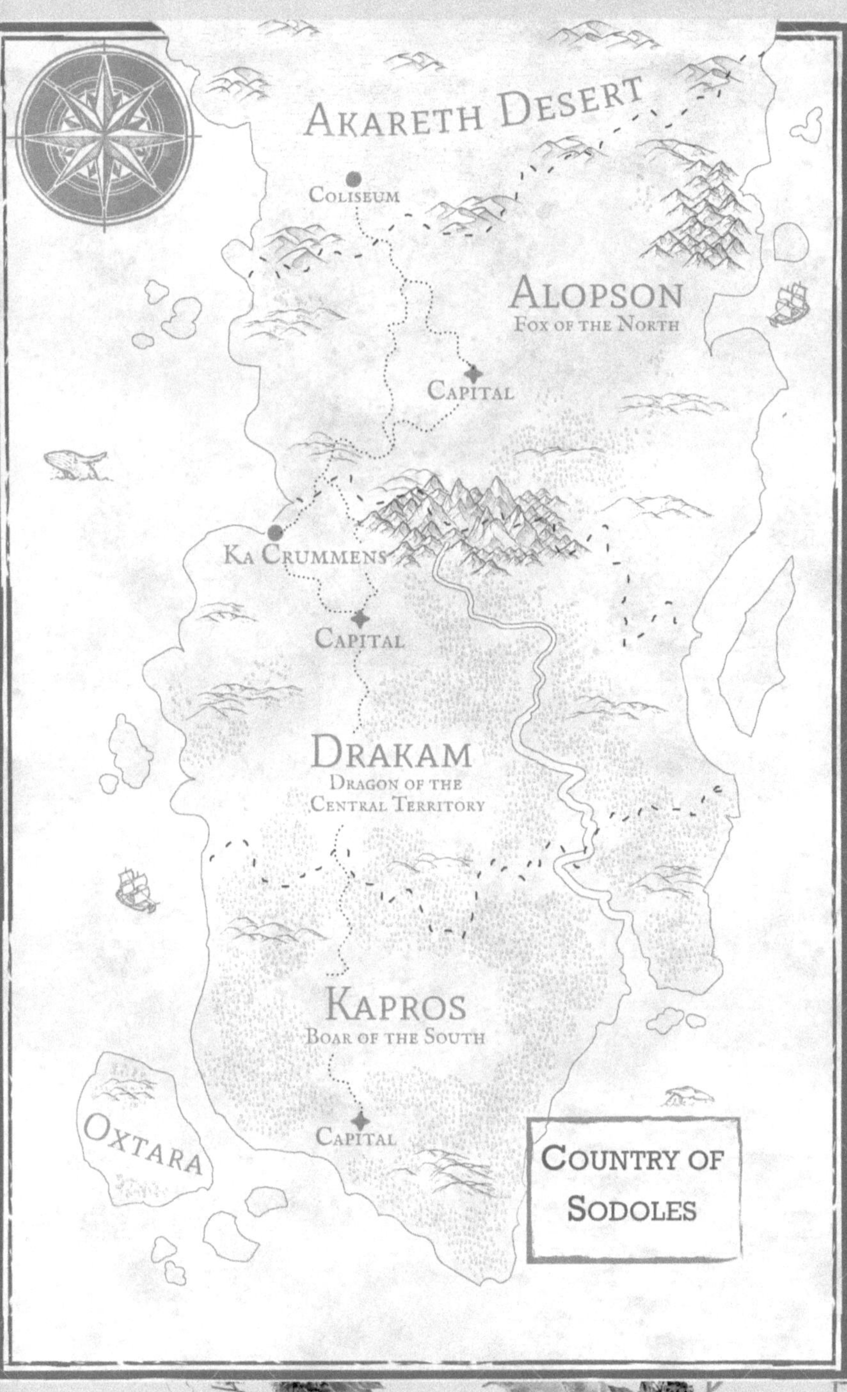

AKARETH DESERT
COLISEUM
ALOPSON
FOX OF THE NORTH
CAPITAL
KA CRUMMENS
CAPITAL
DRAKAM
DRAGON OF THE
CENTRAL TERRITORY
KAPROS
BOAR OF THE SOUTH
OXTARA
CAPITAL
COUNTRY OF
SODOLES

WHAT CAME BEFORE

(book one synopsis)

Thaeia believed herself to be cursed by the gods to live without magic in a world where everyone is blessed with power on their twelfth birthday. Not only didn't she receive a gift, but an invisible void came into being around her that temporarily swallowed the magic of anyone that gets too close to her. The people of her small island reacted with fear—especially her best friend's father, who declared her cursed, forsaken, worthless. He poisoned his son against her, stealing away the one person she thought would be by her side forever.

Nor didn't want to turn on his best friend, but he feared Thaeia's void. What if the gods curse him just for being her friend?

The two grew up at odds, at best avoiding each other, at worst, trading insults—and even blows—each burying the pain and guilt of what they were doing to each other. Thaeia never left the island due to her surrogate mother's warnings about the outside world, but in one night, everything changed. On her deathbed, Thaeia's surrogate mother revealed a half-destroyed family crest that was with Thaeia when she was left on her doorstep as a baby.

So, with her mother figure gone, Thaeia decided to set out to find the answers to her past. She ended up traveling with Nor (reluctantly) and one of her only friends from the island, Halee. Both of them travel north to compete in the magic games that only happen every five years. Thaeia doesn't intend to go that far, aiming for the large port city of the central territory to try and book a ship to a kingdom across the sea that bears a crest vaguely similar to the one her surrogate mother gave her.

Along the way, Nor runs into an old flame, the captain of House Kapros, Valsan. Valsan and three of his fellow guards are also traveling to the games, and Valsan is as eager to reconnect with Nor as Nor is with him. With Valsan's gentle prodding and advice, Thaeia and Nor begin to realize the fear and anger between them needs to be healed, that they love each other still, and that they need to find a way back to their friendship before it's too late.

Thaeia's young friend, Halee, an Animal mage, also meets the handsome and bashfully charming Miles, a plant mage. The two instantly form a crush that blooms into a real connection.

As they travel, Nor and Thaeia work through their friendship with plenty of bumps along the way. But when Thaeia arrived in the port city, the storm season was rolling in, preventing her from leaving. So, she's talked into staying with her friends, agreeing to go to the Magic Games to cheer them on.

She was having a good time, considering that maybe her mother was wrong, and it wouldn't be too bad for her out here in the world, even with her curse. Thaeia celebrated with her friends, enjoying her freedom. But after waking with a raging hangover, she discovers she enrolled herself to compete in the games while in her drunken stupor—and her first match is to be against the top mage —Keir, the son of the Lord of the most powerful House in the country.

With her Void, and the extensive training she received from her surrogate mother growing up, she was able to beat Keir, catapulting herself to epic fame. All seemed great until the next day, at the start of the team competitions. Explosions rocked the coliseum, injuring many, killing some—the obvious target being Thaeia.

Before she passes out from pain and blood loss, she sees the telltale red flames of Keir's magic. Is he coming to help her? Or was he part of the attack against her?

In book two, we pick up right where we left off ... So here are the final few paragraphs from book one just as the group competition of the magic Games is about to start. Hopefully this settles you back into the world and what's happening.

Enjoy!

THAEIA

The mallet begins its descent. Why does it seem to be moving so painfully slowly?

There's a deafening sound. I'm knocked from my feet.

My ears are ringing. Dust and debris billows from the west wall. I shift, coming to my knees. There's blood on the ground. Another drip splashes down from my head. Oh, it's my blood. What's going on?

My legs wobble, but just as I find my feet, another boom rocks the Coliseum. Screams begin to break through the high-pitched tone in my ears. Wiping the blood from my face, I blink through the dust. It's chaos. People are shoving and scrambling over each other, trying to get out of the Coliseum. The entire west wall of the arena is caved in.

Is that ...? Yes, there are bodies trapped under the rubble. Nor is there, using his magic to lift the larger pieces of stone as others drag the bodies free.

Stone and sand fly through the air as another explosion rips the north wall apart. Without thinking, I sprint across the arena. If this is someone's magic, I have to stop it. I stumble as another loud boom sounds to my right, and more screaming rips through the air. It's happening all around me. Too fast. The explosions are coming too quickly and too spread out. I skid to a stop, turning a tight circle. I need to help. I need to stop this. I can stop this if I can just find out whose magic this is. Scanning the crowd, I look for anything suspicious. Someone concentrating. Anything. Any clue. I freeze as the smell hits my nose. Powder. Powder and metal. This isn't magic. This is man-made.

The world around me erupts in white light, fire, and pain. The wall in front of me explodes, and as I'm sent flying through the air, I hear my name screaming on the wind. Nor. He needs to get out of here. Everyone needs to get out of here. Where's Halee? The others? Who would do this?

I don't feel myself hit the ground. There's just burning and a never-ending loop of agony as skin rips, bones break, and muscles tear. Nor calls my name again. My head falls to the side. Everything is blurry. I blink, trying to clear my vision but all I see is haze, smoke, dust, fire. The edges of my vision darken. There. There's a bright point of red light. Not the angry color of the fire burning around me, but a pure red, like light shining through a brilliant ruby.

Darkness closes in, and as I black out all I have left is sprit and hope ... hope that this isn't the end.

CHAPTER 1

KEIR

Is she dead?

Smoke, ash, burning embers, and dust obscure the arena around me. I sprint towards where I saw Thaeia go down, ignoring the stabbing pain along my left side. I'm pretty sure a few of my ribs are cracked, but I'll live. My left hip is bruised but I'm still able to move, the adrenaline taking away most of the pain and allowing me to run without too much of a limp.

The surface of a large chunk of sandstone wall grates against my palm as I brace and vault myself over the rubble. A scream rings out from up in the stands, followed by a pop. There's a grumble of noise, then several shouts as people panic, calling up their magic which only adds to the chaos. Then everything quiets as others use their power to calm and direct the massive crowd from the destruction of the Coliseum into the tent city sprawled to the east. The shift between fear and bravery, between panic and calm, has been teetering one way then the other ever since the explosions began.

My eyes water, and my red Spirit flames reflect back onto me through the thick smoke. Gren growls, and a moment later, both he and Hich puff out as my flames extinguish and my magic snuffs out.

Well, Thaeia is alive.

Waving my hand, trying to clear the air, I stumble to keep from stepping on Thaeia's outstretched arm. I drop to a knee. Fuck. There's so much blood. The screams of the people trapped in the wreckage blend with the once again rising shouts of the panicking spectators attempting to flee the Coliseum. As I look over Thaeia, the noise fades. Her right pant leg is torn, revealing swelling from her knee to her ankle that is destined to become a deep bruise. That's probably broken. There's blood pooling from a deep slash in her right side, and her right arm is bent at an awkward angle. Her shoulder looks dislocated.

At least her skin is warm and not clammy as I brace my hands on her arm and joint, moving slowly until I feel the bone line up. There's a loud pop and crack as I twist and push, and her shoulder slides back into place. I wipe my hand across her face, trying to clear some of the blood seeping from a cut along her hairline, but I only manage to smear soot and sand into the blood.

The noise settles, and I know my father's Emotion magic is sending a sense of calm across the crowd.

"Keir!" My father, the Lord of Alopson's voice rings out from behind me up in the stands. "Find my son!"

Sorry, Father.

Thaeia's head lolls against my shoulder as I haul her into my arms. I'm about to stand when the desert night breeze clears the air before me for just a moment. There's just enough light from the fading day to illuminate Valsan as he meets my gaze from the other side of the arena. His eyes flick to Thaeia before snapping back to my face. We stare off for a single moment before he nods then jerks his head to my right. That simple move gives me permission to take her—because while I've known Valsan for many years, and consider him a friend, I know if he thought I meant Thaeia any harm, he'd come for my head. My lips press tightly as I nod back just as the smoke thickens again, obscuring Valsan along with everything else around me.

I plant my foot, stand, and take off. Skirting debris and giant chunks of destroyed wall, I duck into a partially collapsed tunnel. I pause to adjust my hold on Thaeia when the wind once again clears the way for me to see back into the arena. Right where I just stood, where Thaeia fell, there are three—no wait, five, grey-clad forms. Smoke blows around them concealing them one moment and revealing them the next. Their cloaks cover them from head to boot, the muted color blending into the dust, sand, and stone around them. Their heads swivel back and forth, one pointing towards the pool of Thaeia's drying blood. I lose sight of them as thick smoke hangs in the air between us.

Pulling back deeper into the shadows, I hide behind a large chunk of fallen ceiling partially blocking me from the arena. Hugging Thaeia's bloody, unconscious body, I do my best to shield her as another break in the smoke exposes the grey-clad forms once again. They lift their heads in unison, glance around, then turn and run off, quickly disappearing into the dust and smoke of the recent explosions.

Who the fuck were they? My thigh muscles bunch with the desire to run after them, to sic Gren on them to petrify them, and drag them before my father. Some instinct whispers inside me that they have something to do with all this, and anger flashes through me so intently, my hands actually shake. Taking a deep breath, I rub a hand down Thaeia's back. Before anything else, I need to get her away from here. I'm about to turn and head deeper into the tunnel when a flash of red catches my eye. Two guards from my House now stand where Thaeia fell, looking around. One lifts their head, calling out something I can't hear, but a second later, Valsan jogs over looking annoyed with a scowl on his face. The three exchange quick words before Valsan shakes his head, gesturing around him to encompass the chaos and destruction before he turns on a sharp heel and runs off. The two Alopson guards watch him go before they turn in the opposite direction and jog off.

Are my guards looking for Thaeia? Me? Those grey-cloaked people?

My hand presses against Thaeia's back. I don't know who orchestrated this attack, but I do know three things: Whoever they are, they are after Thaeia; People have died, and that won't stand; And I will give my life to protect the woman in my arms.

From the arena, the slapping of running feet draws near. I tense, shifting closer to the wall to protect my back, ready to set down and defend Thaeia if necessary. A woman with wild eyes, soot-stained skin, tangled hair, and blood dripping down her arm, runs right by. She doesn't slow, and I'm not sure she even saw me.

Shuffling back, I maneuver Thaeia over my shoulder so I can move faster. She sways across my back as I make my way down the tunnel, my free hand trailing the sandstone wall to help me find my way in the dark. If I had my magic, my red Spirit flames would illuminate the tunnel, and my loyal basilishounds would lead the way out.

My hand flexes around Thaeia's thigh. As long as she is near me, my magic will stay dormant, but that's okay. The absence of my magic means she's still alive. But in order to keep her that way, I have to get her out of here. And not just out of the Coliseum, out of the desert, and to ... where? Do I take her to my estate? To House Alopson? She's from Kapros. Do I try to get her home? My chest expands as I take a deep inhale. This is going to be ... tricky. I'm a pretty high-profile person. Okay, I'm very high-profile. People are looking for me. Who do I trust? My father? Of course I trust him. But do I lay Thaeia at his feet and take that chance? I trust Valsan, but he has entrusted me with Thaeia's safety for now. So, do I take her to Valsan's tent? No. Too obvious, though I don't doubt the Kapros captain's ability to protect her.

A small smile twitches my lips. Valsan really is nauseatingly good, and it still annoys me that he continues to refuse to leave Kapros and come to Alopson to work for me.

I shake my head, knowing at some point I'll need to reunite Thaeia with Valsan and her group of friends, and together we can all decide the safest way forward.

The flickering of flames ahead draws my focus. I creep along the edge of the tunnel as I approach the opening that leads to the camps. Poking my head out into the cool evening air, I blink against the light of glowing arsine torches that weren't there a few hours ago. There is a torch placed every few paces around the outer border of the tent city.

Those went up fast.

As I scan the area, a red-clad guard of my House walks along the perimeter, dropping in and out of the bright white torch light. Just as he's about to dip out of sight, he turns and walks back the way he came.

Father works fast. It seems we are in lockdown. Smart.

A young man, a boy actually, stumbles between the tents, heading for the perimeter. The guard holds up a hand, and when the boy doesn't stop, he gently grabs the young lad's shoulder. "You need to stay in the camp, son. Are you here with anyone?"

The boy's eyes fill with tears, and he bites his lip. "Yeah, but I lost them in the crowd. There was so much pushing and shoving and yelling. I couldn't breathe. There was so much smoke."

The guard lifts his head, keeping his hand on the boy's shoulder. He calls out, and in a matter of seconds another Alopson guard strides over. As they exchange a few words, I use the distraction to slip from the tunnel. Ducking between a tight row of tents, I make my way steadily southeast. Without breaking stride, I whip a blanket off the top of a stacked pile. With a flutter, the scratchy fabric settles over my head and around Thaeia. I clutch the blanket in front of me like a cloak, tilting my head down, keeping my steps steady. The lack of my red Spirit flames is a disguise in itself, but I'm not taking any chances. My shoulder is hot and sticky from Thaeia's blood, so I pick up my pace. I'm surprised by how quiet it is, but when I skirt around a dark, quiet tent, angling towards my own, I spy a mage walking slowly between the tents, her left arm raised. As she passes a torch, I recognize her. A Serenity mage.

Making sure to keep Thaeia out of her range, I stick to

the shadows as much as possible. I move through the Drakam camp, eventually crossing into the Alopson section. A quick glance to my left reveals patrols of my father's guard continuing around the perimeter with the occasional green-clad Drakam guard walking by as well. I recognize Marcus, one of the guards of House Alopson, with his left hand clenching and unclenching, adding his Halcyon magic to help keep the peace.

The adrenaline is wearing off, and my injuries are starting to make themselves known. Thaeia is getting heavy. My thighs strain as I trudge through the sand until my private tent comes into view. Keeping my head down, I look left, right, then poke my head into my tent. Finding it empty, I duck inside. With a shrug of my shoulders, the blanket flutters to the ground. The glowing embers in the stove provide enough light for me to see, and my boots make sandy imprints on the carpets as I cross the large space, carefully setting Thaeia on my bedding.

Quickly crossing back to the entrance, I secure the flaps to make sure no one barges in unannounced. Throwing a few fresh logs into the stove, sparks dance as I gently blow to help the flames catch. On my way back to Thaeia, I lift my shirt, wincing at the bruising along my ribs, but it's not too bad. I'll see a Healer at some point. Looking down at the battered woman laying in my bed, my heart aches. Healing magic won't work on her. I need to get her to Valsan, but I'll wait for things to calm down at least a little before I either bring him here or attempt to get her to him.

Of course, if Thaeia would be so kind as to wake up, I could ask her what she wants to do and we could come up with a plan together ... but she's worryingly pale and unmoving.

Cracking my neck, I kick my boots off and fill a basin. The water sloshes gently as I set it on the floor near Thaeia's head. My fingers skim across her cheek. "Come on, Fox Slayer. Wake up. Open those golden eyes for me."

Her eyes remain closed, her breathing shallow, but she moans in pain, her nose scrunching before relaxing, and she falls back into deep unconsciousness.

I sigh. "Okay. You keep resting. I'll patch you up as best I can."

Grabbing one of the thin towels near my bathing supplies, I flex, ripping it into long strips. The soft swish of the material running through the water soothes me as I slowly work my way from Thaeia's hairline down her neck, cleaning the worst cuts first, making sure all the dust and sand are clear. The basin is already tinged a dirty pink, so I toss the water on the open section of sand near the stove.

Over and over, I refill the basin, cleaning Thaeia. With careful fingers, I maneuver her shirt over her head, averting my eyes as much as possible. I drape another thin towel over her chest, then carefully examine her injuries. Her bruised and bleeding skin enrages me, and my fingers flex with the desire to call up my magic and send the Spirits out to hunt down whoever did this, but at the same time ...

She is so beautiful. Lean muscles cut down her arms and across her stomach, but she's still somehow soft. Her shallow breaths cause her full breasts to rise and fall under the thin towel. With gritted teeth, I manage to get her clean down to her waistband. My back is tight, and I swallow around a building headache. Her pants were already tight, but now they're sticky with blood, and her right pant leg is torn and burnt.

I find myself yearning for her eyes to blink open and for her to snap some pithy remark on my impropriety. Glancing at her face, I shake my head with a small smile. "Feel free to punch me when you wake up, Fox Slayer, just know I'm doing this with nothing but purely good intentions."

My gaze travels from her tangled hair, across her bruised forehead, taking in her arched eyebrows, the slope of her nose, the curve of her lips, the rise of her cheeks. I recall her brilliant laughter in the bar tent that night. She was radiant, the crowd drawn to her joy. I couldn't keep my eyes off her. Still can't.

Even bruised and broken, she's perfect.

I shake my head. "Okay, Fox Slayer. I'm doing this with *mostly* good intentions. But it seems you have entranced me with a magic all your own."

Unbuckling her thigh sheath, I palm one of her throwing knives before I set the rest to the side. The steel glints in my hand, and I pause, staring at the four inter-locking circles embedded in the blade. There's something familiar …

The tearing sound seems overly loud as I cut her pants off, leaving her underwear on, because I'm a gentleman. It's a struggle to get her free of the ruined fabric without jostling her too much, and by the time I wrestle her free, I'm puffing and sweating slightly. It's deeply concerning that she hasn't stirred yet. What if there's internal bleed-ing? What if she never wakes up? What if she dies here in my tent?

I breathe through my spiraling thoughts, dipping a fresh piece of torn towel into the basin. The water is cool against my fingers, calming me, but then my movements slow, my hand hovering over her hip. Water drips onto her skin as I just stare wishing she'd wake up, that she'd smile or rage or cry or hug me or hit me … something. I can't stand seeing her so broken, so still, so …

Gripping the wet cloth tight, I lower my slightly trembling hand and finish cleaning her one torturous inch at a time. Eventually, I sit back on my heels, satisfied. Okay. I should brace her leg in case it is broken. But that wound on her side needs stitching. A bruise colors her shoulder from being dislocated, but it will heal fine in time. The cut on her head has stopped weeping blood, and now it's just a slow oozing. There are several superficial burns dotting her skin, but luckily—and I have no idea how—none of the burns look too bad.

I blink my exhaustion away as best I can, reaching over to the small sewing kit next to the basin. With a small swish, the tie falls away, and I unroll the folded leather. I frown at the slight shaking of my hand as I pinch the small needle between my fingers, but then I freeze as a conversational tone with a hint of tension sounds from right outside.

"Maybe he's made it back to his tent."

My back stiffens with a jerk of muscle as the voice draws nearer and another one calls out, "Lord Keir?"

Adrenaline spikes, allowing me to move lightning-quick. Tossing the needle into the folds of the kit, I fold the leather over itself. I grab a few blankets and throw them over Thaeia. I toss some pillows around her as I call out, "Yes?"

There's a soft murmur, "Oh, thank the gods." Then his voice rises. "Sir, are you injured?"

"Nothing too bad. I'm fine. I just came here to change." The shadows of the two guards move to the front of my tent, and I bark, "Is there something you need?"

There's a pause, and their shadows turn to look at each other before one says, "Your father is looking for you. But if you are hurt, he will want you to see the House Healer."

My nose wrinkles. I really dislike our family Healer. Lafayette has been with our family for years, his stooped form haunting our halls as he shuffles about. I look around, panic scattering my concentration as I call out, "I'm sure Lafayette is busy. I'm fine. Nothing too bad."

The guard outside coughs, "Regardless, he'll make time for you, my lord. Once you've seen the Healer, we are to escort you to your father's tent. He has called a meeting of the Houses."

Rolling my shoulders, I sigh. I imagine after today's events, my father will have at least one guard on me at all times from here on out. Glancing at Thaeia, I rub a hand over my face. This is getting trickier and trickier.

With hurried movements, I pull a blank piece of paper from one of my many notebooks. My writing is rushed and sloppy, but I shove the note into Thaeia's hand, curling her fingers around the paper. Sliding a pillow under her head, I arrange the blankets and extra pillows over her, covering her completely. Stepping back, I make sure my bed simply looks rumpled and messy. No one should come in here, knowing I like my privacy, but just in case ...

With a wince, I yank my bloody shirt over my head and drop my pants to my ankles. I kick free, quickly running a wet piece of towel over my skin, amazed that I made it through those explosions with minimal damage. I have Hich to thank for that. My loyal hound had whimpered a second before the first blast even went off. He'd pulled on the strength of my magic, almost draining me then and there, but it allowed him to solidify long enough to slam me to the ground. And while his and Gren's Spirit bodies couldn't fully block the flying debris, they hovered over me, keeping me from getting up before the second and third blasts ripped through the air.

Without looking, I grab a new shirt and pants, foregoing underwear as I dress quickly in the red and black colors of my House. Father will expect me to dress according to my station, representing House Alopson as the future head of our territory. My position as the forthcoming Lord of Alopson has never felt as real or as heavy as it does right now.

Doing my best to shake off the growing shadow of my future, I stuff my feet back in my boots, taking one last look at my bed where Thaeia lies hidden. I should tell my father. He'll know what to do.

But why does my heart kick faster at that thought?

I stride across the tent which is large enough for me to slip from Thaeia's Void before I reach the entrance. My hounds appear at my sides with soft growls, which is good because I'm never without my basilishounds. If my guards were to see me without my Spirit flames, there would be questions. Gren's growl goes deeper as his head turns back to look where Thaeia is hidden. A soft clicking sound from me brings his attention back to me. I shake my head, whispering, "Leave it."

Gren's ears twitch, but he drops his head, sticking to my side, Hich trailing close as I unlatch the flaps and duck out into the darkness of this nightmare of a night.

CHAPTER 2

NOR

Wiping my eyes, I clear my vision of the blood trickling from a cut on my eyebrow. My right shoulder throbs from where a large chunk of the Coliseum wall slammed into me after the first blast. Valsan had thrown me to the ground, shielding me from the worst of the debris.

With a glance to my right, I see Val on his knees, his large hand wrapped around the arm of a woman with glazed eyes. His back flexes as he tugs her gently, trying to free her from the rubble that has her pinned. His shirt is torn, and there's already a deep bruise spreading across his ribs. He needs a Healer. He took that damage to protect me. Warmth spreads through my chest, but then it morphs into anger over the senseless violence inflicted today.

Lucas and a few other Light mages illuminate as much

of the Coliseum as they can, Fire mages joining in. Nezera has duplicated themselves, directing people to safety. Harland uses his thread magic to wrap and secure a bleeding wound on a man's leg, and a soft song floats on the night air as Kat uses her Siren magic to lead people to the exits that have been cleared of debris. Others have used their magic to suppress most of the flames from the explosions, but smoke and dust still hang heavy in the air. Others still send their power out to try and keep the panic at bay, but every now and then, a snap of magic flares and shouts ring out in fear before calm simmers everyone down again.

My arm trembles as I lift my left hand. Dust, blood, and ash coats my skin, nearly obscuring my tattoos. I'm close to my limit, but I will push until I have nothing left —that's the least I can do. I was within Thaeia's Void when the blasts went off, preventing me from shielding myself or the others. Rolling my shoulders, I look around. I'm one of the lucky ones. I might be a bit battered and bruised, but I'm alive, so I'll use my magic now to help until I can't anymore.

The large block of sandstone lifts as I draw up my Gravity magic. My stomach churns with the weight of the object, like there's a tether extending from my gut to the large piece of broken stone. It vibrates in the air, threatening to slip from my control, but Valsan is there, helping the woman to her feet. Gritting my teeth, I force my magic to move the stone from over the woman and the man I lo —admire.

With a grunt, I let go, and the giant hunk of stone slams to the arena floor, sand and dust billowing out, obscuring Valsan and the woman for a moment. I wave my hand to clear the air, seeing Val sweep the swooning woman into his arms before striding to the entrance of one of the many tunnels to pass her off. Triage tents have already been set up around the tent city, Valsan having volunteered our tent as one of the locations for the wounded to receive treatment from any Healers, Menders, and Restorers present. It's chaos, but controlled chaos now that the explosions have stopped and various calming magic hangs heavy in the air.

I blink, shaking myself out of the fog of exhaustion. Who could have done this? And why? No, I suspect I know why. I saw Keir leaning over Thaeia, and in that moment I almost crushed the lord. But there was a second where Keir and Valsan made eye contact, and Val's small, tight nod allowed me to rein in my rage and my magic. If Val trusts Keir, then I have to as well—because if I don't, I'll either collapse in terror, or run out of here to find Keir, lord or not, and squish him with my Gravity magic until he's no more than a smear of blood and goo in the sand.

No, right now, I need to focus on helping those I can.

Sorrow presses at me from the inside out, making it hard to breathe, but at the same time, I'm oddly tranquil thanks to the magic pulsing around the arena. It's an odd combination that makes my brain tingle with confusion. Anguish sharpens my focus, driving away the false serenity. There were those I couldn't help. The image of Anton's broken body flashes through my mind for the hundredth time. The Strength mage from our team didn't make it. He'd been standing directly to Thaeia's right, and he'd been torn apart by that first blast. Two other competitors from our opposing team died too, as well as several spectators who were seated closest to the explosions.

Yeah, I'm one of the lucky ones.

Valsan runs a hand through his black hair, tying half back. He turns as someone calls his name. The captain of the guard of House Alopson strides over, pale face covered in dust, her long blond braid spilling down her back. Daria's tattoo scrolls around her wrist spelling out, ORRIKEUM, for her Allusion magic. Her four stars flex as she clasps hands with Valsan.

"We need help over here!"

Spinning away from Valsan and Daria, I jog on shaky legs towards where the shout came from. A young woman holds the hand of a man on the ground. His foot is crushed under a section of collapsed wall, and his skin is clammy, his eyes wide with pain.

Lifting my left hand, I grunt. "Hold on, I've got you." My magic swirls in my gut, but I only manage to get the stone a few inches off the ground before it starts wavering. I grit my teeth, sweat trickling down my spine as I force my magic to hold. The woman yanks on the man's arm, tugging him out from under the hovering hunk of rubble. White dots dance at the edge of my vision, but I'm distracted by movement. At first, I assume it's just black soot mixing with my sweat to drip down my arm, but another glance reveals ink darkening my forearm. My third star outlines then fills in as the man finally scoots free, falling into the arms of the weeping woman. The stone thuds to the ground, and I double over, breathing through the exhaustion.

The woman helps the man to his feet, securing his arm over her shoulders as she says, "Thank you. Thank you so much."

I nod as they hobble off. I'm still dizzy, but I have a little left in me yet. I take the time to look around. The west wall of the arena was caved in, but we've cleared everyone that was caught in the rubble in that section, including the three bodies of those who didn't survive. The east wall had minimal damage that is now mostly cleared to allow people to exit. The north wall sits completely collapsed, a giant section of the seating area closest to the arena just ... gone. My gaze travels up. Drakam and Kapros got hit the hardest, the Alopson section barely touched. Significant? Maybe.

A hand lands on my shoulder, and I sigh into the familiar touch. Valsan steps in close, his wood-smoke and coffee scent overpowered by sweat, dust, ash, and blood. Still, I lean into him as he says, "I'm in awe of you. It's times like this I wish I had a more active magic. I can't help but feel slightly useless."

I turn into him, gripping his chin, his beard scraping my already tender skin from using too much magic, but I don't care. I never imagined Valsan had moments of weakness. He is so sure, so strong, so confident ... but the sorrow in his eyes reveals his vulnerability, and it nearly knocks me off my feet. "Val, your mere presence instills calm. The people of Sodoles trust you. They need you. I ... I ..."

A small smile ticks the corner of his mouth. "Yes?"

My fingers flex on his jaw before I playfully push his face back. "*I* need you. Okay? Happy?"

He presses a quick kiss to my lips, hovers, then kisses me again, going deeper, sliding his tongue against mine. All my aches and pains are forgotten as I let myself sink into Valsan's strength. When he pulls away, he rests his forehead against mine. "Yes, Nor. That makes me very happy."

I drop my hand, and his eyes shift. Grabbing my wrist, he holds it up between us.

"Nor! You have a new star!"

I manage a small smile and a slight nod. That doesn't seem important right now. People have died. So many are hurt. Thaeia ... I'm so tired.

Valsan sounds far away as he grips my shoulders. "Hey. You've pushed too hard. Come on. Let's get you to a Healer, or a Restorer. Yes, some Restoration magic will do you good."

"I'm fine." I don't sound fine. I sound exhausted, so I force some energy into my voice. "We have to make sure everyone is clear of the rubble. What if—" My head snaps around, and I nearly stumble from the wave of dizziness. "Where is Halee? The others?"

Valsan's hand lands on my back. "I saw Miles shuffle Halee out of the Coliseum. She seemed okay. Maybe a little banged up, but she was on her feet, and her eyes were clear. I'm sure the others are doing their jobs, helping where they're needed."

I run my hand through my hair, and even that small movement seems to take too much energy. "Do you think she's alive?" We both saw Keir sprint into the arena and scoop a limp Thaeia into his arms. The question is, who else saw? And is she alive? Pooling tears turn the destroyed Coliseum blurry, and I try to swallow them down. "She was so pale. There was so much blood. I couldn't tell ... was she breathing? Who did this, Val? Oh, gods."

He grips my arm, pulling me across the arena, dragging me into an empty tunnel. My back hits the wall, and I sink down, knees bending into my chest. I feel empty but calm, but I know that's just magic. Val crouches in front of me. "We have to believe she's alive. I trust Keir." He wraps his big hand around my calf. "Nor, I trust him or else I would have gone after her myself." I nod, my head feeling much too heavy. "But, Nor"—he squeezes my leg, and I lift my gaze back to his face—"we have to be careful. Whoever orchestrated this has shown their hand. They want her eliminated at all costs. And *we* brought her here. Everyone has seen us together. Daria said Lord Alopson has called a meeting of the Houses. We have to go."

I blink at him. "Okay. I mean, I don't want to let you out of my sight, but I can go back to the tent—"

"No. You were requested to attend. Everyone in the two teams that were present in the arena when the blasts went off has been summoned." The dark thought spills into my mind, *those that survived.* Fuck whoever did this. Val goes on, "Lord Alopson has already set his guards along the perimeter of the tent city. No one is being allowed to leave. House Drakam is assisting in patrols."

I can't help but notice the tightness around Valsan's eyes as I ask, "Are there other Kapros guards that came to compete on their own?"

He nods. "I have Aimee rounding them up, but there are only six."

"Six is better than none."

A tired smile lights his eyes for a moment. "Yes. I just wish ..."

As the lowest House, Kapros never has a large presence at the games. Lady Kapros didn't even bother attending this year. Which, now that I think about it ... was her absence deliberate? Coincidence? If *I'm* thinking it, then the other Lords surely are. So, not only are we from the same territory as Thaeia, she arrived here in Valsan's carriage with the captain of House Kapros whose

Lady is absent during an unprecedented attack in the neutral zone.

I ask, "How likely is it that we're going to be arrested at this meeting of the Houses?"

"Arrested? Unlikely at this point. Held for questioning? Probable. We'll—"

I slap a hand over his mouth as a low voice whispers from the arena just outside the entrance to the tunnel where we're crouched. "Find her. We need the body for proof." Running steps pass by, and I pull Valsan closer, deeper into the shadows. He shifts, and the glint of a dagger flashes in his hand. I reach for my magic, but the power is resistant to rise. It's sluggish, like trying to pull your boot out of sucking mud, but I yank, ready to attack anyone that comes into the tunnel. A grey-clad body peeks around the entrance to the tunnel, a hood hiding their face. Looking over their shoulder, they wave someone over, and another similarly clothed form appears. Who the fuck are these fuckers? The two creep towards us, and I press my magic against them to block them from coming any further, but Valsan holds up a hand, and I pull back slightly. He stands, stepping into the center of the tunnel, and I grip the wall, forcing myself to my feet. Val cocks his head.

Wait. Where am I? What's going on?

I shake my head, clarity sweeping back through my mind as Valsan focuses his Confusion magic away from me and on the two still approaching us. They slow, looking around, the one on the right scratching his head.

Valsan asks, "Who are you looking for?"

The one on the left shakes his head, but the one scratching his head says, "The Void? I think."

My back snaps with tension. These fuckers have the answers we need.

Valsan asks, "Why?"

Again, the one on the left shakes his head, his hand slapping over his mouth. The other one looks at the ceiling in confusion. "Why? The order. We're following orders. We have to find her."

"Shut up!" The man on the left grabs the other by the cloak, shaking him.

Val takes another step, and I plant my Gravity magic between him and the two cloaked men, creating an invisible wall that will crush either man if they attempt to charge Valsan. I clench my hands to keep from collapsing as a spasm rips through my stomach.

Valsan's calm voice urges, "Whose orders? Who wants her?"

The one on the right opens his mouth, but then both men stop, their arms dropping to their sides, their eyes going blank. I recognize the magic, but I can't move fast enough. My shout bounces off the arched ceiling. "Val!"

"I know." He sprints towards them as I drop my Gravity shield.

Too late. The Compulsion magic takes control of the two men. They each swipe a dagger from the folds of their cloaks, slashing their own throats. Blood pours down their grey cloaks, their eyes wide, their mouths open in silent objection. Whoever did this has very strong magic, or access to very strong magic ... so basically any of the Houses.

The men collapse, the occasional twitch of a hand or foot the only indication of resistance as they bleed out. Valsan and I kneel before them, each taking one. The rough, grey fabric is generic and cheap. The man I'm searching has brown skin, brown eyes, and brown hair. He's a medium build, and I lift his left arm, reading, EMTHARACTH, Intellect. No wonder he was able to resist Val's Confusion magic. I pat him down, finding nothing beyond the dagger he used to take his own life.

Sitting back on my heels, I glance at Valsan. "Anything?"

He shakes his head as he stands, then helps me up. The world spins before settling. I force my grip to relax around the bloody dagger. I do a double take, my eyes going wide as I stare down at the blade, blood dripping off the shiny steel.

"Nor, what is it?"

Lifting the dagger, I rub my thumb over the base of the steel. "This ... this is Saph's mark. This is one of her blades."

Valsan's voice is sharp. "The woman who raised Thaeia?"

I nod, my full attention on the four interlocking circles shining up at me. "There were rumors of her exceptional weapons craft before she moved to the island, but ... She never made a weapon in all the years she lived on Oxtara. Never."

Valsan picks up the dagger from the other dead man. "So, why do these men have Saph's weapons? And is this clue meant as an intentional misdirect, or a warning, or a sloppy mistake?"

I blink at the shining steel in my hand, Saph's mark staring up at me. What does this mean? How is Saph connected to all this? *Is* she connected? Is this just coincidence? Surely not. None of this makes sense, but I'm snapped from my spiraling thoughts as Val takes my hand, his skin is warm against mine as he tugs me closer before moving quietly towards the exit. "We need to get to the meeting, but we need to regroup first, find the others. We need a game plan. We need to be a united front before walking into the lion's den ... or the fox's den as it were."

"Wait. Maybe ..."

Sand scrapes under my boots as I skid to a stop, turning back around. Valsan doesn't resist though I see the question in his eyes. I kneel back before the dead men, ripping their cloaks off, throwing one to Val who catches it against his chest with a smile. "Good idea."

He grabs one man by the arm, dragging him to the wall within the darker shadows. It won't hide them for long, but it will be a while before they're found, hopefully. The scent of blood clings to my nose as I sweep the grey cloak around my shoulders and pull the hood over my head. Turning, I see Valsan has done the same. With a nod, we move back towards the exit, his growled whisper rippling down my spine, "We need to be careful, Nor. Right now, we're just pieces on someone's game board, and until we have more information, we can't allow them to use us."

I blink at his harsh profile inside the fold of the hood. He is *mine*, and I won't lose him. I won't lose anyone else. All I can do is nod, not sure if he even sees my acknowledgment. We remain silent as we break out into the desert night air, but only make it two steps before my throat closes, a sickly-sweet scent watering my eyes. My stomach turns, and I fall to my knees, acid scorching my throat as I vomit into the sand with a wet splat. Valsan staggers, but stays on his feet as a woman comes at us from where she was hiding behind a tent. "I've been looking for more of you grey fuckers. This time, one of you is going to tell me what I want to know *before* you take your own worthless lives."

Vesper? I hold up a hand, but choke on her poisonous vapor. I reach for my magic to push her poison away from us, but my power sputters in my gut, only making me more nauseated. I'm at my limit.

Shit.

CHAPTER 3

NOR

VALSAN TUGS HIS HOOD DOWN, and my fingers shake as I do the same. Vesper frowns. "You two were part of this?"

I jerk my head from side to side, her poison causing sweat to break out all over my body. Valsan staggers again, but holds up a hand. "No. We confronted two men dressed like this. They killed themselves when we questioned them, so we took the cloaks to infiltrate and hopefully get answers."

Vesper cocks her head, shifting her weight, kicking her left hip out and resting her hand there. I'd laugh at her sass if I wasn't in so much pain. Slowly, the nausea lessens, and I manage to sit back on my heels, gasping in deep breaths of poison-free air.

With a tap of her finger to her thigh, Vesper narrows her eyes at us. "One slip-up, and I'll have you puking up your intestines."

Valsan holds out his hand, hauling me to my feet as he says, "Fair enough. Has anyone told you to report to Lord Alopson's tent?"

She shrugs. "Yeah, but I figure it's gonna take a hot minute to gather everyone Lord Alopson wants in attendance, so why not poke around a little first?"

Valsan frowns. "Don't get yourself in too deep. Just go to the meeting, answer their questions, and go home. This doesn't have to be your fight."

The night air brushes across my face. I'm so grateful for the cool breeze, I don't even mind the fine grains of sand that strike my face.

Vesper stands tall, dropping her arms at her sides. "Not my fight? My best friend's leg was crushed. I don't know if even a Healer will be able to fix her. I saw a man with half his arm missing. A young man died in my arms before I could pull him from the rubble. So don't you stand there and tell me this isn't my fight. Now, I figure you and your merry band of friends are my best bet to draw out, if not the ones who did this, then someone who knows someone who knows something. You are my best bet at getting answers ... and vengeance."

I blink at her, my tired brain trying to follow her words. She wants to, what? Join us? Use us?

Valsan cocks his head, and I'm ready this time, but his Confusion magic steers clear of me. Vesper's brow furrows, and she licks her lips, looking around. Valsan places a gentle hand on her arm. "Why don't you just go home?"

She stares at Valsan, blinking. "Why? I told you. Vengeance. Payback."

"What do you want with Thaeia?"

"Thaeia?"

"Who wants her?"

"She survived? How the hell would I know? I'd just as soon stay far away from her, but if this is tied to her, then ..."

Valsan holds her for a moment longer before dropping his hand and stepping back with a nod. He tugs his hood back over his head, and I do the same as he says, "Okay then."

Vesper's brows scrunch, but she just shakes her head at Valsan as the three of us stay low and quickly move into the press of tents. Vesper peels off to the right, whispering over her shoulder, "Hold on." She ducks behind a colorfully striped tent, then a few seconds later comes back with her own grey cloak thrown around her shoulders and shrouding her head. Must have been one of those she found and questioned earlier.

We move silently, making our way through the Drakam camp, drawing ever closer to the Kapros section. A tight formation of a dozen Alopson guards approaches, directing people to triage centers or to their tents. One has their left hand raised, their tattoo spelling out the word for Tranquilize. They must not be using much of their power since those around them are still standing, but I'm sure it's helping with keeping the populace calm and well, Tranquil.

With our heads bowed, we duck down a side path between tightly packed tents before any of the guards see us. It's eerily quiet back here. The tent to my right glows with the soft light of a torch inside, hushed voices whispering within. Most of the other tents are dark, the entrances secured. A dark mop of hair pokes out of a tent as we pass. The man looks around, but upon spying us, stumbles back inside with wide, panicked eyes, the flaps of his tent snapping shut.

Just as we cross into the Kapros section, a trio of grey-cloaked people rushes by, ducking in and out of the shadows. My muscles tense, and I turn, ready to run after them, but Vesper halts me with a hand on my arm. "You two go on to the meeting. I'll follow those goons and see what I can find out. I'll rejoin you before too long."

Valsan narrows his eyes. "No."

Her brow raises, but her shoulder hitches up with indifference, and the three of us move silently after the cloaked forms. They continue in a straight line, aiming ... shit, right for our tent. Valsan's hand lands on my right arm, and we turn, cutting through the shadows, picking up into a sprint. Planting my boot, I swivel at the next turn, kicking up sand as we cut the trio off. They skid to a stop, cloaks flaring around their bodies before settling. Valsan holds up a hand, and the three relax at the sight of our cloaks. The one in the middle asks, "No luck?"

Valsan shakes his head, and Vesper says, "You neither, obviously. What now?"

My lips twitch with a smile. This woman is fearless.

The one on the right shoves his hood down, revealing a shaved head, brown skin, brown eyes, and a short black beard. "We have a few more hours until we're supposed to report back, so we keep looking."

The one on the left rolls their shoulders, a light feminine voice coming from under her hood. "It's so weird feeling so calm when I know I should be tense as if I'm dangling over the pits of the Everafter. Plus, this Compulsion magic is uncomfortable. I'm not too keen on finding out what happens if we fail."

We all stand in silence. I have so many questions, but I

don't know what will trigger the Compulsion magic. We have an opportunity here. I have to say something. "I overheard there's a meeting happening soon between the Houses. Are we in danger of being sold out?"

The one in the middle cocks his head, and my muscles bunch, ready to crush them if my question has raised suspicion, but the woman turns to her companions with the beginnings of panic in her voice. "Are we?"

The middle one shakes his head. "No. We're protected, for now at least. Those Lords will talk circles around each other, games within games, strategies, chess pieces being moved. We are hieeerrrr"—he grabs his head—"Damn, that magic is strong." After a second, he drops his hands. "What I mean is, we are"—he tenses—"*their*?" When nothing happens, he goes on, "Best option of finishing the task."

I feign meekness, slumping my shoulders, toeing my boot into the sand. "And we're sure she didn't die in the explosions? She *was* right in the thick of it."

The woman shakes her head. "There was no body, so it was either recovered—in which case we need to find out by whom, or she survived and is in hiding."

The bald man grimaces. "If she survived, I can't imagine she'd be in any shape to get up and run off under her own power. I just hope one of the other Houses doesn't have her." It's a struggle to keep myself from reacting to that nugget of information. My skin actually tingles with the need to know *which* House these hunters are working for and how high up that order came from.

Valsan nods. "We need to keep looking. You three head to camp Drakam. See if there's anything there. The three of us will continue to scope out camp Kapros, then we can work together to clear the Alopson section."

The middle man speaks, his voice low with a thread of command. "Remember, if we find her alive and in the hands of another House, we're to take her out, quick and silent. No trace. The other Houses can't gain control of the Void, and her death can't be traced back to ... our boss."

I rise onto the balls of my feet, willing him to say the name, to tell us which House is calling the shots here. But, without another word, the bald man pulls his hood back up, and the three turn to leave. I angle towards Valsan, and in my mind's eye I recall his bruises and cuts now hidden under the grey robes. I remember the fiery red of the explosions, hear the screams, see Thaeia running, and then ... My chest tightens. These bastards—whoever they are—are involved, they are hunting Thaeia. There was no hint of reluctance around the talk of killing her. What if they find her? What if they get to her first?

No!

The tents, the wind, the soft crunch of sand underfoot ... it all fades as rage courses through my blood. My magic still sits heavy and tired, but I rip it from my gut, ignoring the pain in my stomach and the white dots in my vision. The three retreating figures don't have time to scream or even grunt. The only sound is a wet splat as they flatten then explode under the pressure of my Gravity magic.

I blink up at the stars. Wait, why am I on the ground? Shifting, I get my elbow under me, propping myself up. Valsan's hand comes to my back, helping hold me up as his soft voice whispers, "You passed out, but only for a moment."

I avoid looking at him. Instead, my head falls to the side, and I stare at the dark stain on the sand. There's some flesh, torn clothing, and bloody bits splattered on the sides of the nearby tents. I've thought about doing that before. I've dreamt of exacting revenge on my father, and just earlier today, I imagined crushing anyone who threatened those I love again. But this ... actually doing it ...

Vesper chuckles, "Woah. Nice." With a nervous glance over her shoulder, she steps closer to us. "But, uh, we should go. Like now."

Val and Vesper each hold out a hand, and together they help me stand. I stumble to the side as the world tilts, but I'm able to stay upright as a voice whispers from inside one of the tents. "What was that?"

Vesper ducks under my arm, bracing some of my weight on her shoulders and practically drags me away from the bloody scene, Valsan on our heels. We turn a corner, sticking to the shadows when that same voice from before says, "What is tha—Oh my gods! Guards! Guards!"

Another voice screams, joining the rising call for help. My gaze is on the ground, and with every step, I see my boots poke out from under the long cloak. For some reason, it almost makes me laugh, imagining my toes are playing peekaboo. Should I be worried about how little what I just did bothers me? I should be worried. But, I feel ... nothing. That was just a task that needed doing, and now it's done.

A little shiver snakes down my spine. I feel Val's eyes on my back, but I can't face him. I can't bear to see the disappointment, the reproach, the horror, or whatever will be in his eyes. I can't. My palms sting where my nails dig into my flesh. I can't.

The sound of running draws my attention, and Vesper drags me behind a dark tent and crouches, taking me with her. I'm still unsteady and a bit dizzy, so I brace by planting a knee into the sand. Valsan's heat presses against me from the side, but I still don't look at him. Vesper leans around the corner, whispering, "Guards. Two Alopson and one of yours, captain."

There's a little shift of muscle from Valsan, but he says nothing. The next second, his grey cloak pools on the ground around his feet. Vesper shoves her hood back, cocking a brow at him. After a long second, she shrugs. "Yeah, good call." An elegant shrug of her shoulders sends her cloak to the ground.

I struggle with my cloak, feeling like a toddler as the folds seem to cling to me. Flinging my arm, I try to dislodge the sleeve, but it keeps getting caught. A twinge of pain shoots up my side, reminding me of my injuries, and the exhaustion of magical overuse threatens to take me down ... again. Nerves and frustration snap through me, and I grip the edges of my cloak, trying to rip it off my body.

Seemingly unaware of my struggles, or simply ignoring my embarrassing fight with the robe, Vesper keeps a lookout while saying, "I'm going to go ahead and go to Lord Alopson's tent. I want to scope out the vibe of who is already there and how it changes as more people arrive. And I'd love to get a front-row seat to the reactions of the room when Valsan enters. Let's see who will readily be on your side and who you should watch out for, so take your time, make sure that tent is full before you two get there."

Finally turning, she looks past me, presumably making eye contact with Val before she nods and creeps off, disappearing into the night.

Valsan still hasn't said anything, and his silence is driving me mad. I want to hear his deep voice, but I'm terrified of what he might say, so I stay quiet. His strong hand wraps under my arm, pulling me to my feet, and while my bones ache, and my gut tightens with magic fatigue, I'm able to keep up as we make our way through the eerily silent camp towards the Kapros section.

A shout towards the edges of the camp shatters the silence. "You can't keep us here! We're not prisoners. We haven't done anything wrong! We just want to go home! Let us through!"

I slow, peering between tents, catching the flash of the green uniform of Drakam. The guard holds up a hand, palm pressed to the chest of the short man before him. A woman stands behind him, her shoulders hunched, her hands wringing behind her back. The guard gently shoves the man back a step, saying, "The city is on lockdown. Please return to your tent."

The short man bows up, thrusting his chest at the guard. "No! You can't do this!" He jerks his head over his shoulder. "May, do it."

The woman shakes her head, her brown curls springing around her head as the guard clenches his left fist. "Don't."

The man shouts, "May!"

The woman flexes her left hand. It's too dark to read her tattoo from this distance, but she hesitates. "Honey, maybe we should just—"

"MAY!"

She flinches, snapping her arm up at the man's command. But the guard shoves the man back, aiming his left hand towards May. The ground shifts, and the Drakam guard starts to sink, the sand churning around his calves. But before the short man can grab May and run, the two gasp, grabbing their throats. The guard's descent slows, then stops. He doesn't try to extract himself, instead he calmly watches as the two continue to struggle. The man falls first, then May collapses on top of him. The guard shifts back and forth, wiggling himself free, drawing a set of cuffs from his belt and a length of rope from his pocket. As he begins to bind the two unconscious people, Valsan nudges me, whispering, "Come on."

The first few steps feel as if May is using her magic on me, causing the desert to try to swallow me. I stumble along, and at first, I think the brilliant white dots have started closing in on my vision again, but a closer look reveals arsine torches burning along the perimeter of the tent city. When did those go up? Who put them up? If I had to guess, Lord Alopson is probably responsible. The thought of facing the formidable lord makes my mouth go dry.

"Oof." I'm pulled to the side so suddenly, I trip over my feet, Valsan's grip the only thing keeping me from falling on my ass. The jarring motion sends pain flaring through my body, and I see two of Valsan before my focus sharpens. My shoulders hitch, and I quickly look away before I meet his gaze. I'm shocked to see the Kapros boar standard snapping in the breeze to my left, just a few tents over. Why did we stop?

"Nor." Valsan's whisper is close.

Unbidden, images of those people splattering under the force of my magic play through my mind again. I steel myself and turn towards him, but keep my head down staring at his thighs. The fabric of his pants shifts with the subtle flex of his muscles, but when he remains silent, I force my eyes to travel up. His torn shirt reveals his broad physique. Traveling upwards, I pause my gaze at his neck, my own throat constricting as I watch him swallow. My eyes trace over his dark beard, knowing the feel of his facial hair against my skin, both soft and rough. His lips are relaxed, not pressed into the tight line I expected. And there are his deep green eyes, practically black in the dark of night. I hold his stare, ready. As if in a daze, I watch his lips part, and I brace for his words.

"Say something." His voice is throaty with concern, and I blink a few times. Confusion keeps me from answering, so he says, "You haven't said a word since ..." His warm hand cups my face, and I nearly sigh into his touch. "Nor, are you okay?"

My forehead crinkles as I once again picture the pile of human sludge—the blood soaking into the sand, pieces of flesh stuck to the sides of the surrounding tents. When I find my voice, all that comes out is, "They were hunting her." He nods, his eyes searching mine. What is he looking for? Remorse? Guilt? Disgust? He won't find it. I'm ... numb. But I know once the shock wears off ... "I'm not sorry."

His expression doesn't change as he says, "You believe you did the right thing."

"I do. But ... do you disagree?" I hate the pleading lilt to my voice, but there's no helping it.

He drops his hand, his eyes hard. "This is my job. This is what I've spent my life training for, but until today, that's all it's been ... training." His hand flexes on his thigh sending heat through my body as he goes on. "This is no longer theoretical. People have died. There is an actual manhunt underway. This is not a game, but someone is treating it as such. Pieces have been moved, bluffs have been called, and damn it"—he runs a hand through his hair—"not only do we not know all the rules of this game, we don't even know all the players. This is dangerous, Nor."

I sway as relief and weariness make me feel like I've been drugged. I mean to keep the insecurity locked inside, but the words slip out. "So, you're not ... angry? Repulsed? I haven't ... fucked things up? I haven't driven you away?"

His expression darkens, eyes snagging at the top of my face near my hairline on the cut I'd forgotten about. His attention draws the throbbing pain back to attention. A hardness steals across his face, lips pressed tight, eyes narrowed as he closes the space between us. If I wasn't so enamoured with him, I'd be terrified by that look, but I know the anger I see in his eyes is *for* me ... not at me. His hand presses to my chest, palm splayed. I can't help myself. My body moves into him, and the second my lips touch his, my world solidifies. As long as I have him, I'll be fine. No matter what. He returns my kiss with gentle lips. Pulling back, he presses his forehead to mine, his soft exhale puffing against my face. The warmth of his touch seeps through my clothes and sinks all the way to my toes as he says, "There will be no driving me away, Nor. Liking you means I like all of you. We will disagree at times, we will fight, and we will communicate our way to a solution. But, Nor"—his fingers curl into the fabric of my shirt as if to hold me in place, but I'm not going anywhere—"let me be clear. We are not in disagreement about what you did."

"Really?"

He steps even closer, his breath fanning my face. "Nor, the Akareth Desert is a neutral land. To enact violence here is—"

"We need a Healer!"

Valsan and I both look towards the shout coming from near our tent. Stepping away from me, Val turns, but I grab his arm, keeping him close for a moment longer. My fingers trail up his side with a feather-light touch, mindful of his injuries. "You don't have to do this at all, you know. No one has ordered you to uncover this plot. You can follow your own advice to Vesper. Go, answer Lord Alopson's questions, fulfill your duties to camp Kapros, and go home. You—"

"Do you not know me at all?"

I chuckle, shaking my head. "I know. I knew my words were futile as soon as they left my lips. And I love that about you. You care." Leaning in, I press my lips to his again, giving in to my desire for a moment. I angle my head, kissing him deeper, my tongue licking, tasting blood and smoke. I'm angry, comforted, and aroused. It's a heady mix that makes the world spin. I feel lighter than my magic has ever been able to make me feel. He opens, and I groan into his mouth as our tongues meet. It's a slow dance of lips, our mouths caressing until finally I pull back, a little breathless. Panting softly, I stare into his eyes. "You are not alone."

"Nor." He leans in, resting his forehead against mine again.

His back muscles tremble under my hand, and I stroke my fingers down his spine. "You need a Healer, Val." He tenses, but I shake my head. "No. Don't argue. You know you're hurt. If we are going to help, we need to be sharp, and we both need to be at full strength. So, let's find the others, get healed up, and hunt down the bastard or bastards who did this."

The smallest smile pulls at his beard as he nods, the press of his forehead warm and comforting before he pulls away. The vulnerability and exhaustion leave his eyes as he stands tall, once more the captain of House Kapros. How does he do that?

He whispers, "At least we were able to confirm one of

the Houses *is* hunting Thaeia. I'm assuming they also orchestrated the explosions, but we can't be sure. There may be more than one entity acting here."

Well, that's a chilling thought. Leaning in, I lower my voice, looking towards the boar head standard flapping over our tent in the near distance. "Is there any way this order came from Lady Daire? Her absence looks suspicious."

Valsan's jaw flexes, and I see the pain in his eyes. But true to his nature, he presses his lips tight, thinking through my words before he says, "I don't want to believe my Lady would do such a thing, but ... I can't rule it out. And you're right, guilt will be pointed at her, at our House, so I need to be ready to face those accusations."

"What will you say?"

The muscles of his face flex, pulling his cheeks into a hard line, steely determination flaring in his eyes—and damn it if my cock doesn't jump at that look.

"What I always say. The truth."

I grin at him, love for this man turning my insides to mush. I do love him.

My emotions must show on my face, because he looks over his shoulder towards our tent then back at me. His eyes have gone soft, and his fingers trace a gentle path across my cheekbone. "Before we go in there, Nor, before we get distracted ..." His touch travels up, lightly caressing the cut along my hairline. "Gods, Nor. It was bad, but ... it could have been so much worse. I've held back because I knew you needed *this* between us to go slow, but after today ..." I swallow. Is he really going to say it? Here? Now? I find myself holding my breath as he looks me right in the eyes. "I love you, Nor."

CHAPTER 4

NOR

THERE'S no ringing of bells, or a chorus of birdsong. The air doesn't smell fresher. The stars are no brighter. But his words, hearing them out loud ... they sink into my chest, nestle into my heart, and take root. That's where Valsan belongs. That's where I'll keep him, forever if he'll let me.

I take a stuttering breath, buttressing myself, letting the words build, but Val grabs my hand and turns, leading me between the tents until ours stands tall and bright before us. Torches lead the way from each direction, reminding me that our tent is being used as a triage station. We push inside our tent and dozens of heads swivel towards us. I count six cots, each holding a body. Valsan releases me, moving deeper into the space, but I stay where I am. The air in the tent is warm from the stove, and the tang of blood coats my nostrils with every breath. A man with ash-dirtied brown hair sits on the ground beside one of the cots, his hand loosely gripping the limp fingers of the woman passed out in the bed. There's a bandage around half her face, dark blood staining the section over her right eye.

Stepping further into the tent, I shift to make room for the Healer to get by on his way to the next cot. He kneels on shaky legs, holding his left hand over the shattered knee of the person before him. Their moans get quieter, then cease as the exposed tendons and muscle knit together, and the skin starts to scab over. The Healer sags, but keeps going. I wonder how many he's helped. How much longer will his magic hold out? Valsan places a hand on the other woman moving from cot to cot. Her tattoo says she's a Mender, and her tired eyes find Valsan as she nods at whatever he says to her.

I scan the large tent finding Owen and Miles packing the last of our bags and tossing them out the back flap to land in the sand with a thud. They are both in new clothes, each wearing the black uniform of House Kapros, their sleeveless shirts bearing the white boar head across their chests. I weave through the cots, and both men pause, stretching their backs. They nod at me as I ask, "Where's Aimee? Halee?"

Owen wipes his forehead, leaving behind a smear of dirt on his already smudged face. "Aimee is loading and securing the carriage."

Miles' eyes dart to the waving flaps at the front and rear of the tent. "On our way here, we passed a family that was struggling to hitch their horse to their cart. Halee insisted she go help and that I come back here to pack— that there wasn't time to waste. I didn't want to leave her, but she ..." His hands clench, his fingers worrying at each other. "She should have been back by now. I shouldn't have ... I need to ..."

Valsan joins us, bracing a hand on Miles' shoulder. "We're not leaving. Not yet. Lord Alopson has called a meeting of the Houses. And Halee was right to help. I'm sure she's fine."

Worry skates down my spine. What if she's not?

Valsan pats Miles before releasing him, looking over his shoulder before moving us all closer to the tent wall, as far away from prying ears as we can get. "We need to be sharp." Valsan's gaze locks on me. "Everything, every reaction, every word, will matter in this meeting. Pay attention, and be ready to come under fire."

I nod, and Miles whispers, "Do you know where *she* is? Is she alive? Is she—"

Valsan holds up a hand. "I'm pretty sure she's alive. I don't know where she is but I know who she's with." When he doesn't say more, Owen and Miles nod, accepting their captain will tell them more if and when they need to know. Miles rocks back and forth on his toes, his eyes glancing out the tent. Valsan nods at him. "Go, find Halee."

Relief falls over Miles' face, and he eagerly spins, slamming right into Halee. He grabs her before she falls. She's breathless, a sweet smile on her face. I release a little sigh, some of my tension easing at knowing she's okay. Halee tucks a strand of hair behind her ear, saying, "Sorry I took so long. The horses calmed quickly enough, but then someone's donkey was throwing a fit so I—"

Miles' lips crash to hers, his hands holding her face with urgency. Halee freezes with obvious surprise, but then her eyes slide closed and she wraps her arms around Miles, pulling him closer. Owen chuckles, turning then kneeling, pretending to straighten an already neat pile of bandages and blankets. Valsan grins, but his shoulders are slumped. He's exhausted and injured. He drops to one knee, digging through his bag as Miles and Halee continue to kiss like it's the end of the world. I turn, finding the Mender as she stands, sending off a newly healed patient, making room for someone else should they come in needing help. Stepping around the cot, I lean into her, asking, "Can you see what you can do for the captain? He'll insist everyone else be seen to first, but we're short on time. He could use—"

She smiles. "Of course." Coming a little closer, she whispers, "You look like you could use a little help as well. Put your hand on his back."

My brows scrunch together, but I kneel to do as I'm told. Valsan smiles, sinking into my touch without looking at me. Miles and Halee finally pull away from each other but keep their faces close as Miles whispers something to her that deepens her blush. The Mender leans over and places her hand over mine on Valsan's back, pressing her other finger to her lips to tell me to keep quiet. I nod, and a second later, my bruises and cuts start to mend, and the pain in my head lessens. Valsan tenses and shifts to look over his shoulder, but I press a kiss to his cheek. "Let her finish."

He shakes his head but remains still. "Sneaky."

The Mender chuckles, patting my hand before straightening and stepping back. "That's all I can manage. You'll need the actual Healer for anything more."

I nod. Both Valsan and I say, "Thank you."

Aimee steps into the tent, also now wearing the black uniform, ash lightening her dark hair, a bruise on her left shoulder, but her back is straight and her eyes are sharp. "Carriage is almost ready. What's the plan, captain?"

Valsan grabs a black shirt from his bag, and as we stand, I note his posture looks stronger. There's now a healthy flush to his skin as he says, "Lord Alopson has called a meeting. Were you able to find our other guards?"

He yanks his ruined shirt over his head, and I have to swallow to keep from drooling. As he pulls on his official uniform, Aimee rolls her neck, cracking her knuckles one by one saying, "Yes, sir. They were helping direct the crowd out of the Coliseum, so I left them to it and told them to report here once they could. Should I go retrieve them?" There's a glint to her eyes that conveys leashed violence. She's out for blood.

We all are.

Valsan shakes his head, pulling his hair tie loose and redoing it. "No. Their presence was not requested, only the heads of the Houses, their captains, and those who were in the arena when the attack happened. Lady Kapros is not here, so I am acting head. Aimee, I'm bringing you as my second. Owen, Miles, I want you to scout the Alopson camp. Stick close to Lord Alopson's tent ... just in case. And keep your ears open for any whispers about *her*."

The two nod, Miles darting a glance to Halee who shifts, dropping her gaze, whispering, "I'll stay here. I'll help where I can. My magic can't do anything for the injured but I have a steady hand and can—"

Valsan shakes his head. "I don't want you alone. You stick with Miles." He leans down, bringing his eyes level with hers. "You are a known friend of Thaeia. We all are, and while I hate to think this of my fellow countrymen, any of us could be used as leverage to find her, to draw her out." Valsan stands, shoulders square. "So until we know more, no one goes anywhere alone. Understood?"

We all nod, and I shift, trying to hide the embarrassing kick of my cock at the command in Valsan's voice. *So inappropriate. Read the room.* And like the smartass I am, my cock responds, *I am reading the room. Look at him. He's so hot.*

Shifting again, I manage to keep my dick from coming to complete attention as Valsan continues, blessedly unaware of my internal argument with my own cock. "And as to our other guards, Kapros has the smallest contingent present. I don't want us all in the same place at the same time. Besides, the people of Sodoles come first. I trust our guards to continue helping and be useful. Aimee, I'll send you to them with a directive once we know more about what the other Houses intend to do."

We stand in a tight circle, Valsan on my left, Owen next to him, Halee and Miles clutching each other's hands next to Owen, and Aimee steely eyed to my right—Thaeia's absence hovers like a ghost between us. Valsan looks at each of them. "Anyone else need healing before we go?"

Halee gasps, and everyone snaps their attention to her. Miles reaches for her, rubbing a hand down her back, asking, "Are you hurt?"

Her wide eyes are on me. "Nor! A third star!"

Oh. Yeah. I have the urge to tuck my arm behind my back—not the reaction I thought I'd have. "Yeah. It doesn't matter right now."

A corner of her mouth dips down in a little frown. "Of course it matters." She wraps her arms around me. "Congratulations, Nor."

I pat her back, letting myself feel a moment of pride,

and as she steps back, everyone around me smiles. Owen reaches over, slapping me on the shoulder. "Congrats, man."

Aimee lifts her chin in acknowledgment, and Miles claps my other shoulder. "Yeah, congratulations."

Valsan doesn't say anything as we reform our little circle, he simply shifts closer so his arm brushes against mine—and that's all I need from him, his presence, his support, his love.

Valsan dips his head, and our circle closes in even tighter. "Thaeia needs us. The country needs us. Today has changed Sodoles forever. Be alert. Consider every moment from here on out as if the other Houses are our enemies, because until we are certain otherwise, they are."

He glances at me, nodding before turning back to the others. "This was an act of war, so we treat it as such."

CHAPTER 5

THAEIA

Somehow, I'm alive. The pain tells me I've definitely not moved on to the Everafter—unless I'm in the pits of the Everafter in eternal punishment, which wouldn't surprise me, but I'm almost certain I am, in fact, alive.

Question is, who else survived? My heavy eyes burn at the thought of my friends hurt ... dead ... gone. The darkness behind my closed lids swirls, and the space around me tilts. I bite the inside of my cheek to ground myself. I can't think like that right now—right now, I have to concentrate on the here and now.

Carefully, I crack open my eyes, but I'm met with more darkness. Where am I? Shifting slightly, I realize I'm on a bed. A plump pillow cradles my head, and the comforting weight of blankets covers me from head to toe. As my eyes adjust, I realize there's light beyond the fabric covering my face, but it's the glow of fire, not daylight. Am I in Valsan's tent?

With a small flex of my muscles, I slowly wiggle my toes and stretch my calves, nearly screaming at the pain that shoots up my left leg. Carefully, I bunch my thighs, working my way up my body. There's a stabbing pain in my side, and my shoulder feels like my arm was nearly ripped from my body. There's a dull, throbbing pain along my hairline, but I'm alive.

Staying under the warmth of the blanket, I clench my teeth, managing to swallow my grunt as I try to roll onto my side. A crinkling draws my attention, and I slowly draw my hand to my chest. There's a piece of paper clutched in my fingers, and when I smooth it out, the soft sound seems overly loud. My eyes have adjusted to the darkness under the covers, but I can't make out the words on the paper.

I count to five, listening. I'm pretty sure I'm alone—wherever I am—so with painfully slow movements, I curl my fingers over the edge of the blanket and slide it down over my forehead until my eyes peek out.

This isn't Valsan's tent. It's bigger. The bed I'm on is the only one in the large space. I ignore the flutter of excitement that builds in my belly when I spy the stack of books to my right. Is this ...?

The blanket slides down to my neck, and I bring the paper before my face.

Thaeia–

You are safe. For now. Don't make any noise and don't leave the tent. I'll be back as soon as possible. DO NOT LEAVE THE TENT.

-*Keir*

Several emotions slam into me, making me dizzy. I'm grateful that Keir was there to help me, if that is in fact what he's done. Or has he kidnapped me for some nefarious purpose? I don't want to think that about him, but I don't really know him, and his father ...

The paper crinkles between my fingers, and I have to take a few deep breaths before I'm able to relax. I'm worried for my friends. I'm angry that someone would go to these lengths to ... I don't know, kill me, I guess. But why? Is my Void *that* much of a threat? Apparently, to someone, yes.

Or am I being a narcissist? Maybe this wasn't about me at all. Sodoles is a big country. Maybe this was a power grab? My head starts to hurt as I realize how little I know about the politics of Sodoles and the three Houses.

I inhale, and the light, earthy scent of the paper in my hand wafts up my nose. Involuntarily, my legs press together. I'm in Keir's bed. The blankets shift over my skin. Oh, shit! I'm naked in Keir's bed, and—a quick sniff confirms it—I'm clean.

I shake my head, whispering to myself, "Get a hold of yourself, Thaeia. It would appear that Keir saved you. He cleaned your wounds." Shifting, the towel over my breasts scrapes against my peaked nipples. "He undressed you." The thought of his hands on my flesh sends heat pooling between my thighs.

I hiss at the sudden jolt of pain that screams up my leg, ripping my arousal away. Bracing a hand on the bed, I get myself to a sitting position, rolling my sore shoulder. The blanket and towel fall away, and I glance down, poking at the deep cut along my right side. Every inhale tugs at my torn flesh. Now that I see the wound, deeper pain shoots up my side, and little white stars begin to dance across my vision. I notice a leather wrap caught in the bunched blanket around my hips. Flipping it open, the slight glint of a needle shines up at me, already threaded.

Shrugging, I reach for it, my hand steady as I pinch the needle between my fingers. This isn't the first time I've stitched myself up, but I think this is the deepest cut I've sewn up. My jaw aches, and I force my teeth to unclench, exhaling as I pinch the edges of my wound together. Blood seeps between my fingers, making my hold slippery as I punch the needle through my skin. My eyes water, and blink away my tears as I sew myself back together. Halfway done, my hand starts to shake, and the pain begins to nauseate me. But I keep going. Sweat beads on my stomach, and I have to use the edge of the towel to keep a firm hold on my slick skin. My muscles clench before I stab the needle into myself again.

Just a few more.

My shoulder throbs with the awkward position I'm in to reach the cut. I blink a few times, trying to clear the darkening edges. Pausing, the trembling needle hovers over my bleeding skin. I take a few slow breaths, focusing on the stack of books to distract me for a moment. As I read the spines, a small smile tugs at my lips. Such a wide variety of books stare back at me, from *History of the Games*, to *The Games Rule Book*, to an epic fantasy. There are a few notebooks in the stack, some of the pages dogeared. The book on the bottom has my eyes widening as I realize it's a romance.

Well, fuck me.

My smirk stays in place as I bite my lip and quickly

finish the final three stitches. With a sigh, I use a torn piece of fabric I find on the ground to wipe away as much of the blood as I can. It's too uncomfortable in this position, so I carefully lower myself to my uninjured side, pulling the blanket over my shoulders and tucking it under my chin. It's quiet outside. Yes, it's nighttime, but the constant revelry of the previous evenings is absent. There's not even the panicked cries I'd expect after what happened today. Is it still today? I think so. It's just so eerily silent.

Keir's note said not to leave, but I need to find my friends. I need to know if they are okay. Yet, if I go to them, and this *was* about me ... I can't put them in danger ... any more danger. If this happened because of me, I need to get as far away as possible. I could steal a horse and run. But where do I go? I assume there are people looking for me, and from the tone of Keir's note, not everyone looking for me is concerned about my welfare. I need help. I can't do this on my own, and my friends would come after me anyway. Smiling into the pillow, I let the fact that I have loving, loyal friends warm me from the inside out. I curl my fingers around the note Keir left me and hug it to my chest. He's a friend, right?

My eyes blink slowly as exhaustion tries to claim my battered body. Before I let myself slip into the darkness, I slide the blanket over my head, enveloping myself in the shadowy warmth, clutching Keir's note.

What if someone finds me here? What if Keir is punished for helping me? What if he's killed? What if ...?

Rage tears through me, banishing my exhaustion and dampening the pain. I shove the blanket off, the material fluttering through the air before billowing off the side of Keir's bed. Bending my legs under me, I shove to my feet before I can process the pain. I wobble as I spy an open trunk with clothes inside, so I aim for it.

One step.

My body seizes in agony as my leg buckles. I crumple to the floor, feeling a stitch pop. My shoulder wrenches as I stupidly try to catch myself, and white-hot pain fires through my body from my toes to the tip of my head. The musty wool scent of the carpet is the last thing I register as my face slams into the floor and everything goes dark ... again.

CHAPTER 6

NOR

VALSAN'S broad back disappears inside the ostentatious tent, Aimee right on his heels. The red-clad Alopson guard standing at the entrance glances at me, and the urge to explain that I was on the team that was in the arena when the explosions went off sits heavy on my tongue. But the guard nods at me like he already knows who I am before snapping his eyes back forward.

With a tightness that threatens to snap my spine, I enter the tent just as the first blush of dawn colors the inky night with indigo. How has the entire night already passed? There are five people poised around a circular table near the center of Lord Ransden Alopson's tent, and others stand around the perimeter. All eyes are turned towards Valsan, but as I enter, a few shift to look my way. Scanning the faces, I find Vesper at the back of the group of contestants that were down in the arena with me just a few hours ago. Her lips quirk as she bites her cheek, her eyes shining with amusement as I make my way towards her. Gretchen, the Fire mage steps to the side, her round eyes slightly glassed over either from shock or exhaustion. Probably both. Two men who were on the opposing team stand at the edge of the group, arms crossed, bodies angled towards each other, whispers passing between them.

The contestants are all huddled together like scared sheep as I weave through them to reach Vesper. I bump her shoulder as I stuff my hands in my pockets. I'm about to ask her what went on in here before our arrival, but Harland shuffles over nervously, his eyes darting around the room before flashing up to my face. He attempts a smile, but it's tight, and there's a sheen of sweat on his face. Poor kid. He jumps as I press my palm to his upper back. Leaning over, I whisper, "Everything will be fine. I'm sure they will ask a few questions, but all you have to do is answer honestly. The real challenge will be having to stand here while the ones in charge argue and drone on." I roll my eyes playfully, drawing out a small but genuine smile from the young Thread mage.

I drop my hand and lean back towards Vesper. "So?"

Her blue eyes narrow, her short blond hair sticking up with sweat and a few slicks of dried blood, but I don't think it's hers. She jerks her chin towards two men at the table. "Keir arrived just a few minutes before you. Lord Alopson nearly collapsed with relief before he steeled that aristocratic spine of his."

Interesting.

She goes on. "They exchanged a few words, and something Keir said shocked Lord Alopson. He tried to hide his reaction, but I saw it. They know something."

Keir's ruby-red flames lick his shoulders, and his basil-ishounds lay at his feet, seemingly relaxed, but their ears are perked, twitching at every soft sound of muffled conversation. Lord Alopson is now angled away from Keir, whispering to his captain, Daria, whose lips are pressed tight. She nods every so often at whatever her Lord is saying. Keir's eyes are on Valsan.

I swallow as the two just stare at each other for a long moment. The larger of Keir's hounds sits up, hollow eyes tilted up at his master. Keir strokes his hand through the hound's head, flames and all, his gaze still locked with Valsan. Jealousy flares in my chest, and I know it's unwarranted, but the feeling scrapes at my insides anyway.

But then Val turns his head and looks at me. The second our eyes meet, his face softens, his affection clear in the small smile that crinkles the edges of his eyes. That one look banishes my doubt and jealousy like water dousing a fire. My shoulders relax, but then hitch up again at Vesper's quiet chuckle. Breaking Valsan's gaze, I look at her, catching her mirthful eyes darting between Valsan and me.

I shake my head, raising a brow, and she shrugs. "You're high maintenance, aren't you?"

She's obviously teasing, but my brows furrow anyway. Fuck. Am I?

Her chuckles get louder, drawing the eyes of several people. She ducks her head, shoulders shaking as she attempts to get herself under control, and I let myself smile with her. Maybe I am, but Valsan doesn't seem to mind. I think he likes *managing* me. I look back towards him, keeping my head down, trying to look from under my lashes, but Val sees and shoots me a wink.

Fuck me.

Vesper shifts a little closer, snapping me from the lust clawing at my stomach. She keeps her head down as she says, "There were mixed responses to your arrival. Lord Keir and the Alopson captain seemed relieved. Lord Alopson barely spared Valsan a glance. He actually seemed more interested in you." I try to keep it subtle, letting my gaze slide towards the lord of the northern territory. His hand rests on Keir's shoulder, and his lips move, speaking to his son, but his eyes are scanning the tent. I drop my gaze before he looks at me, and Vesper continues, "There were also a few scowls when Valsan entered." I remain tight-lipped as she lifts her head slightly, aiming her gaze at Lord Severn Drakam. He stands to Keir's left, his arms crossed, his shoulders slumped, adding to the overall exhausted aura around him. His black hair, streaked with grey hangs limp around his face, and his brown skin—the dull color of the underside of an oak leaf—is pale. The lord of the central territory looks like he's about to fall over, but there's fire in his muddy, brown eyes—eyes staring at Valsan. Vesper tsks. "See?"

I nod as she jerks her chin towards Lord Drakam's captain who looks bored. His green vest with the dragon emblem is disheveled, the third button down looped through the wrong hole, and his hands are stuffed in his pockets. His vacant gaze is on the table, seemingly not at all concerned with what is happening around him. Vesper whispers, "The Drakam captain took what I would call an aggressive step towards Valsan, but Lord Severn held him back with a shake of his head."

Again, interesting, but I'm not used to these games, these meetings where words mean more than what's actually said, where eye contact can convey a silent order. I'm out of my depth, but the stakes are too high for me to flounder. Just like back home in the quiet bay behind Thaeia's house, I need to learn to swim or I'll drown.

Vesper shifts, moving her gaze towards the group of contestants in front of us and to our left, but Lord Alopson clears his throat, keeping her from saying whatever she was about to tell me. Everyone goes silent, turning their attention to the tall, commanding Lord of Alopson.

"Thank you for coming." His deep voice carries across the giant tent even without him raising his voice. "The events of a few hours ago were horrible and unacceptable. I have called you all here so that the three great Houses of Sodoles may work together to find those responsible and bring them to justice. Lord Drakam and I have decided to cancel the remainder of the Games." Shadows from the flickering arsine torches cut his pale skin with shadow, making his cheeks look sharper, his blue eyes darker.

The distant expression on the Drakam captain's face melts away, his eyes focusing on Lord Alopson. "You've started this meeting even though one is still not here." The words are harsh, but his face is relaxed. It's such an odd delivery, I almost chuckle. I have to grit my teeth to keep my hysterical laughter from bubbling out. The captain goes on, his entire body relaxed, but his voice snapping out like a whip. "Why are we wasting time here when the Void is out there somewhere?"

My nails dig into my palm, but despite my rising anger towards the Drakam captain, I feel calm, focused. Strange.

Lord Alopson shifts, and once again, all eyes turn his way. "We are here because our people look to us, and in order for us to lead them, we need to work together. The people come first."

The Drakam captain's fingers flex before falling limp

once again. "The *people* won't be safe until the Void is found. We need to—"

"That's enough, Silas." Daria, Alopson's captain, glares at the Drakam captain. Seems there's no love lost there. "You are here as your Lord's second. Act like it."

Silas's eyes narrow, and his jaw flexes. It's just a moment of outward rage, then it's gone, the placid look falling back over his face. I blink, slowly—too slowly—looking around the room as Lord Alopson says, "Lord Severn and I have already spoken, and each of our Houses has sent every guard available to patrol the tent city. They are also working with civilian volunteers to help keep the people as calm as possible."

Silas plants his palms on the wood table, leaning in casually, his posture opposing the animosity in his voice. "And how long do you think that calm will hold? The longer you keep these people *prisoner* here, the higher the emotions will rise. Do you want a riot?"

Lord Alopson simply raises a brow, then leans forward, mimicking the captain's stance, placing his left hand on the table. The Lord of Alopson must be in his late fifties, but the muscles of his arm flex with strength as he displays his stars. Twelve. Twelve stars climb his arm, curling around his shoulder, the final one brushing his neck. Lord Alopson keeps his eyes on the Drakam captain until the man looks up from the Lord's tattoos to meet his gaze again. The captain is smart enough to lean back, crossing his arms as Alopson calmly says, "Captain Silas, there will not be a riot because *I* won't allow it. *I* will keep the peace"—the fingers of his right hand trace his tattoo, the letters spelling out AKUTHERUM, Emotion.—"and I will hold the peace of this entire city for as long as necessary. The safety of our people is my first concern."

Holy shit! Lord Alopson is using his magic on the entire tent city? Well now this whole strange exchange makes more sense. And now I know why I feel like punching Silas but at the same time am too relaxed to follow through. The silence is heavy, broken only by the occasional shift and shuffle of feet on the thick carpets.

Silas narrows his eyes at Lord Alopson. "You presume to use your power on u—"

His mouth snaps shut in surprise, and Harland jumps as an armor-clad warrior appears out of thin air right in front of us, red flames outlining the Spirit. Another pops up in the tent, and another, and another. They turn, bowing to Keir before walking right through the walls of the tent. Lord Alopson, with his hand still braced on the table, looks around the room. "My son is adding another layer of security. His Spirit warriors have agreed to patrol. Keir will know the moment any trouble arises outside of what I can control."

Silas scoffs, and he's about to say something else, but Valsan steps to the table, Aimee at his side, her steely eyes traveling over both Lords and their captains. Valsan stands tall, his broad shoulders filling the space around him, his posture relaxed but ready. Gods, he's glorious, even exhausted and in the midst of a room full of predators.

Valsan's deep voice resonates with calm authority. "Lord Alopson, Lord Drakam, how would you have us proceed? Because while said with the wrong tone"—his forest-green eyes flick to Silas who cows under the reproach—"the Drakam captain has a point. While powerful, Lord Alopson's magic does have a limit, as does everyone's, and we should work towards sending the people home quickly."

Lord Alopson nods, finally leaning away from the table and crosses his arms. "Agreed. In a few hours, I will hold a memorial in front of the Coliseum. It will give the people something to rally around, bring them together, and make them more amenable. As to clearing the area and sending the people home ..." He glances at Lord Drakam whose tired face doesn't shift or change other than the flexing of his jaw like he's grinding his teeth. When he doesn't say anything, Lord Alopson turns back to Valsan. "Recommendations?"

Silas scoffs. "Why are you asking him? Lady Kapros isn't here. You all can't tell me that isn't suspicious. Has anyone questioned the good captain?" His eyes snap to me. "Maybe we should start by questioning everyone from Kapr—"

The larger of Keir's Spirit hounds growls, stepping towards Silas. Keir, arms crossed, looking so much like his father, asks, "Are you accusing House Kapros of planting those explosives?"

My gut churns with my magic as Silas returns Keir's stare, sneering, "Are you not?"

Valsan clears his throat. "Lady Kapros is not here to defend herself, but if it will ease the minds of the other Houses, you are welcome to search my tent and my belongings as well as those of my guards. I have already sent word to my Lady, informing her of what happened." He did? When? "And I can arrange for a representative from each of your councils to come to Kapros and speak with her if that is your desire. I'm confident my Lady will provide any aid needed to find those responsible." When no one responds, Val continues. "As to what we can focus on right now ... I suggest we start with the contestants in this room. We will question them individually, sending them back to their tents once they've spoken with each of us. Then, Lord Alopson, Lord Drakam, myself, and our seconds will convene. While we do this, I suggest each House select a dozen guards, or in my case, the eight I have, to set up a search point in front of the Coliseum. We should pair them off, mixing Houses so no pair has two from the same House. We'll start with the Kapros section of the tent city since they are closest to the exit. After the memorial, each person, cart, wagon, or carriage will be searched before allowing them to leave."

Keir steps to the table. "And in the spirit of cooperation, I will share with you that I've already called on the Spirits of those who died in the attack. It's ... unadvisable to pull a Spirit so soon after death. The pain, the fear ... it's all still very close to the surface. Some haven't realized they are dead. It can be ..." His eyes glaze over, but then he waves his hand, snapping himself from his thoughts. "The Spirits saw nothing before their deaths. Everyone's focus was on the Master of Ceremonies and the starting gong."

Keir's words bring that moment to the front of my mind. The anticipation, the excitement of our first team match, and with Thaeia! ... And then ...

A sharp tsk sounds from the other side of the table. Of course it's Silas. "And why should we trust you, son of Alopson? You were seen drinking and celebrating with the Void. Are you two friendly? Are you—"

"Captain Silas!" The soft sense of calm lifts for a moment. Keir's father's face reddens with anger, his poised facade cracking for a moment. Then his shoulders roll down his back, and the blanket of serenity settles around me once again as Lord Alopson says, "I understand your anger and frustration. I too am eager to find those responsible. Moments like this can feel wasted when action claws at our bellies. But we must be smart. Patient. Whoever did this acted swiftly and under our noses." His blue gaze slowly travels around the tent. "This attack was coordinated. There was power and influence behind this." He pauses, meeting the gazes of everyone around the table. "Power that I wield as well. I know I'm not above suspicion, and will answer any of your questions ... after we've talked with the contestants."

His words hang like a noose from a gallows. Lord Alopson believes one of the Houses ordered this attack. Valsan, Vesper, and I *know* it was one of the Houses, but which? Could more than one be working together? Is Lord Alopson trying to put the scent off himself? I wouldn't be surprised if House Drakam was involved, but that's just because I hate Captain Silas.

Lord Alopson wraps one arm around his waist, the other elbow planted on his forearm as he scratches at the day's worth of stubble on his face. "I have sent word to my House, doubling the border crossing guard to help get people through as quickly as possible."

Lord Drakam grunts, speaking for the first time. "I've done the same."

Valsan's deep voice has me involuntarily standing taller as he says, "As soon as we're done here, I'll do the same as well."

Lord Alopson turns towards us, his eyes traveling over me and the other nine contestants huddled against this side wall. He opens his mouth, but is cut off when a woman to my left sheepishly raises her hand to shoulder height, her body hunched in as if terrified to be calling attention to herself. She was one of the contestants on the opposing team, and I'm not sure if she's been to a Healer or if she was spared most of the damage from the blasts, but she seems unharmed.

Lord Alopson smiles, nodding his head at her. "Yes?"

She drops her hand, clasping them before her. "Tereza, my Lord. Um, I was just wondering, um ... this checkpoint and the searches, and, um, well ... what are you looking for?"

Lord Alopson's smile falls, his eyes turning serious. "We're looking for any residue or materials that can be tied to the explosions. There have also been cloaked individuals seen slinking around the Coliseum and through the tent city. No one knows who they are or who they are working for, but we are also looking for anyone in or tied to this group."

The woman bows her head, nodding, but Silas growls. "But we all know that whoever did this probably set the explosives during the storm before slipping away. They're most likely not even here anymore. That's what I would have done."

Vesper chuckles under her breath. "Really? That's what he would have done? Tracks. He would run. Coward."

I bite my cheek to keep from laughing as I nudge her shoulder. "Shh."

Lord Alopson's captain crosses her arms. "So you would have us just let everyone leave under the assumption the guilty party is already gone?"

Silas scowls, but his shoulders remain relaxed. "Of course not!"

Daria rolls her eyes. "Then stop wasting our time."

Silas' top lip curls. "This entire meeting is a waste of time when we should be out there, looking for the Void, for that Thaeia woman." He turns his gaze to Lord

Alopson who plants his hands on his hips as Silas continues, "And if you don't have your people searching for her,
you should. House Drakam is, and when we find her, she
will answer for her crimes."

Lord Drakam remains silent, his gaze on the table.
Who's running the show in Drakam? Because right now, it
seems the captain is calling the shots.

And then I catch it ... Lord Drakam's jaw clenches, his
fingers gripping the table with white knuckles as his eyes
dart to Valsan before falling back to the table, his body
relaxing. It was such a quick glance, I didn't have time to
read his expression. I can't stop my eyes from finding
Valsan whose stare bores into Silas as he asks, "Crimes?"

Lord Severn's eye twitches, but still, he says nothing as
Silas snorts. "Yes, captain. Crimes. That woman—"

Lord Alopson's voice cracks like a whip. "Captain Silas.
You have been disrespectful and disruptive this entire
meeting. You are dismissed."

That last word is spoken on a growl, and the tent goes
silent. Silas shifts, visibly struggling to keep his mouth
shut. His head swivels to look at his Lord, but Severn
keeps his gaze on the table, letting the Lord of Alopson
command his captain.

My head hurts. Who in their right mind would want
this power, this responsibility of ruling? Who would
choose this? Well, I guess, the Lords and Lady of Sodoles
were born to their title. But, still.

Silas stalks from the tent, grumbling, "I didn't want to
be here anyway. I have more *important* things to do."

He's referring to Thaeia, and everyone knows it
because Vesper leans into me, her voice pitched low. "This
doesn't look good for your girl."

I look around the room from the still silent Lord

Drakam to Keir who seems calm enough, but his Spirit hounds are pacing around his legs betraying his nerves. Lord Alopson stands tall, commanding the room, not even a bead of sweat betraying the immense power he's using right now. My gaze slips back to Lord Drakam, and I can't help but wonder at the strange dynamic between him and his captain.

Lastly, like a moth to light, I turn to look at Valsan. He meets my gaze, and gives me an almost imperceptible shake of his head before he looks away. We have to find Thaeia. We're running out of time.

CHAPTER 7

KEIR

THE TENSION in my father's tent is cloying. I feel each of my Spirits patrolling the tent city and take comfort that at least for now, all is fairly calm. Hich's essence tickles the back of my legs, and Gren remains on alert, eyes and ears aimed at the tent flaps through which Silas just left. The Drakam captain's attitude and accusations stirred my rage even through my father's calming Emotion magic, and Gren is ready to chase down and petrify the scowling captain at my command.

Good dog.

Shifting, my crossed arms flex as I itch to get back to my tent—to get back to Thaeia. If I can time it right, I can get Valsan to her right now. I glance at the Kapros captain again, but he's looking at Nor. Something passes between them, but then Nor is distracted by the woman standing to his right. Vesper? I think that's her name.

My father clears his throat, and the room snaps their attention to him. He nods to Nor. "You first." The tall islander squares his broad shoulders, nodding, then my father looks at the rest of the contestants. "The rest of you wait here." He turns towards Severn and Valsan. "I have arranged for a small private tent just outside, backed against the dune. Let's go."

Severn ducks his head and literally drags his feet as he leaves with Valsan on his heels. I wait for another pointed look from the Kapros captain, but he keeps his gaze forward as he walks out into the early morning light. Damn it. How ...

Wait ... maybe ...

Turning, I'm surprised to see my father still at my side. Snapping my spine straight, I ask, "What do you need from me?"

His eyes soften, his hand grasping my shoulder. "You *are* okay? Truly? You've been to the Healer?"

I nod. I saw the pompous, hunched old man on the way here at my guard's insistence. "I'm fine, Father."

His eyes track over my face before he leans in, pulling me into a hug. I stiffen. My father has never been one for public displays of affection, but perhaps this attack has rattled him more than I thought. His voice rumbles out. "I'm so glad you're safe, son." My brows pinch as I awkwardly pat his back, but then his voice drops. "Go. Make sure she's safe. We'll get her out."

With a final squeeze, he lets me go and exits the tent without a look back, Daria on his heels.

When I first arrived, before Valsan got here, before the meeting, I told my father about Thaeia. I hadn't planned to say anything, but the words just came out on a desperate whisper. I wasn't sure how he would react, but beyond the slight widening of his eyes, he did nothing. Said nothing. I wasn't even sure he heard me until just now.

He's right. I need to get out of here. Without drawing attention, I use my magic to mentally link with Hich. *"Bring Nor to my tent."*

I share the image of Nor with my giant hound, and his ear twitches, the red flames flickering with the movement. Out loud, I say, "Go, join the patrols." Hich stretches, his front claws scratching at the rug, his haunches raised high. Then he saunters from the tent, walking right through one of the canvas walls. Gren yips, and I stroke a hand through his head, the tingle of my magic caressing my fingers. A few of the contestants eye me with expressions ranging from wariness to awe. Forcing a weak smile, I nod at them. "If you'll excuse me." I turn with Gren close to my side. Aimee, the scary Kapros guard and Valsan's second, narrows her eyes at me but remains unmoving as I pass. Shoving out into the already sweltering heat of the earliest part of the day, I gasp as the dry air scorches my lungs. The sister star has crested the horizon, half its mass and double rings filling the sky. The tip of the sun, a blazing red ball, peeks over the rolling dunes, the haze of heat and sand turning the morning sky orange.

The Alopson guard standing outside the tent snaps to attention. "My lord. If you'd just wait a moment, I'll have a guard escort you."

I clench my teeth to keep from rolling my eyes. My father didn't have the chance to call off my protective detail after I shared who I have hidden in my tent. And even if he had, that order would have looked suspicious. So, I'll figure it out. Power tingles down my spine, and a flaming Spirit warrior appears at my side. Keeping my gaze on the Alopson guard, I wave a hand at the Spirit. "No need." The guard shifts, and I'm sure he's wondering if this counts towards my father's order to keep me protected, but I don't give him the chance to argue. I walk away, Gren at my side and the Spirit warrior trailing behind me, the flames of my magic illuminating the sand under my feet and the canvas of the tents as I pass. My feet sink into the sand with each step, pulling at my boots. I'm so tired. I used a lot of magic yesterday—or I guess that was two days ago—in my match against Thaeia. I used *too* much magic. And now, with the Spirits patrolling, my spine aches, making each step a little more painful than the last. But I know my limits, and I still have a long way to go before I'm tapped out.

So, I push on.

The booming voice of the Master of Ceremonies fills the air. "Attention citizens of Sodoles. Thank you for your continued patience and cooperation. In light of the horrible events, the remainder of the Games have been canceled. But rest assured, the leaders of our great Houses have committed to restoring the Coliseum and each look forward to seeing you perform in five years. For now, please have your belongings packed and be prepared to be searched as you leave today. Again, we thank you for your patience and cooperation."

There's a short pause, the echo of her enhanced voice hanging in the air before she repeats the announcement. I tune it out, and Gren growls, solidifying my focus as my tent comes into view. I chuckle, looking down at my loyal basilishound, mentally connecting with him. *"You're going to have to learn to like her, buddy. She needs us, though I get the feeling she would never admit to needing anyone."*

Gren's ears droop as we step into my tent. The flaps

close with a whisper of sound, and I only take one step inside before both Gren and the warrior puff out in a cloud of red and black smoke. My head whips around. Thaeia's power shouldn't have reached us from my bed.

"Shit, lordling, you scared me."

Thaeia's voice is strong, drawing me to where she stands in front of my wooden chest. The tan skin of her back and side is exposed for a glorious moment, and I catch the rough stitches climbing along her ribs before she lowers the shirt she's pulling over her head.

My shirt.

Gods. She's wearing my clothes—the green and black bruise on her leg peeking out of my pants rolled up at her ankles, the waist sitting loose above her wide hips. This woman ... She wakes up, alone in a strange tent. She stitches herself up, and gets herself dressed ... all after barely escaping death.

I think I'm in love.

She turns, a small wince pulling at her eyes as she curls her fingers over the long sleeves of the lightweight shirt she just slipped on. She notices me staring at her fingers, and she relaxes her hands. With a slow exhale, she begins to roll up the sleeves. I'm so entranced, I actually startle when she says, "My friends?"

"I was just with Captain Valsan and Nor. They're okay." Her breath hitches on an inhale. "I don't know about the others. I'm sorry."

She nods, then cracks her neck, and I find myself staring at the long column of her throat. "Thank you, Keir."

My gaze snaps to her face. She shifts, keeping most of her weight off her injured leg. The purple bruise above her left eye, melting into her hairline, sends a fresh wave of anger through my blood. I stalk towards her, and she shifts again as I reach for her, my fingers brushing over her cheek. Her gold eyes flick between mine, tension building as the silence stretches. She shivers as my touch moves to caress her lower lip, then trails over her chin, down her throat.

She swallows, the movement bobbing under my finger. "Keir?"

"You shouldn't be moving around. Come, lay back down." Her lips twitch with a suppressed smile, and I shake my head, my own smile lifting with my mood. "Not like that. You need rest, and you're safe here ... for now."

Her eyes flash with fear for just a moment before she wipes it away with a smirk. "You undressed me, lordling."

I recognize her words for what they are—a distraction. And it works. The image of her bare body comes into full focus in my mind, and my dick kicks against my pants. She's so warm, so close ... and injured. I get myself under control, curling a gentle hand around her elbow, steering her towards my bed. "I did, and you can get back at me later. Right now"—I stop us in front of my rumpled blankets—"you need rest."

There's defiance in her eyes, but her injuries win out, and she slowly lowers herself to sit with my help. Her jaw tenses as she props herself on her right hand, breathing slowly through her obvious pain. I look around, searching for evidence, and finding none, I ask, "Have you taken anything for the pain?"

She shakes her head, her hand wrapping around her stomach, her hair falling over her face. With hurried steps, I cross and kneel in front of a small box, flinging it open with a soft scrape of wood on wood. Glass clinks as I riffle through neat rows of bottles before I find the cloth packet. Filling a glass with water, I shake a small amount of the powder into the glass, then on second thought, add a little more.

Thaeia's gaze is still on her lap when I return. Dropping to my knees, I shove the cup under her chin, and she takes it without looking. Her hand trembles, sending the water sloshing against the edge of the glass. My hand wraps around hers, holding the cup steady. Slowly, her head lifts, and my chest hollows out when I see tears clinging to her lashes. My fingers tighten around hers.

"Thaeia?"

She sniffs, using her free hand to wipe away the tears before they can fall. With a little tug, she pulls free of my grip and throws back her head, gulping the pain reliever down. I reclaim the empty glass, setting it on the ground before taking her hand back in mine. She drops her gaze again, watching my thumb rub back and forth over the back of her hand. Her skin is soft and browned by the sun. At first sight, I was attracted to Thaeia, wildly so, but it's quickly becoming more. It's unnerving how much of my mental space she takes up. We stay still and silent for several minutes, and I realize that despite the tension between us, this moment is ... nice. I'm at ease sitting here with her, no words, no magic, just us.

She takes a deep breath, and I'm proud of myself for keeping my eyes on her downturned face, and not her breasts as they swell with her inhale. She lifts her gaze, her golden eyes finding mine, determination straightening her back as she says, "I want to trust you, Keir." I bristle that my honor is even a question to her, but then I remind myself that she doesn't really know me. We just met a few days ago. And after everything that has happened ... she has a right to be wary. Thaeia blinks a few times, shifting on her ass, my blankets curling around her hips. "You've helped me, and I ..."

She falls silent, and I squeeze her hand. "What do you need, Fox Slayer?"

My lips quirk with a smile, and she returns it. For a beautiful second, her eyes sparkle and her body relaxes. Then the moment passes. Her lips pull into a tight line, and her shoulders slump. But she holds my gaze as she asks, "Was this ... did those people die ... was this about *me*?"

CHAPTER 8

THAEIA

I HOLD MY BREATH, not sure I want to know the answer to my question. I mean, I suspect, but to hear it out loud …

Just a little while ago, when I woke with my face planted in the carpet, I managed to haul myself to my feet, fix my popped stitch, and only swayed slightly as I limped to Keir's trunk. I was able to find some clothes and dressed with muffled grunts of pain. But already, under Keir's attention, I'm starting to feel stronger, not so alone.

The pain meds are helping as well.

Keir shakes his head. "I don't know." I raise a brow, and his fingers tighten on my hand again before he continues the gentle strokes with his thumb. "Not definitively. But yes, it's likely this was about you."

Before I can stop it, a chuckle bubbles from my lips. My head falls back, and I stare at the ceiling of Keir's tent, aiming my manic anger at the skies. "Really? Of course.

Gods! You're just gonna keep piling on, huh? Just when things were going so well. Ugh!" Closing my eyes, I let my head fall forward. "Sorry."

Keir's soft voice curls around me. "Don't apologize, Thaeia. It's okay."

Peeling my eyes open, I look at Keir. "No. No. I can't waste my anger on the Gods. I need to focus. How bad is it?"

"The Games have been canceled. The city is on lockdown. The Houses are convening right now. They are questioning the contestants that were in the arena. My father is holding a memorial in a few hours, then the people will be allowed to leave once they have submitted to a search."

I study his face, and though there is no outward change, I sense there's something else.

"And ...?"

He licks his lips, which threatens to steal my attention. "And, House Kapros is withholding judgment until more is known. House Drakam suspects House Kapros. It doesn't look great that Lady Daire didn't attend the games this year. Drakam is also placing blame ... on you."

"Of course they are. Blame the freak." Taking a slow breath, I run my hands through my hair. "Though I'm not surprised." I force myself to stare into his bright blue eyes as I ask, "And House Alopson? Where does it stand?"

Keir's stroking thumb stills. "I'm with you, Thaeia. I can't help but agree that Lady Kapros' absence looks ... suspect, but that's not on you. I want whoever orchestrated this found and brought to justice."

Saph's presence whispers in the back of my mind.

"And your father?"

My arm tingles all the way to my shoulder as Keir's

thumb begins stroking the back of my hand again. He begins to answer, but a familiar voice cuts him off.

"Lord Keir?" My neck cracks as I whip my head around at the sound of Nor's voice coming from outside the tent.

Keir rises, his movements smooth and graceful. Crossing the large expanse of his quarters, his flames flare along his shoulders, the smaller of his dogs appearing with a low growl. Keir undoes the ties at the entrance, holding one of the flaps open. Relief floods my body, and I start trembling as Nor pushes into the tent, the second of Keir's dogs trailing behind him. Nor glances back at the fiery Spirit basilishound. "There you are. I assume this is where you were trying to lead me?" Nor turns back to Keir. "This fella was waiting outside the interrogation tent. He made eye contact with me—which was terrifying by the way—before huffing and started walking this way. He kept looking over his shoulder, so I followed. Then he just puffed out. I—"

"Nor!"

The pain is inconsequential as I launch myself into a stumbling hop across the tent. Keir's Spirit fire extinguishes, and the dogs puff out. Nor's eyes go round, but his arms reach for me as I slam into his large, warm body. He's okay. He's alive and he's okay.

His hands press to my back, holding me close. "Thaeia? Well that explains the disappearing, reappearing dog act. Wait. You're shaking. Are you okay? I've been so worried. I"—he shifts, but I keep my face buried in his chest—"we need to get her out of here. You heard what that Drakam captain said about Thaeia. It wouldn't take much for him to stir up trouble, raise a rabble ..." Fear spikes through my chest, making my knees weak, but Nor holds me up as he continues, "We need—"

Keir cuts him off. "I know. Nor, right?"

I feel Nor nod, and one of his hands leaves my back. "Yes, sorry. It's nice to meet you, officially."

"You as well."

Nor sways as the two shake hands, then his arm wraps back around me. I draw in a breath, catching smoke, blood, and dirt, but under it all lies Nor's comforting eucalyptus scent. Shifting back, I reluctantly hobble out of Nor's embrace and look him over. "You're okay? Really?"

He nods. "Yes. I've seen a Mender. I'm tired, on the edge of exhaustion, but I'm okay. But you ..."

I shake my head. "And Halee? The others?"

"All fine."

My mouth falls open as I pant out a breath in relief. I look Nor up and down again, my gaze snagging on his arm. I grip his wrist, yanking him towards me. "Nor! A third star!"

The fingers of his right hand brush along the outline of his new star, and while there's a little smile on his face, he's not smugly excited as I thought he'd be.

Keir claps Nor on the back. "Congratulations."

I almost expect a mocking tone to lace that compliment. Keir has ten stars. Three must seem paltry to him, but his expression seems genuine. Is this guy really real?

Nor's hand drops, and he slides his arm from my grasp. "That isn't important. Others weren't so lucky. Thaeia, people died."

Like a dark cloud passing in front of the sun, the three of us sober. Keir crosses his arms. "Nor's right. This attack is unprecedented. We need to get you out of Akareth."

I cock a hip. "And where do you imagine it would be

safe for me? Drakam is out. Kapros will be watched, so I certainly can't go home. Alopson—"

"My father knows you're here, Thaeia." As if my blood iced over, my body freezes. Lord Ransden Alopson knows where I am. Keir continues, "I told him, only him. No one else knows. I swear. He will help get you out. We just—"

Nor rubs the back of his neck. "Shit."

His voice melts the ice in my veins with a tingling rush. I turn around, hopping with every other step as I make my way back to Keir's clothing chest. The pain meds are working, and I need to take advantage of my increased mobility. Kneeling, I expertly buckle my thigh sheath around my left leg, the blades Saph gave me already tucked into their homes. Then, I shove my hands into the chest, riffling through the neatly folded piles of mostly red cloth. With little flutters of sound, each garment sails over my head as I pick it up and toss it away.

There's a hint of amusement in Keir's voice as he comes closer. "Can I help you find something?"

"I need a cloak, or something to disguise my features." Another shirt flies over my head. "I can't stay here."

My heart nearly beats out of my chest as I wrap my hands around a length of black fabric. It's just a long rectangle of cloth, but it will work to wrap around my shoulders and over my head. What I wouldn't give for another sandstorm right about now. Standing, the tent swirls, and I brace my left foot behind me until the dizziness wears off. I snap the fabric in front of me, crossing my arms to fling it around my shoulders, but Keir grabs it, stalling my efforts. Panic claws at my ribs, and I can't seem to take a full breath. I need ... I need to get out ... get away ... run ... run ...

I try to yank the fabric free, but Keir holds tight as he says, "Thaeia. Calm do—"

This time, when I pull, Keir lets go. "Don't tell me to calm down! I'm being *hunted*!" Everything inside me is screaming to stay away from Keir's father. Shaking my head, my soft mumbles fall from my lips. "I should never have left home. Saph was right. I'm so stupid." If Lord Alopson knows where I am, I can't stay here. The memory of Saph's hate-filled eyes when she spoke of Ransden Alopson flashes through my mind. I take a deep inhale, the breath catching at the twinge of pain along my ribs. "Thank you for helping me, Keir. Honestly. I don't know how I'll be able to repay you, but one day I will." The black fabric settles over my head, and I tuck my hair behind my ears.

I aim for the exit, but Nor grabs my upper arm. "Thaeia, slow down."

Keir steps to my other side. "I shouldn't have told my father without talking to you first, but you were unconscious, Thaeia ... for a long time. I was so ... I didn't know what to do. He'll help. I promise."

My eyes dart between Nor and Keir. The silence stretches until Nor shifts. "I feel ridiculous even asking, but Keir, could I talk with Thaeia alone for a moment?"

Keir's eyes fall to my face. I'm not sure how my expression is reading right now, but he nods, a little smile lifting his face as he shrugs at Nor. "Sure. I'll just leave *my* tent. I should make sure my Spirits are seen patrolling anyway." His touch glides down my arm, then his fingers wrap around my hand, giving me a quick squeeze. "We'll figure this out, Fox Slayer." And with that, he strides from the tent, his red flames licking at his shoulders and over his hair, competing with the orange-red of the rising sun.

Nor draws me across the tent. My mind is busy working through options, trying to clear the cloud of fear, so I don't notice I'm once again sitting on the floor until Nor plops in front of me, crossing his legs. The sand under the carpet shifts under my ass as I lean my back against Keir's low bed.

Nor reaches over, cupping both my hands in his. His mouth opens, but before he says anything, I cut him off, needing to ask, needing the extra reassurance. "Valsan is okay? Halee? The others?"

A soft smile slides across his face. "Yes."

"Good. That's good."

His smile fades, but his hands on mine remain steady. "Talk to me Thaeia." I glance towards the entrance, then look all around the tent, irrationally sure someone is listening in. "Thaeia?"

Okay. Here I go. Shifting side to side, I lean in, dropping my voice. "There's a crest. No, that's not the right place to start. Saph wasn't Saph. I mean, she was Saph, but that wasn't who she was before."

Deep furrows pinch Nor's brows. "What?"

Pain begins to push against the meds, and I rub my fingers into my temple. Stretching my leg, I massage my knee. I'm pretty sure my leg isn't broken, but fuck, it hurts. Nor frowns, glancing around before shoving back to his feet. I watch him without seeing what he's doing as I try to gather my thoughts. Nor sits back down, recrossing his legs and holding out a half-filled glass. "For the pain."

I shake my head. "I took some already."

"Take more. You need it."

"How much did you put in there?"

"Three pinches."

I crack my neck. That's still within a safe amount ... I

think. The cut along my side pulses with pain along with my heartbeat, and I shrug. Grabbing the glass, I swallow the powdery water in three gulps. It's cool and refreshing, but I involuntarily shiver from the bitter aftertaste. Nor digs a hand into his pocket, producing a ginger cookie of all things. I smile as he hands it to me, saying, "Found it in one of the boxes over there. Your lord has a stash of snacks. Good ones."

Keir has a secret stash of snacks? That's it, I'm marrying him. The sweet and spicy cookie melts on my tongue, the bitter taste of the drug forgotten. Swallowing, I realize I've eaten the entire cookie. Nor chuckles, handing me another. "Let's clean him out. He can afford more."

I snatch the treat from him, inhaling the ginger scent before taking a small bite. Nor gets back up, rummages around in Keir's belongings, and comes back with an open tin, the golden rounds of ginger cookies within. In his other hand, he clutches a paper sack. When he sits back down, he holds the open end of the sack towards me, and when I peek inside, I nearly scream with delight. Chocolate. My hand dives in of its own volition, and my fingers come out slightly smeared with the dark treat. The little square of chocolate in my hand is dusted with ... I inhale ... chili powder. Hurriedly, I swallow the ginger cookie I was chewing and take a little nibble of the chocolate. A moan slides from my lips—I can't help it.

Nor laughs quietly, popping an entire square into his mouth, his dimple crinkling his cheek as he smiles around his chewing. "Your lord has good taste."

I roll my eyes. "He's not my lord." His left brow cocks up as he licks some chocolate from his lips. I look at the half-eaten cookie in my right hand, and the piece of chocolate in my left. "But he will be."

I meet Nor's eyes, and we both smirk, each popping more chocolate into our mouths. I chew slowly, knowing I've been stalling—and Nor has let me. But I have to tell him. I have to get this off my chest. So, I lick my fingers clean, leaning back against Keir's bed.

"Saph knew something about my past. She didn't get to tell me everything before she died. In fact, she told me very little, but what she did say made it very clear ... she hated Lord Ransden Alopson."

CHAPTER 9

NOR

THAEIA TELLS ME EVERYTHING, our treats forgotten. She tells me Saph's real name, Rhenara, and about her past in Alopson. And that Lord Alopson was the reason she left and changed her name. Thaeia tells me about her so-called family crest ... all of it.

It's a lot. When she stops talking, I just look at her. She's bruised and battered. At some point she took my hand in hers, or maybe I reached for her. I don't know. There are shadows under her eyes, and her hair is a wild tangle of messy, knotted waves. But her spine is straight, and there's fire in her gaze. There's a little smear of chocolate in the corner of her mouth, and the warmth of her hand rests lightly in mine. That simple contact seems to be grounding us both.

I click my tongue. "Okay. Okay. So ..."

She shakes her head, her shoulders shrugging. "So?"

Because I don't know what else to do, I chuckle. "Yeah. I have no idea. I don't see how you're getting out of Akareth without someone in a position of power agreeing to hide and help you. Right now, I think that's Keir."

She presses her lips between her teeth. "But with Keir comes his father. He obviously trusts his father. I'm not going to be the wedge driven between them. Does Valsan not have enough 'clout' to get me out? He's well-liked and respected. Maybe ...?"

Something inside me sours at the thought. Valsan *is* well respected. He's also good and honorable and kind. I don't doubt that right now, he's trying to think of a way to get Thaeia out.

Thaeia shifts, responding to my silence. "Yeah, you're right. It feels wrong to ask that of him."

I raise a brow. "I didn't say anything."

"It was on your face, you love-besotted buffoon."

She laughs, but my smile falls. "Love huh?" Her laugh dies off, her fingers squeezing my hand. When she remains silent, I sigh. "I feel silly talking about this, what with everything going on. You're in actual danger here, Thaeia. I—"

"Just tell me."

"Valsan told me he loved me." My entire body tingles with warmth as I say that out loud. He loves me. Holy shit.

I'm jarred from my thoughts when Thaeia's hand cups my cheek. "That's great, Nor. Right?"

I smile, my dimple forming under her warm hand. "Yes. Yes it is." Her arm drops, and I shake my head. "But I didn't ... I mean I wanted to but ..."

"You'll get the chance, Nor. But even without the words, I'm pretty sure he knows how you feel. I can see it. I'm sure he does too."

Taking a deep breath, I nod. "Thanks. And if we ask, Val will help. He'll help even if we don't ask. That's just who he is. We can't do this on our own."

She smirks. "Val, huh?" I laugh, shaking my head, but she launches forward so quickly, my breath wooshes out with a huff as she crashes into me, arms wrapping me in a hug, her body curling into my lap. "Thank you, Nor."

My lips press to her hair. "For what?"

"For being here."

I nuzzle her head with a chuckle. "How's this for our first adventure together?"

She laughs, but it hitches like tears hover just below her mirth. "It's not boring, that's for sure."

We sit quietly. Her fingers trail over my third star, her touch light, almost tickling. With each pass of her finger over my tattoo, I feel more settled. Still, I'm unsure how to move forward, what to say, what to do? And I think Thaeia has stalled as well because she's unusually still and silent.

After a while, I clear my throat, her hair fluttering under my lips. "Okay, so I can create a diversion. I'm good at calling attention to myself. If I make enough noise and make a big enough fuss, you should be able to slip from the tent city. You'll have to avoid the main roads, or probably roads all together, but if you can get into Alopson we can meet up somewhere. If I haven't been arrested, that is. *Someone* will meet up with you, and if you can get back to Ka Crummens, you can get on a ship, any ship, to anywhere. I'll give you what money I have. Buy passage anywhere yo—"

"Nor."

"Thaeia, don't."

"Don't what?"

"Don't do what I know you want to do. Don't be brave.

Don't be stubborn. This is dangerous. People have died. Someone or several someones want you eliminated."

Thaeia's breaths are even, and she's quiet for several heartbeats, then she pulls away, scooting out of my lap. Despite the heat of the stove and the quickly warming day, there's a moment where I'm chilled by her absence.

"I know. But if I run, if I manage to get away—which with my luck, the gods wouldn't let that happen—I'd be running forever."

"Not necessarily. We just need time to figure things out, to—"

"I'm going to let Keir help."

"And his father?"

She shrugs. "I don't know if Saph's hate for Lord Ransden is tied to me, or my curse. In fact, now that I've taken a moment to calm down, it can't be, right? Whatever happened, happened a long time ago. Saph left Alopson years before I was even born." She chuckles, and I can tell she's trying to sound confident, but her eyes still hold uncertainty. "I just panicked before."

"Well if anyone has good cause to panic ..."

She smiles rolling her eyes before turning serious. "If Keir says his father will help, then I'm going to pull this thread and see where it leads. I can't say I'll be able to completely trust Lord Alopson, but I ... I trust Keir. Am I being stupid?"

I cock my head, scratching at my stubble. "I don't think so."

"Great. Way to make me feel better." Her voice drips with sarcasm, and we both laugh. But as our laughter fades, I just stare at her.

I think my plan is better. She should run, and run far. I search her face for any crack, any slip of vulnerability that will allow me to talk her out of placing her life in Lord Alopson's hands, but all I see is steely determination.

I hate it, but I know Thaeia, so I nod. "Well, you're not in this alone." Lifting my arm, I clench my fingers into a fist. A brilliant grin lights up Thaeia's face, her gold eyes sparkling. Her left arm rises, and she bumps her fist to mine.

Pulling away, she runs her hand through her hair, her fingers getting stuck in the tangles. She winces as she tries to work out some of the knots, but I shake my head. "I think that's a lost cause. You're going to need coconut oil and a long bath to tame that bird's nest."

She sighs, her hands falling to her lap, her gaze snapping to the stove. "It's too hot in here."

I have to agree, the building heat of the morning, added with the heat of the stove, makes it near stifling in this tent. Crawling over the carpets, I grip the warm handle and pull the little stove hatch open, using the poker to spread the nearly spent logs apart, snuffing out the fire.

A deep voice cuts through the tent from the entrance. "I'm afraid that will do little to alleviate the heat. The day has barely begun, but it is already sweltering."

Almost comically, Thaeia and I spin to face the owner of that voice. There he stands. Lord Ransden Alopson. He's tall and broad, backlit by Keir's Spirit flames. Keir shoots an apologetic look towards Thaeia, but she's staring at Lord Alopson. Then we both actually realize *who* just entered the tent.

I jump to my feet, and when Thaeia shifts and starts to struggle to stand, I hurry to her side, gripping her elbow. But Lord Alopson's voice halts our efforts. "Please, don't bother. Rest." His salt-and-pepper hair is neatly tied back, his expensive red and black embroidered clothes sharp and unwrinkled, a stylized fox on the breast of his sleeveless tunic. A small smile lifts his lips, showcasing where Keir got his good looks. "But you'll excuse me if I don't get closer." He keeps his gaze on Thaeia. "You see, at a time like this, calm and order are crucial. My magic—"

Thaeia holds up a hand. "It's okay. I understand. Trust me. I understand."

The smile slips from his face, a look of pity flitting across his eyes. Thaeia stiffens. She *hates* pity, I should know. But she presses her lips between her teeth and remains silent. Lord Alopson's blue eyes—a shade darker than his son's—assess Thaeia before he jerks his head at Keir. "The uniform."

Keir rolls his shoulders, sliding a small pack from his back, the canvas whispering quietly as he opens the flap and reaches inside. Lord Alopson crosses his arms, his presence filling the tent even from a distance, making me feel small, like prey. It makes my skin itch with the desire to leave, to take Thaeia and run. Keir crosses the tent, only making it three steps before he hits Thaeia's Void, and his Spirit flames and his hounds extinguish. I blink, realizing I didn't even notice her Void this time, and it has been days since I last felt any pain at the sound of her voice. I'm finally slipping free of my father's abuse.

Keir walks right past me, eyes on Thaeia. He holds out the bundle of clothes, and she takes them, clutching the red material to her chest. She glances down then back up at Keir, her brows high.

Before he can answer her unasked question, Keir's father turns to me with a blank expression. "You lied."

A tingle of fear travels from the tip of my head to my toes, but I keep my spine straight and maintain eye contact. "No. I didn't know where Thaeia was when you interrogated me."

There's the slightest twitch of the muscle over his right eye as he says, "Interrogation is a bit dramatic. We civilly asked questions imperative for the safety of Sodoles."

My legs feel like they're about to give out with fear, but I hold Lord Alopson's gaze. A bit of my anger slips out. "Sure. Slap whatever platitudes you want on it. And Lord Drakam never opened his mouth. Or was he using his magic to pull power from a Memory mage, or a Truth mage, or ... Wait. How are you even here right now? There's now way you could have questioned all the contestants so quickly. Surely your son could have relayed any message you ..." My words trail off as I remember who I'm speaking to, so I drop my gaze, adding, "Sir."

To my utter surprise, Lord Alopson's mouth quirks with the smallest of smiles. "You're perceptive." He glances at my tattoos, and oddly enough, I have the urge to hide my arm behind my back as he says, "You'd be an asset to my House."

There it is. The words I've longed to hear, coming from Lord Alopson himself. But they fall hollow and empty at my feet. My dream has shifted, changed. I no longer care about the prestige of House Alopson. Valsan's smiling face appears in my mind. I blink, realizing Lord Alopson is still talking.

"I left my captain to finish the *questioning*." He smirks around the word before continuing, "And yes, Severn might have been using his Channel magic, but I suspect he was just being his useless self." I fight to keep the shock from showing on my face. Was that a slip, or did Lord Alopson actually mean to say that about Lord Drakam? Seems the Houses are more divided than I thought. He stares at me for another long moment before he shifts just enough to look at Thaeia. His fingers press to his temples, rubbing with deep, slow circles. There's a slight shake to his hand as he lowers it. Is the great Lord Alopson finally reaching his limit? How much longer can he possibly hold everyone within his Emotion magic?

Crossing his arms, Lord Alopson smiles, all evidence of any weakness now gone as he says, "As to why I'm here right now? I had to see for myself what my son has gotten himself into." Keir drops his head, but Thaeia stands tall, holding the Lord's gaze. Alopson jerks his head at the bundle of clothes clutched in her arms. "That's the uniform of the guards of House Alopson. This is how we're getting you out." Smart. I should have thought of that. "It was my son's idea."

Keir shifts, lifting his eyes, not to his father, but to Thaeia, a slight blush staining his cheeks at the pride in his father's voice. I understand. I've been yearning to hear that tone in my own father's voice for ... too long. It doesn't matter. Not anymore.

Thaeia drops the red trousers on the carpet at her feet, holding the shirt against her chest, gauging the fit as she says, "My face will still be exposed."

Keir clears his throat. "That's why we'll wait till night to move you. Guards deal with a certain amount of anonymity. People tend to see the uniform and not much else."

Thaeia raises a brow before turning her back to us. "And what about those who do bother to pay attention?"

We fall silent, and a thought jumps to mind. I rub my hand down my face with a groan. "Well ..."

When I don't go on, Thaeia rolls her eyes. "What?"

"You're not going to like it."

"I don't like any of this."

Lord Alopson's deep voice, laced with impatience, breaks in. "If you have an idea that will help, please share."

I sigh again, cracking my neck as I turn towards the Lord. "Can you get your hands on summer poppy? Either the seeds or oil or lotion?"

Thaeia groans, and I wince at her in apology. Keir looks between us. "I think our House Healer has some summer poppy oil. Why?"

Thaeia presses her hands to her head dramatically. "Oh man."

My shoulders hitch as I wince again. "So, ah, well, Thaeia is allergic."

Lord Alopson crosses his arms. "How so?"

Thaeia lifts her head with a mirthful chuckle. "If I come in contact with summer poppy, I get real itchy, and"—she presses her hands to her cheeks then pulls them away a few inches—"I swell up."

Keir's brows furrow. "Sounds painful."

Thaeia scratches her scalp, her fingers getting tangled in her messy hair. "It is."

I interject. "But, you'd hardly recognize her. She gets really puffy."

Thaeia drops her head back, staring at the ceiling. "Ugh. This sucks, but it's a good idea."

Lord Alopson nods. "Then I will make sure you have the oil before we move you. How long does it take to …?"

Thaeia and I glance at each other, small smiles lifting our lips as we both say, "Not long."

She turns to face the Lord. "A matter of minutes, and without lamb's bay lotion to soothe the effects, I'll be swollen for hours."

Turning around, Thaeia's arms cross before her, grabbing her shirt. As she lifts it over her head, I nearly growl at the sight of the long, stitched wound up her side. Parts of her flesh are red from surface burns, but at least those don't seem too bad. Her battered skin disappears again as she slides on the new shirt. When she turns back around, the red fabric with the Fox emblem hugs her large chest, and she holds out her arms. "Another problem. No sleeves." Her left hand waves at Ransden. "Kind of a giveaway."

My brows scrunch. "We could draw one on you."

Thaeia's eyes go wide. Falsifying stars is a criminal offense. There are always those few who ink themselves, trying to drive up prices for services using their magic, but if you're found out, your business and your reputation are ruined. If reported, falsifying stars will land you in jail. It carries a death sentence. We take our gifts from the Gods very seriously. But still, Thaeia's life is *already* on the line ...

She's shaking her head, clasping her hands behind her back as if to keep me from drawing on her arm right now. "I'll endure the poppy, but that ... drawing a ..." Keir grabs her arm, pulling her hand into his. The panic drains from her eyes, and her posture softens. Those two have it bad for each other. I think of my own obsession with Valsan, and Halee finding Miles. At least some good things have come out of all this pain and chaos.

Keir's calm voice seems to settle Thaeia further. "It's okay. Faking a tattoo *is* an option, but one I think we can avoid if we wait for nightfall. It'll be cooler then. You can wear the uniform jacket without drawing suspicion."

Lord Alopson steps forward a single step, staying outside of Thaeia's Void, but Keir actually startles, letting go of Thaeia as if afraid of his father's disapproval over that small touch. The moment passes quickly, then Lord Alopson steps back, his shoulders brushing the secured flaps of the tent.

Thaeia bends over, unbuckling her thigh sheath, setting her beloved knives to the side before she reaches for the fastening of her borrowed pants. Keir clears his throat, and I grip Thaeia's wrist, saying, "You don't have to change right now. You have several hours until nightfall."

She looks up, her cheeks turning pink. "Oh. Yeah. Sure. Guess I'm just anxious." Dropping her hands from the waistband of her pants, she stuffs them in her pockets, looking at Lord Alopson. "Why are you helping me?"

There's not a twitch or hitch of muscle. Lord Alopson's posture remains tall and unmoving as he considers a moment before saying, "First, I need you to answer a question for me, Thaeia." He pauses, and Keir stiffens. There's something in Lord Alopson's voice ... There's a tightness behind his eyes, and he sounds ... bitter.

If I need to, how quickly could I get out of Thaeia's Void? Will my magic even rise if I call it? There's no way I'd come out alive if I attack a mage with twelve stars, but the way Lord Alopson is staring at Thaeia ... if he makes a move against her, I'll die protecting her.

And, it seems my instincts are correct. Keir strides away from Thaeia, not aiming for his father, but to the side of the tent. I count. Nineteen steps. He stops, turning so he can watch Thaeia and his father. He's using Thaeia's Void to shield himself from his father's magic, but all it will take is one step for him to access his own power. Keir crosses his arms, his tattoos flexing with the movement.

The tent seems to grow smaller with the continued silence as father and son stare off.

Then something settles inside me. I feel light, centered, sure of myself and what to do—like how I used to feel when Thaeia would laugh as we bobbed on our boards in the warm sea waiting for the perfect wave. My feet move, and when I come to Thaeia's side, I interlace our fingers, letting her know I'm here. I'm with her. Her hand is a bit clammy, but she gives me a little squeeze as she looks Lord Alopson right in the eyes. I'm so proud of her, my friend. My best friend.

Lord Alopson meets her stare, holds it, then flicks his gaze to her thigh sheath. When he looks back at her, there's a split-second of ... fear in his eyes. Then it's gone. I'm not sure I even saw it, but his voice rumbles with a hint of the emotion he wiped from his face.

"Where did you get those knives?"

CHAPTER 10

THAEIA

The urge to turn and run shivers through my body. My gaze drops to the well-worn hilts of my small knives. What should I say? The silence stretches. Lord Alopson stands still, waiting. Nor shifts at my side, his hand gripping mine tightly. Keir's eyes are on my thigh sheath, and the look on his face tells me he sees nothing special about my blades. But his father obviously does. He *knows* where they're from. But what am I going to tell him? I need to say something.

Think, damn it!

"They were a gift."

Lord Alopson cocks his head. "Hmmm. Very nice blades. May I see one?"

A bead of sweat creeps between my shoulders, gaining speed as it trickles down my spine. The ludicrous thought pops into my head—*Sure, you can see one*. I envision throwing one of my knives at the Lord, imagining it thudding wetly into his chest. *No. Stop it.* I force my clenched hands to relax.

Luckily, I'm saved from answering Lord Alopson as Keir shifts, dropping his voice. "As fascinating as you may find Thaeia's knives, Father, don't you think this can wait? There are more pressing—"

"Yes, you're right." The intensity in Lord Alopson's eyes melts away, replaced with a relaxed smile. He wears both faces so easily. Which is his real one? Which is the mask? Lord Alopson crosses his arms, the movement pulling his shirt tight against the width of his muscular chest. "Thaeia, stay in my son's tent." Keir clears his throat, and Lord Alopson actually smirks. "Please. Keir will retrieve you when the time is right. Do not leave until then, and make as little noise as possible. Don't give any passersby reason to suspect someone is hiding in Lord Keir Alopson's tent." I bristle at the threat, but with no other immediate options, force myself to nod. Keir is risking a lot by helping me. It's the least I can do—do my best to make sure we're not caught.

Lord Alopson's turns, his hand paused at the flap of the tent entrance as he adds, "Nor, I suggest you return to your own quarters and let us handle Thaeia's extraction. People will expect you and your group to be searching for Thaeia. So search. Use the memorial to ask around. Draw suspicion away from my son." Nor's hand flexes around mine, and I know he hates the idea of leaving me here just as much as I do.

Lord Alopson has no such qualms. He has spoken, and he expects his word to be obeyed. Alopson snaps, "Keir, with me."

And with that, the imposing lord pushes from the tent.

Keir, ignoring the command—or at the very least, delaying following his father—crosses to me. He grips my shoulder lightly, and I ignore the twinge of pain as he nods. "I'd like to reassure you and say everything is going to be fine. But ... what I will say is that I will do everything I can to get you out safely."

Nor's grip relaxes slightly, and a tiny bit of my tension drains from my back. When Keir makes no move to leave, I vaguely register Nor slipping his hand from mine and stepping back. Keir's brilliant blue eyes darken as he takes another step closer, our boots brushing. If I did have magic, this is how I imagine it would feel. Excitement. A rush of anticipation. Blood racing. Heart pounding. Feeling so alive, right on the edge of something ... amazing.

Keir's hand brushes up from my shoulder, caressing my neck. I shiver. Nor is right here. Keir's father is probably waiting impatiently outside. But all I want is for this moment to stretch into eternity, for Keir to keep looking at me like ... that.

His light touch raises goosebumps on my skin. Then his grip tightens, holding the side of my neck with what I interpret as a possessive touch. Blue eyes, the color of shallow water sparkling with sunlight, dart from my eyes to my mouth. I'm melting. Right here, I'm going to dissolve into a puddle on Keir's very expensive carpet. When he leans in, I hold my breath, but at the last second, his lips detour. The side of my face flares with heat as the bristles of his two-day-old scruff brush against my cheek. Leather and dried grass. His scent wraps around me like a breezy summer day. His lips tickle my ear as he whispers, "I'll be back for you, Fox Slayer."

Keir presses a quick kiss to my cheek, spins around,

and walks away. His Spirit flames flare around him as he steps from his tent, and Gren, the smaller of his two hounds, looks back at me, his snout curling in a silent snarl. I can't help but grin at the flaming dog, wiggling my fingers in a little wave as the hound strides outside with his master.

The tent is once again quiet, and I feel Nor grinning behind me.

"Don't say it."

"What?"

I turn, hopping to stay off my throbbing leg. I point my finger in his face, his smile widening into a brilliant grin, his dimple creasing his cheek.

"Just don't."

Playfully slapping my hand out of his face, he chuckles. "Oh, come on, Thaeia. You were putty in his hands. You are beyond smitten. And with the young lord of Alopson! You do like to live dangerously."

I roll my eyes. "Like you can talk. Have you decided on a location for your bonding ceremony?"

His grin freezes, panic clawing across his face. "What?"

I slap a hand over my mouth to keep from barking a laugh. "Gods, your face! I'm joking, Nor. I love Valsan, and I love you two together. But just know, I want to help pick out the design for your ring."

Color blooms across his cheeks, and his large hand scratches at the back of his neck. He shakes his head. "Shit, Thaeia. Val and I are still so ... new. And with everything going on right now ..." His hand drops, and his gaze snaps to my knives. "What do you think Lord Alopson wanted with your knives?"

Picking up one of the blades, the pad of my finger runs over and over the four circles of Saph's mark. "I'm sure he recognized the symbol. I bet his wheels are turning with how a woman with no magic from a tiny island in the middle of nowhere got her hands on a set of blades made by Rhenara." I put the blade down and hold out a hand. He takes it without reservation, helping me hobble into his embrace. "But that doesn't matter right now." I wrap my arms around him, letting him help hold me up. Propping my chin on his shoulder, I stare blankly at Keir's bed as I whisper, "Lord 'intimidating' Alopson was right. Go. Be with our friends. Help keep them safe. And ... find the time." The warmth of his hand strokes up and down my back, his chest expanding against mine with his even breaths. "Find time to be with Valsan. Lean on him, and let him lean on you."

"And who will you lean on?"

Keir's smiling eyes flash through my mind, but I say, "Myself. Saph raised me to rely on myself. I'm strong, Nor. I can do this." Now, all I have to do is have faith in my own words. "And as soon as we are reunited, I'll gladly lean on you and our other friends."

Nor sighs, burying his face in my neck. "I don't want to leave you."

My next breath comes on a shuttering inhale, tears threatening to steal my words, but I remind myself of what I just told Nor. I'm strong. I can do this.

"I know. I don't want you to go, but we'll see each other soon." I hope.

His hands come to my shoulders as he leans back enough to look at my face. "Do you know Elchor, in Alopson?"

My brows scrunch, and I shake my head. Nor looks around, then takes my arm, helping me take a few steps closer to the cooling stove. Kneeling, he draws his finger through the exposed sand, sketching a rough outline of what I recognize as the northern territory of Sodoles. He pokes his finger into the sand at the top of his drawing. "We're here." A line in the sand snakes downwards with the movement of his finger. "And this is the only road in and out." Lifting his hand, he moves to the right, pressing his finger back down. "Here's the capital of Alopson, Farcrest." I nod as he moves his finger slightly up and to the left. "Here's Elchor. It's close enough to the main road that strangers are commonplace. It's large enough to disappear in, but small enough that you can walk from border to border in under an hour. If you're running, you can clear Elchor in thirty minutes." His meaning has my fingers tingling with adrenaline, my fight or flight response flaring even though there's no immediate threat as he says, "That's where I'll be." Laying his hand flat against the sand, he wipes away the map. Brushing his palms against his pants to clean them, Nor stands, jaw tight, eyes narrowed on me. "I'll wait at an inn called The Happy Hare. Come find me, Thaeia. I'll only wait a week, then I'm coming to find *you*."

I open my mouth to protest, but he mimics my earlier move, shoving his finger in my face. "No. I'm serious. I will find you, Thaeia. I'll storm House Alopson. I'll search all of Sodoles if I have to." He raises a brow, the beginnings of a smirk twitching his lips. "I'll get Valsan involved." He lets his grin take over his face. "I'll get Halee involved."

"Oh, that's unfair."

He chuckles, shaking his head, dropping his hand. "Still. It's not an idle threat. So don't make us hunt you down."

Swallowing, I ignore the mountain of challenges before me, whispering, "Whatever it takes, Nor. I have to clear my name, not just for me, but for you ... and everyone who's helping me. And I think if I can find out who I really am ..."

Stepping close, his lips brush against the top of my head with a soft kiss. "I know who you really are. You're my best friend." Before I can start crying, his mouth curls into a smile. "You need to wash your hair." I smack his chest, and he huffs a quiet laugh. "I love you, *Void*." Another kiss presses to my head, then his blurry form strides away, my pooling tears obscuring Nor as he pushes from the tent.

Now, I wait.

Alone.

CHAPTER 11

KEIR

It's hot—like the kind of hot that could melt the sand into glass. I'm standing in a puddle of my own sweat on this raised stone platform, my father to my left, and his captain, Daria flanking him on his left. My Spirit basilishounds lay at my feet, and even though they're dead, they seem to be weighed down by the heat as well. It feels like my boots are melting into the stone, and I glance up with the hope that the great Coliseum behind us will grace us with her shadow. But no, the sun is high. There's no escape.

My father really should have picked a better time for the memorial, but he wants to get these people out of here as soon as possible, so .... here we are. The hot wind dries out my lungs, and the sand in the air sticks to my skin. The crowd shifts constantly, wiping sweat from their faces, fanning their shirts. The only Weather mage present tries to create cloud cover, but there isn't enough moisture in the air to fight the searing heat of the sun. A few Air mages send breezes through the crowd, but the hot wind does little to alleviate the growing discomfort. I'm not sure how long the mages my father employed to help keep the peace will last. They are all exhausted from pumping out their Peace, Calming, Harmony, Serenity, and Halcyon magic. But the press of the crowd and the oppressive heat of the day will eventually cause tempers to flare. Emotions will inevitably overpower the magic if we don't wrap things up quickly and get all these people out of the desert. If the thread-thin peace were to snap now ... I shudder to think of the chaos.

The exposed skin of my father's muscled arms glimmer in the harsh sunlight, fat beads of sweat dripping from his fingers. I can almost imagine those drops sizzling as they hit the stone. Concern edges my shoulder blades closer together when I notice the tightening around his eyes. The amount of magic he has expended in just the last day is enormous. He must be nearing his limit. I know I am. I'm feeling the effects of having so many Spirits active for so long. It is usually just Hich and Gren who I don't even register, but now there are dozens of Spirits walking the perimeter and peppered throughout the crowd before us.

Straightening my back against my exhaustion, I listen with half an ear as my father speaks a few carefully curated words, accompanied by the occasional sniffle and sob from the crowd as he commends the sacrifice of each life lost, listing each name and their House. The air shimmers as my father steps aside, making room for the white-robed priest to take center stage. The woman looks on the verge of passing out, her robes damp from her sweat. She raises her arms, bows her head, and rattles off the quickest prayer I've ever heard.

And then, it's over. With the desert sun beating down on us, everyone shuffles away, dismantling what few tents still stand. People gather their belongings to join the quickly growing line snaking around the Coliseum. With a squeeze to my shoulder, my father walks off in the direction of his tent to meet with Lord Drakam and Captain Valsan before they leave. I can't go back to my tent. Not yet. I have to stay out of Thaeia's Void. My Spirits need to be seen around camp. People fear my Spirits and respect my power, and while I don't thrive on others' fear, if that's what it takes to keep people in line right now, I'll take it.

I shrug off the throbbing ache in my spine, watching Nor clap a Kapros guard on the back—Owen, if I remember correctly. The two walk off, heads bent towards each other, whispered words passing between them.

A small group of people distracts me. Two men shove at each other while a woman stands to the side waving her arms, her voice growing louder. From where I am, I can't hear what's being said, but their expressions tell me what I need to know. Tensions are running high and all the calming magic is starting to fail. I find the energy to trudge through the sand towards them, and with a thought, I send one of my Spirits to the group just as a third and fourth person enter the shoving match. The bright red flames flare, stalling the fight as everyone pauses and backs away from the Spirit. This particular Spirit has Blood magic, which is why I chose her. She lifts her left hand, her hollow eyes tracking each person. One by one, they go stiff as the Spirit takes control, holding them immobile for me as I approach.

I stop before them, crossing my arms, Gren growling

on my left. "Please return to your camps and prepare to leave. There's been enough violence."

Through my Spirit, I release the Blood magic just enough to get a nod from each before I let them go completely. They rush off with heads bowed, but the woman pauses, glancing back at me with a frown.

"Sorry, my lord."

I nod at her, but keep my face blank until she hurries away. It is only then I let some of my exhaustion and pain leak through for just a moment. The muscles of my forehead relax, and my eyes slide closed. I'm so tired.

A throat clearing behind me snaps my eyes open. Turning, I'm faced with a woman, her long blond, braided hair falling over her shoulder. The bartender from the other night. She shifts from foot-to-foot, her hands in her pockets.

I raise a brow. "Is there something you need?"

She snaps to attention, the change in her demeanor startling. Both of my hounds perk their ears at her as she steps forward, holding out her hand. "Name's Layla." Her calloused palm presses to mine as we shake hands. I nod, ignoring the feel of something smooth held between our hands. Layla continues, "Before I left, I wanted to thank you for all you've done, you know, after the attack and all."

She drops her hand, leaving behind ... something that I curl my fingers around, shoving both my hands in my pockets as I say, "It's my duty."

She smiles. "Still. I thank you. And"—her head drops slightly, and her voice lowers—"if you happen to see our Shanty Princess, please let her know the door to my place is always open to her."

The scrape of whatever Layla gave me presses against

my skin as I tighten my grip. "I'll pass that along if I do see her."

With a sharp nod, she turns and walks away, and I continue my patrols. I wait a full ten minutes before I draw my hand out of my pocket. Sitting in my palm is a dark brown leather medallion. The dragon emblem of House Drakam looks up at me, and when I turn the medallion over, there's an embossed image of a flaming tankard of ale with the words, The Dragon's Breath Tavern, curving along the bottom edge. The left side of my mouth lifts in a little smile as I place the medallion back in my pocket. This will make Thaeia happy. And I find myself wanting to make her happy ... always. She's known too much fear, too much hate.

For the next few hours, I walk the camps with my hounds, itching to get back to Thaeia. Thanks to the Houses actually working together and the eagerness of the citizens to leave, the camps clear out surprisingly quickly. The sun sets, and I've never been so happy to see her brilliant light go. My clothes are soaked through, and I feel disgusting, worn out, and just ... ready to leave all this behind.

A shout snaps my attention to the south, and when I turn, there's dark smoke rising from the Kapros camp. I groan under my breath, "What now?" I don't know where the strength comes from, but I manage to pick up my pace to a fast jog. As I get closer, a thread of fear sends adrenaline through my blood, and I start sprinting. Skidding to stop, I nearly topple over as the deep sand covers my boot, halting me much too quickly. Hich and Gren whine, and with wide eyes, I stare at the hungry flames quickly eating away what's left of Valsan's tent.

CHAPTER 12

THAEIA

F ROM THE DARKNESS beyond the walls of the tent, I can tell the sun has set ... finally. I've gone through all of Keir's things, twice. I read a short book about a young boy who finds a dragon egg and cares for it until it hatches. It was a sweet story, and I couldn't help but imagine Keir reading this book as a child, then going out on little adventures to find his own dragon egg. After finding a comb amongst Keir's things, I spent what felt like hours working the dried blood and nests of tangles from my hair.

Now, I stare at the ceiling in boredom from where I'm laying on Keir's bed. My fingers lightly press to my scalp, and I wince—my head is still sore both from the cut along my hairline, and the amount of tugging it took to get my hair unknotted. Absently, my hand drops, rooting around in a small bag of popped corn that's propped against the bunched blankets. The savory turmeric powder coats my tongue as the treat crunches between my teeth. At least I have snacks. I took another dose of the bitter pain reliever less than an hour ago, but the corn is helping to wash away the chalky taste.

I'm feeling pretty good right now.

Grabbing another kernel between my fingers, I lazily bring it towards my mouth, but freeze mid-air. I hold my breath, listening. Yes. There it is again. There's someone outside the tent … and they are trying to be quiet, which means they're not supposed to be here.

Dropping the corn, I slip off the bed and kneel on the floor. With slow, calculated movements, I lift my thigh sheath off the low table, strapping it on while straining to listen. The metal of the final buckle is cool under my fingers as I hear it … the commanding whisper. "Go. I'll cover the back."

A light rustling at the entrance tells me my time is up. And I can't shimmy out the back. *Fuck. Okay. Deep breaths. Calm. Think.* Luckily, even with the setting of the sun, the night has decided to hold on to the heat, so there was no need to light the stove. I've been sitting in the dark in my boredom, and now I'm grateful for the shadowy interior. Staying crouched, I hobble to the side of the tent, and once I'm in place with a clear view of the entrance, I shift my feet to plant them into the rug, my bare toes spread to ground me. I'm still in the guard uniform top, which might help me here, but I'm wearing Keir's loose pants. After Keir and company left earlier today, I shimmied into the uniform pants, but only got them halfway up before stepping back out. They were tight and uncomfortable, and I figured I'd have time to change later.

Whatever. Nothing I can do about it now.

The tent flap moves, and a second later, a cloaked form ducks inside, their hooded head swiveling side-to-side. The person takes two steps and pauses. Their head cocks, then they lift their left hand.

Fuck.

When they realize their magic is gone, their body jerks with tension. Their right hand reaches into the folds of their cloak, their head scanning the tent. Their panicked voice whisper-yells through the quiet of the night. "She's here!"

There's a pop to my left, and a gleaming blade punches through the fabric of the back wall of the tent, right over Keir's bed. Unless I cut my own exit and run, I'm trapped. I think I like my odds in here more than out there. I slip through the shadows, rushing the first cloaked figure. I palm one of my blades, and to make sure I have a clean shot, I snap my fingers with my free hand.

The dark cloak swirls around their body as they turn towards the sound. There's nothing but shadow within the deep hood. The blade leaves my hand with a whisper of wind, and in seemingly slow motion, it flips end-over-end. I rush forward, ready to make sure my strike is true, and a voice in the back of my head wonders if this will change me. I've never killed anyone before.

The knife thumps into their chest, and a second later I'm on them. Jumping, I slam a knee into their stomach and follow them as they fall back, their deep hood falling back slightly but not enough to reveal their face. My injured leg protests as I land on top of them, my knee pressed to their sternum. I already have another blade in my hand, and the hilt is sturdy in my grip as I reach into the hood. Grabbing hair, I hold them as they weakly kick out under me. The heels of their boots make little scuffing noises against the rugs. I lean in, inhaling the cheap wool scent of the grey cloak. "Why are you after me?"

They try to shake their head, and the movement causes the hood to fall back. Pain-filled eyes stare up at me as their mouth falls open. A gurgling sound comes out. I punctured their lung. Frustrated, I shake them by the grip I have on their hair. "Tell me!"

A grunt and a series of thuds and thumps come from behind me, and I assume the second assailant has made their way in. But from the sounds of it, they've gotten themselves tangled in Keir's bedding.

The person under me kicks a little harder, their thighs flexing from where I have them pinned. Their hand slaps at my leg, then scratches at their cloak, fingers seeking ...

I press my blade to their throat. "Don't."

Their hand closes around something, and as soon as I see the hilt of a dagger emerge, gripped in their fist, I slice my knife across their neck. I make sure it's deep enough, trying my best to ignore the wet ripping sound of flesh under my blade.

From behind me, the second attacker growls, "You bitch! We were going to bring you in alive, but no—"

There's a squish, then they go silent. The bloody blade I ripped from their comrade's throat now sticks out of their right eye. They stand there, staring blankly as their brain catches up with what just happened. Then, they crumple. I nod with a slow breath, whispering to myself, "Nice shot."

While retrieving my blades and cleaning them off, I listen. Thankfully, all seems quiet. But when will these two be missed? Will there be more? Unbuckling my sheath, I let Keir's pants slip from my hips and do a shimmy-hop into the too tight pants of the Alopson guard uniform. I have to be ready. I look between the two bodies as I strap my sheath back onto my thigh, slipping the two knives back in their places next to the others, all six in a line—waiting.

My gaze lands on the body near the bed. Keir's blankets are strewn across the floor from where they got tangled and dragged themselves free. There's little blood from that one, but the first one made a mess. Keir's rug is ruined for sure.

Keir.

How will he react to all this?

I look at the one sprawled on the rug. Leaning down, I pick up the dagger they tried to pull on me. I gasp, holding the blade up to the light. Four interlocking circles decorate the steel. What. The. Fuck.

I force myself to sit, crossing my legs, breathing away the tension from behind my eyes, from the back of my neck, from my shoulder blades, from my spine, from my hips ... The blade—one of Saph's—twirls in my hand. Saph said she was from Alopson. She worked for Lord Alopson. Does this mean he's behind all this? Why? I feel like I'm trying to put together a puzzle, but I'm missing more than half the pieces and I have no idea what the finished image is supposed to look like.

I glance at the bodies, lives now ended because of me. Well, let's be honest, this is on them. They attacked me. I simply defended myself. Funny, I thought I'd be sad or even traumatized about killing someone. Or disgusted, or panicked, or remorseful. A small smile lifts my lips.

I'm proud and more than a little impressed with myself.

With a deep sense of calm, I look from one body to the other, not sure if I'm talking to them or to myself. "If it's you against me, I'll bet on me, every time."

CHAPTER 13

KEIR

Luckily, Valsan's is the last tent in the Kapros section, so there's no threat of the fire spreading. My panicked gaze flits around as I approach the roaring fire. My thighs tremble with relief when I spy the Kapros captain. Nor stumbles from the tent, a pack in hand. His body doubles over, shaking with coughs as he tosses the bag onto a small pile of charred belongings. Nor turns, coughing into his hand, aiming to return to the tent, but Valsan grabs the back of his shirt, tugging him back. Leaning in, Valsan says something, and Nor nods. Both men collapse, sitting in the sand, soot dirtying their clothes, faces, and hands. Owen paces to the side, his left arm held out, wisps of Ice vapor streaming from his fingers, but the dry desert air and heat of the flames eat his magic before it can do any good.

I walk over, calling a Spirit with Elemental magic. I

send them to the tent, and they quickly take control of the fire. Valsan lifts his head, but keeps his hand pressed to Nor's back. The Kapros captain coughs, the rattling sound and the black smears on his face telling me he too fought those flames to save at least a few of their possessions. His deep voice is tired as he says, "Thank you, Keir, but don't bother. There's nothing left to save, and there's no threat of it spreading. Don't waste the power. It'll die out soon enough."

Nor breaks into hacking coughs that shake his entire body, and Valsan rubs his back. I direct my Spirit to leave the flames and yank on my magic to allow the Elemental Spirit to summon a small amount of water from the minuscule amount of moisture in the night air. The floating bubble drifts to the two seated men, and they each lean forward, slurping from the water sphere until it's gone.

Nor swallows. "Thank you."

I nod at the charred remains of their tent, only a few flickers of flames left. "Was anyone hurt?"

Valsan shakes his head. "None of us were here. Owen and Nor got here first, started pulling stuff out. Aimee and I got here shortly after. I sent her"—his dark green eyes lift to my face, a hard look stealing over his features—"to hunt." I shiver at the thought of the intense female guard, and I almost feel bad for whoever did this ... almost. Valsan goes on, "Miles and Halee are securing our carriage. They'll be here soon."

Thank the gods, but still ...

My gaze falls to an open crate just outside the smoking remains of the tent. The edge of the crate is black and charred, a pile of grey cloaks spilling out, some half-burned. I turn back to Valsan who shakes his head. "Not ours."

I raise a brow. "I wouldn't think they'd be out in the open if they were. You're not that sloppy." I lower my voice, knowing sound travels at night in the desert. "No one saw who did this?" I look at Owen who shakes his head. Nor does the same. I sigh. "You know what this means."

Nor hangs his head between his arms braced on his knees. Valsan takes a slow inhale, but it does nothing to lessen anger in his eyes. "Yes. And it didn't work."

Thaeia *should* be safely tucked inside my tent, so she wouldn't have seen the smoke. And the wind is pulling the scent away from the Alopson camp, so hopefully she hasn't smelled it. Either way, whoever did this was unsuccessful in drawing her out—*if* that was the intent. I need to get back to her.

Nor leans back, rotating to grab a large pack. One of the straps is burnt, but not all the way through. He tosses it at me, his green eyes bright against his soot-stained skin. His voice is so low, I lean in to hear him spit out, "Get. Her. Out. Of. Here. We'll take care of ourselves. She needs to get into Alopson ... safely."

The squeak and rumble of their carriage approaches, and I seize the silver lining of this latest tragedy. "Come to House Alopson. Let me set you up with a resupply of what you'll need to get home."

I see it in Nor's eyes as he realizes I just gave them an excuse to come to my estate ... to meet back up with Thaeia. Nor nods almost imperceptibly at me in thanks as Valsan says, "Thank you, Lord Keir. We are honored by your generosity."

"We've known each other for more than ten years. I think we can drop the formalities. It's just Keir." I crouch, making sure he sees the sincerity in my eyes. "I understand, Valsan, that you and your guards need to return home to Lady Daire, but please know, my House is open to you and your friends"—I make eye contact with Nor, then shift my gaze to look at the wide-eyed girl sitting on the carriage with Miles. Halee. That's her name. The sweet girl I met when they first arrived at the games. That feels like weeks ago instead of days—"for as long as you need."

Valsan smiles, but it's strained as he says, "Thank you, my friend. House Kapros is in your debt. *I* am in your debt."

I squeeze his shoulder. "Nonsense. You would do the same for me. Now, I must go."

Nor's teeth grind so hard, his jaw flexes. I understand his need to protect his friend, and I hope the look I give him conveys that I will do what I must to make sure Thaeia is safe. He holds my stare for a long second before nodding sharply.

My legs protest as I rise, lifting the pack that I assume is Thaeia's, and the Elemental Spirit evaporates as my magic slips. Hich even wavers for a second before solidifying again. I'm almost tapped out. I need to get to Thaeia. Forcing my body forward, I walk blindly, letting my hounds lead. The desert night shimmers around me, the blues, blacks, and greys swirling with my exhaustion.

There it is. My tent. Thaeia. Hich sticks to my side, but Gren stops, backing up as I approach the flaps of my tent. I chuckle. "I know, boy. But I think my magic is going to give out soon anyway. You know I'll call you back as soon as I can."

He whines, but drops his head and follows, his snout

brushing against the backs of my legs with a tingle of power. I love my hounds, and I hate the void that's left inside me when they're gone, but my need to see Thaeia overpowers that ache.

Shoving into my tent, I'm greeted by a rustling, and I huff a breath of relief when Thaeia stands from my bed. She shifts weight off her injured leg, staying on the other side of tent, concern crinkling her eyes. "What's going on? Can we leave yet? Oh, good, you've got my bag. I've been going crazy in here all by myself. I—"

I hold up a hand with a tired smile. Opening my mouth to fill her in, I smack my lips when no sound comes out. Gren and Hich puff out, and the ever-present flames that lick my skin extinguish. Thaeia shuffle-runs to my side. The tent tilts, and as the carpets rush towards my face my last thought is, *Are those ... dead bodies?*

CHAPTER 14

KEIR

I'm pulled from the darkness, and I blink a few times, focusing on the woman staring down at me. Thaeia shifts, and I realize my head is in her lap, her fingers brushing through my hair. Now this is not a bad way to wake up. A slow smile travels across my face, and my hand presses against the back of hers, stalling her fingers.

"How long was I out?"

"Not long. A few minutes. Ten at most."

"Good. We need to go."

But I make no move to get up. Thaeia begins to run her fingers through my hair again, and I nearly close my eyes, as she asks, "Keir, why is my pack burned, and why do you smell like smoke?"

With a grunt, I shift, sitting up. "Someone set fire to Valsan's tent."

"What!" Panic and fear widen her eyes, and she leaps

to her feet. I stand a little slower, closing the space between us, grabbing her arm to keep her from running out into the night. "It's okay, Thaeia. No one was hurt. They're fine. Most of their stuff was lost, but there's an upside." She blinks at me, a doubtful smirk on her face. I rub her arm in reassurance, and the touch seems to settle her as I say, "In the wake of Valsan and his crew losing most of their supplies, I thought it was only right to insist they come to House Alopson so that I may resupply them before they continue on to Kapros."

Her eyes sparkle with her smile. "You are kind indeed, Lord Keir."

I snort. "Just seizing an opportunity."

Her face falls into serious lines. "Seriously, thank you, Keir."

I say nothing. I don't have the words to explain the intensity of my need to protect her, to make sure she's happy, to ... I don't know. We stand for a moment, close, staring. Our breaths sync, and I feel trapped by her gaze in which I'm all too happy to stay, but my gaze is pulled over her shoulder, breaking the spell. "So, what's the story there?"

She rotates to look at the two bodies laid out near the side of the tent. Turning back to me, she shrugs. "Don't know. I heard them snooping around outside. One came in the front and the other ..." She waves a hand at the rear of the tent where the canvas is split and hanging limp. "I tried to question the first one. Got nothing. The second ... I didn't give him the chance. I searched them both. Nothing except ... a small dagger on each."

I blink. "Well, okay. Are you hurt?"

She shakes her head with a smile. "Nothing new anyway."

My grip tightens on her arm. "Gods, Thaeia. I'm sorry. I should have been here. I shouldn't have—"

"Keir." My eyes snap to hers. "It's fine. I'm fine. We're both doing our best here." Her head drops, and she stares at her boots. "This isn't my fault, but this is happening because of me. I've put my friends in danger. I've put you in danger. You're too important to be mixed up in all this. I ... what I mean is ..."

Oh, Thaeia.

My hand cups her cheek, and she melts into my touch. This. I want this. I want her to find peace in my touch. Gods, I want her. And I want her to want me. Slowly, her gold eyes lift back to mine, the depths shining with ... uncertainty. Leaning in, I whisper, "I'm still right where I want to be." She blinks fast, the sheen of tears fading, and she swallows with a tiny nod. Reluctantly, I drop my hand, stepping back. She needs a distraction.

My eyes travel down her body and back up again. A small smile quirks my lips. "I must say, that uniform ..."

She glances down at the too tight pants, and the Fox crest blazing across her chest. Looking back up, she meets my eyes, and I'm certain I'm unsuccessful in hiding the heat in my gaze. She smirks. "Seeing me in your House colors doing it for you, lordling?"

I lick my lips. "Yup."

A laugh bubbles out, and she smacks her hand across her mouth to muffle the sound. I grin, jerking my chin over my shoulder. "Come on. The camps are almost empty. We need to get you out of here so the guards can break down my tent."

The laughter dies, and her smile fades. Damn it. Her arms wrap around her stomach. "The bodies."

Oh yeah. I keep forgetting about the two dead bodies

in my tent. That's how distracting Thaeia is. I crack my neck with a small smile. "If you wouldn't mind moving out of range? Let's see if I've recovered enough to do this."

"What?"

I shoo her across the tent, and she rolls her eyes. But she moves to the other side of the tent. Hich and Gren appear, their attention immediately going to the bodies. Kneeling, I look them over.

Thaeia asks, "Do you recognize them?"

I tilt my head, pointing at the one closest to me. "This one looks familiar, but I can't place them. The other? No."

"Damn."

I stare at the bodies for another minute before standing and taking a small step back, making room for the Spirit I call forth. The Spirit looks around, and I nod at the bodies. She sighs, no sound coming from her, but her lips puff out and her shoulders slump. In life, this mage used her power to break down trash and refuse. She created mineral-rich compost to feed the gardens and fields. And now I'm asking her to do *this*. Asking—that sounds so polite. It's *my* magic that's holding her here. It's *my* magic that directs her power. I'm in control here. She is ... my slave. A sad smile lifts her lips, and she raises a hand. She reaches for me, aiming to pat my shoulder, but her translucent fingers slip right through my body. I feel her reassurance, but it does nothing to quell my guilt. Turning, the mage holds up her left hand, and the bodies collapse inward. My nose wrinkles as flesh peels away, exposing bone. The grey cloaks fade, pull apart, then turn to dust. Muscle breaks down, and eyes liquidate, sliding back into the skulls. In a matter of seconds, there's a puddle of human goo staining my carpet. My back twitches and then spasms, nearly buckling my left knee.

The fleshy remains evaporate, and the bones crack, collapse, and turn to dust.

The mage turns to me, bowing, and I release her. She fades, leaving behind two large, vaguely body-shaped piles of powdery remains. My flames flicker, and Gren disappears. My knee gives out, and I fall, catching myself in a kneeling position.

Thaeia whispers, "Can I?" I nod, and she runs to me, Hich fading away, and my flames dying with her first few steps. Her strong arm wraps around my shoulder, the other pressing to my chest. "Keir?"

I force a smile into my voice. "I guess I'm not as recovered as I thought. Gonna need a bit more rest."

Her fingers caress my chest through my shirt, and I curse the fabric for keeping her touch from my skin. "That was ..."

My face falls. "She didn't like using her magic that way. She only ever used her power to help, for the benefit of her town. This was ... dirty. I ..."

"Keir, she was helping. Those people, whoever they were, tried to take me against my will, and when I put up a fight, they tried to kill me."

I nod, but the melancholy stays. "I know. It just feels so ... wrong to use my magic to manipulate theirs." If this is how Lord Drakam feels every time he uses his magic, there's no wonder he wears a perpetual frown on his face.

Her fingers curl into my shirt, her other hand leaving my shoulder to cup my cheek. Her nails scrape my beard scruff, and I find that I like the scratching sound it makes. Her eyes dance between mine with what I can only describe as wonder. She blinks, opens her mouth, then closes it. What is it she's struggling to say? Have I done something wrong? Her fingers flex against my chest, then grip my shirt. I lick my lips, ready to ask her what's wrong, what she needs ... but then her gold eyes come closer, her gaze falling to my mouth.

Oh gods.

She tastes like the sea as I lick some of my coconut balm from her lips. Seems Thaeia got into more of my things while I was gone. I love it.

She pulls back too soon. Eons of her lips on mine would not have been long enough. Her breath is a little heavy, but no heavier than mine. We stare at each other before she drops her gaze. Her hands fall, and her fingers curl against the base of her palm like she's reaching for long sleeves that aren't there. She whispers, "Sorry. Um. You said we need to go, so ..."

She stands, and I follow. I want to pull her back to me. I want to take that kiss deeper. But she's right. Later. There will be time for more later. Bending down, I grip the edge of the ruined carpet. "Help me?"

She takes the other edge, and together we lift and shake the heavy rug. We both cough as the bodily remains fall to the underlying sand, some billowing into the air.

"Ew." Thaeia gags, spitting.

Holding a hand over my mouth, I chuckle. "Why was your mouth open?"

"Blech. I don't know. It just was."

Crouching, I mix the remains into the thick sand, doing my best to ignore the bone-grey dust getting stuck under my nails. Flinging the carpet back down, I stand, catching myself before I wipe my hands on my pants. Instead, I cross to my small wash station and use the last of my water to clean off at least some of the day's grime. There'll be more water in my carriage for the journey home. It's not a long trip from here to my estate, two days if you take your time, but our guards always make sure my carriage is well stocked.

Stepping to Thaeia, I can't seem to stop my hand from caressing her bare shoulder as I say, "Let's go. We'll go right to my carriage." Reaching into my pocket, I pull out a small glass vial with golden liquid inside. I hold it out, and she swallows, her eyes going tight as she takes the summer poppy oil. She resists opening the stopper, so I give her space, walking away to rummage through a small sack. I find what I'm looking for, holding up the jar. Thaeia tilts her head in question, so I explain, "You mentioned lamb's bay lotion helps."

A softness drifts over her face, gratitude in her eyes. So lovely. I think I'll forever crave that look, the look that says I did something that makes her happy. She sighs. "Yes. Thank you."

I smile with a nod, placing the soothing lotion in her pack. She rolls her shoulders as she pulls the stopper from the container. It makes a little popping sound, and her nose crinkles. Even from here I can smell the sweet scent of the poppy oil.

"Here goes nothing."

I hold up a hand. "Wait."

She pauses, the vial tilted, the oil hanging at the edge. She rights the container as I once again close the space between us, whispering, "You sure you're good to do this?"

Swallowing, then standing a little taller, she nods.

I can't help it. I step even closer, and her breath hitches as I smile. "Yeah. You're good, Fox Slayer." My smile grows to a grin. "Yeah." Just one more taste—because who knows what the future holds, right?

My lips caress hers. I keep my eyes open so I can watch as hers slide closed, and a moment later, I do the same.

We kiss with soft touches, not the desperate tangle I was expecting. The fire is there, but this is ... savoring. My entire body is both relaxed and tingling. My hand curls around her throat, gripping the back of her neck, my lips pressing a little harder. She moans, and my skin lights up with pleasure. If this goes on, I won't be able to stop.

Like a starving man forcing himself away from a feast that he's only gotten a small taste of, I pull away, stepping back. I lick my lips, tasting my coconut balm again. I'll never be able to use that balm again without getting hard. Oh well. Small price to pay.

We both glance at the bottle of oil still in her hand. She tips it over, and the golden liquid quietly glugs into her waiting hand. She rubs the oil on her face, the sheen giving her a dewy glow. After rubbing the oil down her neck, she pours more into her palm, spreading a bit more over her cheeks.

I take the half-empty vial from her, shoving the stopper back into the top. When I look back up, my eyes go wide. "Yikes."

She smiles, but her skin is tight, so it makes the gesture look strained. She's so ... puffy. Her cheeks are so rounded, they press against her swollen eyes. Her neck is bloated too. She tries to roll her lips, opening her mouth, trying to stretch her skin. "Yeah. I know." She holds her fingers over her face, scratching at the air. "So itchy!"

I take her hands. "I'm sorry. But you really are unrecognizable."

"Silver lining, I guess." She pauses, concern filling her inflamed eyes. "What about your Spirit flames? Out in public?"

My thumb traces little circles over the back of her hand, noticing her puffy fingers and her inflamed hands.

"I'm just about tapped. For the first time in my life, even if I were outside of your reach, I think it would be an effort to call up my magic right now. As an excuse, this time, the truth works in our favor."

Slowly, reluctantly, I back away. Leaning over one of my trunks, I pick up the red guard coat, tossing it to Thaeia. She catches it, wincing slightly, and I ask, "When was the last time you took pain meds?"

"A few hours."

She shrugs into the coat, and I pick up the small pouch of pain powder, slipping it into one of her jacket pockets. Then, I turn, quickly stuffing a few books into a pack, along with a change of clothes, and some toiletries. I go to the crate where my stash of treats is hidden.

I go still. Thaeia clears her throat, and I turn, brows raised as I face her. "You cleaned me out, Fox Slayer."

She shrugs. "Nor helped. And they were delicious."

My head falls back with a bark of laughter, the sound bright and happy. She hobbles to me, pressing a fat finger to my lips with a soft giggle of her own. "Shh. If someone hears you, they'll think you've lost your mind, in your tent laughing at yourself."

My eyes darken, and before she's able to pull her finger away, my tongue darts out, licking her skin. It's slightly warmer, and the sweet poppy oil coats my tongue.

She yanks her hand back. "Keir!" She's flushed, and she shifts like she wants to press her thighs together. Fuck me. Even puffy and blotchy, she steals my breath.

"It's fine. I'm not allergic. Just wanted one more taste."

Her lips part on a gasp, but then she snaps her mouth closed, shaking her head. "You are a distraction."

"A good one I hope."

She just shakes her head again, but there's a smile

pulling at her swollen lips. She shoulders her pack, and grips mine by the top loop. I go to protest, but remember she is supposed to be my guard. She would carry my pack. The rest of my things will be delivered to my rooms once my father's entourage arrives home.

I say, "Follow me. Stay close, but not too close. About two paces back. If someone stops us, stand at attention behind me. Avoid eye contact while still paying attention. Guards look but don't see ... if that makes sense."

She nods, her swollen eyes focused. So I go on. "Let me do all the talking. But hopefully, everyone is too busy breaking down the last of camp, and we'll get to my carriage without any issues."

I turn. Still slightly distracted. Oh, who am I kidding. That kiss. All I can think about is doing it again. More. I need more of my Fox Slayer. My eyes slide closed as I fight to get my wayward thoughts under control. After a deep breath, I open the tent flaps. Looking back, I smile reassuringly, a single brow raised in a silent question. She straightens her spine in answer, so I step out into the night, hearing Thaeia follow two strides behind.

I try to shake off the feel of her lips on mine. My cock presses against my pants as I imagine licking her skin, sucking her nipples, drinking her arousal ... My boot catches on a small mound of sand, and I nearly trip. I force my concentration to my surroundings, trying to see into the dark of the night, listening to the wind, the chirping of the occasional desert insect, the shifting of the sands over the dunes. But that kiss ...

My father's tent—the only one still standing besides mine—comes into view. I mumble, "Shit. Okay. Okay." There's a line of carriages, each bearing the Fox emblem of House Alopson. Two pull away, the jingle of the harnesses pass us, and one of the drivers waves to me. I wave back, heading straight for my carriage that sits second from last in line. A few people clad in expensive red clothing mill about the horses hitched to my carriage. I recognize them as members of our council. One, a woman named Teris, turns towards us as we approach, and she tilts her head, her voice high with shock. "Lord Keir, your magic?"

I stiffen, but I force my stride to remain even. I roll my shoulders, but before I can answer, my father's voice draws near as he steps from his tent. "My son has expended much magic over the past few days. We take for granted his strength, but even Lord Keir has limits."

I stop before my father, and Thaeia halts two steps back. The urge to shift my weight from foot to foot spreads down my spine, but I manage to remain still, standing at attention, my gaze sweeping each person without looking them in the eyes. My father glances at Thaeia before he steps back, and without a word, I stride to my carriage. Eagerly, I reach for the handle, but Teris tsks. "Just a single guard? Surely Lord Keir requires additional protection at a time like this."

I bristle, and from the corner of my eye, I see my father open his mouth, but I beat him to it. "The absence of my flames"—I stride forward, counting, and catch Thaeia retreating a few steps. Reaching the now wide-eyed woman, I poke Teris in the chest, backing her up as I continue to count until flames flicker over my skin—"does not mean I am helpless. As you can see, I can still call my gift when necessary."

Teris bows. "I apologize, Lord Keir. I did not mean to imply you were weak. I'm simply thinking of our House, of the safety of our Lord and his line."

I fight to keep from rolling my eyes. That's how they all see me. The heir. The next in line. Their future Lord. But I'm more than my name.

Gren growls, and Hich circles the counselor. I gesture at my hounds. "Thank you for your concern, Teris, but as you can see, there's no need for me to waste the time or talents of any additional guards, not when they're needed to ensure the continued safety of our people. I'm more than capable of protecting myself."

With that, I step back, maintaining eye contact with Teris as my flames extinguish and my hounds disappear in a puff of black and red smoke. Walking away, I duck into my carriage without another word. The carriage bobs as Thaeia pulls herself into the driver's seat, and a sliver of worry tightens my chest. She can drive a carriage, right?

I hear a soft flick of the reins, and I wait for someone to call out, to stop us, but I sway gently as the horses pull the carriage into motion.

With action comes some relief, but it's short lived as Thaeia taps on the roof, saying, "The check point."

I shift, settling closer to the open window. "Let me do the talking."

Her tight voice calls down. "I know."

The line is long, but not as long as I expected. There are guards from each House, their red, green, and black uniforms spread across the wide road, quickly and efficiently searching each vehicle before sending them on their way. A black-clad guard of House Kapros sees our carriage and waves us forward, so Thaeia steers the horses around the line, and stops before the guard.

There's a small carriage to our right, three people standing near their single horse. Their shoulders are slumped and their eyes are tired. A red-clad Alopson guard searches their packs set in a row in the sand. Another Alopson guard slowly makes their way around the carriage as a green-clad Drakam guard finishes patting down one of the three, moving to the second.

The Kapros guard standing before my carriage nods at Thaeia, and as another green-clad Drakam guard comes over, the Kapros guard says to him, "This carriage is clear. Lord Keir is traveling alone with his guard. Captain Valsan inspected his carriage and packs before they left camp. They're good."

Valsan did no such thing, but I add another tally to the long list of debts I owe him. We've done each other many favors over the years, and of course we're not keeping score, but he's a good friend, one I wish would come work for me.

The Drakam guard shifts. "Still."

The Kapros guard's jaw flexes, but she rounds the carriage to the right. From my peripheral, I see the Drakam guard turn. I force myself to remain relaxed. Luckily, his gaze slides right over Thaeia as he bends to look under the carriage, then steps to the door, peering inside.

I smile. "I'd be happy to step out if you would like to search my carriage."

He backs up, shaking his head. "No, no, my lord. You're good. Please get home safe."

The Drakam guard doesn't give Thaeia a second look, confirming what my father said earlier, guards—even to other guards—are often invisible. For the first time tonight, hope blooms in my chest as Thaeia snaps the reins. The Coliseum slowly shrinks behind us as the dunes close in around her. I almost laugh at the absurdity of our current situation. We just slipped through the first checkpoint with more ease than I could have hoped for. But, someone still wants Thaeia dead. She's being hunted, and here I am sitting in my carriage while she drives out in the open.

The horror of the attacks on the Coliseum are now in the past, but will forever mar our memories, our country. What we're heading towards ... I'm not sure.

My mind drifts back to that kiss. Mmm. More of that would be nice.

CHAPTER 15

NOR

A GUST of hot wind tugs at the scarf wound around my head, and I reach up to slide it off. Scratching my scalp, I sigh. The sun set hours ago, but the edges of the sister star's rings still poke above the horizon, adding their pink and blue hazy light to the night sky. The carriage sways, and I plant a hand on the seat, twisting to look over my shoulder. Aimee, arms crossed, swaying with a natural rhythm to the movement of the carriage, stares at me before turning her disgruntled gaze on the desert.

She'd returned from her 'hunt' empty-handed and angry. She said she ran into the Drakam captain, Silas, but after a forced search, found nothing on his person that indicated he had anything to do with the fire. Aimee had flexed her bruised hand, showing off how she made Silas submit to a search, and I couldn't help but smile. He deserved that and more. Aimee obviously believes he had something to do with our tent burning down. And I agree. There's nothing to base my claim on besides a gut feeling. And we can't do anything against a House captain with just a feeling.

Looking beyond Aimee, I see the single horse pulling a smaller carriage up the winding road behind us. They are several lengths back, far enough that I can't make out the facial features of the two guards sitting on the driver's bench, and as they lean in to talk to each other, their words are lost on the desert wind. The other Kapros guards who came to the games to compete are in that carriage, and will follow us as far as the break off for us to head east to House Alopson. They will continue south to House Kapros to report to Lady Daire.

Behind them, the road is empty, the last of the Drakam and Alopson carriages and carts having not yet left camp. The Coliseum stands tall between the dunes, its sandstone walls seem to glow in the moonlight. It looks almost sad to me, like it's unsure that after what happened, if anyone will ever come back to grace her halls and arena with sport and fun. Gripping the rail, I lean out, but a curve in the road tucks the Coliseum behind a large dune, folding the massive structure into the embrace of the desert.

Until next time ... hopefully.

Valsan's hand lands on my thigh, and I turn back around, trying to settle into the bench seat. He gives me a little pat, but instead of pulling away, he lets his hand rest there. The heat of his palm is almost scorching with the heat that's stubbornly clinging to this sandy wasteland even with the sun's absence, but the discomfort is worth the contact between us. Valsan keeps his eyes forward on the empty road. Having waited for the entire Kapros camp to leave, then dealing with the fire, put us far behind the last wave of people who left before us. Valsan's left hand expertly holds the reins as he says, "I'm sure she made it out, Nor."

I can only nod. Word would have traveled if the Void had been found, right? Unless ... no. No. I have to believe she got out. Valsan's fingers trace back and forth in a soothing caress over my thigh. My dick twitches, but my swirling thoughts keep my lust at bay. So many people lost their lives, more than I thought. Twenty-seven dead. Even more injured, but luckily the Mendors and Healers were able to take care of everyone ... well, almost everyone. Thaeia. She'll have to heal the slow way.

From the corner of my eye, I glance at Valsan. Once we get to Alopson and meet up with Thaeia, what then? Valsan and the others can't stay in Alopson. They have to get back to Kapros, back to the capital, Loudare, back to House Kapros and Lady Daire. But what about Thaeia? Will we be able to take her with us? Will she have to stay under Lord Alopson's protection? And if so, for how long? Should I stay in Alopson? Go with Valsan? And there's Halee. I should make sure she gets home safely. But how can I leave Thaeia behind?

Around and around, my thoughts press against my skull until a dull ache begins to build. I crack my neck. And on top of everything, I still haven't told Valsan how I feel about him. The desire to tell him I love him has been sitting in the back of my throat since he first said it to me, but there's been no time.

I turn to look more fully at Valsan, taking in his strong profile. His beard is longer now, and my fingers flex with the urge to run them through it. I could tell him right now. I could just blurt it out. It's three short words.

His cheek twitches, and his fingers dig into my thigh before picking up their little caresses again. He doesn't look at me, but a slow smile overtakes his face as he says, "I feel you staring, Nor."

Shifting, I bend my left leg to settle my weight on my hip. The movement causes his hand to slide down my inner thigh, and my cock once again takes notice. My three stars flex along my forearm as I interlace my fingers with his, holding him against my leg. He glances at me with a little smile on his lips, but he does a double take when he notices my serious expression.

"Nor, what is it? Are you okay?"

Just say it.

"I love you."

Valsan blinks at me, his mossy-green eyes nearly black in the shadows of the night. We sway with the motion of the carriage, just staring at each other. *Why isn't he saying anything? He heard me, right? Oh, gods. Say something.* His fingers flex around mine, and anticipation has me wound tight as he opens his mouth.

But Owen's chuckle floats from inside the carriage, cutting Valsan off. "Finally. Shit, Nor. Took you long enough." A light slap cracks through the night. "Ow. What was that for?"

Halee's soft voice responds, "Don't eavesdrop."

Owen says, "How could I not? It's so quiet in here. Sound travels in the desert."

There's a pause, then Halee huffs. "Well, you didn't have to say anything. You interrupted their moment."

"If they didn't want to be interrupted, they could have waited fo—"

Aimee barks from the back of the carriage, "Shut up, Owen."

Hopefully the dark of night is hiding my blush. This is not how I imagined this going. I should have waited. What a stupid moment to say something so important. I've blown it.

Valsan squeezes my fingers, bringing my embarrassed gaze back to his face. There's a soft smile on his face as he lifts our twined hands, pressing a kiss to the back of mine before bringing them to his lap. "I love you too."

I don't know how to respond. I was so worried about saying the words, I didn't think about what comes after. Absolutely all thoughts drain from my mind, and I forget how to speak as Valsan scoots across the seat, pressing his thigh against mine, his hand tugging mine to feel his hard length pressing against his pants. Leaning in, his deep voice whispers against my ear, "I wish I could properly show you how your words have affected me."

My dick leaps to attention, and I'm instantly, painfully hard. Fuck. I really should have timed this better. Valsan leans back, resettling, once again facing the road, the horses clipping along at a slow trot. I need ... my fingers press against his cock through his pants, and the fabric darkens as precum leaks from his tip. I lick my lips, eager to taste him. I want to drive the man I love wild. As much as his pants will allow, I wrap my hand around him, squeezing. Val's lips fall open, his head falling back slightly.

Owen's obnoxious voice calls out, "Sure is quiet out there."

Miles says, "Owen!"

Halee tsks. "Seriously?"

Well, I'm not stopping now, so I say, "Then fill the

silence. I'm sure you have at least one story you haven't told us yet."

I stroke Valsan, and he grunts, "Yes, tell us a story, Owen. Loudly."

Blushing, I shake my head with a grin, as Owen says, "Okay." Then understanding hits. "Ohhhhhh. Shit. Sure, okay. I get it. When you need a good *story*, you need a *good story*."

Aimee chuckles as Owen's voice rises. "So, there I was, on patrol in the small town of Eshax. Night was falling fast ..."

I stop paying attention as Valsan undoes the fastening of his pants. My hand dips inside, wrapping around him, my palm spreading his wetness over his head and down his length. I stroke him, my own core pulsing with desire as his hips kick up. Damn it. My oil is in my bag which is secured to the back of the carriage. Oh well, I'll make do. Giving him another pump, I then pull my hand free, and he watches as I flatten my tongue against my palm. I can taste him on my skin as I slowly lick from wrist to fingertip. Valsan mouths, *Fuck*, but no sound comes out as he watches me lick myself again, and again. I swirl my tongue around my mouth, gathering saliva as I slip my hand back inside his pants. He's hard in my palm. He's perfect.

With my other hand, I completely undo his fastenings, pulling him free. Leaning over, a long stream of spit drips from my mouth. The motion of the carriage sends the saliva swaying. I watch in fascination as it connects with his dick, wrapping around his length, some breaking off to splatter his shirt. More of my saliva leaks onto his cock as his fingers thread through my hair, scraping my scalp. My mouth actually waters as he tugs gently on my hair. I watch my tattoo stars flex as my left hand pumps up and down Valsan's cock, the dark curls at his base slicked to his body. His length gleams in the moonlight, and I grab his balls with my other hand, scraping and pulling slightly. His hips punch into my fist, and a low growl vibrates from his chest. The sheer possession in that sound makes my cock uncomfortably hard. It makes my skin tingle. It makes my heart swell with knowing how much he wants me. *Me.* All of me.

In the background, Owen still weaves his tale, but all I can think about is the cock in my hand and how much I love this man. Another stream of saliva drips from my lips, landing on his tip, and I swirl my palm over his head before gripping him tightly, sliding all the way to his base. With a hiss, his fingers tighten on my hair, inducing just the right amount of pain. I have a split second to flash a grin at him before he pushes my face onto his cock. He thrusts, hitting the back of my throat, and I struggle to swallow around him.

Halee's high-pitched voice calls out, "And then what happened?"

I nearly snort a laugh around Valsan's dick, but I'm stuffed full. Shifting, I make myself more comfortable, laying my chest against his right thigh, my left leg tucked under me on the bench, my right foot planted on the floor to give me leverage as I bob up and down. His taste fills my mouth, his wood-smoke and coffee scent drowning me. He surrounds me. I'm obsessed. I'm in love. I suck, hollowing my cheeks, and he shoves me harder as he rolls his hips.

I did this to him. Simply by telling this amazing man that I love him made him hard. And giving him pleasure has me on the edge of orgasm.

I'm dizzy with the knowledge that his desire is mine,

and I suck him down with every press of his hand against the back of my head. I nearly slip free as his fist releases me, but I keep licking and sucking. I barely keep my groan from escaping as his hand travels down my back. His fingers tickle at my lower spine as he moves my shirt out of the way so he can touch my skin. I let him slip from my lips so I can lick up the underside of his length, flicking my tongue up the slit of his head. His cock jerks in my grip.

Valsan's hand leaves me, and despite the stubborn heat of the desert night, despite the sweat that's coating my skin, I want his hand back on me. Just as I wrap my lips around his sac, his hand returns, slipping between my pants and my ass.

Oh, fuck.

His wet fingers delve between my crack, and I imagine how he must have just sucked on his fingers for me. I tongue his balls, then swallow his cock with one bob of my head. His finger presses into me, and I rub my aching length into the bench seat. Wrapping my hand around his base, I seal my lips to my fingers circling his cock and pump my hand and mouth together making sure to hit every delicious inch of him. Another finger slips inside my ass, and pleasure curls up my spine.

I scrape my teeth over his length, rubbing my cock into the seat. My body is wound tight, my toes curling in my boots, my stomach clenching. I'm close. Val pumps his fingers inside me, and I pick up my pace, my breath puffing from my nose every time he hits the back of my throat. Valsan's fingers curl, brushing against my spot, and a low, growled whisper floats down to me.

"Now, Nor."

Yes, sir.

My boot scrapes against the floor as blinding bliss rips through me, my cum drenching my pants as Valsan erupts in my mouth. I swallow, trying to take all of him, but some leaks from the corners of my lips. Licking him clean as I come down from my shattering orgasm, Val slips his fingers from me, his nails scraping up my back, caressing my neck, then combing through my hair.

This man is perfection.

His hand tucks under my chin, lifting my head, and I'm immediately met by his lips. He kisses me, long and slow until finally pulling away. Tucking himself back into his pants, he wipes his hand against his thigh. It doesn't do much.

I jolt forward as something wet hits me in the back of the head with a splat. Reaching back, I grab at it, turning to see Aimee looking off into the desert. She glances at me, and winks—she actually winks. The wet shirt slips from my fingers in shock. Valsan picks it up, wiping his hands off, then passes it back to me. I run the fabric over my mouth and clean off my hands.

I snap the shirt out, intending to fold it, when I realize it's one of mine. I spin around, and while Aimee is turned away, I see the slight shaking of her shoulders. I ball up my shirt and chuck it at her. It hits her shoulder, and she jumps away. "Eww, Nor. Gross." She pinches the fabric between her fingers and tosses it off the carriage.

Well, there goes that shirt.

Valsan chuckles, draping his arm over the back of the seat, and I take the invitation. Sliding over until I'm pressed against his side, his hand wraps around my shoulder, fingers tracing small circles over my sensitive skin.

Owen's voice rings out, still telling his story. "I shit you not, he landed in the biggest pile of horse crap I've ever seen. Only the top of his head poked out, one arm flailing as he tried to extricate himself from the excrement. Ha!"

Miles and Halee laugh with Owen, and Aimee's chuckle joins in. A small smile lifts my lips as I snuggle into Valsan, whispering, "Love you."

He squeezes me. "Love you too."

CHAPTER 16

KEIR

Home looms on the horizon.

Before we crossed into Alopson, I'd climbed up to sit on the driver's seat with Thaeia. She'd reapplied some poppy oil when we drew close to the border, but she didn't issue even a single sound of complaint, though I know she was in pain.

The guards of my House stood at attention, all eyes on me, thankfully paying Thaeia no mind. One guard stood before the horses, his gaze dropping to his boots then flicking up to me, then back at his boots, over and over. Another guard walked the length of my carriage, peeking inside, under, then around the other side. In just a matter of moments, we were in Alopson.

That was hours ago, and Thaeia has been quiet, her mottled skin slowly losing its puffiness, but her eyes still remain a little swollen, and one cheek is rounder than the other. Her sudden words have me jumping in the seat. "*That's* your home?"

I smile at the surprise in her voice. Looking at my sprawling estate with the capital city of Farcrest spilling to the south, I shrug. "It's not much, but it's home."

"It's ... greener than I expected."

I point beyond my estate towards the city. "Farcrest was built on an oasis. There are aquifers far below ground and springs feed up all throughout the city." I lean out, plucking a bright yellow night-blooming desert flower and tuck it into her hair.

She smiles, ducking her head. "I don't think one of your guards would be wearing flowers in their hair, Lord Keir."

Bringing my body closer to hers, my lips brush her hair as I whisper, "Then I shall keep it safe and return it to you in a more appropriate and *private* setting." She shifts, pressing her legs together, and as I inhale, I'm hit with the intoxicating aromas of the sweet flower and her natural sea-salt scent. I wrap my fingers around the flower, slowly drawing it from her hair, and reluctantly sit back. The blush on her cheeks is beautiful, and I can't wait to see her entire body flushed with desire. Damn. I'm hard and achy, tempted to have her pull over into a dark corner of the grounds so I can taste her.

But then I remember ...

Reaching into my pocket, I pull out the leather medallion and pass it to Thaeia. "With everything going on, I forgot to give this to you."

She takes it with one hand, turning it over, a puzzled look on her face. "What is it?"

"It's a token from the barkeep." Her eyes light up with recognition. "Her tavern, The Dragon's Breath, is in the capital city of Drakam." Thaeia's lips curl in a little snarl, and I chuckle. "Still, regardless of the location, you have an ally there."

She shifts again, readjusting the reins in her hands, sliding the medallion in her pocket. "I'll take all of those that I can get."

Nodding, I direct her to drive the team around the edge of the property. The sandstone walls glow under the moonlight, the sculpted shrubs creating sectioned hedges across the acres surrounding the giant house. Drought-tolerant trees flank the main drive leading to the circular entrance. We get a quick peek of the wide, climbing stairs that rise from the drive to the towering double doors, each carved with detailed images of foxes. As we turn a corner, the hedges hide the grand entrance from our view, and the horses continue their steady trot around to the rear of the estate, their hooves crunching quietly against the tightly packed, sandy path.

Thaeia's fingers fidget with the reins. "No big home-coming for the son of Alopson?"

I shake my head. "Nah. The staff knows I don't stand for useless ceremony."

"They might not find it useless ... welcoming home their lord."

I smile, and it feels good. It feels like a luxury to be happy in the aftermath of such tragedy. "Maybe, but it always seemed silly to ask them to drop everything to basically watch me arrive. Too exhausting—for me and the staff. So all that pomp and circumstance is saved for official events, meetings and greetings, and such."

Thaeia's voice hitches a bit higher, but her smile doesn't quite reach her eyes. "All those families sending their sons and daughters to catch the eye of the handsome young lord of Alopson?"

"Handsome, huh?"

She tsks at me. "You know you're good looking."

"But I find myself only concerned with your opinion."

She blinks at me a few times before facing forward. I chuckle, trying to put her at ease. "And as for those suitors, there haven't been as many as you'd think."

By the tightening at the edges of her eyes and her hands around the reins, I realize that was the wrong thing to say. She shifts the reins to her left hand, waving her right at me. "You don't have to play it down for me, Keir. It was just a kiss. You are a lord. You will rule over the most powerful House in Sodoles someday. I'm not under the illusion that we are—"

"Thaeia." Her mouth snaps shut, but she still won't meet my eyes. "I was joking. Sure, suitors have been sent. I won't deny that ... because I won't lie to you. But none have worked out. Most have had the emotional depth of a tide pool. And more than once I've had a suitor break down into tears, confessing they had a lover back home that they were forced to leave in the hopes I would elevate their family's standing by choosing them." My shoulders slump. "And the worst part is that every one of them thought I'd force them into a bonding because they were pretty, or their family had connections, or their magic was unique ..." My hand clenches where it rests on my thigh, and I look at Thaeia's profile. "I'm not that kind of man."

She doesn't turn to face me, but her voice is quiet, serious. "I know."

A wave of relief pours through me at those two soft words. She sees me. I release my fist and let my fingers fall around her wrist, noticing her fingers are still a bit swollen. Her gaze flicks to me before going back to the road as I say, "Thaeia, about earlier ... about that kis—"

A horse whinnies from the stables, cutting me off. The team pulling my carriage perks up, their ears twitching at the calls of their stable mates. The area is dark except for a few flickering arsine torches lining the paths.

"Stop here."

Thaeia pulls back on the reins at my command, and I hop down, my legs tingling at the contact after several hours of sitting. Holding up a hand, I help Thaeia down, forgetting for a moment that I wouldn't be helping one of my guards down from the driver's bench. But having her hand in mine is worth it. I jerk my head to the right. "See that stone arch?" Thaeia glances over then nods. "Wait there. The horses have probably woken the stable hand. Give me a few minutes. Okay?"

Again, she nods, then strides to the shadowed archway, only the slightest limp reminding me of her many injuries. She quickly disappears into the darkness, and my skin tingles with unease at not being able to see her, so I grip the lead and take the horses into the stable yard. No sooner do I have the line secured and the first trace undone, before the stable hand emerges, rubbing her eyes, her hair flat on one side from where she was sleeping on it just moments before. She smiles, running her hand along the horse's flank. "Welcome home, sir. I'll take it from here." I grab both our packs, slinging them over my shoulder as I step away, trying to keep my pace even and unrushed, but her voice stops me. "I was sorry to hear about what happened."

I turn back to her. "Yes, it was horrible."

"Do you know who did it? Why? It's just so—" She

shakes her head. "Sorry, sir. I know you're tired and have much to do. And it's late. Please excuse me."

I accept the escape, taking my leave, but making a mental note to come back and speak with her later. Arabell is young still, only fifteen, but she grew up in House Alopson. I've known her her entire life. She will readily spill the gossip floating around the House. But right now ...

My boots are nearly silent on the sandstone walkway as I reach into the dark shadows of the deep alcove. Thaeia's fingers wrap around mine, and she comes into view one inch at a time as she emerges into the faded light of a nearby torch. I give her a little tug, indicating for her to follow, and I can practically feel her tension through our clasped hands.

The chirps and clicks of night insects fill the silence. A soft, warm breeze whispers through the shrubs, carrying the scent of the night blooming desert lilies on the air. The light trickle and splash of a nearby fountain bubbles gently, adding to the calm of the evening.

After just a few quiet minutes, I reluctantly let my hand slide from Thaeia's. "Stay here for a moment." She doesn't answer, and I catch her curling her fingers over the sleeve of her guard jacket. I stride away, hurrying my steps until I come to a heavy arched wood door. I forgot to count my steps, but I think I'm far enough away from Thaeia for the magic to work. I press my hand to the flat metal plate on the door, waiting for the telltale click. When I hear it, I shove the door open, bending down to grab a rock to keep it from closing and locking again. My arm flexes as I raise it towards Thaeia. "Okay." She reaches me quickly, taking my hand, and the slide of her skin against mine settles me slightly.

Pulling Thaeia into the pitch-black hallway, I kick the rock, and the door slides shut on silent hinges. Her fingers tighten around my hand before relaxing. I lead her down the dark passage, and once we're far enough away, that same click tells me the door has relocked.

I can't see her, but I feel Thaeia shift to face the door. "What was that?"

I move our twined fingers so our hands are pressed flat against each other. Lifting our pressed palms before us, I lean in, guessing where her face is and whispering against her cheek, "All the doors in the estate are magically coded to the Alopson line. My father, my grandfather, my father's sister, her children, my brother, and me. Long ago, before I was born, a Metal mage crafted each panel to recognize the bloodline of Alopson." I pause, a little frown pulling at my lips. "Much to the chagrin of my mother. Wedded members of the family are not included in whatever magic the mage worked. It's a little thing, but I think it made my mother feel … left out." I slide my hand down her palm, stroking her wrist before gripping her lightly. "Come on."

I know every nook, every hall, every hidden passage, every room of this giant estate, and though I move with confidence, I feel Thaeia's hesitance pulling against my hold on her hand as I lead her through the darkness. It takes longer to get where we're going since I stick to the narrow passages hidden between the stone walls. But finally, the door I'm seeking comes into view. Again I release her, my fingers tingling with the absence of her touch. Holding up a hand to indicate she should stay where she is, I cross to the door and press my hand to the metal panel like before. It clicks, and I hold it open as I wave Thaeia forward. She gasps as she steps inside.

Making sure the room is empty, I pull her into the towering space, checking that the door closes behind us, and listen as we walk away, only letting out my held breath once I hear the lock click. Letting go of a gaping Thaeia, I jog across the room, skirting the tables lining the center of the open area. I check the main door, making sure that too is locked before turning back to face Thaeia. Her mouth is open, her eyes wide as she tilts her head back to look up and around the warm wood bookcases climbing three stories, curving iron stairs traversing each level. Glassed-in, burning arsine spills light along the walkways, and a few unlit lanterns dot the empty tables, their chairs pushed neatly in place.

When Thaeia's attention finally turns back to me, I smile, holding out my arms. "Welcome to the private library of House Alopson."

CHAPTER 17

THAEIA

My brain can't seem to wrap around what I'm seeing. Books. So many books. It's a wonder this room hasn't sunk into the desert under the weight of them all. I know Keir is watching me, but I can't peel my gaze from the towering shelves as I step further into the room. Running my hand along a shelf to my right, my fingers trace over the polished wood shelf, clear of dust, each spine perfectly in line with its neighbor. This entire section—which must hold scores of books—seems to be comprised of children's tales and folklore.

"You will have plenty of time to explore later."

I jump at Keir's voice so close behind me. I didn't hear him cross the room. Turning, I'm met with his amused smile before he spins and starts up the nearest staircase. The soft metallic sound of his boots hitting the metal stairs echoes around the room, and assuming he wants me to follow, my boots add to the tune. Looking down, I nearly chuckle. Even the stairs are beautiful. Each one has little designs carved into the metal, allowing little peeks of light to shine through from the bottom floor. I'm so entranced by the stairs, I don't realize I've reached the top. I look around the second floor, realizing Keir has walked off to the right along the balcony that overlooks the first floor. Leaning over the smooth metal railing, I look up, seeing the third floor mirroring this one.

Amazing.

I grip the rail, shifting to follow Keir, but something stops me. My knuckles turn white against the black metal railing, and the intricate scrollwork of the baluster blurs as sudden tears fill my eyes. This metalwork smells like Saph. I wonder if all Metal mages' magic smells the same. Her absence carves into my chest, and everything just feels like ... too much.

The blurry shapes of Keir's boots come into view, and his hand falls over mine where it's still got a death grip on the railing. "Thaeia, what's wrong? Is it one of your injuries? What do you need?"

I shake my head, keeping my gaze down, trying to wipe the grief from my voice. "It's nothing. Just been a long couple of days."

He doesn't say anything, just stands with me in silence, letting me breathe. With a final big inhale, I feel a painful pull along my ribs, reminding me the pain meds will wear off soon. I'll take another dose before I go to sleep, wherever Keir plans to set me up, but tomorrow I'll start weaning off. If I don't feel the pain, I could do something to make my injuries worse.

Finger by finger, I release my grip, and Keir slides his hand under mine, gently leading me down the aisle. As beautiful as the metal work is, I'm not up to looking at it right now, so I focus beyond. There are no windows on the first floor, but a series of arched windows flank the second and third floors, letting in twinkling starlight. I imagine the morning light in here is glorious. From up here, I can see a pattern on the first floor—the tiles laid to reveal a stylized fox that looks like it's running across the room.

Keir notices the direction of my attention. "When my ancestors built House Alopson, they really leaned into the whole fox theme. Which, why? The only reason the fox was put on our standard in the first place was because my great, great, great, many times over great-grandmother saw one on one of her trips abroad. She was so enamoured, her bonded smuggled twenty foxes back to Sodoles. But of course, Alopson is not the right climate for the poor little animals, so when they started dying, my great, great, whatever set them free."

My mouth drops open. "So your family is the only reason we have foxes roaming around Kapros?"

"And some parts of Drakam. But, yes. I mean, at least the other symbols make sense. While dragons aren't real"—he winks at me, and my entire body tingles—"that we know of anyway, they are a symbol of strength and power."

I scrunch my nose. "But a boar?"

"At least you have boar in Kapros. It makes sense. And while they are small compared to other predators, they can take down prey three or four times their size. Never underestimate a boar."

We stop in front of a plain wood-paneled door with one of those peekaboo window things fastened from the inside. Keir grabs the handle, the latch clicking as he opens it. No magic metal panel on this door. He drops my hand, steps inside, and places our packs on the floor. Turning, he clasps his hands behind his back. "Hopefully, this will suit your needs. I'll announce that the library is off limits to staff for a while because, hmm, I don't know. Um, some rare books have gone missing and we're doing a complete inventory overhaul ... or something. I'll figure out meals too. But if this is not to your liking, I'll find—"

"Keir, it's perfect. More than I could have asked for. More than I deserve."

And it is. The room is, in a word, cozy. The stone floor is mostly covered by worn, threadbare rugs, their wine, cream, and deep blue patterns adding warmth. A small, empty fireplace sits to my right, yet more foxes worked into the stonework. As I step into the room, I run my hand over the plush velvet two-seater couch, the sapphire-blue fabric copying the jewel tones from the rugs. To give my hands something to do, I pluck a cream-colored pillow off the sofa and hug it to my chest as I take in the rest of the room. A large wood bed sits along the same wall as the fireplace, the blue blankets neatly tucked. Leaning over, I inhale the soft scent of the single desert lily propped in a white vase that sits on the small table next to the bed.

Keir points at a small door next to the table. "There's a bathroom through there. Nothing extravagant, just a shower, toilet and sink, but it'll get the job done."

Just the word, shower, makes my bones groan with the desire to stand under a spray of hot water. But I resist shoving into the bathroom and stripping right now, instead taking in the rest of the room. Across from the bed, a tall armoire nearly brushes the high ceiling, and I smile as I make out the carved fox running across the doors. The back of the room is framed by a large window, the panes wavy, obscuring the grounds of the estate beyond while still letting in light.

Keir steps around me, gripping the heavy blue velvet curtain and pulls it over the window, sinking us into darkness. The light from the still-open door allows my eyes to adjust fairly quickly, and I realize Keir is ... nervous.

Clutching the pillow with my right hand, I run my left over the fox carving in the armoire doors. "You weren't kidding. About the foxes." A soft chuckle escapes his lips, and I turn to face him. "Really, Keir. This is amazing. It's perfect. I don't know how to thank you."

He sketches a stiff bow, suddenly stiff and formal. "Just make sure you rest. Sleep as long as you can. Recover. I'll have breakfast brought to you. Your friends should be here soon. I'll have them set up in the east wing. You'll be reunited. We'll figure out the next steps later ... after you've rested."

My brows pinch together. What's going on with him? Is this it? Is he already pulling away? I'm sure being back in his home has made him really realize how impossible 'we' are. Still. I thought I'd have a little more time to *explore* the lordling.

He steps forward, some of the formality draining from his posture as his eyes go dark, matching the deep blue tones splashed around the room. His fingers brush my cheek, and I shiver. Leaning in, he reaches around me while pressing his lips to my cheek, whispering, "Sleep well. See you tomorrow. Lock this door behind me, just in case."

And then he's gone, the tap-tap of his boots descending the metal stairs fades then stops, followed by the click of the main library door opening and an identical click as it relocks.

What the ...? Wait. Whose room even is this? What-ever. I'm exhausted. I grab my bag, lugging it towards the bathroom, but I freeze. There on the nightstand, next to the vase with the lily sits the yellow flower Keir picked for me earlier. It's a little crushed, two of the petals bent and bruised, but the cheerful color is bright against the warm wood of the table. My finger brushes the velvet petals, and a rush of affection skips through my blood, raising the hairs on my arms. He's just so ...

I sigh like a love-sick heroine in a sappy romance book as I walk into the bathroom. My pack slips from my grip, thudding to the floor. Nothing extravagant? The sand-stone tiles are large and clean, bleeding right into the large walk-in shower where the same wavy glass as the window out in the room provides light and privacy. There's room for two in there. I bite my lip, definitely not picturing Keir's naked body dripping wet, washing every inch of my skin before using his tongue to ...

I strip the guard jacket and shirt off, letting them pool on the floor at my feet. The mirror hanging over the pedestal stone sink reflects the angry stitched cut on my side. Seeing my wound makes it throb, and when my gaze travels up, I notice my still slightly swollen face. I pull the jar of lamb's bay lotion from my pack, setting it on the small shelf built into the wall next to the sink. I might just use that entire jar ... after my shower. Quickly, I shake some of the pain powder into my mouth, grimacing at the bitter taste. Leaning over the sink, I slurp some water, swallowing a few big mouthfuls.

I disarm, frowning at the daggers I swiped from the men who attacked me before putting them next to my thigh sheath holding my throwing knives. Hopping from side to side, I kick my boots off and shimmy out of the tight guard pants, wincing at the deep bruise spanning from my knee to my ankle. At least it's already turning greenish yellow. That means it's mending. A groan—half disgust-half pleasure—slides from my lips as I peel my underwear off. The tile is cool under my feet, and the spray of water is freezing as I turn the faucet. But I just stand there, shivering, watching the dirty water swirl down the drain. As the water slowly warms up, my body relaxes, and I realize there's a real danger of me falling asleep on my feet here in this shower.

I must have zoned out, because the next thing I know, I'm being hugged by the soft mattress of the bed, the warm blankets tucking in around my clean, naked skin. I blink lazily, looking at the plastered ceiling. The intricate scrollwork starts to stretch and blur. I blink again, and the ceiling clarifies, but my eyes don't open after my next blink. I'm clean. I'm in the softest bed ever made. I'm pretty sure I'm safe. I'm ...

I rouse from sleep, but keep my eyes closed, rolling over, not sure how long I've been out. But I'm still tired, so I'm ready to slide back into oblivion as soon as I get comfortable again. When I inhale, I smell dried grass and leather. Keir. Was he here? Is he here? I slip back into sleep, reaching out, fingers grazing the edge of the bed. A soft voice, which I'm pretty sure is all in my head, whispers, "It's okay, Fox Slayer. Sleep. You're safe."

CHAPTER 18

NOR

AFTER ARRIVING the night before last, Keir set Halee and me up in small but comfortable rooms in his family's private wing here at House Alopson. Though exhaustion pulled at me, my eyes refused to stay closed. I tossed and turned for what felt like an hour before kicking the blankets off with a frustrated huff. With the foggy memory of the abbreviated tour Keir gave us, I somehow found my way to the guest quarters. I stood at the end of the long shadowy hall, the dim torches doing nothing to tell me which room Val might be in. Embarrassed, I was about to turn around when my gaze caught on a shaft of light coming from under the third door down on the right. Taking a chance, I knocked. When the door swung open, Valsan blinked at me, taking in my disheveled hair, wrinkled shirt, and loosely done up pants. Stepping back, he silently ushered me into his room, the door softly clicking shut behind me. Val crossed the room, leaning over the small desk where he must have been working. "Couldn't sleep?" I shook my head, my blurry mind forgetting his back was to me, but all the same, he answered, "Me neither."

He extinguished the lamp, plunging us into darkness, but somehow he found me. He always seems to find me. Wrapping his fingers around my hand, he guided me to his bed. I heard the rustling of clothes, and I assumed Val was undressing, so I did the same, stripping to my underwear. The swish of blankets being pulled back fluttered through the air before he pulled me onto the soft mattress. He curled around me, his bare chest pressing against my back, and he tugged the blankets around us. As soon as his arms wrapped around me, I laced my fingers with his, our joined hands pressing to my stomach. With his breath on my neck, I immediately fell asleep.

We slept through the entire day, waking shortly to eat a quick meal that had been delivered to his door at some point. Valsan stepped out for an hour to check on Aimee, Owen, and Miles who were bunking in the guards' quarters, and to send a message to Lady Kapros. As soon as he returned, he peeled his shirt over his head, kicked off his boots and pants, and crawled back into bed. Without a word, he held the blankets open in invitation—one I greedily accepted. We curled into each other once again, and slept the rest of the night away.

Now, in the dining hall, my knee dances under the table as I push my eggs around my plate, my fork making little scraping sounds. Halee slides onto the bench next to me, quietly setting her plate down. She picks up her fork, but doesn't begin to eat, just stares at her sausage link.

I ask, "You okay?"

"Hmm?"

I shift to face her. "Halee, what's wrong?"

"Oh. Nothing. Not really. I just ..."

I lower my voice. "Thaeia?" While we're the only ones at this table, the small dining hall is fairly full with the murmur of conversation and the clink of utensils carrying through the wood and stone room.

Halee's fingers begin tapping her thumb, and she nods. She blinks up at me, and though I try to keep a brave face, she must see something in my eyes. Her back straightens, and a wide smile spreads across her face. "I'm sure she's fine. There's a lot going on. I never really thought about how busy a House must be, but the constant bustle is ... overwhelming. I don't know how Keir lives like this."

I shrug. "I'm sure the privacy of their family wing helps. And besides, the lord grew up with all this. I'm sure it's normal to him."

She looks around at the dozens of people enjoying their breakfast and the efficient staff that scurries around delivering food and clearing plates.

"I guess, but still ..."

I smile, scooping some eggs into my mouth. Halee digs the edge of her fork into her sausage, cutting off a small piece, then spears it and delicately chews. I have the sudden urge to make Halee smile, to wipe away some of her nerves, so I ask, "Where's Miles?"

That does the trick. Her cheeks turn pink, and her lips curl in a small smile. "He's running an errand for Valsan."

"You two seem ..."

I wink, and the pink in her cheeks turns red. "He's ..." She sighs.

My dimple creases my cheek as my grin grows. I

nudge her with my shoulder. "I'm happy for you. I like him. You two are good together."

She ducks her head, her black hair falling over her face for a second before she tucks her curls behind her ear. "We are. I think ... we've talked and ... he's going to ask for a few more days of leave. He's going to come to Oxtara with me."

"Meeting the family?"

"Too soon?"

"Not if you feel it's right." If I had family worth a damn, I'd want Valsan to meet them.

"I ... I'm planning to go to Loudare with him when he goes back to House Kapros. There's a school in the capital that is accepting applications for scholarships. If I can secure a spot, they'll provide room and board as well as a meal stipend. If not ... I'll figure something out."

"That's amazing, Halee. If there is anything I can do to help, let me know."

"Thank you, Nor. Have you and Valsan talked about ... things?"

I'm back to pushing the last of my eggs around my plate. No. We haven't. The past day spent in his bed was quiet ... comfort for the both of us. Should we have taken the time to talk? No. I don't think so. Something inside me knows that yesterday was exactly what we needed. Nothing more, nothing less.

Halee's small hand falls over mine, stalling my absent movement. "You love each other. You'll figure it out."

Maybe to a nineteen-year-old, love conquers all. But I know better. Despite my persistent cynicism, I know Valsan is worth fighting for. *We* are worth fighting for. So, I smile, dropping my fork to take her hand in mine. "You're right. We'll figure it out. Thank you, Halee."

A throat clears behind us. Halee and I were so engrossed in our conversation, I didn't hear or see Keir come up.

"Sorry to interrupt." He waves at the empty spot on the bench on my other side, his Spirit flames fluttering along his fingers with the movement. "May I sit?" I want to tell him it's his house and he can do as he pleases, but I just nod. He swings a leg over the seat, his hounds settling under the table, the red glow of their flames illuminating the space around us. Keir braces his forearm on the table, leaning in to speak softly. "I'm on my way to attend an emergency vote on releasing funds for the families of the victims of the attack." I'm about to ask why he's telling us this, but then he adds, "After, I'm going to check on her." Halee starts tapping her thumb, and Keir smiles. I imagine this look on his face is well practiced to put others at ease. And, it works. Halee's middle finger pauses on her thumb, and she smiles back as Keir says, "Would you like to come?"

Halee practically bounces in her seat as she nods, her food forgotten. But when he shifts to stand, she reaches across me, resting her hand on Keir's forearm. I almost snatch her hand back, my brain screaming at me that she's going to be burned, but the gentle flicker of Keir's magic swirls harmlessly around her skin. She whispers, "Before you go, I wanted to say, thank you. For everything. We are in your debt. We are not from your House. You had no obligation to help us."

Keir's eyes harden, the blue darkening as he shakes his head. "I had an obligation as a human being to help other human beings in need. Houses have nothing to do with it."

I take in the heir of Alopson. His smooth, pale skin.

His perfectly styled black hair. His piercing blue eyes. His cut jaw that's flexing with the conviction of his words. His tailored clothes that boast the colors and symbol of his House. His fit physique that speaks to his strength. Even his polished boots. Everything about this man showcases a person raised in wealth and privilege, groomed to lead. Yet, he has this vulnerability, this ... heart. Will he be able to hold on to that part of himself?

I recall what Thaeia told me about Saph and her mysterious falling out with Lord Alopson. Is Keir's father hiding something dark behind the polish of his House? And is Keir hiding something too? For Thaeia's sake, I hope not.

Keir looks out the window to our right and stands. "I shouldn't be more than two hours." He shifts his gaze to Halee. "In the meantime, one of our mares is about to foal. If you're interested—"

Halee leaps from the bench. "Yes, please. My magic can help her, and the chance to feel that first flutter of awareness as a new creature enters our world ..."

Her eyes shine with excitement, and I lick my lips, smiling. "May I join you?"

Halee's voice is louder, higher with her energy. "Yes! Of course!"

Keir presses his lips together, failing to hide his smile. "Then I shall find you there after my meeting." With long, purposeful strides, the young lord of Alopson leaves the dining hall, his hounds padding behind him. More than a few eyes follow him, each holding pride and respect for their next Lord. Keir is well-liked. I can see why. No matter how often I tell myself to be wary, to be cautious ... I can't find any holes to poke in the near-perfect man. It's both comforting and annoying.

Halee spins, but her excitement shifts to something else, something softer. I know what that look means.

Miles makes a beeline to us, plate in hand. His shirt is a little damp around the neck and down the center. He must have been doing drills with the Alopson guards. At least that's where Aimee said she'd be this morning. Leaning down, Miles drops a kiss on the top of Halee's head. "Morning, gorgeous." He sets his plate on the table, but remains standing.

Halee's grin gets impossibly bigger. "Morning."

These two make me smile, spreading warmth through my chest.

Miles looks between us. "Where are you headed?"

Halee's thumb resumes its tapping, and she shifts from foot to foot. "One of the mares is about to foal."

Miles' nose wrinkles. "Not something I'd like a front row seat to, but I get why you're excited." I chuckle, and Halee's pink cheeks go round with her grin. Miles presses his palm to the wood table, and right between his fingers, a thin green stem curls upwards. Long white petals unfurl, revealing a bright yellow center. It's a cheerful looking flower, and Miles plucks it, leaning over to tuck it behind Halee's ear. As he does, he plants a solid kiss on Halee's lips. "Have fun. I'll find you later."

Owen's hoot can be heard from the other side of the dining hall. Halee's blush deepens, and Miles rolls his eyes. With a bright laugh, Owen jogs over and throws his arm over Halee's shoulder, tugging her into his side. "My sweet Halee, why do you waste your affections on this one?" Owen jerks his thumb at Miles who crosses his arms with a shake of his head. "Run away with me, my lady. I'll show you delights he knows nothing ab—"

Miles playful shoves Owen. "That's enough." He gently tugs Halee from Owen's arms into his own.

Owen holds up his hands with a grin. "Ah, alas, it must be love." With a chuckle, he slides onto the bench and starts eating Miles' breakfast. Miles rolls his eyes again, then presses another sweet kiss to Halee's head. "See you later."

Halee bobs her head in a nod before turning to me, her fingers tapping out her embarrassment. But she's smiling, her eyes sparkling. She's happy, her voice excited. "Ready?"

I sweep my arm out. "After you. Though I have no idea how to get to the stables from here."

Halee goes still, her head tilting to the side with a slight flexing of her left hand. A second later, she bursts into motion, aiming for the door to our left. "This way."

I guess I'm going to spend the morning watching a horse give birth.

With a grin, I wave goodbye to Miles just as three people join him and Owen at his table. They seem to know each other, picking up conversation as I follow a nearly jogging Halee. As we turn down a juncture in the hallway, I pause. Something from the corner of my eye pulls my attention to the end of the long passage. I stare, my magic swirling in my gut, ready. Nothing. Maybe I imagined it. Still, I can't help but look over my shoulder as I catch up to Halee.

CHAPTER 19

THAEIA

The smell of coffee drags me from sleep. I curl into the fluffy blankets, sinking into the soft mattress, considering for a second to just stay in bed. But the coffee scents wafting to me are too tempting. Throwing the blanket back, I notice the sharp line of daylight peeking around the edges of the velvet curtain. I have no idea what time it is, or even what day. Coffee first. All the rest later.

There's a silky robe draped over the end of the bed, and I snort. Reaching for it with a smirk, I can just imagine Keir imagining me draped in this useless—

"Ohhh."

A thin layer of fluffy material lines the robe, and as I slide it on, it sits light against my skin but hugs me with warmth.

"Not bad, lordling."

The smooth stone floor gleams under my bare feet as I

shuffle across the room, following my nose. The pain meds have worn off, but the sleep has done wonders. The wound in my side still aches, but it's bearable. I can walk with only the barest limp, and my ribs must have been bruised, not broken because I can take almost a full breath with just a small pinch of pain. When I reach up to scratch my scalp, I run my fingers over my face. It's back to its normal size, and all the itchiness is gone. My jaw pops as I yawn, stretching my arms wide, cracking my back. Gods, I feel ... better. Sore, but good.

A beautiful wood tray sits on the low table in the seating area. An intricate inlay of crushed pearl stares up at me from the tray's surface as I lean over to grab the carafe. The trickling sound of the dark roast pouring into the glass cup fills the room, and when I pick it up and hold it between my hands, the warmth seeps to my very soul. I take a sip, and moan. It's slightly bitter with a hint of cherry and oak and ... vanilla. Perfect.

It's only after my cup is half empty that I realize there's a folded note on the tray. I hold the cup of comfort in my right hand as I pinch the paper between the fingers of my left, flipping it open.

Thaeia—
You didn't lock the door.

Oops. I didn't realize I was that exhausted. I shouldn't have forgotten something so important. But a glance at the door shows the latch turned to the locked position. Hmm. I guess Keir has a key.

I hope you slept well. You slept the entire day,

and last night. You were still a little red from the poppy oil, so I applied some lamb's bay lotion. And yes, I realize the liberties I keep taking while you're unconscious. ~~I can't seem to keep my ha~~ I promise I'm only trying to care for you.

My face is lit with my smile. He tried to cross it out, but I can read it. Can't keep his hands off me, huh? I take another sip of my coffee, my lips pausing on the rim of the cup as I realize I'm feeling something beyond the hum of arousal—Warm affection blooms in my heart. I ... I really like him.

Feel free to just rest and relax, or you're welcome to start browsing the library. I have a meeting with my father and the council, but I'll stop by later.

The coffee turns sour on my tongue. Lord Alopson. I still don't know what he did to cause Saph to run for her life, but he's been nothing but kind to me. Is he using me to some end? I don't know. I can't see the endgame. I don't know who the players are, and I don't know what piece I am ... I feel like a pawn, but ...

I blink, finally getting to the last line of Keir's note.

Your friends are here. Everyone is safe.
-Keir

I exhale, realizing my cup is empty, so I absently refill

it. There's a light crackle of flaky pastry as I pick up a buttery roll. I don't really taste it, but I'm sure it's delicious. My mind is just too full of questions to fully appreciate the decadent breakfast Keir brought me. I hold the roll between my teeth as I flip the lock. The metallic click sounds overly loud, and for a moment, adrenaline readies my muscles in case someone is in the library beyond this door. I don't consider how ridiculous I look as I peek outside, flaky roll in my mouth, cup of coffee in one hand. I should have grabbed one of my knives. Or at least put on a pair of socks. My toes curl as I step onto the warmer wood floor outside my door. I'm greeted by silence and the smell of books. So many books. Creeping to the metal railing, I peer up first. So many people fail to look up. No one ... at least no one within my line of sight. There's no noise either, just the curling wood buttresses holding up the intricate coffered ceiling. Peeling my eyes away from the beauty, I look down. The sunlight from the arched windows spills down on the empty tables, the bookcases seemingly staring up at me wondering what I'm doing lurking around instead of perusing all the knowledge neatly arranged within their shelves.

The telltale click of the magical metal lock snaps me from my thoughts. I back up, slowly closing the door, but keep it cracked. On silent hinges, the main library door opens. A leg appears as someone moves to come inside. Keir steps into the library, the soft light of the morning sun washes over him, and I swear he glows.

Pulling the door open, I return to the railing. His gaze travels up, and our eyes clash and hold. He smiles, and something like relief shifts his posture. "Good, you're up." His eyes snag on the robe. I realize the belt has loosened some, and the opening dips low between my breasts. I like the hunger in his eyes. I'm pretty sure it's mirrored in my own, so I leave the robe in its current state. Keir blinks, pulling himself from his daze. "Are you up for some visitors?"

His words have me clutching the robe tighter around my chest, securing the belt. Before I can answer, a squeal shatters the peace of the library.

"Thaeia!"

Every bit of tension pressing against the inside of my skin leaks away as Halee bursts into the library, nearly shoving Keir out of the way. Stuffing the last of the roll into my mouth, I chew quickly—too quickly. A flaky crumb lodges in my throat, and there's no stopping the coughs that try to dislodge the traitorous pastry. She runs for the stairs, and I eagerly move to meet her, swallowing around my coughs. The quick tap-tap-tap of her feet climbing the metal stairs is a happy sound, announcing our reunion. Halee doesn't break stride as she looks around, but her mouth drops open. "Wow."

As soon as Halee reaches the landing, she's in my arms. She's so small. So thin. Seemingly fragile. But I know better. This girl is strong and resilient. I hug her tight, breathing her in.

"Why do you smell like horse?"

She steps back, a beaming smile on her face. "Oh! I helped a mare give birth. It was wonderful!"

"It was ... messy." Nor's voice snaps me around.

I was so wrapped up in my friend, I didn't hear the two men come up the stairs. When I look up, Keir's standing off to the side next to a smiling Nor. Tears pool in my eyes, causing the room to go blurry, but as soon as the fat tears drop down my face, everything sharpens into focus.

Halee slips back, making room for Nor. My knuckles

brush his as we bump fists, then he yanks me against his chest. He's solid, and warm, and smells like soap. His breath tickles my neck as he asks, "You okay?"

I nod into his shoulder. "Yeah."

Nor gives me a tight squeeze then steps away. I brush my hands down the silky robe. "Let me get dressed and we'll catch up."

Rushing back into my room, I head towards my pack that's propped up in the corner of the little sitting area. Halfway there, I pause. There on the blue velvet sofa lies a bundle of clothing. I'm curious, but the need to pee hits me like a kick in the stomach, so I speed walk to the bathroom, relieving myself with a sigh. A glance in the mirror shows my skin is back to normal, and I splash some cold water on my face to help the coffee wake me up. Tying back my hair, I return to the main room. I pick up the new clothing, finding a pair of lightweight pants that have a surprising amount of stretch. There's also a linen tunic with slits up the sides. It's a seafoam blue that I imagine will match Keir's eyes.

I pull on the clothes. They smell like Keir—like leather and dried grass. Fuck. That's not going to be distracting or anything. The pants are *tight*, the stretchy fabric hugging the lines of my legs from hip to ankle. At least the tunic hangs low, covering my ass. I have to admit, the clothes are comfortable. I do a little spin, then bend my knees into a squat. And I can *move* in them. Well done again, lordling.

Securing my thigh sheath, I check under the bed, then by the sofa, looking for my boots until I recall kicking them off in the bathroom last night. I peek back in, but they're not there. I walk back out, hands on hips, looking around. There they are, placed neatly by the door.

Oh, lordling. My insides melt, and my heart actually skips a beat as I stare at my boots, running my hands over the clothes he brought me. I do a slow turn, taking in this lovely little room where Keir made sure I'd be safe. What is this thing between us? Can it be anything serious? He's definitely long-term material, but someone like him with someone like me ...?

I shake off my wandering thoughts. Kneeling in front of my pack, I pause for just a second, then reach in and along the back, digging my fingers into the hidden pocket. The worn piece of silk that Saph gave me curls in my hand along with the paper with the crest of the kingdom of Kivel. My homeland? I stuff the silk and the paper into the waistband of my pants before returning to the library. Keir is gone, and when I peer down at the first level, Nor says, "He's up on the third floor. Said there's a book he wanted. How anyone can find a specific book in all this ...?"

Awe fills Halee's voice. "I think it's wonderful."

I look around the library. "I agree."

Keir's voice calls down from what sounds like far back on the third floor. "Thaeia. Come up here. I think this might be something."

CHAPTER 20

KEIR

THAEIA IS DISTRACTING. The clothes I brought her hug her curves. She shifts in the chair next to me, leaning over the table to read what must be an engrossing paragraph in the book before her. But her movement brings her scent to my nose—vanilla and sea salt. I curl my fingers around my book, trying to ward off the sudden urge to lick her. Usually, it's the words on a page that pull my attention away from the world, but even books can't compete with the woman sitting next to me. And it's not just physical. She gets lost in a book as easily as I do. She cares for her friends, seems to have a fierce loyalty, and despite everything, is quick to laugh. Gods, her laugh. How can a sound send my heart racing and at the same time bring me such peace?

Focus, Keir.

Earlier, when I showed her the old book I found, she tentatively took it from my hands, squeezing it closed. She seemed almost ... scared. I didn't understand why until she pulled out a chair and sank into it. Joining her at the table, I'd asked what was bothering her, and with a deep breath, she told me her story.

Nor took the chair on the other side of Thaeia while Halee sat across from us. I got the feeling Nor knew this tale already, but the little gasps from Halee told me this was her first time hearing about Thaeia's past. Or I should say, the shadowy secrets of her past.

For a moment, I got hung up on Saph/Rhenara's connection with my father and the fact that those grey-cloaked attackers had carried Saph's blades. My father has never mentioned someone of that name, and a sliver of doubt sliced through my stomach. Looking at the worn-out crest on the scrap of silk, and comparing it to the drawing of the crest of Kivel, I couldn't come to the same conclusion as Thaeia. They have little to nothing in common. But I did understand her need to make some kind of connection. I just think she made the wrong connection.

We've been sitting in this little study area on the third floor of the library for a few hours, and we've accumulated quite the pile of books that's spread out on the table. Nor flips the page of the book before him, but he seems distracted, his eyes not really focusing on the words. Halee is curled up in the overstuffed chair behind us, her eyes closed, her face relaxed in sleep, an open book in her lap.

The tapping of Thaeia's finger on the page of her book draws my attention back to her. The book before her is even older than the first one I found, it's binding fraying, some of the words faded from countless fingers passing over the pages.

She says, "Look at this. Maybe ...?"

I lean over. For the briefest moment, I think about resting my hand on her thigh, but press it to the table instead. I read the words over Thaeia's finger.

The mage was close to her limit, the third time she'd done so in a fortnight. The only way to keep her from pushing herself to the breaking point was to force her to stop. She was a dedicated mage, and insisted she had more, unable to see the danger she was putting herself in. She was with child. We had to stop her. So determined was she, she ran, but you can't outrun it. She cried. She cried for her magic, even knowing it wasn't permanent. It was necessary for her safety. For the safety of the babe.

I read it again. I read the passage before and three pages beyond. There's no further explanation, but ... Lifting my head, I meet Thaeia's hopeful eyes. "This is something."

She blinks, shifting in her seat. "It's so vague. Why isn't there more? Why were they so careful with their words? What does it mean?"

The smooth leather of the cover caresses my hand as I pick up the book, looking at the spine. "I don't know."

Nor reaches towards me. "Let me see."

I hand him the book as I push away from the table with a scrape of my chair and head down an aisle. Thaeia comes after me, leaving Nor at the table and Halee sleeping in her chair. I crouch, running my finger over dozens of spines. Not finding what I'm looking for, I stand, moving down. I reach up, drifting my finger over these books, but again, nothing.

I grumble, "There should be more."

Thaeia looks up at the books, then at me. "More what?"

"More books by that same author. I know there are more. I haven't sought them out since I was very young and in my studies, but I know ..."

We search row after row, but come up empty-handed. It doesn't make sense. To keep the limited staff allowed in this wing out of the library, I made up the story of missing valuable books and a necessary inventory check, but it seems there *are* actually books missing. But *when* did they go missing, and why?

When we return to the table, Nor stretches, then stands. "I'm going to head out. I don't think I can read another word. I need to move."

The light coming through the window has dimmed. Has the day already worn away? We missed lunch, and are about to miss dinner.

With a gentle shake, Nor wakes Halee. She wipes her mouth, blinking until she remembers where she is. "Oh. Sorry. I thought I was all recovered, but I guess I'm still a bit worn out from ... everything."

Thaeia smiles. "Understandable. I slept for an entire day. Why don't you and Nor go eat. I'll see you tomorrow?"

She turns to me with the question, and I nod. "I'll bring your friends here anytime you wish. As long as it's safe to do so."

Halee stands, lifting her arms over her head with a yawn. "Great! See you tomorrow, Thaeia."

Nor rests a hand on Thaeia's shoulder, the two friends holding eye contact for a long moment before he says, "That book ... the passage ... it's something." His eyes dart to the open book still on the table.

Thaeia nods, her face absent of a smile, but she doesn't look dejected either. "Yeah. It's something."

Nor and Halee leave, their footsteps fading. We're too far back in the upper stacks to hear the automatic lock click into place, but I trust that Thaeia and I are secure in the safety of my library. Her eyes are on the book, her teeth worrying at her bottom lip. I pick up the book, snapping it closed, holding it spine out. "This is a clue."

She squints. "What?"

I tap the worn gold letters stacked down the spine. "This author. He's not from Kivel. He's a Drakam author." Thaeia's brows climb her forehead. "And that's not all. I'm certain there are other works by this author, and I'm certain we had them in this library. Yet, they are not here. At least, they are not where they should be."

"Could they have been put away in the wrong spot?"

"Possibly. But we keep things very organized." I look around, not really seeing the library around me. "I'll search every shelf if I have to ... just to make sure." I face Thaeia, setting the book on the table so I can grab her shoulders. "But, Thaeia, this is a clue. It means something that the author went out of his way to keep from actually saying anything about a Void. And it means something that his other works are missing. I think Saph was right. At least in the past, there might have been others like you."

She stares at me, and I can't read her expression. Is she excited? Wary? Scared?

Her muscles flex under my hand, then her lips are on mine. My eyes widen in surprise, but before I can appreciate the moment, she pulls back, licking her lips. "Thank you, Keir. For everything. You are ... surprising."

"In a good way, right?" I smirk, but her gaze drops.

Her voice comes out softer, almost like she's embarrassed. "You've done so much for me, my friends. You are ... I mean all this ..." She waves her hand around the room. "You didn't have to—"

I grip her chin, unsettled at her train of thought. "Thaeia, look at me." Her eyes slowly travel up until she meets my gaze, her teeth worrying at her bottom lip. "I helped you because it was the right thing to do. It *is* the right thing to do." Her eyes dart away, but I hold fast to her face. "And I'm helping you because I want to. You owe me nothing." Leaning in, I make sure her attention is back on me. "Do you understand?" She nods, but my heart slams into my stomach when I see tears shimmer in her eyes. "Thaeia?"

She tries to shake her head, but I don't let her go. Sniffling, she wipes her face. "I'm sorry. I am grateful, but that's not what this was. I ... Ugh. Gods, I feel so stup—"

I kiss her. Slowly. I savor her taste and swallow her startled gasp. "Oh, Fox Slayer, I simply wanted to be clear that I expect nothing from you. That doesn't mean I don't want you. Gods, Thaeia, never, *never* question my desire for you."

Her breaths come out in shallow little pants. Her fingers tighten around my shirt, pulling me towards her, and I go like an accolade to their god. Our lips brush again, and I can't keep my hand from threading through her hair, scraping her scalp to tug her closer. Gods, she tastes so good. I lick her lips, and she opens for me. Our tongues dance, and she moans into my mouth. My cock weeps at the sound, and I press my hard length into her stomach, letting her feel what she does to me. Her hips roll against me, and I bite her lip.

"Fuck, Fox Slayer."

Her lids are hooded, her mouth wet and swollen from my lips and the scrape of my day-old scruff. Her gaze falls to my pants, seeing the obvious bulge. When she licks her lips, I snap.

Her throat is smooth under my grip, and when she swallows, I squeeze. I push her until the backs of her thighs hit the table. My cock jerks as I keep pushing, bowing her back until I have her laid out before me. So beautiful. Her fingers curl around the edge of the wood, and her breath hitches beautifully as I shove her shirt up to expose her belly. My skin tingles as I watch hers erupt in goosebumps. I lick from her waistband to her navel, gentling my lips around the angry line of the wound in her side. Most of her bruises have faded, but this injury will stay with her. It will scar and tell the story of her strength.

My breath flutters lower, and her head thumps against the table with a gasp. "Keir."

Kneeling, I yank her boots off, and they thud heavily somewhere behind me as I throw them over my shoulder. I need her. In my mouth. Squeezing my fingers. Clenching my cock. I need her whimpers and her screams. I peel her pants off, groaning at the absence of underwear.

"Fuck, Thaeia." I'm usually much more eloquent than this, but she seems to have struck me dumb.

My hands press on her inner thighs, spreading her. She's wet, and my hunger for her is all consuming. I look at her face. She's watching me, her chest rising with her panting breaths. Then, she sits up, gripping the hem of her shirt, pulling it over her head and laying back down. Her breasts fall slightly to the sides, and with her eyes still on me, she palms them, pinching her nipples.

My fingers dig into her thighs, and I bite my cheek to keep from coming. My voice is gravelly, a deep growl as I lean forward. "Hang on tight, Fox Slayer."

CHAPTER 21

THAEIA

Keir's eyes land on my pussy, and he dives for me. My core clenches as his tongue drags between my folds, flicking my clit. My hips buck off the table, but his hands spread me wider, controlling me, eating me like a man starved.

The sight of him between my legs is an image I'd be willing to die for. I want to keep watching, but as he stiffens his tongue and spears me, my head involuntarily falls back. There's a flutter and thump, and I worry for Keir's precious books as one falls from the table to the floor, but then his lips wrap around my clit and suck.

All thought leaves my brain as sparks tingle from my core and shoot outward to my fingers and toes. The wet sucking sound of him attacking my pussy is obscene. I love it. His hands wrap under my thighs, and I'm yanked harder into his face.

Fuck.

My hands find their way into Keir's hair. I grip tightly, grinding into him with every lick and suck he laves on me.

"Keir. Oh, fuck. Keir. More. I need more. I need ..."

Instead of more, I'm left cold and throbbing as Keir stands. His mouth and chin glisten with my arousal, and he licks his lips as he pulls his shirt over his head. The muscles of his chest flex as he toes off his boots, then shoves his pants to his ankles, kicking them free. His thick cock twitches against his stomach, precum leaking down the tip.

My pussy is pulsing in time with my heartbeat. I feel like I might come just from the way he's looking at me. I bite my lip. With a flex of his thigh muscles, he's on me. My eyes clash with his, and I'm struck with what I can only describe as wild desire in his gaze. An animalistic groan rips from his lips as rough hands grab my wrists and pin them to the table over my head. He looms over me, rubbing his length through my folds, coating himself in my wetness. My hips roll into him, needing the friction, needing him, but my position on the table is awkward, and I can't move much.

With slow, teasing drags of his cock between my legs, he groans, "So wet for me. I've fantasized about this, but the reality ..." His jaw clenches, and he grinds his length against my clit. My head smacks against the table as pleasure shoots all the way to the top of my head. "Thaeia, look at me." Slowly, I drag my gaze back to his, little panting breaths escaping my lips. "You're going to take all of me." It's not a question, but my head bobs anyway, my body lighting up with anticipation. With a deep rumble that sounds almost like a purr, he rotates his hips, lining himself up. With a single thrust, he drives into me. My back arches off the table, pleasure curling my toes as he fills me. "Gods, Thaeia. You're so wet, so tight. So fucking good." Without pulling back, he grinds against me, hitting my clit again. My head falls back, and a scream tears from my throat. The books look down on us as Keir draws back and slams back into me so deep, it cuts my scream short, turning it into a gasp.

My limited sexual experience has not prepared me for this moment. I'm ... efficient at getting myself off, and the few partners I've had—I can count them on one hand— left me feeling ... underwhelmed. This is ... *more*.

The table screeches across the floor with every pump of his hips until the edge hits a bookcase. Books rattle with his next thrust, and I see stars. A few topple to bounce off the table then flutter to the floor. I wrap my legs around his hips, hooking my ankles, giving me leverage to lift into his thrusts.

"Yes, Thaeia. Yes. So good. You're taking me so well. Look at your pussy pulling me inside your wet heat. Listen to how wet you are."

He moves faster, his words driving me towards the edge. My feet flex, and I dig my heels into his lower back as shock waves build between my thighs. Keir leans over me just as more books tumble from their shelves, several striking his back before falling open on the table to either side of us. He doesn't slow while shielding me from being smacked in the face by the falling books.

One hand releases me, sliding between us. His thumb presses to my clit, and I fall over the edge. Light shatters inside me until there's nothing but pulsing pleasure. Sheer bliss radiates under my skin, causing my back to arch off the table into Keir's chest.

He loses his rhythm, punching his length into me. I

watch as his jaw flexes. His eyes find mine, and they turn the deep blue of stormy waters. He holds my gaze as his orgasm rips through him, his raspy voice growling my name. Watching him come drives me to another orgasm, and I clench around him as he jerks inside me.

Keir relaxes while keeping the bulk of his weight from crushing me. I let my free hand trace down his sweaty back, and the fingertips of the other hand he still had wrapped around my wrist travel down my arm in a delicate caress. He presses a kiss to my neck, and shifts back slightly to look at me. "Are you okay?"

I smile, squeezing his hips with my thighs. "Are you?"

He laughs. "I'm perfect." His lips fall to mine, kissing me slow and deep. My legs release their iron grip from around his hips. With his lips pressing little kisses to my mouth, he wraps an arm around my back, lifting me with him, helping me stand as he steps away from the table. "Come. Let's get cleaned up."

I glance at the mess of books around us, but he shakes his head. "We can put this all back together later." Tugging my hand, he leads me through the stacks towards the stairs. His ass muscles flex with every step, and I bite my lip. I never knew sex could be like this. I mean you hear things, and I've read my fair share of romance, but I figured it was all over exaggeration.

Keir's half-hard cock bobs with every step. Running my tongue over the roof of my mouth, I wonder what he would taste like right now with our combined release coating him. The metal steps leading down to the second floor are cold under my bare feet. Making our way towards my room, I pause halfway down the balcony, tugging him and pressing his beautiful ass against the metal railing. I can just picture the pretty little indentations he'll have there when I'm done. I drop to my knees, my still-healing leg protesting a little. But it's worth the discomfort as his shocked eyes watch me. I suck his half-hard cock into my mouth. His head falls back, his hands gripping the rail so tight, his knuckles turn white.

"Fuck, Thaeia."

I let his length slide out until I can suck hard on the tip, tasting myself and his cum. It's a heady mix, and I lick him from balls to tip. Wrapping my hands around the scrolling metal posts, I pin Keir between me and the railing. He's fully hard again, and when I suck him this time, he hits the back of my throat.

"Gods, you look so good like that, taking my cock so deep."

My hips involuntarily press forward. Apparently, I have a thing for praise. I manage to swallow, constricting around him, and he grunts, bucking into my face. I work him hard and fast, releasing one hand to press between his shaft and balls. He stiffens. "Thaeia. I'm going to come."

It sounds like a warning—one I don't heed. I press a little harder with my finger, and suck him deep. His salty cum explodes in my mouth, and I swallow it all, wondering if that will earn some of the approval he gave me either.

It does.

He slides out of my mouth, his thumb tracing my bottom lip. "So good."

Fuck. My pussy clenches at those words, some of his cum along with my renewed arousal drips down my thighs. His eyes follow the trail of wetness sliding down my skin, and he smirks.

"Does my Fox Slayer need to come again?"

CHAPTER 22

KEIR

WE DID MAKE it to the bed eventually where I coaxed two more orgasms from Thaeia. Her flushed skin, damp with sweat brought about by pleasure—pleasure I gave her—is now one of my favorite sights. That, and the way her eyes go round, her head tilted back, baring her neck, and her lips dropped open on a silent scream as she comes. That's beauty incarnate.

After a quick shower, we settled back in the rumpled bed, her warm body fitting against mine. We've been silent for a while, but it's not uncomfortable. She's relaxed, languid, her hair cascading over my arm, her hand limp on my stomach. My fingers trail from her shoulder to her elbow and back again. Her even breaths tickle my chest hair, and our legs are entwined, the sheets twisted between us.

I keep up my caresses as I say, "I should have told you before … I'm on the shot."

She stops breathing for a moment, then her voice comes out shaky. "Good. That's good."

I chuckle, nuzzling her hair. "Don't sound so terrified of having my babies."

Thaeia shifts, trying to pull away, but I hold her close as she says, "Keir, we've known each other a week, barely a week. I'm—"

My chuckles turn into a full-blown laugh. "I'm joking, Thaeia." She relaxes slightly, and I resume my caresses up and down her arm. "I just wanted you to know. You don't need to worry. There's enough on your plate right now."

Thaeia inhales deeply, and on a slow exhale she scoots closer, pressing her breasts more firmly to my side. "Thank you. I should have asked. That was irresponsible of me."

I kiss her hair. "If I had lapsed on my shots, I would have stopped. It might have killed me, but I would have taken you with my fingers and let you spend hours on my face." Her muscles flex, her thighs rubbing, and I smile, loving how well she responds. "I would have spilled on my books before risking something like that before talking about it first."

She reaches up, scrubbing her eyes. "Fuck, Keir, are you for real? How can you be real? I think I've somehow conjured you to life from one of my romance novels."

"Hmm. You show me your favorites, and I'll do my best to live up to the expectations."

She pinches the bridge of her nose. "Fuck." I smile, calling up certain scenes I've read over the years that I wouldn't mind trying with her. Thaeia's fingers trace little circles around my navel. My muscles twitch. It tickles. She huffs a little laugh, and I smile at the ceiling as she asks, "So, whose room is this?"

"It's had a few different lives over the years. When this library was added on to the estate—years ago—this room was constructed as a records room."

She hums. "This is too beautiful a place for records."

I chuckle. "It wasn't back then. The way my father describes it, it was utilitarian. Apparently, the bathroom was added just so the librarian didn't have to walk all the way through the family wing every time nature called."

"Have I kicked your librarian from their home?"

I shake my head even though she can't see it. "When my parents got bonded, and my mother moved here, she took over the library and slowly converted this room into what it is today. She expanded the bathroom, added the shower, had the window reframed, and made it ... hers. She loved books." I try to keep the undertone of sadness from my voice, but I don't think it worked.

Thaeia shifts, placing her hand on my chest and propping her chin on the back of her hand, her eyes searching my face. "That's where you got your love of books."

I shrug. "I guess. Sure. But my father loves to read as well. He was the one who read to me every night when I was young." My fingers comb through Thaeia's hair as I try to dispel some of the emotions this conversation is drawing to the surface of my heart. But she has shared her past with me, her hurts. So I'll do the same. "When I say my mother loved books, I mean even more than her family. She hated court life. She was not from Sodoles. My father met her on one of his travels over-seas. To hear him tell the story, they fell hard and fast for each other, and though she objected at first, he managed to convince her to come back here with him.

They were bonded within a week." The story is just free-flowing from me now, some of my long-buried pain leaking out with each word. "She left when I was very young. Seven or eight. I don't really remember. My memories of her are random and scattered." I chuckle, but it's not a happy sound. "Once, when she didn't know I was watching, she came here, to her beloved books, but my father failed to leave the door open for her. I'd never seen her look so angry. She slapped the metal lock panel over and over, mumbling about bloodlines and outsiders. I didn't really understand at the time, but once I got older, long after she had left, I realized that she hated it here."

Thaeia's eyes never leave my face. I feel no judgment from her, not even pity. She's just listening. She's letting me talk through this, giving me space to feel.

I crack my neck. "I think my father saw the writing on the wall, and to try to appease her, he appointed her as ambassador. And for a while, I think it helped. She was gone more than she was home, but she got to see the world. She always brought home crates of books, and for a few days at least, she'd be happy. But then ..." I blink at the ceiling, letting go a little more of a mother I barely remember. But not for the first time. Throughout my adult life, I've released parts of her she left behind in my heart. "One day, she left and never came back. I don't know if my father knows where she is. In fact, I don't even know if she's still alive."

Thaeia rolls off me onto her back, but keeps her side pressed to mine, seemingly knowing I'm craving the contact right now. She looks around the room, and I have to catch my breath as a shaft of moonlight reflects in her gold eyes. Her voice is quiet, reverent. "It's a beautiful room. And there's love in the library. It's warm here, inviting."

I nod. It is.

"I vaguely remember her waking me up in this bed. I think I'd come in here because I missed her, but I don't recall the exact emotion." I close my eyes, inhaling. "I remember smelling dust. Not dirty or musty, but the dry scent of old books. I remember lips pressed to my cheek, and whispered words to wake me up. I remember ... brown eyes with long black lashes." I open my eyes, tilting my head on the pillow. "Huh. I hadn't realized I can't recall her face anymore."

Thaeia's hand slides under mine, lacing our fingers. We lay in silence, and I'm oddly at peace. Usually, after drawing up such deep emotions, my mind would continue to spin out for hours, even days. But right now, I'm calm. I'm just ... here, with Thaeia. My Fox Slayer.

A loud gurgling sound comes from Thaeia's stomach. I prop myself on a forearm. "Shit. I'm sorry. I failed to bring you lunch, and sexed you right through dinner."

She laughs, and the sound is so light and happy, I hope it sinks into the walls, infusing into the library forever. "It's okay. I'll take the sex over food anytime." Her head falls to the side, aiming her smile at me. "And that's saying something, because snacks are life."

I grin, leaning over her. "I was that good, huh?"

Her eyes darken. "I don't think you need any further boost to your ego ..." I get a little closer, my lips hovering over hers as she breathes, "But yes. Yes you were." Her gaze turns playful, and my heart tugs with longing, longing for more of this.

I shift my body, settling between her thighs. Trailing my lips over her chin and down her neck, I whisper against her skin, "Well we better make sure it wasn't a fluke."

Her head presses back into the bed, giving me more of her neck to explore with my tongue. She tastes like salt, and her throat vibrates with her hum of pleasure. That might be my favorite sound.

Her breathy voice has my half-hard cock stiffening as she says, "Yeah. We better make sure."

CHAPTER 23

NOR

A GUST of wind knocks into me, and I shield the side of my face with my hand. Stinging sand pelts my skin. I really miss home. I miss the humidity of all things. This desert air makes it feel like my lungs are irreparably scorched. During a break in the wind, I glance up. Thick, grey storm clouds hang low in the sky—so low it feels like I could go onto the roof of House Alopson and brush my fingers through them. I've never seen clouds move so quickly, as if they're racing to get from one coast to the other.

Looking over my shoulder, I frown at the long stretch of the exterior of the private family wing of the estate. The crisp sandstone walls blend with the arid landscape, the brush of light green foliage softening the hard edges of the building. I haven't seen Thaeia today, and I wonder if they found anything else after I left the library last night.

I crack my neck, absently working my way towards the stables. The passage in that book was vague, very carefully worded, but it had to refer to someone with a Void. Thaeia isn't the first. The question is, why has this information been hidden? And by whom?

A high whinny draws me from my thoughts and three more horses join in as the wind kicks up again. The horses must sense the coming storm. Does Alopson get rain this far north, this close to the Akareth Desert?

In answer, a fat raindrop smacks me in the face. Just a single drop, but I have a feeling it's heralding more to come.

Aimee lifts a hand. "Easy." The horse in front of her snaps its head up, yanking on the lead, but Aimee holds firm, keeping the horse from getting tangled in the traces. Its partner is already hitched to the carriage, seemingly unbothered by the erratic whipping wind. Valsan steps around the horses, deftly buckling the harness, but he pauses as if sensing me. His head swivels over his shoulder, and his smile sends my heart into my toes then back into my chest with a rush of lust and love. Just from his smile. Fuck.

Valsan turns to Owen. "Finish up here."

Owen grins, opening his mouth, I'm sure ready to say something lewd or sarcastic or both, but Valsan holds up a hand. Owen manages to swallow his words, but it takes an effort. I can't help but laugh as Valsan heads towards me. Meeting him halfway, he walks right into my space, his hand cupping my face, the scruff of my beard scraping his calluses. His lips brush mine once, then again before he pulls back. "Missed you."

I raise a brow. "I was in your bed just a few hours ago."

"Still." He kisses me again, and I smile against his

mouth. For the second night in a row, I slept in Valsan's bed, at least one part of my body touching him at all times. I've never slept so well. And that's all we've done ... sleep. We've found comfort and peace just knowing the other is there.

The wind picks up, jingling the tack, the horse throwing its head back again, stomping its hoof. A few more raindrops plop onto my head, and I look up. The clouds are darker and lower, still moving quickly across the sky like seawater being sucked outward before a storm surge. Valsan runs a hand through his hair only for it to fall back over his eyes again. He usually has it tied back, and he huffs in annoyance as he tries to tuck the wayward strands behind his ears, but they're ripped free again by the wind. "I should just cut it."

"No." There's a bit of bark in my voice, and Val smirks. Though I surprisingly enjoy him topping me, my own dominant side tends to come out in bursts. My fingers dive into his hair, combing it back from his face. I fist the strands close to his scalp and yank. "I like your hair."

His dark green eyes flash with need, and I pull his hair again. He grunts, his eyes on my mouth. "Then I'll reconsider."

My lips pull up in a smirk, and he returns the look. After a moment, I let him go, reluctantly taking a step back to catch my breath. I didn't come here to seduce Valsan, but ...

His voice cuts off my thoughts. "We're leaving."

I nod, a list immediately forming in my mind of everything I need to do, but then I catch Aimee securing packs to the carriage, and a horrific thought tightens my chest. Does he mean 'we' as in him and his guards, or 'we' as in us? Is this the moment I'm left behind? I guess I *should* stay with Thaeia ...

"Nor?"

I blink at Valsan, realizing his hand is on my shoulder. "What?"

He cocks a brow. "I said your name three times. You got lost in your head again, didn't you?"

My eyes dart between him and the carriage. "I just ..."

"How long do you need to be ready to go?"

My eyes snap to his and hold. He pats my shoulder. "Of course, if you want to stay, I'll understand." The next gust of wind brings a wave of rain that hits hard then moves on. Valsan looks up. "I'd prefer to wait out this storm. There are reports of another hurricane making its way towards the southern coast." Two big storms so close together? This is going to be a long storm season. "It's supposed to make landfall tonight, which means we'll be hit with this erratic weather for the next few days. Regardless, we need to leave. Soon."

His eyes turn serious, and I brace, sensing bad news.

"Word from Drakam says Severn is threatening to close his borders. He's still blaming Kapros for the attack on the Coliseum, though he has no proof. Right now, he doesn't need it. Tensions are high, and he's using the fear and anger to drive suspicion at Lady Kapros." My jaw flexes. More like his captain, Silas is whispering in Severn's ear. "Apparently, Severn has tripled his guards at our border, and Lady Kapros has responded in kind. I need to get there before Severn or Daire pushes the other too far."

A shiver slides down my spine all the way to my feet. I glance at the gleaming estate, the sandstone glowing against the dark backdrop of the stormy sky. "And Lord Alopson?"

"Is walking a fine line. Some on his council are calling for him to join with Severn and demand Daire step down." Lady Kapros hand over control of our territory? What would that mean for us? "Others are of the mind that Alopson should stay out of it and concentrate on securing their own borders. Lady Kapros has 'requested' Lord Alopson intervene and force Drakam to keep his border with Kapros open. Lord Alopson refused, saying the Kapros-Drakam border was not his concern."

Valsan steps closer, dropping his voice. "One of his council members accused me of carrying out Daire's plot, and of sneaking Thaeia out of Akareth. Because how else could she have gotten through the checkpoints?" He rolls his eyes, but I see the worry behind them. "Before I could deny it, another councilor accused Lord Alopson of the same thing." Val's cheek twitches with a flash of anger. "Everyone on the council pointed blame at someone else. They are divided."

My brows furrow, and I click my tongue. "What I don't understand is how Thaeia became a suspect in this. She was down in the arena with us when those blasts went off. She almost died!" I catch my shout, lowering my voice. "It doesn't make sense."

Valsan sighs. "They need someone to blame. Thaeia is different, and that makes her an easy target. And Lady Kapros ... the lords find guilt in her absence from the Games."

Crossing my arms, I shift from foot to foot, trying to dispel some of my anger, and under that ... shame. I hated Thaeia for her differences. I feared her. I hurt her. So it shouldn't surprise me when others do the same. Maybe I *should* stay. What if the council turns on Lord Alopson and his son? The two lords are strong, some of the strongest mages I've met, but the Alopson council has twelve members, all powerful in their own right. What if they discover Thaeia? What if ...

I'm spinning into a loop of horrible scenarios, and Valsan presses his hand to my chest. "Hey, if you—"

A deep rumbling—the kind of sound that you sense at the base of your skull before you actually hear it—comes from the estate. A second later, a shout rings out.

"Earthquake!"

We all turn just as a deafening crack splits along the outer wall of the estate. A blur passes on my right, and I nearly jump out of my skin until I realize it's Aimee. She's in a full-out sprint, heading towards the crumbling building, the erratic winds carrying stone dust in every direction. Owen is not far behind, and I dig my toes into the ground, ready to push into a run to follow, but Miles' shout from behind us stops me.

"Fire!"

A curl of smoke snakes into the air, then another strong burst of wind smacks me in the face with the scent of ash. Flashbacks of stumbling through our tent to grab Thaeia's pack flit through my mind. The choking smoke, the heat of the flames pressing against the barrier of my Gravity magic.

Miles has the lead of one of the carriage horses, pulling the team and carriage away from the smoking stables.

What the fuck is going on?

Quickly tying off the horse team, Miles runs into the stables, his Plant magic creating vines that burst from the hard-packed sandy ground. The writhing plants wrap around the doors, yanking them open then smacking the horses' flanks to get them moving.

I'm frozen for a long moment. Another section of the family wing collapses, leaving the interior rooms open to the elements like a dollhouse. There's the room I was given—though I haven't really used it since I've been sleeping with Valsan. There's the bed I was supposed to sleep in, one of the legs hanging off the edge of the splintered floor, the blanket waving in the wind. Halee's room next to mine, gapes open as well, her pack hanging over the edge, hanging where it's caught on a jagged piece of stone. Water sprays from a broken pipe in her bathroom, adding to the rain quickly soaking the dozens of rooms left exposed to the elements.

As another fissure snakes up an adjoining wall, a Stone-like substance chases it, and I see Aimee, hand pressed to the building, sending her Petrification magic to reinforce the cracks. The earth pitches below her with another Quake, and she's thrown into the air, but she quickly regains her footing. An olive tree shutters and falls into a crevasse. A crack like lightning tears through the air, and a wave of Owen's Ice spears into the sky, securing a section of wall that was about to fall.

I turn just in time to see Valsan disappear into the stables. I hadn't even realized he'd run off. Snapping out of my stupor, I follow, running around back where the smoke is the thickest and the fire is eagerly eating the wood structure. Horses scream from inside, two more bursting through the open doors, their tails raised as they thunder off into the desert. I hear Valsan's hacking coughs, and worry pushes me faster. My magic swirls in my gut, and when I lift my left arm, my power slams into the bulk of the flames. I compress the Gravity around the now sputtering fire, and with a flex of my hand, the flames extinguish. A woman runs up, skidding to a stop at my side, throwing her left arm before her. The clouds swirl overhead, and for a moment I wonder if I need to worry about a tornado on top of the fire, but then rain falls from the clouds, extinguishing the last of the flames licking along the stable's roof. A glance at her tattoo reveals the word, VATHRAR, Weather.

But she falters, her hold slipping. The rain spreads, and I'm drenched in seconds. A boom goes off to my left. I blink the water from my eyes, trying to make sense of what I'm looking at.

It's like something out of a twisted fairytale. A giant scorpion snaps its tail, the venomous tip dripping viscous liquid. It towers over the estate, its many legs scrambling as it climbs to one of the roofs. Its pincers snap with the sound of rock striking rock. It's deafening. The windows along the top floor shatter, and the scorpion stumbles as one of its many legs breaks through the roof. In its panic to get free, the giant insect writhes, large chunks of sand-stone breaking and tumbling to the ground. With another snap of its claw, the scorpion crawls over the many build-ings of the Alopson estate, its bulbous tail curled, poised, ready to strike.

A horse screams as it escapes the still-smoking stables, the shrill noise drawing the attention of the giant insect. It changes course, and I stumble, arms outstretched to keep my balance as the scorpion leaps off the roof, legs scram-bling. How does something so large move so fast?

The scorpion slams its tail into the ground, but the horse dodges, galloping into the desert. Valsan lifts his arm, and the enormous insect shakes and flails its tail as the Confusion magic stalls its attack. The horses still hitched to the carriage toss their heads, rearing up in fear. They're going to get tangled and hurt themselves, or worse, the scorpion is going to kill them. Sprinting across the wet ground, I slide right into the side of one of the horses, fingers quickly undoing the tack. Freeing one horse, I step back as it bolts. I'm halfway through getting the second horse free, when a thundering crack splinters the ground, the gaping opening spreading and coming right for me. Valsan loses his concentration for just a second—just enough time for the scorpion to snap its pincers and thrust its tail at the carriage.

Valsan shouts, "Nor!"

With a grunt, I create a Gravity shield over myself and the horse. The black venomous tail slams into my magic, and I feel the impact in my gut, almost doubling me over. With shaking hands, I get the last two buckles undone, and the horse tears off. The scorpion's tail crashes against my barrier over and over. It hurts.

A hand grabs the back of my shirt, yanking me away from the carriage. Valsan yells, "Leave it. It's not worth it. My Confusion magic is only making it angrier." He tugs me back again just as the scorpion drives its tail into the ground missing us by a foot. Ripping its spike from the earth, the black plates of the giant insect shimmer with rain as it raises its tail again. This time it smashes into the carriage, wood shattering, wheels collapsing, leather ripping. Pieces of the roof get caught on its tail, and the scorpion whips around, flinging shards of carriage all around the grounds. A large chunk of metal flies towards us, and I get my Gravity shield back up just in time to block it.

The enormous insect clicks and snaps, turning back

towards the main estate. Valsan shouts in my ear. "We need to find the mage doing this."

I shake my head, rain flinging from my hair. Forget that. My stomach clenches as I pull on my magic, condensing the Gravity around the scorpion. I hold my breath, my lungs burning, my teeth grinding as I crush it from all sides until it explodes in a mess of bits of carapace and goo. With its death, the pieces start to shrink back to normal size, the magic broken.

I assume more help has come when I catch movement from the corner of my eye, but when I turn, my vision narrows with infuriating focus. Did I just see what I think I saw?

CHAPTER 24

NOR

SOMEONE DRAPED in a grey cloak bursts from the cover of a dense shrub and sprints around a corner. My boots thud against the ground as I run across the stable yard.

Valsan shouts again, "Nor!"

I can't afford to stop. I can't lose sight of the grey cloak.

Shit, where did they go? There! A flash of dark fabric to my left. I slip on the wet sand, stumbling a step before I'm able to kick back into a sprint. Have I lost them? The rain passes over me in a curtain, obstructing the world around me, but then a gust of wind parts the water just long enough for me to catch the flutter of grey fabric fleeing around another hedge. Flexing my left hand, I hear a satisfying, "Arghhh."

I round the corner. A small smile teases my lips as I'm met with kicking feet hovering in the air before me. The grey hood obscures their face, but I can fix that. I rotate my hand like I'm turning a door knob. The struggling person swims their arms, but it doesn't help as my Gravity magic spins them upside down. Their cloak flips over their head, and they grasp at it but miss. I snatch the fabric as it floats towards the ground and toss it away. Closing my fist, my magic pulls the floating man towards me, his face turning purple from being upside down. His legs kick at the sky, his arms flailing. He's panicking, which is working in my favor since he hasn't yet thought to fight back.

Even knowing what will happen, I ask, "Who are you working for?"

In anticipation of the Compulsion magic triggering a suicide attempt, my Gravity magic pins his arms to his sides. From my peripheral, I see the brilliant red of one of Keir's Spirits, the rain obscuring them except for the flickering Spirit fire as they run by trying to help gain control of this chaos. I ignore the Spirit, focusing on my captive, but instead of trying to take his own life like the others, he snaps at me like an animal. His teeth elongate, sharpening, and I glance at his wrist. THROMKKURKOTHEUM. Transformation. Shit.

He snaps at me again, snarling, "Where is she?"

My magic pulses from me on a wave of fury. "Who sent you!"

He howls as I slowly crush him. Blood drips from his snout, his fangs still trying to snap at me. I squeeze tighter, and his howl cuts off on a whine. I take a step closer, confident in my magic. "Tell me."

He growls at me, foam gathering around his mouth. But then he just kind of … stops. His eyes glaze over, and his tongue lolls from between his teeth. Did the Compulsion magic take hold and trigger a heart attack or something?

A soft voice from behind startles me. "Who is your master?" Halee stands next to me, her thumb tapping along her fingers, but her eyes are hard and trained on the floating wolf-man. There must be enough beast within him for Halee's Animal magic to take hold. Interesting. His unfocused gaze turns to her, his mouth opening and closing, but no words come out. Halee coaxes, "It's okay. You can tell me."

He starts panting, but his eyes remain glazed over. "I—"

A yelp rips from his throat. His body goes rigid, pain shooting through his eyes, then he hangs limp. Halee whispers, "What happened?"

The rain picks back up as I lower the body, the fur melting into his skin, his claws shrinking back into nails. When he slumps onto his stomach, we see an arrow protruding from his back where it pierced his heart. Halee jumps, squeaking in surprise as a red-clad Alopson guard bursts through the pouring rain and sprints past us. "The roof!"

I look up in time to see another person cloaked in grey, bow in hand. They turn to flee. Catching up with the guard, I call out over the pounding rain. "Your magic?"

She shakes her head. "Earth magic. If I use it here, I might collapse this entire wing. There are still people inside."

Okay then. I gather my magic, a small spasm of pain rippling through my stomach. I'm not sure where on the roof to aim, so I spread my reach as far as I can. I have to increase the press of Gravity over the roof enough to stop the assailant but not so much that I'll cave in the ceiling.

I take a deep breath, but Valsan's voice stops me. "I've got them."

Val's hair is plastered to his face, his clothes slicked to his muscular body, vengeance in his eyes. Gods, he's glorious. He smirks at me as he tilts his head upwards. "They're immobile, no idea why or how they ended up on the roof. We should go help them down."

The Alopson guard chuckles as she wipes the rain from her face only for water to drip back into her eyes. "Thank you, captain. I'll go."

Val nods. "I'll hold him from here." As the guard walks away, I release my magic, letting it settle in my gut.

Halee squeezes water from her hair. "I saw the scorpion from all the way across the estate. I felt it. Gods, it was so angry. I don't know if I could have subdued it."

Valsan says, "Nor took care of it just fine."

I preen at the praise as Halee sighs. "Well, the horses have calmed now that they are in the safety of the desert away from all this chaos. I'll go see if I can convince them it's safe for them to come back."

The rain lightens to a drizzle, but the steam coming off the baked ground swirls up and conceals Halee as she walks away. I puff out a breath, rain water spraying from my lips, and Valsan's gaze drops to my mouth. "You look good wet."

My cock jerks, and I'm thankful for the crazy weather since my soaked pants hide the spot of precum that leaks from my head. But then his brows furrow, and he cocks his head.

Just a minute later, the Alopson guard's voice comes from the roof. "Shit." Val and I look up at the guard who's peering over the edge at us. She raises her hands. "I don't know what happened."

Val asks, "What?"

She glances at the roof behind her, then back at us with a shrug. She flicks her hand at us, signaling us to back up. We take two steps back, and a second later, a dark shape thuds to the ground with a sickening crack. The rain has turned the cloak a dark charcoal. Their eyes are open and blank, lifeless.

Val glances at me, and I shake my head. "Wasn't me."

Kneeling, Val pulls the hood all the way down and hums. He looks up at me then back at the body. Pointing at their mouth, then the skin around the eyes and ears, he says, "Looks like poison."

I blink the rain out of my eyes. There are little sores oozing around the eyes and ears, and though the rain is doing a good job of washing it away, there's froth spilling from their lips. When Valsan shoves the sleeve of the cloak back, it reveals the word, EMKACTH, Insect. He claps his hands. "That explains the scorpion."

I look up at the roof, down the line of olive trees that flank this wing of the estate, then back the other way. What we don't know is who killed this mage. Was it another of the grey-cloaks, or ...

Miles joins us, his eyes taking in the body before he runs his hand through his dark hair. "Same faction from the Coliseum?"

Valsan stands, clapping his hands again. "Seems like it."

Miles tilts his head. "So we have to ask how they made it through the checkpoints, or ... were they already here?"

The unsaid part of that sentence implies Alopson's involvement. Would he attack his own home to cast suspicion away from him?

I glance at the Insect mage, water and blood pooling

around them. There's the crunch of boots on grainy, wet earth, then the Alopson guard reappears, wiping her hands on her pants before waving at the dead body. "I'll take care of this."

For a moment, I wonder if she did this. She's an Earth mage, but magic is not the only way to administer poison. I flex my hand, readying my power. I open my mouth, but she beats me to it. "I didn't do this. My magic can't do this. You're welcome to search me, though there was plenty of time for me to dispose of a bottle of poison, so you should also check the roof and surrounding grounds. But, I didn't do this."

Some unspoken command passes from Valsan to Miles who steps forward, palms lifting in silent command. The guard raises her arms out from her sides and stands still as Miles pats her down. Just as he steps back, a Spirit approaches, bowing. Her slightly transparent form flickers in the wind, the ruby-red flames licking along her outline. She holds out her left arm for us to read, THRITHR. Truth.

The guard nods, facing the Spirit, her posture tall and confident. "I didn't kill this mage."

The Spirit's pinky finger twitches, then she turns to us and nods.

Valsan asks, "Did you see anyone else on the roof or nearby?"

The guard shakes her head. "No."

The Spirit nods again.

Valsan points at the dead Insect mage, asking, "Have you ever seen this mage or know anything about these grey-cloaks?"

The guard glances at the body, taking a long look, then shakes her head. "No, to both questions."

Another nod from the Spirit confirms she's telling the truth. Well, this mage's power sure is useful. She shimmers, blinking out before reappearing, a bit more transparent than before. Valsan says, "I think Lord Keir is reaching his limit." The Spirit dips her head, and Valsan bows. "Thank you for your assistance"

Returning the bow, she puffs out leaving behind a black and red vapor that's quickly dispersed by the wind. Valsan nods at the dead body, speaking to the guard. "You'll handle this?"

She nods, and Miles, Valsan, and I turn, heading back to the stables. The wet sand crunches and squishes under my boots. I step over a piece of the carriage door, stopping next to Valsan, hands on hips, taking in the destruction.

The carriage is completely destroyed, large holes gaping in the ground from the scorpion's tail strikes. Metal and wood and leather pieces spread in broken bits across the ground. I follow Valsan's and Miles' gazes to the scattered packs that were secured to the rear of the carriage. Some of them must have gotten caught in the scorpion's tail or pincers or legs, because they are shredded. Others lay mostly disintegrated in a big glob of venom left behind by one of the tail strikes.

Aimee joins us, Owen right behind her, and when he sees the carriage and their belongings, he tsks. "Are we cursed?"

Aimee's face doesn't change, she just turns to Valsan. "The Quakes have stopped, and the family wing is stable, for now. A lot of structural damage"—she faces me—"but no one was hurt." I let out a shuddering breath as she continues, "Owen and I reinforced what we could."

Owen rubs the back of his neck. "My ice won't hold for

long in this heat, but other mages of House Alopson are already working on repairs."

Aimee points towards where they just came from. "The center of the shockwave seems to have come from outside the guest suites."

Another sheet of torrential rain hits us, but we hardly notice, all of us already soaked through. Aimee rubs her tattoos, jerking her head towards the private family wing of the estate. "Lord Keir single handedly kept that section from completely collapsing. He had four Spirits working to reinforce walls or counteract the tremors. He sent even more Spirits out to search the grounds." There's a note of awe in Aimee's voice, and I feel the same way. I know he's not the type to keep a running tally, but the list of debts we owe that man just got longer. Aimee continues, "Keir's Spirits found the grey-cloak responsible for the Quakes, but she took her own life before they could capture her."

Owen shakes his head like a dog, water spraying from his hair. "So we're calling these thugs, grey-cloaks?"

There's a break in the rain. It just stops, the thundering sound cut off so suddenly, my ears ring for a second. Aimee dips her head at the carriage remains. "That bug did all this?"

Owen crosses his arms, Ice crystals climbing his left arm, creeping over his shoulder, betraying his emotions. "What if it was deliberate? What if someone doesn't want the captain to leave?"

Valsan rubs his hands together. "I think it was coincidence. We just happened to draw the scorpion's attention, and good thing we did, keeping it mostly away from the estate. I'd rather lose the carriage and a few belongings than people's lives."

Aimee crosses her arms. "And if this *was* at least partially targeted towards you, captain?"

Dread spreads through my gut, swirling with my magic-induced nausea. Valsan shrugs. "If ... and that's a big if, we were targeted here, they must have known I'll get my hands on another carriage. We'll go on horseback if necessary, so at best, they've delayed our departure. So that begs the question, what were they buying time for?"

I glance towards where I left the Alopson guard with the body. "The grey-cloak with the Transformation magic was after Thaeia. Maybe they thought you were going to smuggle her out? If they have reason to believe she's here, it's easier to pin her in and try to get to her here instead of chasing her across Sodoles. I don't know. None of this makes sense."

With a flex of his fingers, the Ice on Owen's hand shatters, the crystals melting as they hit the ground. Valsan sighs. "What is it, Owen?"

He shakes his head, but a little stain of pink tinges his cheeks. "Nothing, sir."

Aimee laughs. "Oh, come on. You have a million tells, and right now, your body is telling us you have some dim-witted, poorly thought-out theory."

The Ice travels across Owen's chest and down his other arm. "I'm just wondering if this might be Lady Kapros." Storm clouds roll through Valsan's eyes, and Owen holds up his crystalized hand. "I know, captain. I know. But she didn't come to the Games—the territory leaders *always* attend. And now this attack ... What if—"

"Owen, that's enough." Valsan doesn't raise his voice, but the command is there.

I toe my boot against a piece of the shattered carriage. "I mean ..." Val turns to me, his jaw twitching. But when he doesn't say anything, I stand a little taller, voicing my thoughts. "There was talk last year that Lady Kapros was pushing to redistribute funds to open our own port in Kapros. The rumors were that she wanted to break our dependency on Drakam and their ports. But I guess the Kapros council voted against her in favor of increasing funds to recruit mages at the Games this year?"

Owen taps his foot, the movement making little sloshing sounds in the sandy puddle. "It was the captain who recommended more funds for recruitment."

Valsan says, "Building a port able to dock ships large enough to cross the seas would be an expense Kapros wouldn't make back for scores of years, if ever. We don't have a natural bay deep enough, so we'd have to dig one. Plus, Ka Crummens is already the established port for Sodoles' imports and exports. Kapros doesn't produce enough of anything to justify our own port for exports, and we'd have to severely underbid on Drakam's import fees to get merchants to come to Kapros. But if we are able to draw more powerful, more talented mages to Kapros, that alone will build our economy and—"

Owen raises a hand. "We know, captain. And I agree, as did our council."

Miles shifts. "And there was Lady Kapros' proposal to … 'bulk up' our guard ranks."

Owen raises a brow at Valsan, who says, "Yes. She proposed to triple our current numbers. I opposed her, and as captain, my recommendation was taken over hers … again." He shakes his head, running his hands through his hair. Of course, the wind chooses this moment to pick up, sprinkling us with a three-second rain shower, then dying back down. "The budget required to expand our guard was needed to supplement our food imports. Our fruit, veg, and meat harvests were not great, but adequate. However, our grain production was well below projection, and we needed those funds to import rice, flour, sugar ...”

Miles shifts his weight to his other hip, a small desert rose sprouting from the ground at his feet as his Plant magic leaks from him. “You’re the best captain in Sodoles. We may not have the largest guard, but we are the best. Kapros is well protected and well-ordered. We didn’t need to expand. We *did* need the food. It was the right call, captain.”

I cross my arms. “Is it possible that Lady Kapros might be using your absence to push her agendas on the council? Without you there ... But then how does Thaeia play into all this?”

Valsan’s face doesn’t change, he just stands there for a long moment before he says, “I ... don’t know.”

CHAPTER 25

THAEIA

The shaking has stopped. I pace for the hundredth time along the second-floor balcony. Absently, I rub my shoulder where the avalanche of books struck me when the first Quake started. Keir's Spirits—two of them—still stand at the main door, guarding it, guarding me. When I peer down, the female tilts her head in acknowledgment, red flames swirling around her hair, before she straightens and snaps her gaze back forward.

I go back to pacing, glancing at the window. Nothing. My nails dig into my palms, so to give myself something to do, I make my way down one of the aisles, stepping over piles of scattered books. Crouching, I pick one up, the leather cover warm in my hand, the scent of paper wafting up to me as I make sure none of the pages are bent before carefully closing the book. I slip it onto the shelf, and repeat the process. Over and over I check the books for damage before putting them away. The mundane task helps pass the time, but my head aches from listening for any sound coming from the first floor.

There—the telltale click of the lock, but not from the main door.

My steps are light and quiet as I jog to the railing, gripping it to peer down. I see the red glow of his flames before Keir and his hounds emerge from the shadows from the rear of the library. My grip relaxes slightly once I see him. He's okay.

His head snaps up, eyes finding me with ease. A soft smile lights his eyes, and I relax even more. His hand slides along the rail, his feet carrying him up the stairs towards me. The brush of his magic slides against my spine, and his flames extinguish. Gren and Hich dissolve, and the guards poof out. A moment later, he pulls me into his arms, being careful of my lingering aches and bruises. Without a word, he brushes his fingers over the scratches on my shoulder, his eyes traveling over me to the books I have yet to put back. My skin pebbles under his touch as he leans in, his breath teasing my hair. "Are you okay?"

I nod. "You?"

He dips his head, and his fingers trail down my arm circling my wrist before taking my hand. Leading me to my room, he leaves the door open as I sit on the sofa. Taking a seat next to me, he angles towards me, his posture snapping straight.

I smile. "Uh oh. That's your lord face."

A little smirk cracks the serious pull of his mouth. "My lord face?"

"You have this ... look you adopt when you're about to talk business. Very serious." He shakes his head, unable to wipe away his smile. I let the light moment stretch before asking, "What happened?"

His smile finally falls. "There was an attack. The same group with the grey cloaks from the Coliseum. Two dead, two in the capital jail. Neither has said a word. Before one of the others died"—Keir's eyes find and hold mine—"Nor said they wanted to know where you are." Dread sinks like Saph's Metal magic in my gut. "There was damage to the estate, but most was relegated to our family wing. There were a few injuries, and we're lucky no one was killed. The stables were destroyed along with Valsan's carriage." His hand slides over mine, his thumb rubbing little circles. "Your friends weren't hurt. They are all safe."

My relief is overpowered by my anger at these attacks. Keir says something about his father closing their border, and I try to pay attention as he goes on, "Lord Drakam was already threatening to close both his borders. There has been word of some fighting at the Kapros-Drakam border, but it has died down for now. Though I wouldn't bet on that tentative peace lasting."

My anger turns to rage, and I pull my hand back so Keir won't feel me shaking. Taking a slow breath, I let it out, silently saying the words Saph taught me right after my twelfth birthday. *Self-control is strength. Master your thoughts. Find power in the peace.*

I manage to get myself under control, and my thoughts solidify with purpose. Peace? That will have to come later. I stand, fingers curling into my palm in reflex, though there are no sleeves to grab. "Take me to the jail." His brow scrunches, but before he can deny me, I take a step back, planting my feet. "The 'grey-cloaks' as you called them, were looking for me. Well, let them find me. Maybe they will talk."

"Thaeia—"

"No. You know this is the right move. This has to stop before anyone else gets hurt. Before anyone else dies."

"We don't know for sure that these people are responsible for the explosions at the Coliseum." I raise a brow, and he drops his gaze. Running his hands through his hair, he sighs. "Okay. It's worth a try. We'll wait for nightfall though." I begin to protest, but his lord face comes back on and I nod ... reluctantly. He smirks, and I roll my eyes, but then he's closer, his fingers grasping my chin. My breath catches as his lips brush mine softly, quickly, before pulling back. "Thank you, Fox Slayer."

I blink, the words falling out of my mouth before I can stop them. "How have you done this?"

"What?"

"Endeared yourself to me so thoroughly, so quickly?"

His smile grows. "It's the Alopson charm."

I let him joke, but I know the real answer to my question. Keir is honestly kind and empathetic. And maybe the way I grew up has conditioned me to crave this kind of affection, but I don't care. Even the Void deserves to have someone look at them like ... this.

Keir breaks me from my thoughts. "Since Valsan's carriage was destroyed, I'm on my way to secure him another. But with the borders closed or closing, negotiations will have to be drawn with Drakam to get Valsan and his group home ... including Nor and Halee." He pauses, uncertainty hooding his eyes, and he shuffles in place. "Would you, what I mean is, if we can find a safe way for you ... I'm not trying to keep you here, not that I don't want you here, I do. I'd actually prefer it if you stayed, at least a while longer, you know, until it's safer, until we have this figured out. But it's not just your safety, though that's important, of course. I want you here with me. Self-ishly. But if you'd—"

"Keir." His eyes climb to my face, and I smile. "I'll stay." My smile grows. "At least for a little while longer. Thank you."

Color stains his cheeks, and my heart flutters. This time, it's me who leans in. He meets me eagerly, our lips pressing, then opening. Our tongues slide and taste, and I moan into the kiss, the first flutters of arousal awakening. Before the moment can bloom into full desire, Keir pulls back, a small frown on his face.

"I wish I didn't have to go right now."

I attempt a sassy smile. "But alas, you must."

He snorts a laugh as he turns. The metal stairs clang under his boots as he jogs down them. Hich and Gren reappear, the red glow of the Hounds and their master spilling along the library floor as they leave through the main door.

Now I'm forced to do my least favorite thing ... wait.

As the hours sluggishly tic by, I get the bookshelves sorted. I have no idea if the books are in the right places, but at least they're off the floor. The sun set a while ago, and I interlace my fingers behind my back, stretching my arms straight, cracking my back. I roll my head from shoulder to shoulder, then hit the stairs. I run down to the first level, barely hitting the floor before I spin and run back up. I sprint to the next set of stairs and run up to the third level, quickly running all the way back down. Over and over I run the three flights of stairs. I pump my arms, feeling the slight pull in my side, but the exertion feels good. I removed the stitches two days ago, and it's healing well. My leg throbs a little, but I'm able to push on. My breaths come faster and my shirt begins to stick to my skin. I keep going but almost slip on the next riser as the memory of the screams, of the fire, of the flying debris all press against my skull. The rhythmic pounding of the metal stairs almost drowns out the roar in my head as I recall the explosions at the Coliseum. The echoes of the searing pain that tore through me that day cause my foot to miss the next step, and I just manage to avoid scraping my shin. But the thought of the two grey-cloaks sitting in the cells drives me on. I hit the third floor again, working through what I'll do and say to them.

After two more rounds, I stop on the second floor, sucking in air as I stalk into my room, ripping my sweaty shirt over my head. I step into the shower, quickly rinsing off. Keir has brought me more of the delightful stretchy pants, and I pair them with a soft tunic that hugs my chest. Just as I tie my hair back, Keir appears at the door, his shoulder leaning against the frame, his arms crossed. I swallow at the delicious sight, but don't allow myself to get distracted.

"It's time?"

He doesn't move, his eyes traveling down to my boots and back up. "What were you doing to pass the time, Fox Slayer?"

"Running stairs."

He chuckles, shaking his head as he pushes off the door. "Can't keep still."

I frown, knowing I'm about to ruin his teasing mood. "It's hard to relax when people are trying to kill you and will hurt your friends to get to you."

His laughter fades. "Fair." He leaves, descending the stairs, and I follow as he says, "There's a back way into the jail. Daria has the only key." I'm about to ask what good that will do us, but he reaches into his pocket and waves a brass key over his shoulder.

I stop halfway down the aisle, giving Keir space to activate the lock, and once it clicks, I hurry forward, jogging through the door. We shuffle single file down the narrow passage, the lock clicking in place once I'm far enough away. This trip through the hidden corridors doesn't seem to take as long as the first time. We repeat the process of him unlocking the door leading outside, and once I step through, my eyes don't have much adjusting to do since night has fallen, casting the grounds of Keir's vast estate into shadow with the exception of low-burning arsine torches dotting the sandy paths.

We don't speak as we cross the vast grounds of House Alopson and enter the capital city of Farcrest. The occasional light flickers behind curtained windows, and a distant clip of footsteps along with the murmur of conversation floats down the streets, but we never see anyone. Keir leads me through his city with ease, never pausing, his posture tall, his stride even.

I try to take in the city. There are sculpted and well-maintained sandstone buildings lining the cobbled streets. The crackle of palm fronds brush against each other in the wind. And though I never see them, the trickle of water fountains adds a lyrical note to the evening air. A gust whips my hair around my face, attempting to pull it from its tie, and sprinkles of rain dust my face. And then it's gone, remnants of the storm with more to come. I'm no stranger to hurricanes, and I know this is just the lull as the tails curl around, and the rear of the storm prepares to wrap around us.

Metal scrapes against metal, and I jerk to a stop. Keir turns the key into a hole in the wall of a nondescript building. I squint. If I wasn't looking at the key sticking out of the wall, I wouldn't know that keyhole was there. Where's the door?

In answer, a whirring sound comes from inside the wall, and much like the floor mechanism in the arena at the games, the wall itself shifts, and an opening slides back. I follow Keir inside the dark building, eyeing the wall as it clicks and grinds closed. Must be completely mechanical since I'm too close for any magic to be at work.

When I look back down the hall, I can't see Keir, so I pick up a fast walk, taking the turn to the right. Blinking, I find myself staring down a short hall, iron bars reaching from floor to ceiling down either side. Barred doors indicate eight cells, two of which hold the mages responsible for the recent attack.

Keir takes a few steps forward, then turns back to face me. His feet are planted, his arms by his sides, but his left hand flexes. I have the urge to remind him his magic won't work with him so close, but he's aware. Still, I appreciate the gesture.

There's a muffled shuffle in the cell to my right, and I'm about to face them, but a gasp from the cell to my left has me turning that way instead as the prisoner whispers, "You!"

CHAPTER 26

THAEIA

I MIMIC KEIR, placing my hands on my hips, staring at the prisoner. "Me."

Their left hand flexes, their face pulling back in anger. "You must die. You are an abomination."

I step to the bars, so close, the scent of iron teases my nose. "You're welcome to try."

The prisoner scrambles away from me, fear dilating their eyes. "No! Get away."

"Bret, it doesn't matter." The voice of the prisoner in the cell behind me is dejected, resigned. "The Compulsion magic will kill us, or they will. Now that we know the Void is here and alive, they can't let us live."

I step back, turning so I can see both prisoners. "So, what can you tell me?"

Bret, the one still cowering against the back wall, clicks his tongue. "Nothing. We will tell you nothing."

Keir says, "Then I'll tell you what I know. I know this was ordered by one of the Houses."

Bret stands a little taller, his misplaced confidence outweighing his fear for a moment. "That's not hard to deduce. But I wonder, young lord, do you stay up at night questioning whether your father is behind this? If Lord Alopson has ordered the hit on your little toy here?"

Keir's pointer finger twitches, but that's his only reaction. I snap my fingers, drawing Bret's attention. "We also know you want me dead, not captured."

The prisoner on the right murmurs, "Obviously."

I look from one prisoner to the other. "Well, if you can tell me who is so desperate to get their hands on me, I'll make this easier on everyone. Why suffer under the Compulsion? Why do their dirty work? Why die for them? Tell me, and let them face me, let them look me in the eyes, let them try to kill me themselves. Seems only fair."

Bret crosses his arms, but stays pressed to the back wall. "It is an honor to carry out our orders. Our master should not have to dirty their hands with your blood. Me, however, I will bathe in it."

Ignoring Bret and the shiver of fear that wants to slide down my spine, I turn to the other prisoner. They look at me, their expression blank, their eyes blinking slowly. They lick their lips. "Will your Void keep the Compulsion magic from activating?"

Bare feet slap against the stone floor as Bret runs to the bars, shouting, "Ethan, don't!"

I keep my gaze on Ethan, shrugging. "I don't know. Possibly. Probably. But I don't know."

Ethan continues to stare at me, and I wait him out. He shuffles closer, but stays out of reach. "You will really face our master?"

I nod, willing him to see my determination. "To stop the violence? Yes."

Ethan blinks at me, and Bret shouts, "Don't!"

Tearing turns my attention to Bret. He has ripped his pants from ankle to knee. A faint glimmer of steel flashes as he pulls a thin blade from a hidden seam. How did the Alopson guards miss that? Keir lunges for the bars, reaching through to stop him but Bret jumps away from Keir, rearing his arm back. The knife sails towards me.

Diving, I feel the brush of air pass my shoulder as the blade sails past ... right into Ethan. Ethan gasps, his feet scraping against the stone floor. The hilt of the dagger protrudes from his neck, blood covering his hands where he grips the blade, unable to dislodge it. His wide eyes find me, his mouth opening with a gurgle. "Our master is Lor—" Blood spurts from his mouth, dripping down his chin as his legs buckle, and he falls.

I shout, "Keir!"

The scrape of the key in the cell is loud, and the screech of the door swinging open is even louder. I barrel inside, hearing Keir follow me. Propping Ethan's head in my lap, I ignore the wet heat of his blood. Ethan opens and closes his mouth, no sound coming out. I lean down, pressing my ear close to his lips, but all I hear is a strangled, "I'm sorry."

His chest rises and doesn't fall. Ethan's eyes glass over as his body goes limp. A strange calm settles over me starting at my head and draping over my shoulders. I yank the blade from Ethan's throat, and his head thuds against the floor as I stand. Striding from the cell, I point the dagger towards Bret's door. "Keir, if you'd be so kind."

Keir pauses behind me. "Thaeia, he's a prisoner." I hold up the bloody blade, anger flashing in my eyes as I wave silently at Ethan's dead body. But Keir shakes his head. "I know, but still."

On a wild hunch, I step around Keir. I walk to the other end of the long line of cells, only stopping once the familiar red glow casts my shadow against the wall. Turning, I face a confused Keir. Gren watches me, his head tilted. Hich barks, his tongue lolling, his tail wagging at me. He takes a step forward, but stops, having learned the boundary of my Void. Avoiding Keir's gaze, I look at the two basilishounds, pointing at Bret with the still dripping blade as I say, "Enemy."

"Thaeia." Keir's voice is shocked, and Hich stops wagging his tail. But Gren immediately turns on Bret, the flames on his back flaring as his fur bristles. Bret makes eye contact with the growling Hound and he stiffens. His mouth falls open as his body Petrifies.

Huh. I honestly didn't think that would work. I didn't think the Hounds would understand me, nonetheless act on my word.

Keir snaps his head towards me, anger in his eyes. "You had no right."

My body vibrates with the desire to close the distance between us, but I force myself to stand still. "I had every right. It's my life they want to take. Besides, the Petrification is temporary, right?"

"That's not the point, Thaeia. They were prisoners of House Alopson. He was unarmed."

I flip the dagger, catching it easily before tossing it again. "Really? You sure about that?"

Keir's eyes narrow. "An oversight that will be addressed. Thaeia, my father and I have extended shelter and protection to you. You aren't even supposed to be here, and now I'm going to have to explain ... this." My chest aches at the venom in his voice. He runs a hand through his hair, Gren flattening his ears, sidling closer to Keir. "The blame rests on me. I shouldn't have brought you here. I'll figure something out. Come on. Let's go."

I blink away the tears burning my throat, watching Keir head towards the secret door. He unlocks the panel in the wall, but before it slides open, Keir says, "Come on. I need my flames extinguished to help hide us."

I meet Gren and Hich's gazes with a frown. "Sorry, fellas."

Keir barks, "Thaeia, don't. Just come on."

Both dogs cock their heads at their master, and while they're distracted, I step forward, and they puff out. Once we get back to the library, the lock on the hidden door clicks, and I stop in the middle of the room, standing on the mosaic of the running fox. Keir keeps going, his stride never breaking as he crosses to the main door, the lock clicking with a press of his hand.

"I'll bring your breakfast in the morning"

"Keir." He freezes, his shoulders stiffening, but he doesn't turn. "I'm sorry."

For a long moment, he doesn't move, but then his head dips in the slightest of nods. Without looking at me, he leaves, the final click of the lock sealing me in the library. Alone.

CHAPTER 27

THAEIA

I'VE SPENT the last two days slowly going crazy. Two days of tension winding my back tighter and tighter. Two days of anxiety poured into reading every and any book that might have the smallest hint of past Voids. Nothing, which drove my jittery nerves into restless apprehension bordering on panic. Keir has come and gone several times as he drops off my meals with hardly a word said to me, then rushes back out to his next responsibility. I don't envy him his position, and I understand his disappointment with me, but my sour mood grows with every silent minute. I just want to talk, to … fix things. I'm on edge, and I don't know how to dispel all this stress.

Last night, I tried to wear myself out, running the stairs again, and when that didn't help, I upended the work table upstairs—the table I can't look at without a throbbing starting up between my thighs—and spent an hour throwing my blades at it. The bottom of the table is now pocked with scores of knife marks, but the churning anxiety in my stomach is still there.

I sigh, looking out the window near my bed, the rain falling sideways, blurring the outside world. The rain and howling wind is starting to sound like voices, whispering to the books, and I feel like they're all talking about me behind my back. I'm sick of it. I'm beginning to hate it here.

The click of the lock followed by the swish of the door opening draws me to the railing overlooking the first floor. I smile for the first time all day when Halee steps into the library, a tray of food in her arms. Keir slips in behind her, making sure the door closes and locks before he looks up, finding my eyes like he's always aware of where I am. He smiles, but it doesn't quite reach his eyes. Even his Spirit flames look a little dull, Hich and Gren a little more transparent than usual. He's tired, but he still finds the time to check on me, to feed me, to keep me safe. Even after what happened at the cells.

I grip the railing to keep from punching it. I feel so godsdamned useless! I want to do *something*. I want to help. No. I want to hunt. After the cut-off shout from Ethan before he died, I'm almost certain Lord Drakam is the one after me, but I can't completely rule out Lord Alopson, what with Saph's past. It's definitely one of the Lords—not Lady Kapros. Ethan was going to say Lord, but which one?

I force my rage into a dull simmer as Halee steps onto the landing. After a one-armed side hug, she moves into my room, setting the tray on the table in front of the sofa. She picks up a steaming bowl, settling into one corner of the velvet couch and blows into the bowl. "This smells great. Thanks for the recommendation, Keir."

I jump as Keir's arm slides around my waist. He inhales deeply, nuzzling into my neck. "I've missed you."

I rest the side of my head against his. "Me too. And I am sorry for causing you trouble. I—"

"I know, Fox Slayer." His lips press to the place where my neck and shoulder meet, sending a little shiver down my back. "I have to work late again tonight, but I'd like it if we could talk. If you don't mind a man slipping into your bed in the dead of night ...?"

I pull away enough to raise a brow at him. "Do you have a particular man in mind?"

My teasing smile slips as his eyes darken to stormy seas. His hand curls around my throat, squeezing just enough for the edges of my vision to spark with little stars. He pulls me to him, his lips brushing mine as he says, "Thaeia, you know who belongs in your bed."

Holy fuck. I'm about to collapse into a puddle of arousal, but Halee clears her throat, snapping me out of it. "You two want some privacy?"

Keir doesn't move, and I'm about to nod and send Halee on her way, but Keir finally releases me, stepping back. My neck tingles, and I wonder if the imprint of his palm lingers around my throat. He bows to Halee, and her eyes go wide, a sweet blush coloring her cheeks as he says, "Thank you, Halee, but that won't be necessary. I have meetings to attend. I'll leave you ladies to your lunch."

With quick, jogging steps, Keir runs down the stairs, his flames bursting along his shoulders and through his hair. His hounds appear mid-stride, and I wonder if they are always hovering nearby, waiting for their master to slip out of my Void. The door shuts and locks behind them.

I sigh, entering my room, flopping onto the couch next to Halee. I lean over, grabbing the second bowl, letting its heat seep into my hands as I blow on the fragrant soup. Halee dips her spoon into her bowl, and it comes up filled with amber broth, white rice, ochre beans, orange carrots, and chunks of white meat of some kind. Halee slurps the soup, chewing, watching me out of the corner of her eye. She side-eyes me, then looks away. Her leg bounces, and she glances at me again. She's acting weird.

I lower my bowl, holding it in my lap, tilting my head at her. She ducks her head, her hair falling to hide her face, but not before I catch her flaming cheeks.

"Halee?"

She ... giggles. The sound is so happy and light, it almost seems out of place among all the stress I've pumped into this room. When she looks up at me, she's got her lip between her teeth, a smile tugging at her mouth. Her eyes are sparkling, and realization slams into me. Setting my soup on the table, I hop across the sofa, grabbing Halee's forearm. Leaning in, I grin with outright glee. "Halee, did you and Miles ...?"

She bites her lip harder before releasing it, nodding with another peel of giggles. I shake her, some of her soup sloshing onto her lap, and I try to brush it off. "Oops. Sorry." Her giggles get louder as she sets her bowl on the table. I shake her again. "And? How was it?"

She covers her mouth with her hand. "Thaeia!"

"What? Come on! I've been stuck in here for days. Give me *something*."

Her face is still bright pink, but she attempts a sassy brow lift. "Are you and Keir ...?"

I grin, calling her bluff. "Oh yeahhhh. In the library, against the balcony, the bed ..." Halee grimaces at the cushions where we sit, and I laugh. "Not yet. You're safe."

We both laugh, and I realize this is just what I needed. My friend and some time to turn off the fear and uncertainty. I missed out on this type of bonding as a teen. No one shared their secret crushes with me. No one sat up with me through all hours of the night to talk about sex and growing up and lust and love and heartbreak and ... all that.

Halee sighs, a dreamy look falling over her face. "Since the guest suites were destroyed, and it will take the Stone and Construction and Metal mages some time to rebuild, I was given a new room. But Miles being Miles didn't like the idea of me being alone after the attacks, so he offered to sleep on the floor."

"Oooh. Yes. Tell me you told him it was silly for him to sleep on the floor when the bed is so big."

She rocks back into the sofa, laughing. "Something like that."

I chuckle. "Yes, girl."

She laughs harder, snorting, and I join her. Eventually her laughter fades to a wistful sigh. "It was ... so many things. It started off sweet and slow, but then things got pretty intense. He took his time." Her hands flex on her thighs before the thumb of her left hand starts tapping her fingers. "He had me practically begging."

"Mmmm."

She grins at me, nodding. "Yeah. It was ... yeah, it was ... I mean I never thought it could be like ... Thaeia, it was so *good*."

I thread my fingers through hers, giving her a squeeze. "I know what you mean. Keir took my expectations and threw them out the window, and then he rewrote what I thought I knew about pleasure." My smile slips. "Though, I did … something. Keir's upset with me."

"He didn't seem too mad earlier."

I shrug. "I guess he's had some time to cool down, but he wants us to talk. Tonight."

"And?"

"What if I make him angry again?"

"So let him get angry. Don't hide yourself. If he's going to love you, he needs to know you, the real you. And if he can't love"—she waves her hand at me—"all this, then he's not worthy of you."

I tilt my head at her. "When did you become so wise?" She blushes, and my grin pulls at my cheeks. "So, oh wise one, specifics, I need them. Spill."

We giggle, each going into too much detail of our recent sexual exploits. If Miles or Keir knew we were divulging all our sexy secrets right now, they'd be horrified—but probably a little flattered too since we can't seem to stop singing their praises. We finish our soups, each nibbling on our bread rolls, taking sips of iced lemon tea between bouts of laughter. We spend hours talking about the boys we like, never once bringing up the fires, or the border closures, or the grey-cloaks. We push all that to the backs of our minds, allowing ourselves to just be girlfriends for a while.

A gentle shake of my shoulder drags me from sleep. Keir stands over me, a tired smile on his face. He dips a glance at my lap, and I realize Halee's head is cradled on my thighs, her mouth slightly open, a small wet spot of drool on my pants. My lips curl up, and I rub a hand down her back. "Halee."

She mumbles something that sounds suspiciously like

'Miles' before she pushes herself off my lap, wiping at her mouth. "Sorry. I don't remember falling asleep."

"It's okay. I passed out too."

Halee stands, stretching, as Keir says, "Miles is down the hall, waiting. He said he's staying with you for safety. I can have guards posted outside your room if you'd pre—"

I bite the inside of my cheek. How can someone be so attentive and so adorably obtuse? I smack his thigh. "She's fine with Miles."

I raise a brow, and a second later his mouth drops open with realization. "Oooh. Okay."

Halee's face heats, and I waggle my brows at her. She laughs, skipping down the metal stairs, the door opening and closing a moment later. Keir flops on the sofa, taking Halee's spot. He kicks off his boots, and I pat my lap. Hesitating for just a moment, he swivels, resting his head on my legs, and I comb my fingers through his hair, gently working through a few tangles. I scratch my nails over his scalp, and he sighs. "You two have a good time?"

"We did."

"Good." His eyes slide closed. "Halee and Miles, huh?"

"That's been building since they met."

"Hmm."

I want to let him rest, but tap his nose. "Go shower. It'll make you feel better. Have you eaten?"

He doesn't open his eyes, but nods. "Yeah. I ate ... something between meetings."

He drifts off, but I give him a little shove. "Shower, then we can talk. Come on."

With a grunt, he sits up. I tug his hand, helping him stand. He shuffles into the bathroom, and a second later there's the soothing sound of running water. I do my best to keep images of Keir's wet, naked body out of my mind, busying myself by setting his boots next to mine, lined up at the door. I place Halee's and my empty bowls and glasses on the tray, then strip down to my underwear, sliding into bed. A few minutes later, the shower squeaks again, and the sound of falling water stops. Keir is downright lickable as he strides naked from the bathroom, patches of his skin still wet where he missed toweling himself off. My core heats, and I swear a drop of arousal wets my underwear. Internally I scold myself. *He's exhausted, you slut. And you need to talk about what happened.* Keir nearly falls into bed, and I scramble to pull the blankets back as he flops onto his stomach. I chuckle as I drape the blanket over both of us. "Long day?"

"Long week."

Yeah. It has been.

Rolling onto his back, he shimmies his body until his head hits the pillow. He spreads his right arm, his eyes closed. "Come here, Fox Slayer."

Gods, I love it when he calls me that. I snuggle into his side, his arm wrapping around my shoulder, his fingers tracing little circles over my skin. He takes a deep inhale. "I want you to know ... back in the cells ... when you offered to hand yourself over, to face your enemy ..." His fingers still, pressing into my skin. "Thaeia, my blood turned cold." I shiver as if his body has actually cooled. Has he thought through the possibility that it could be his father who is pulling the strings of the grey-cloaks? He puffs out a breath. "Then Bret pulled out that dagger—a glaring lack of discipline from my guard. And then Gren!" Keir chuckles, his chest rumbling under my ear. "I can't believe he obeyed you, and so readily."

My body tenses up. "I put you in a bad spot. I was so

..." I sigh. "Honestly, I didn't think Hich or Gren would listen to me, but I needed to do *something*."

He chuckles again, and I melt a little more. "I get it. And you have every right to be angry, Thaeia. You've been dealt a bad hand, and life keeps punching you even when you're down."

I kiss his chest, the short hair tickling my nose. "But I have my friends, and I have you, Keir. You make me feel ... worthy. Gods be damned. I don't need them as long as you look at me like you might die if you can't kiss me."

He tilts my chin up, bringing my lips to his before whispering, "Worthy? Thaeia, you are beyond compare. And if you ask it of me, I will lay Alopson—no, all of Sodoles at your feet."

I kiss him, sucking his bottom lip between my teeth before licking. "Having you occasionally on your knees for me is enough."

I sink into the heavenly mattress as Keir flips our position, kissing my neck, working his way down. "As my lady wishes."

I giggle, slapping his back, then lightly grabbing his hair to pull him back up. "Wait, wait. While I'm tempted, really tempted, I think we should talk first." I can't believe I'm stopping Keir from going down on me, and I internally slap myself as I ask, "What happened, with the prisoners?"

He shifts, settling against my side, fingers twirling a lock of my hair. "The guards assumed the Compulsion magic took Ethan, and I didn't correct them. I told Daria that Bret got belligerent during questioning, and Gren thought I was in danger, which technically is the truth." He takes a slow, deep inhale, letting it out slowly as if he's releasing the strain from the last few days.

I blink away the burning behind my eyes. "I am sorry for causing you trouble, Keir. You went ou—"

"It's fine, Fox Slayer. I understand. Really, I do." He grabs my hand and brings it to his lips. "We're okay, right?"

His readiness to forgive and move on only causes the growing pit of guilt to expand in my stomach. "Keir."

He sits up, cutting me off. I follow, and we shift, facing each other. His hand cups my cheek. "Thaeia. We'll figure this out. We'll find out who's behind this. You will be safe." My skin heats as his fingers slide down to lightly grip my chin. "Do you believe me?" I can't speak around the lump in my throat, so I nod, and he lays back down, pulling me back against his chest into our original position. "Good."

He takes another deep breath, and by the time he lets it out, he's asleep. He twitches, stress furrowing his brows before he relaxes back into whatever dream he's having. Does Lord Alopson know his son is here with me? Does he know his son is sleeping with the Void? I can't picture the imposing lord not knowing everything that goes on in his House. Has his magic picked up our emotions when we're together? How deep do Keir's emotions go where I'm concerned? Because mine ...

What if Keir's father is the 'Lord' Ethan was about to tell me was his master? If so, why did he help me escape Akareth? What does the Lord of Alopson want with me?

Or is it Severn Drakam?

Drakam or Alopson?

Saph's angry eyes play through my mind as I recall her venomous tone when talking about Lord Alopson.

I stare at nothing, feeling like the captive in that adventure book I read as a kid, wondering if Lord Alopson will show up in the morning to lock me in the cells ... or to kill me. The line from the book plays over and over in my mind, replacing the character's name with my own.

Good night, Thaeia. Good work. Sleep well. I'll most likely kill you in the morning.

CHAPTER 28

KEIR

I TIPTOED out of the library this morning while Thaeia
still slept.

Guards walk along every hall, within sight of every
door. I glance through a window, and there is a red-clad
guard of our House patrolling the grounds. Father has us
on lockdown.

I yawn, tugging on the clean tunic I changed into after
leaving Thaeia's room. The fabric is stiff and uncomfortable, the high collar scratching my neck, the blood red of
the shirt clashing with the brilliant color of my Spirit
flames. Gren growls, mirroring my mood. My hand ghosts
through his head, and we both calm a little from the
gesture.

After the incident at the cells, Gren slinked at my side,
ears back, eyes beseeching. I've spent the last few days
reassuring him I'm not mad at him. I wasn't even mad at

Thaeia, not really. Okay, maybe a little, at first. But I don't blame her. Ethan was right, we could not let them go free with the information on Thaeia's whereabouts. Most of my anger came from my lack of control over the situation. Thaeia is turning my world on its end, and I can't help but feel shaken, like I'm standing on the deck of a ship in turbulent seas with no land or calm waters in sight. At any moment, I might lose my footing, and I'm unsure what that will cost me.

"She *demands* I intervene?" My father's voice spills from the council chambers, and my body jerks. Hich cocks his head, ears alert, and Gren shifts his body in front of mine.

When I step into the room, my father glances at me with a nod, simmering anger in his eyes. What have I walked into? His face is impassive, his posture stiff where he stands at the head of the table, literally lording over his council. He glances down the long table flanked with his council, two seats empty. Daria, his captain, stands to his right, her body angled to face her lord, but I know she's paying attention to everyone in the room. Her voice is even as she speaks, "Lady Kapros sent word an hour ago. Lord Drakam closed his southern border. Lady Kapros objected and doubled her already tripled guard at the border. She claims Drakam's guards attacked. Drakam says her guards struck first. Regardless, there are conflicting reports of injuries and deaths."

My father shifts. "And do we have any corroboration to these reports?"

"We do not."

"And Lady Kapros *demanded* I intervene? Those were her words?"

Daria nods, her face passive. "Yes."

Julien, a council member who has served our family for two generations, sits two seats down from my father on the right. His arms are crossed, his silver hair styled back. He does not look happy. In fact, more than half the people in this room have scowls of varying degrees on their faces. Julien scoffs, drawing the attention of everyone in the room. "Let them squabble. We need to focus on Alopson."

My father ignores Julien, speaking to Daria, "Captain, please let Captain Valsan know about these developments. Tell him he is welcome to attend this meeting."

With a snapped salute, Daria strides from the room, speaking quietly with the two guards posted at the doors. One steps into the room, feet slightly spread, hands clasped behind their back, gaze ahead, seeing but not looking. The other remains out in the hall as Daria walks off.

Julien clears his throat, the fingers of his right hand tensing on the table. "Lord Alopson, this meeting was called to discuss Nisha."

My gaze snaps to one of the two empty seats. *Yes, where is Nisha?*

A tiny twitch of my father's left fingers has Julien shifting back in his seat. My father stares at the older man. "*I* called this meeting for many reasons."

Lafayette, our ancient family Healer aims his cloudy gaze at me from where he sits to my father's left. "Yes, my lord, but I think we can all agree that Nisha's death should take precedence."

Wait. Nisha is dead? Hich sits, his ears alert, his eyes blazing with Spirit fire as I ask, "What happened?"

Teris, the woman next to Julien starts to speak, but has to clear her throat, tears in her voice. "Nisha was found dead last night."

Julien's hand flexes on the table again as he aims angry eyes at me. "In the hall of your family wing." He leans forward. "Outside *your* precious library."

I do not react, outwardly at least. Inside, I'm vibrating. Not only was Nisha in the restricted family wing last night, someone killed her practically under my nose. I keep my body relaxed, my voice even. "What was Nisha doing in the family wing?"

Silence spreads, pressing against the walls until Teris sniffles. "She was probably going to confront the Void."

I can't help the tightening of my jaw. "What do you mean?"

Lafayette's condescending voice cuts in. "Lord Keir, I don't doubt your heart was in the right place, but Nisha came to a few of us just yesterday. She had been paying attention, watching. Meals going into the library, empty trays coming out."

I raise a brow. "I am conducting inventory due to—"

Julien clicks his tongue. "Missing books. Yes, we know."

Lafayette continues, "Nisha saw you and your Kapros friends coming and going. A few times, your Fire was suspiciously absent."

Gren circles around me as I say, "I have taxed myself these past few days. Even I am allowed a few moments of weakness."

Why isn't my father saying anything?

Teris wipes at her eyes, her tone angrier. "You've never shown such *weakness* before. Not until the Void. Nisha suspected you were hiding her in your library. She went to find the truth, and the Void killed her."

I take a step closer to the table, leaning over to press my left palm into the warm wood. "Excuse me?" My jaw cracks as I grind my teeth. With a thought, I send two Spirits to the library to guard Thaeia.

Teris drops her gaze. Julien swallows, fear evident in his eyes, but he says, "We will give you the chance to produce the Void and hand her over for trial."

My body goes still, my flames blazing higher. "No."

Julien chuckles, delight glittering in his gaze. "Fellow councilors, now you see Lord Keir has been swayed by a pretty face to the detriment of this House. I move for the council to recognize that Lord Keir has been compromised and should be removed from these proceedings to be followed by a vote of no confidence."

My father leans forward, drawing every eye to him as he braces his hands on the table. "Julien, that's your future lord you're speaking of. Take care."

Julien glances at me before turning back to my father. "His position as head of House Alopson is not written in stone."

I'd like to see Julien try to take my House. He'd be hard-pressed to find support outside a few within this room. And even if he did rally a rebellion, my magic can overwhelm whatever they throw at me.

A few other council members turn to my father, silent challenges in their eyes. My father looks around the table, his features unreadable. Lucia, who's sitting across from Julien, crosses her legs, leaning back in her chair. Though she is younger than the other members, she carries herself with the confidence of someone with seasoned experience beyond her years. "While I do not agree with our lords' decision to keep Thaeia's presence from us, we must think logically. Why would the Void go to such great lengths to hide her presence only to kill a council member and leave the body out in a hallway?"

Julien shrugs as if he's speaking on the weather. "She's obviously desperate and panicking. She blew up the Coliseum. Her body count is rising. Who knows what she'll do next. I wouldn't be surprised if she has a network of mages working for her. It was probably her that coordinated the attack on the estate. We are all in dang ..."

Julien's words trail off as my father curls his left hand into a fist. Everyone relaxes into their chairs, anger draining out of their faces as he says, "You are the one who sounds desperate, Julien. We were all there during the attack at the Coliseum. Did any of you see the Void plant the explosives?"

Teris shakes her head. "No, but—"

Lucia taps her fingernail on the table. "Did any of you see her set off the explosives?"

Silence.

My father asks, "And without magic, how do you suppose Thaeia is coordinating all these attacks? Are you implying my son is helping her in this?" More silence, though I know at least three of the council members would accuse me here and now if they thought they had the support. With a little shift of his feet, my father faces our Healer. "Were there physical wounds or signs of a struggle on Nisha's body?"

Lafayette shakes his head, and Lucia asks, "So, Healer, how *did* Nisha die?"

Lafayette presses his thin lips together. "There was poisonous gas in her stomach and lungs."

Julien cocks his head at my father. "None of this matters! You lied to us, bringing that thing t—"

I wave a hand. "You were not lied to, you just weren't told. I don't need the council's approval to have a guest in *my* home."

Lafayette snorts, his wrinkles deepening. "You do when your actions place the House in danger."

Armand who sits closer to where I stand, huffs. "Julien, Lafayette, stop the theatrics. Just admit it, you're scared shitless by the Void. That's why you want her gone. This has nothing to do with the attacks."

Teris goes still, her eyes narrowing. "Of course we fear her. Who knows what her Void is capable of? Her existence is a threat to—"

My flames ripple down my arms, pooling on the table. "She didn't do it."

Jacob, speaking for the first time, asks, "Which crime?"

Facing him, I hold his gaze with ease. "Any of it. All of it. She's innocent."

Jacob cocks his head. "And how can you be so sure?"

"Of the attack on the Coliseum? Because she almost died."

Lafayette drones, "But conveniently, she didn't. A fantastic way to shift suspicion away from her."

I ignore our cantankerous Healer and his ridiculous statement, keeping my attention on Jacob. "And as to Nisha's death last night. I was with Thaeia. All night."

The room goes silent, and I know I've just handed out the perfect ammunition against me, but Thaeia isn't here to defend herself. Someone has to. Julien drops his head, but I catch the grin spreading across his face.

The tension in the room stalls as Rhain strides through the doors, everyone shifting in their seats as the councilor moves through the room to stand behind their empty chair near the center of the table. Rhain was appointed to my Father's council a few years before I was born, and early on, my father had some kind of fallout with them. It didn't cost them their seat, but there's always been a thread of tension between them and my father. Rhain stands tall, their blond hair braided down the center of their head, little gold hoops decorating the plaits. Their gaze travels down one side of the table then the other before they speak with a shrug of their shoulders. "The safety and security of House Alopson should be our first priority." They glare at me before aiming their stare at my father. "So, last night, after Nisha was discovered murdered, I sent word to Lord Drakam and Lady Kapros. They know the Void is here."

Well, fuck.

CHAPTER 29

KEIR

THE ROOM IS silent after Rhain's revelation.

Armand's brows pinch. "On whose authority did you contact the other territory leaders?"

Rhain grips the back of their chair. "Authority? Isn't it our *responsibility* to safeguard our people?"

Armand shakes his head. "Yes, but we do make decisions unanimously. We are a *council*."

Rhain ignores him. "Once we hear back from the other territories, the Void will be our bargaining chip. We—"

Daria pushes back into the room, Valsan at her side. The two take in the tension of the room with quick, efficient glances. Daria takes up her post next to my father, and Valsan moves to stand next to me at the opposite head of the table. Daria slips her hand to rest on the hilt of her sword, steely eyes on Rhain. In just a few moments, she's assessed who needs her attention. Her Allusion magic is formidable. She could suggest Rhain should go sit on a cactus, and they would, but Daria likes her weapons. I make a note to introduce her to Thaeia ... if the opportunity ever arises. I think they'd get along.

My father presses his palms into the table. "Rhain, you overste—"

Rhain smirks at my father. "*You* have risked your territory, your people for the sake of one, magicless girl? Not even one of our own?"

Hich lowers his body, poised in a crouch, hollow eyes fastened on Rhain. Pushing his hands off the table, my father stands to his full height. "As Armand said, you are a council. You are *my* council, each of you either appointed by me or my father. You all have served House Alopson over the years, some longer than others, but each of you brings different perspectives, opinions, and talents to the table." He flexes his left hand, his stars rippling up his arm. "But *I* am Lord. *You* are advisors. Rhain, you have forgotten your place. You have stepped over a line." My father shakes his head. "Rhain. Don't."

He must have caught some intent through Rhain's emotions, and I brace as Rhain takes a big step back, sparks cracking along their fingertips as they call on their Electric magic. The sparking bolts snap along Rhain's fingers, growing larger as they lift their left hand. Everything seems to slow down. I meet my father's eyes, waiting for him to unleash his magic to calm the room, but he just raises a brow at me, dipping his head slightly. He's letting me lead.

Rhain clenches their fist, their eyes blazing at my father as lightning curls around their hand. I don't give them a chance to throw it. All I have to do is think it, and

Hich barks. The piercing sound makes everyone but my father jump. Rhain turns at the sound.

Mistake.

Hich's eyes flash pure white, and Rhain goes still, their mouth frozen in an open objection, their body creaking as the basilishound's power of Petrification hardens Rhain's body. The room has fallen silent, several councilors staring in horror at Rhain's statuesque form. Others have their gazes turned down, staring holes in their laps.

I step out into the hall, jerking my head at the two guards. "Please take Rhain's body to the holding cells."

They snap to attention then quickly stride into the room, tilting Rhain back, lifting them between them and silently carrying them out.

My father sits, and all eyes turn back to him as he says, "I will handle the situation with Thaeia. As far as this council is concerned, she is off-limits. She is under the protection of House Alopson."

I blink at my father before schooling my features. Yes, my father helped me get Thaeia out of Akareth, and while he knew I had Thaeia in our library, he never asked about her. To place her under the protection of our House is a huge declaration—one I'm grateful for. But there will be repercussions. I take a slow breath, pride filling me. I don't know where this will lead us, but I'll stand with honor alongside my father in defense of the woman I ... do I love her? What we have might be working towards that. But there's been so much stress, so much drama, danger, tension ...

My father goes on, his gaze traveling around the table. "This is your one warning concerning Thaeia. You won't get another. If I find out any of you have gone behind my back, if you try to harm her or sell her to Drakam or

Kapros ... You won't receive the leniency Keir showed to Rhain."

My father lets the threat hang in the air, and everyone looks properly cowed.

"Now." My father turns to the woman standing in the shadowy corner behind him. The Displacement mage is slumped in on herself, her eyes blinking slowly with her exhaustion, but she attempts to stand taller under my father's gaze as he asks, "Senna, have we received anything back from Severn on my request to allow Captain Valsan and his guards through his territory?"

Valsan shifts next to me, crossing his arms. Senna nods, her blond hair swaying around her face. She's a few years younger than me, in her late twenties, but these past few days have worn her ragged with the amount of messages she's had to send and receive from the other territories. There are shadows under her eyes, and her pale skin is so washed out I can see the blue of her veins. She licks her chapped lips. "Yes, sir." She glances towards the doors where Rhain's body was just carried away. "But just so you know, I didn't send their message. I ... faked it."

Surprise shoots down my spine. Valsan chuckles under his breath, "Good girl."

My lips twitch as I try to hold back my smile, and I have to admit, Valsan's deep rumble of praise ... does something for me. I get why Thaeia responds so well to my praise. And now my mind is wandering down that road, the desire to sink myself deep inside her pooling low in my core.

Reluctantly, my focus redirects as Senna continues, her voice wavering, "The messages Rhain wanted me to send to Kapros and Drakam seemed ... important." Her eyes flick to her feet before rising back to my father's face.

"Your signature was absent, and … it just didn't seem … right. I'm sorry. I was going to bring the messages to you before I actually sent them. I didn't mean to withhold, and I promise I've never faked sending any message you've given me. I swear it. I just … I …"

Tears pool in her eyes, panic lacing through her words. My father lifts his hand, settling his large palm on her shoulder. She blinks, slumping slightly, and I'm sure her look of relief is aided by my father's magic. He gives her a little squeeze. "Senna, I believe you, and I thank you for trusting your instincts with Rhain."

A tired smile lifts one corner of her mouth, but it falls with her obvious exhaustion as she holds out a piece of paper, her hand shaking slightly as my father takes it, eyes traveling over the words as Senna says, "This is the reply from Drakam to your request. He will allow Valsan through, but Silas, the Drakam captain, insists on escorting them to the Kapros border."

Valsan's earlier grin falls. I can't imagine he's happy about having to travel the length of Drakam under the scornful eye of Silas, but it's a way for him to get home.

My father looks at Valsan, silent communication passing between them before Valsan nods his assent. Folding the paper and tossing it, my father lets it float to the table where it lands with a silent flutter. He leans over, plucking a pen from its holder, scribbling a quick note on the back. Handing the message back to Senna, he says, "Agreed. This note will let Silas know to expect Valsan, his guards, and two guests at the border in"—he cocks his head at Valsan—"two days?"

Again, Valsan nods.

Senna pinches the note between her fingers, the paper crinkling slightly with her trembling. She opens her palm, resting the folded message in the center. Her jaw clenches, and sweat beads on her brow, but the paper curls in on itself, getting smaller and smaller like it's being sucked into the center of her hand. With a little pop, the note implodes, and Senna sighs. "It's been delivered."

My father places his hand back on her shoulder, and I suspect he's feeding her more of his Emotion magic, helping calm her, reassure her, relax her. "Thank you, Senna, for all your hard work. Go, grab a meal. Take a shower. Get some rest."

She licks her lips again. "What if further communications are ne—"

"Senna, rest. We can use the birds."

She wrinkles her nose. "They take half a day to get to the capital of Drakam, more than a full day to get to Kapros. I am much more efficient, my lord."

My father gently shoves her towards the door. "Indeed, you are, Senna, but you will be of no use if you pass out from overuse. So, rest."

With a sigh, she shuffles out.

Turning back to the table, my father calmly says, "You're all dismissed. Keir, Valsan, please stay."

Chairs screech as the council members push back from the table. Without a word, everyone files from the room, a few subtly glowering at me, but Gren's growls put fear back in their eyes. Daria leaves last, posting up outside the doors before closing my father, Valsan, and me alone in the council room.

I cross my arms. My father waves his hand at the empty table. "Valsan, would you care to sit?"

The large captain shakes his head, pacing three strides to the right before returning. "What do you plan to do about Thaeia?"

I'd like to know the answer to that as well.

My father asks, "Do you want to take her home?"

A painful emptiness spreads through my chest. Will Valsan be able to get her there safely? Will she leave?

Valsan cracks his neck. "We should ask her, but I fear it is too dangerous for her to try to cross the country right now."

I try and fail to keep the eagerness from my voice. "I agree."

Valsan smirks at me, a knowing look in his eyes, and I wonder how much he knows about Thaeia and me. And then I look at my father who is ... smiling at me. I'm thrown off kilter, my cheeks heating as I glance from Valsan to my father. I may be thirty-two, but right now I feel like a little boy who was caught admitting to his crush. The two men continue to grin at me in silence until I feel like I'm going to melt into the floor from embarrassment.

Finally, they sober, the moment of levity passing as Valsan rubs a hand down his face. "Thank you, thank you both for all you've done. Not only is Kapros in your debt, consider me personally indebted to you as well."

I clap him on his back, an easy smile lifting my face. "We're not keeping score, my friend."

Valsan returns my smile, the corners of his eyes crinkling. I drop my hand as my father comes around the table, coming to stand before us. "We must be careful, concerning Thaeia." I feel bad talking about her when she's not here, but my father goes on, "Someone killed Nisha when she got too close to Thaeia."

The inflection in his voice raises my hackles, and my flames flare, but I keep my voice calm as I say, "It wasn't me. And it wasn't Thaeia."

Valsan asks, "When did this happen?"

My father says, "Last night."

With a nod, Valsan says, "Nor was with me last night, Aimee and Owen were in the guards' barracks—easily confirmed, and I believe Miles was with Halee in her guest quarters. They will be a little harder to confirm. I can retrieve Miles if—"

My father shakes his head. "You and yours are not suspects, captain."

Stiffening even more, I fight to keep my hands from clenching. He trusts Valsan but aimed that veiled suspicion at me?

Turning to me, my father says, "Relax, son. I didn't think it was you. You read too much into my words." He's reading my emotions, but he's not forcing me to calm down. He's letting me feel every moment of unease. I have to find my calm all on my own. I get halfway there, but then my mind starts to spin as my father turns back to Valsan. "Go, ready your people. You're expected at the border crossing soon. I'd hate to give Silas any excuse to act out."

Valsan's eyes flash, but he wipes the emotion away. "Thank you. Let me know if there's anything I can do. Please inform me if Thaeia decides she wants to return home ..." He turns to me with a kind smile. "But I think she'll stay, at least for a little while longer. The advantages to staying far outweigh the dangers of leaving."

Gods, I hope so.

Valsan squeezes my shoulder, and I return the gesture. I like Daria. I trust her. But I've always felt Valsan belongs here. I haven't hidden my desire to have him come work for me, but he's always turned me down, happy with his work in the south. And he has done exemplary work with the Kapros guard.

When he doesn't release me, I pull myself from my thoughts, focusing back on his face. There's a serious pull to his eyes as he leans in, whispering, "It's still a long way down the road, but when your time comes, and if you still feel my services will be useful ... ask me again."

I'm frozen with shock as he walks away, slipping from the room, leaving me blinking stupidly. My father snaps me out of my stupor as he asks, "What was that about?"

I shake my head. "Nothing. At least nothing to worry about right now."

He raises a brow. "Hmm. Because it sounded like you might have finally worn him down."

I shrug. "I didn't even ask ... again. But maybe. Like I said, it doesn't matter right now. Daria's position is safe." I crack a smile, though I feel very little actual joy.

"You'll be great, Keir. When it's your time to rule, it'll be up to you to find the right people to support you, to challenge you, to back you, to push you ..."

I flop into the nearest chair, Gren laying at my feet, Hich sitting at my side. I prop my elbow on the table, wiggling my fingers, watching the flames dance over my skin. My father stays standing, and we remain silent for a few long minutes until he finally says, "Your emotions are jumping around, but your frustration is at the forefront."

I run a flaming hand through my fiery hair. "The Coliseum, the attacks here, the skirmishes at the borders, Nisha's death ... nothing adds up."

My father sighs. "That's because you don't have all the information." My gaze snaps to his face. Another deep sigh heaves from my father's chest, and he waves a hand. "I don't have all the pieces either, but ... I have my suspicions. There are things you should know. There are things I ... need to tell Thaeia."

There's guilt in his voice. Why? What does he know?

Daria knocks on the door, poking her head in the room. "Sir? They are almost done with repairs to the damaged wing. You're needed for some final decisions."

He hides it well, but I see the exhaustion behind my father's eyes. I stand. "I can go."

"Thank you, but you should go to the library. Catch her up on everything. It might be later tonight, but I'll try to join you both for dinner?"

I nod, frustrated at the interruption, the image of his guilty eyes playing through my mind, his hesitant words spinning over and over. I guess I'll have to wait until tonight to learn my father's secrets.

The day speeds by, the first few hours eaten up with Thaeia, our conversation too brief, many of her questions remaining unanswered, frustration at having to wait eating at both of us. After I left Thaeia, I went to the stables, checking in on the reconstruction and with Arabell to see if there were any changes or modifications she wanted to make before the Stone, Construction, Metal, and Natural mages finished their work. I then rode into the city, visiting a family that lost their mother to the explosions at the Coliseum. It was meant to be a quick trip, delivering the funds finally approved to support those who lost loved ones, but the young boy, just having turned twelve, was eager to show off his new Hardening magic. And I was happy to allow him the distraction from his grief.

Only three days a mage, and the boy could already harden his entire body to resemble tree bark and sandstone. He could change his left hand into marble, and if he concentrated hard, his little tongue poking between his lips, he was able to harden my shirt with his touch. Though it just made the material feel like it was soaked in salt water and left to dry in the sun, it was something, and quite impressive for a mage so new to his power. Before I knew it, two hours had passed as I let the boy play with his magic, allowing him to show off for me.

I smile at the memory as I reach out to press my palm to the metal lock on the library door, but a sealed note tacked to the wood stalls my hand. Pulling it free, the wax snaps as I open the folded paper. My shoulders slump, and I crumple the note in my fist, pushing the door open. According to the note, my father won't be joining Thaeia and me for dinner. He's been called to the city and won't return to the House till morning.

I toss the balled-up paper on the closest table. Gren growls and Hich yips a happy bark. Looking up, there's Thaeia smiling down at me from the third floor. Her shirt is damp with sweat, forming to her curves, making my mouth water with the urge to lick every inch of her salty skin.

Grinning up at her, I plant my hands on my hips. "Have you been throwing knives at the tables again?"

Her eyes shine with her smile, evaporating my exhaustion. "Maybe." She looks towards the door behind me. "Let me guess, your father can't make dinner."

I shake my head. "Not tonight."

She must hear the frustration in my voice because she starts to make her way down the metal steps, each soft clang bringing her closer to me as she says, "I'm sure as soon as he has the time—" She hits the second floor, and she reaches up, tying back her wild mane of hair, exposing her neck. I almost lick my lips as I take a step towards the stairs as she continues—"he will fill us in."

Hich sits, his tongue lolling in a happy grin, but Gren backs up. I aim an apologetic look at my hound a second before he puffs out and my flames extinguish. Climbing the stairs, I meet Thaeia half way, my hands sliding around her waist. With her one step higher than me, we are eye to eye. Her gaze bores into me, her breath fluttering over my face, her fingers combing through my black hair.

I examine her relaxed face, asking, "How are you so calm about all this?"

She shrugs. "Unless I track your father down and demand he tell me everything right now, I'll have to practice patience." She huffs a laugh, her fingers still scraping along my scalp. "Saph used to say that out of all the things she tried to teach me over the years, patience seemed to be my hardest subject."

"She loved you."

Thaeia's hand stills, and a small frown dips her lips. "Even when she didn't have to."

My fingers slide around her wrist, bringing her hand down to press her palm against my chest. "That's what a mother is supposed to do."

She blinks at me, and I tense as I realize my words sounded like I'm looking for pity, but she simply curls her fingers into my shirt. "You've had another long day, lordling."

The tease in her voice lights me up, and I pull her body against mine. Her soft curves mold to my harder plains, her muscles tightening as her breath catches. I smile, seeing the bright blue of my eyes reflected in her gold ones. "The day's not over yet."

She leans in, and my cock jumps as her lips whisper against my mouth. "No, it's not. I'm starving. Where's dinner?"

I chuckle, grabbing her ass as I back her up. She struggles to climb the stairs backwards, but I don't release her. "On the way."

She smiles, and as we hit the second floor, her lips brush against mine. "How much time do we have?"

I palm her breast through her shirt, the weight heavy and perfect. My thumb grazes over her nipple, drawing a beautiful gasp from her. "Not enough. Not nearly enough time."

Her lips pull down in a teasing frown. "Later then."

My cock jerks again in protest. I lean in, squeezing her breast. "Or, I could push you to the floor and take you right here. I could drive into you"—I roll my hips, pressing my hard length into her stomach—"and rut you hard and fast."

Just the mental image of Thaeia spread and pinned beneath me has precum leaking from the head of my dick. I ache for her, my entire body coiled, ready to pounce. She glances over my shoulder towards the door before finding my gaze again.

"Do it."

CHAPTER 30

THAEIA

MY PUSSY THROBS as wicked delight flares through Keir's eyes. The next moment, his hands curl around the hem of my shirt, pulling it over my head. Before the garment even clears my eyes, one of his hands curls around my back, and his leg snakes around the back of my knee. He literally sweeps me off my feet, following me to the floor, his arm around my waist preventing me from smacking my head.

His other hand grips my chin, forcing me to meet his bright gaze. "Say Gren, and this stops." I smile, both at his thoughtfulness and at the safe word. I'm sure Gren would hate us using his name like this. It almost makes me laugh, but Keir's serious gaze keeps my laughter at bay. "What do you say if you want me to stop?"

"Gren."

"Good girl."

My core pulses at the praise, and then his mouth closes around my nipple, biting softly. A rush of wetness slicks between my thighs, and I'm shocked at how quickly my climax approaches. I manage to hold off my orgasm as I moan, arching into the pleasurable pain. His hand pulls out from under my back and presses to my chest. Holding me down, his other hand skims down my stomach until his fingers curl in the waistband of my stretchy pants.

His eyes darken with command. "Stay."

My body melts, completely giving in to whatever Keir wants of me. I'm jerked downwards as he yanks my pants down to my ankles, then pulls them off, tossing them over his shoulder. I don't see where they land, and I don't care as he rises over me, still fully clothed. He watches me as my gaze travels down to his hard cock straining against his pants. His voice is gravelly as he grabs himself through the material. "Is this what you want, Fox Slayer?"

I bite my lip, nodding.

He strokes himself. "Say it."

"I want your cock."

His hands pull at his fastenings, freeing his glistening length, precum slicking the head. My hips lift, aching for him to fill me. I'm so wet, my arousal drips down between my ass cheeks. I'm on the verge of begging when his large hands grip my waist. He thrusts. His cock drives deep, and my back arches off the floor. My mouth falls open on a silent scream as Keir fucks me hard and fast, just as promised. His grip is bruising, and my back scrapes against the hard floor.

I want more.

His hips slam against me, his eyes on his cock sliding in and out of my pussy. "Fuck, Fox Slayer. You are exquisite."

I clench around him, pleasure sparking through my core. His next thrust is so forceful, he nearly loses his grip on my hips. Leaning over me, the library is blocked by the beauty of the man fucking me. I'm right on the edge, my orgasm teasing at the edges of my awareness.

He pulls out, denying me my release, but before I can protest, he flips me around. I somehow have the awareness to turn my head just as my face is shoved to the floor. His hands come back to my hips, lifting my ass and thrusting his cock back inside me in one brutal move. My hands scramble at the floor, but he reaches around and grabs one, securing it to my back in an almost painful hold. I'm pinned, immobile. My mind is blissed out, relinquishing complete control to Keir. All I can manage are grunts and moans of pleasure with every wild thrust of his hips. His own grunts match mine, but his go lower, bordering on a growl.

Vaguely, I hear a knock on the door. Oh yeah, dinner.

"Ignore. It." Keir's gravely voice barks the command, each word punctuated with his cock slamming so deep it's almost painful. "You will eat when I'm done with you."

Fuck. Me.

I angle my head as best I can to look at him, my neck straining against his punishing hold. "Yes, sir."

Just as I hoped, my words unleash him. His grip tightens even more. He draws my arm back until it extends on the edge of pain. With every drive of his hips, he pulls me back, forcing me to meet his wild thrusts. My shoulder aches, and my knees will be bruised tomorrow. *Good.* I want the reminder of this moment.

"Keir. Keir. Fuck. Oh, fuck. Keir." His name comes out like a mantra, like a prayer. I'm wound so tight, the pleasure-pain drives out all thoughts except the need to come.

The slapping of his hips against my ass is tempered by his grunts, the fabric of his pants rough against my sensitized skin. My pussy actually drips onto the floor. I'm beyond words, just gasping with his thrusts. Tears prick the backs of my eyes as my orgasm refuses to crest.

I'm burning. I'm melting. I'm dissolving into ... nothing and on the verge of exploding into stardust all at the same time.

Keir's thumb presses against my clit, circling roughly. His growled voice pierces the fog of my pleasure, his lips close to my ear. I hadn't realized he'd moved to drape himself over my body. "Fox." Thrust. "Slayer." Thrust. "Mine." Thrust. "Now, come for me."

He pinches my clit, his cock driving deep and steady, and finally, I fall. I shatter. A scream wells up, but no sound comes out. My mouth hangs open, and white pinpricks of light wink along the edges of my vision. Sparking tingles erupt from my core and shoot down to my toes, to my fingers, and the top of my head. I'm held in suspension as my body pulses, the pleasure going on and on.

Keir thrusts, holds, and grunts, "Thaeia."

My name on his lips as he comes has me lighting up again, extending my orgasm as Keir empties himself, his thighs flexing against the backs of my legs.

His grip loosens as I slowly come back to myself. Wrapping an arm around my chest, he sits back on his heels, gently pulling me with him, keeping my back against his front. His lips trail light kisses down my neck. "My amazing Fox Slayer. You slay me."

My brain is slow to register ... anything, but the next thing I know, I'm in Keir's arms, and he's striding into my room and straight through to the bathroom. The shower squeaks on, and he carefully sets me on my feet under the hot spray of water. My legs wobble, but he holds me until he's certain I won't fall over.

"I'm going to go get our food. I'll be right back."

I blink, realizing he still has his clothes on, and they're quickly soaking through. I blink again, nodding, and he jogs from the room. Just a few moments pass before the smell of roasted meat and fresh bread has my stomach grumbling. Another second later, Keir steps into the shower, now naked. I realize I've just been standing here as his soapy hands move down my body, cleaning me. He takes his time with me, but he quickly scrubs himself before shutting off the water and drying us off.

Wrapping me in the light, fluffy robe, he shrugs into a second robe then leads me into the sitting area, depositing me on the velvet sofa. When I lean forward to grab one of the plates, he presses a gentle hand to my shoulder, shaking his head. He sets a plate on his lap, picking up a fork and spearing a piece of meat that's coated in seasoning, the center red and dripping with juices. It's flavorful and delicious, settling my growling stomach. Keir feeds me, all the while his other hand stokes lightly over my thigh. When everything on my plate is gone, he hands me a glass of wine. I cup it, snuggling deeper into the sofa. Only then does he pick up his plate and start to eat.

I wake just as Keir settles me into the bed. Did I drink the wine? I don't remember. My robe is gone, and he is naked as well. Pulling me into his arms, I breathe him in as he pulls the blankets up.

The world might be going mad around us, but here in each other's arms, I'm pretty sure this is as close to absolute bliss that I'll ever find.

CHAPTER 31

NOR

Tilting my head back, I watch the stars blink against the black velvet night sky.

Two days ago, in the rush of packing to leave House Alopson, we barely had time to say goodbye to Thaeia. Even though at that point almost everyone in the estate knew she was a 'guest' of Lord Alopson, Thaeia was sticking to her perceived safety of the library. Thaeia and I bumped fists before I pulled her into a tight hug. We said nothing, and when I felt her inhale shudder with oncoming tears, I gave her a squeeze and stepped back, giving Halee room to step into Thaeia's arms. That's when the tears started. Thaeia and Halee cried into each other's hair, sniffling their goodbyes and promises to see each other soon. I had to clear my throat several times, determined to make it out of the library without balling like a child.

When the tears slowed then stopped, Owen swept in, lifting Thaeia off her feet. We all chuckled as Owen said his goodbyes, lamenting their missed opportunity in the forest. I didn't know what he was talking about, but it brought a smile to Thaeia's face as she playfully punched him in the shoulder. Miles awkwardly hugged Thaeia next, his tall frame bending so he could pat her on the back. Thaeia whispered something to him, to which he blushed before stepping back. Aimee held out her hand, clasping Thaeia's forearm with a nod.

Thaeia's smile turned watery as she turned to Valsan. Launching herself at the captain of the Kapros guard, Thaeia hugged Valsan tight. He returned the embrace as she said, "Take care of him. Of them both."

Halee wiped at her eyes, and Miles pulled her into his side. Valsan looked over Thaeia's head, meeting my gaze as he said, "I will."

I shift on the carriage seat, recalling the affection and heat in Valsan's eyes. Next to me, his breathing is even, his arms crossed, his eyes closed, the reins threaded through a metal hook. Val doesn't move or even open his eyes as he says, "You're restless."

Counting my breaths, I dispel some of the frustration clawing at my skin—and not all my restlessness is from the near-constant low-level hum of arousal that being around Valsan causes. No. I'm irritated at Captain Silas. After two hard days of travel, we arrived at the border expecting the Drakam captain to be waiting and ready. But we've been held here for two hours now, the green-clad Drakam guards telling us Captain Silas was held up and would be with us 'soon.'"

Aimee paces next to our new carriage on loan from Lord Alopson where it's parked on the side of the road, her eyes on the barricaded border crossing. Guards from Alopson and Drakam stand on either side, eyeing each other. But then a burst of laughter comes from our right as one of the Drakam guards laughs at something Owen says. Good old Owen. Halee and Miles' whispers float from inside the carriage.

I'm about to jump down to stretch my legs, but Silas finally saunters up to our carriage, a large bay horse trailing behind him by a lead. My jaw flexes as I fight to keep from sneering as Silas' eyes narrow at the seemingly sleeping Valsan. When Val doesn't move, Silas clenches his fists. "Nap time's over. Let's move."

Owen strides over, swinging the carriage door open. Grabbing the handle, he plants one foot on the step, his body swinging as he hangs off the side like a sailor leaning out from the rigging, looking for land. Owen smiles, sweeping his hand towards the border. "Yes, by all means. And we thank you for taking time out of your busy schedule to see us safely to our border."

At Owen's sarcastic tone, Valsan opens his eyes, shifting to take up the reins. Aimee smacks Owen on the back of his head before climbing onto the rear seat. Owen disappears into the carriage, the door clicking shut. Halee's soft voice floats out, but I'm unable to make out her words as Valsan flicks the reins, not waiting for Silas. The scowling Drakam captain hastily swings onto his mount, the giant bay sidestepping at his sudden movement, almost unseating Silas. He kicks his horse into a trot, positioning himself on our right flank, his voice rising with unnecessary volume. "Let them through."

The Alopson guards salute to Valsan as we pass, and even a few Drakam guards join in. Then, we're across the border, Silas trailing us with five of his guards following.

We travel in silence. For hours, the carriage sways and creaks, the horses maintaining a steady trot, their hooves clopping out a beat like drums. The day passes slowly as we head towards Rokvale, the capital city of Drakam. I can't seem to relax the tightness in my back knowing Silas is just behind us. I don't turn, but I imagine his cruel eyes boring into me and it makes me want to squirm ... or to use my magic to knock him off his horse. The dryness of the desert air gives way to a slight humidity, nothing like Oxtara, but enough to ease the scratch in my throat and burning in my lungs. I'm not sorry to say goodbye to the arid north.

Valsan takes a slow breath, his soft voice startling after so many hours spent in silence. "It's starting to smell more like home."

Movement draws my attention as Owen pops his head out the window, his brown hair fluttering in the breeze. "I was just thinking the same thing."

Silas scoffs, and the urge to crush him courses through me as he says, "We're just missing the faint stench of fish and seaweed, mud and gull poop. That's when you know you're in Kapros."

My fingers curl into a fist, and Aimee shifts, aiming her hard gaze at the Drakam captain. Silas just keeps on smiling, about to say something else. One more word, and I'm going to punch him with my magic.

But Valsan pulls on the reins, turning our carriage to the left. Silas barks a curse, and his horse tosses his head as he dances to keep away from the wheels. Valsan urges the horses into a faster gate as the occasional twinkle of light comes from the far-off capital city.

Silas gets his mount under control, his scowl

furrowing his brow. "Captain Valsan, what do you think you're doing?"

Valsan doesn't look at the Drakam captain, but his knuckles are white where they grip the leather reins. "We've been traveling with little to no rest for almost three days. Rokvale is close. I'd like to get there before morning and allow the horses time to rest. My people could use food and rest as well."

Silas whips his horse into a short canter, drawing in front of us and stopping. His five guards fan out behind us. The fingers of my left hand dig into my thigh as Valsan pulls the carriage to a halt. Silas points at us. "Going through the city will slow us down. We are going around, and our first stop is not scheduled for hours."

I raise a brow. What schedule?

Valsan stares at Silas. "I wasn't aware of a schedule."

Silas rolls his eyes. "One of my guards was sent to inform you of the travel schedule."

Valsan shrugs. "They didn't."

Silas' horse dances, and the captain struggles to keep him in front of our carriage. "Of course they did! You dare accuse m—"

Both doors of the carriage open, and Miles and Owen step out, gazes trained on Silas. Aimee stays where she is, but her posture says she's ready. I flex my left fingers, but Valsan holds up his hand, the gesture holding everyone where they are as he says, "You don't have to believe me, but the horses are tired."

Silas glances at the team, noticing the sweaty foam around their harnesses. With obvious reluctance, he shakes his head. "I'm not allowing you into the House Drakam estate."

I run my tongue along the back of my teeth. I wouldn't

even want to go to House Drakam, and I'm about to say as much, but Valsan beats me to it. "I am not asking that of you, captain. We have a place we can stay."

Silas' eyes narrow. "Where?"

"A tavern in the city. I know the owner."

Silence vibrates in the air between Valsan and Silas like a string pulled too tight, ready to snap. Finally, the Drakam captain snarls, "Fine. Let's go."

Without waiting for Silas to move, Valsan clicks our team into motion, and Miles and Owen jump back onboard. Silas' horse snorts as it hops out of our way, and Silas hangs precariously off the side of his saddle before losing his seat. The thud of his body hitting the ground is so satisfying, I sit a little taller, a smile tugging at my lips. As we roll past the grumbling Silas, he leaps up, gripping the dangling reins of his horse and yanks on them. "Stupid animal."

Luckily, we're only moving at a fast walk when the door to our carriage slams open again, and Halee leaps out. Miles is right behind her, reaching for her arm but missing as she jerks away and sprints right up to Silas. Two of the Drakam guards move their horses around to flank their captain, but they remain mounted. Valsan pulls the carriage back to a stop as Halee reaches up, gripping Silas' horse's bridle. Her hand soothes down its face as she says, "Don't you dare blame him. He moved to get out of the way. What, you expected him to just stand there and get run over? It's not his fault you couldn't keep your seat."

Silas goes to yank the reins again, but Miles places his hand on his shoulder. A third Drakam guard comes around, leaping from his horse, clenching his left hand. He has Sound magic, and I imagine he could inflict serious damage if he wanted to. I'm ready to knock him out.

Halee keeps stroking Silas' horse, ignoring the building tension around her. "He doesn't like you much, you know. Maybe if you were a bit kinder to him, your horse would do more to work with you than against you."

Silas takes a step towards Halee, trying to shake off Miles' grip. "How dare you presume to—"

Halee straightens. "I don't *presume* anything." Silas' horse bows its head, bending at the knees and slowly lowers to the ground. Halee's hand settles between the horse's ears. "Until you learn proper manners, he is on strike."

Sweet Halee, defender of all animals. I snort, unable to hold back my laugh, and even one of the mounted Drakam guards cracks a smirk before fixing her face into a neutral stare. Silas gives a tug to the reins, but his horse doesn't budge. Turning his frustration back to Valsan, Silas sweeps his hand at Halee and his lounging horse. "Control your people, captain."

Valsan clicks his tongue. "You're welcome to walk."

I have to sit on my hands to keep from wrapping my fingers around the back of Valsan's neck and pulling him to me for a kiss.

Silas tosses the reins at Halee and crosses his arms. "You are here under the grace of Lord Drakam. Don't push me or I *will* bring you to House Drakam ... as my prisoners."

The curved edge of the sister star's rings peeks over the horizon, lending us the slightest hint of bluish-white light as the morning dawns. Valsan looks at Halee who looks at Silas as she holds out the reins. "Don't hurt him. I'll know, and you don't want to see me angry." To punctuate her threat, dozens of ravens spear into the sky from a nearby copse, their black wings nearly invisible against the still mostly dark sky. A fox barks, and ... something roars behind us.

Silas shifts, flinching slightly, but keeps his gaze on Halee. A slow smile creeps over his face. "The little Animal mage has fangs."

I see his intent to take another step towards her, and I construct a Gravity shield between him and Halee. Silas runs into it, his body jerking to a stop. He turns his gaze to me, eyes narrowed. But then Valsan clears his throat, and Silas looks around, really looks. Ice encases Owen's entire left arm. Vines have sprung from the ground and curled around Silas' ankles. The horses of the other Drakam guards refuse to move, no matter how the guards urge them. At some point, Aimee left her post on the back of our carriage and now has her hand wrapped around the shin of a Drakam guard sitting on his horse, his lower leg stiff as wood from her Petrification magic. One of the Drakam guards has their left hand raised, and dense smoke curls around their arm, obscuring their tattoo so I'm unable to read what magic is at play.

My stomach pinches with a spasm of pain as I isolate the Gravity around each of my friends and encase them in a protective bubble. My leg bounces as I let my vision go wide, waiting for someone, anyone to make the first move.

Silas steps back, and some of the tension dissipates as he says, "We're wasting time. If you want to feed and rest your horses so badly, tell your people to stand down, and let's get moving."

Valsan gives a nearly imperceptible nod, and all our people release their magic. But I keep my Gravity shields in place until everyone is back on or in the carriage. Silas' horse gets to its feet, and the Drakam captain swings into the saddle, casting an apprehensive glance to the carriage and Halee within before gently nudging his steed into a walk.

With a groan of the wheels, we move forward as the sky continues to lighten. By the time the sun crests the horizon, clouds have gathered and the wind is a steady howl through my ears. Rokvale is a well-ordered city. The streets, for the most part, are clean, and the occasional sounds of the capital waking up ring through the wind. A bell chimes to our right as a woman opens the door to her bakery, the sweet scents of pastries making my mouth water. A man walks past us going in the opposite direction with his head bowed, his arms filled with bolts of colorful fabric, most of which contain at least a thread of the green of Drakam. A dog barks, and I bite the inside of my cheek to keep from smiling as Silas blanches at the sound.

Valsan steers the carriage around turn after turn as if he knows this city as well as Loudare, the capital of Kapros. We make another left turn, and a familiar image comes into view. A wooden sign with the image of a flaming tankard of ale swings in the breeze, bringing to mind the nights in the desert at the bar tent ... before everything went to shit. We pull behind The Dragon's Breath Tavern. Everyone clamors out of the carriage, Halee trying to hide a yawn behind her hand. Silas and the Drakam guards dismount, a few stretching as Silas says, "Three on, two off."

Two of the guards peel away, walking down the street to go do gods knows what. Three stay, their posture stiff, watching us. I have the urge to push them back with my magic, just to have some breathing room, but Valsan claps his hands. "Miles, Aimee, tend the horses. The rest, with me."

My knees nearly buckle at the command in his voice, and he shoots me the tiniest wink, knowing full well the effect he has on me. Valsan, Owen, Halee, and I stride into the tavern with Silas and his three guards on our heels. A blond head pops up from behind the bar, and the barkeep smiles at us. Wiping her hands on a rag, she comes around, heading towards us, nodding curtly at the Drakam guards as she holds out a hand to Valsan. "It's good to see you, Captain Valsan, though I'll admit, I wasn't expecting a visit so soon." She ticks her gaze to Silas. "Captain."

Silas doesn't respond, and Valsan says, "Good to see you too, Layla. We're only passing through, I'm afraid. We could use a short rest. A few hours."

She cocks her hip. "Your ride out back?" Valsan nods, and she says, "Sure thing. I've got a few rooms" She looks at our group. "But you'll have to share."

Valsan nods again. "Not a problem."

My body tingles with the anticipation of climbing into bed with him, but the spark of arousal is doused when Silas speaks. "*My* guards and I will not need a room. Just food."

The barkeep frowns. "My cook hasn't arrived yet, but I might be able to find something." When Silas doesn't respond, she wipes her hands again, jerking her head towards a dark hall to our left. "Captain Valsan, you know where the rooms are, upstairs. All four rooms are free. Bath is the last door on the right. They're all unlocked. Help yourselves."

"Thank you, Layla." Valsan shakes her hand before heading towards the hall, never once glancing at Silas. I follow as the Drakam guards sit at a table, Silas angling himself so he has a straight view of the hall leading to the stairs. Great. How am I supposed to get any rest knowing this creep is down here glaring at us?

Val's back muscles flex as he climbs the stairs, and once we reach the second floor, a short hall stretches before us. Valsan rests his hand on the knob of the first door on the left. "Nor and I will take this one. Halee, you and Miles will take the next one." Halee's cheeks tinge pink as she scoots past us and slips into her room. "Owen, you take the one on the end on the right, and Aimee will take the one across from Nor and me."

Owen taps his chest in a lazy salute, heading towards his door. "Sure thing, captain. But I don't think I'll be able to sleep with captain sour-face downstairs."

I don't bother to hide my smile this time as Valsan says, "I want to leave in four hours. Make sure you're rested and alert when it's time to move on."

Owen nods, disappearing into his room. Boots treading on the stairs announce Miles and Aimee a few seconds before they hit the top. Valsan points to the door Halee went through. "Miles." Then he points to the room across the hall. "Aimee."

Miles goes into his room without a word, but Aimee crosses her arms. "I'm on watch."

Valsan nods. "You want relief?"

"How long?"

"Four hours."

She shakes her head. "I've got it." And with that, she walks back down the stairs, fading into the shadows like a ghost.

When I turn towards our room, I startle at the empty hallway. Pushing through the door, it closes softly behind me, and I reach back to lock it. My eyes stay on Valsan who stands next to the bed, his broad back on display as he pulls his shirt over his head. He folds it, and I swallow as he sets it on a chair, his eyes never leaving me. "It's been a long night, and Silas has tested my patience." The muscles of his abs flex, and my gaze follows the dark dusting of chest hair trailing downwards to dip behind his waistband. The fabric of his pants shifts as his cock begins to swell. I can't pull my gaze away as he growls, "I need you, Nor."

My feet move without thought. My cock aches, and my body hums in anticipation of what Valsan is about to do to me.

CHAPTER 32

NOR

"CLOTHES. OFF." Valsan's low bark of command has me rushing to yank my tunic over my head. I kick out of my boots, and drop my pants and underwear to my ankles, stepping on them to free myself. Valsan has removed his boots, but his pants are still on. I lick my lips as he moves one hand to his waistband and flicks the fastening open.

I force my eyes to his face and nearly groan at the hunger in his eyes as I say, "Do you want my magic, Val?"

"Mmm." His hand slips into his pants, and he grips himself. "Yes."

I step closer, my cock bobbing before me. "Do you want my mouth, Val?"

He strokes down his length, and my hips jerk forward with sheer desire. "Yes."

"My ass?"

He yanks his hand out of his pants and wraps his palm

around my neck, pulling me into him until his teeth graze my jaw. "I want all of you, Nor." His lips press to mine, but instead of the crushing passion I expect, the kiss is gentle, sweet. He licks at me, his arms wrapping around me, and I hold him just as tightly as our tongues taste and savor. I inhale his wood-smoke and coffee scent, and I fall with him as he backs us to the bed and lays down. He whispers against my mouth, "Take off my pants."

Gladly.

My knuckles graze his skin as I peel the last of his clothes off. Instead of throwing them to the floor, I fold his pants and set them on the chair because I know that's what he'd want. Climbing back onto the bed, I straddle Val as he reaches up and cups my cheek. "I love you, Nor."

Like two stars colliding, we come together, kissing and holding each other tight. Our cocks press together, leaking onto our stomachs. My magic swirls readily as I use it to float the bottle of oil out of my pack. In mid-air, the cork pops out, falling silently to the floor. The golden liquid dances between us, and I catch it in my palm. When I reach down and grip us both in my hand, he groans. I lick his lips, whispering, "Again." I stroke us, and he gives me what I want—that same throaty groan. I pump my fist with a little twist. Val props himself on an elbow to watch me jerk us both. It is an intoxicating sight.

While keeping his eyes on my fist moving over us, he runs his fingers through the oil hovering in the air. My asshole clenches in anticipation, and a moment later he reaches around. I press my chest to his to give him better access as he slides his fingers between my cheeks, circling them around my hole before pressing one inside me. My fist tightens around us as I push back into his touch, my hips rolling with pleasure. I stroke us in time with his finger thrusting into me, and when he adds a second, my body shudders and my toes curl.

I kiss him, moaning into his mouth as he pumps his fingers, spreading them, preparing me. But I'm already ready. My thighs shake, and my stomach clenches as my orgasm threatens to crest. I bite my lip, and Val slides his fingers from my ass. I give us one more stroke, the sight of our dicks in my hand almost sending me over the edge again, but I manage to hold back. I need him inside me, and I want to paint him with my release. I want to mark him as mine, over and over. Forever. Always.

I shift, releasing my dick so I can line him up at my entrance. Lowering myself slowly, I groan at the delicious stretch as his head breaches my hole. I stop, bearing down and clenching around his tip. His hands grip my hips, his teeth bared as he growls and slams me down. My head falls back with a grunt, and his fingers dig into my flesh as he says, "I had every intention of taking you hard, of testing your limits ..." I flex around his cock, squeezing him, a dribble of cum leaking from my dick to drip onto his stomach. "But now I find myself wanting to savor you, Nor."

My heart stops, then gallops away, the beat drumming inside my head. "I am yours, Val. Only yours." With a flex of my legs, I rise, feeling every delicious inch of him slide along my inner walls. Just as the rim of his head presses against my tight hole, I begin to slide back down. My entire body shivers with the pleasure that shoots from my core. When I'm fully seated again, I grind on him, using my magic to pull at his balls and press into his entrance, seeking his pleasure spot. His hips buck, punching him even deeper inside me, and I grin. "You can test my limits next time, Val." Leaning forward to kiss him, the movement slides me up his cock. "Anytime, Val." Rolling my hips, I lower back down. "Always, Val. I love you."

One of his hands comes to my head, gripping my hair, the other presses to my back, holding me as he takes control of the kiss. I try to move, to create that wonderful slide of his cock inside me, but his hold on me limits my movements. Instead, he bends his knees, planting his feet on the bed and bucks up into me, thrusting long and slow, hitting me so deep, our teeth clash.

My body is molten fire. My balls pull up tight, and I know I won't be able to hold back this time, no matter how badly I want this to last forever. He doesn't let me pull back too far, so my lips brush his as I say, "Val, I'm going to come. Please." I don't know what I'm pleading for, but Val presses harder on my back, pushing me onto his cock as he thrusts into me. That. That was what I wanted. I drive my magic into his ass as his cock hits me so deep, my vision blacks out for a moment. Throwing back my head, I erupt, my body shaking with pleasure as my cum spurts between our pressed bodies. My hot, sticky release rubs into our skin as Val continues to pump inside me.

Lightly gripping his hair, I tug. "Come for me, Val. Come inside me. Let me feel your hot release."

My magic presses against his prostate, and he gasps, "Fuck, Nor."

His hips slap against my ass, and his cock jerks inside me as his orgasm sweeps through him. I watch in awe as Valsan's jaw flexes, his eyes struggling to stay on my face when I know they want to roll back. He's beautiful. He thrusts again and again as I extend his climax, massaging his G-spot with my magic. Slowly, I withdraw my power, and his body goes lax. I let myself fall forward, collapsing on top of him. We're both sweaty and sticky, but neither of us moves.

After a moment, I realize I might be heavy, so I roll to the side. He slides out of me but keeps a hold of me, not allowing me to go far, keeping my chest pressed to his side. He presses a kiss to my hair, and I sigh as he says, "We should shower and rest."

Lifting my head, I see the light from the window spilling across the floor and realize at least one of our four hours has passed. He's right. We should shower, but I can't seem to get my body to move.

A kiss presses to my forehead, waking me. I didn't realize I'd fallen asleep. I blink against the bright after-noon sunlight streaming into the room. Valsan stretches under me, and I feel every muscled inch of him. He runs a hand down his face, scratching his beard. His voice is rough from not enough sleep. "Time to go." A grunt pushes from my throat as I literally peel myself off him, standing, stretching my arms over my head. Valsan chuck-les, propping himself on his forearm. "You're making it very *hard* not to drag you back into this bed."

He drops his smirk to his half-hard cock, and I grin, sending a gentle pulse of my magic to stroke him. He growls, jumping out of bed so quickly, I have no time to evade—not that I want to. His arms wrap around me, and his lips press to mine for a quick blissful moment, then he pulls away. "Let's go. We have a long way to go to get to Loudare."

We shower quickly and dress even faster, and as we go downstairs, the sounds of laughing and conversation drift up to us. The main room is nearly full. All the tables are occupied, and all but three spots at the bar are full. I'm unsurprised to see Owen at a table with five other people.

They are strangers, to me at least. I don't know if Owen has ever met a stranger. The person sitting to his right throws their head back with a barking laugh before lifting a tankard of ale and taking a long drink. Owen lifts his own glass ... water, taking a sip. While he may appear lighthearted and carefree, I know he's on edge. His eyes keep sliding to the table on the far side of the tavern where Silas and his guards still sit.

Silas sees us and pushes his mostly empty plate away before standing, his ever-present scowl in place. His guards follow suit, and before Valsan says anything, Silas barks, "We've wasted enough time. If you're hungry you'll have to—"

Valsan walks right past him, slipping a few coins across the bar. "Thanks, Layla."

She drops them in her pocket before sliding a small bag across to him. "You bet. Come back to see me when you have more time. We'll let loose a bit, like the old days, yeah?"

Valsan chuckles, and I wonder what Valsan really letting loose looks like. He takes the bag, meeting my eyes then nodding towards the door. As we push out of the tavern, the scents of bread and what I think are dried meats waft from the bag in Valsan's hand. Seems Layla has packed us lunch.

Our carriage is out front, Aimee sitting in the driver's seat, the reins held loosely in her hands, but her hard eyes watch Silas and his guards. The door to The Dragon's Breath opens behind us, and raucous farewells spill out into the street, following Owen as he joins us. Aimee hops down, nearly bumping shoulders with one of the Drakam guards as she makes her way to the rear of the carriage, taking her usual seat.

As Silas and his guards mount up, Miles and Halee exit the tavern, blinking against the bright sunlight. Halee rubs her eyes, and it looks like the short rest just made her more tired ... unless she and Miles chose to use their time for other things. I smile, adjusting myself as I recall how Valsan and I spent part of our short break.

With all of us mounted and ready, we pull away from The Dragon's Breath, winding our way through Rakvale. A few people stop to stare as we pass, no doubt wondering about our little procession. As we pass a little cafe with tables spilling out into the walkway for people to enjoy their lunch, a woman leans across her small table. Her hand covers her mouth but it does nothing to muffle her words as she says, "That's Captain Silas! And is that the captain of the Kapros guard? Did you hear what happened at the Games? Do you think it was Lady Kapros?"

The woman sitting across from her glances at our carriage, and when she catches me staring at her, drops her gaze, whispering back, "It *is* suspicious that she didn't attend the Games this year, isn't it?" Her eyes dart back to us, then at Silas and his guards. She picks up her plate and drink. "Let's go inside. It's too hot out here anyway." Her companion looks at us and nods, picking up her lunch, and the two women disappear inside the already-packed cafe. I roll my eyes with a shake of my head.

After a few minutes, the swaying of the carriage lulls me into a relaxed state—I'm sure the orgasm earlier also helped—despite Silas scowling at us from atop his horse. I can't help but notice he's being nicer to his mount, even occasionally dropping a hand to pat the gelding on the neck when he thinks no one is looking. I cough, bringing my hand to my mouth to hide my grin.

Within an hour, we are free of the capital, and being back out on the open road allows me to relax even more. Though, as I shift on the increasingly uncomfortable seat, I have to admit I'll be glad when our journey comes to an end. I could go an entire year without ever looking at another carriage. I sigh, brushing my hair back, letting the breeze hit my face. Staring up at the sky, I notice the fast-moving clouds. I wouldn't be surprised if we get rained on before nightfall. We have another two days of travel before we reach the Kapros border, and I doubt Silas will let us dawdle … not that Valsan would either.

After another few hours, a loud screech overhead has us all looking up. Fear shivers down my spine, and I wonder if we are indeed cursed as the prazar flies low, casting us in shadow before lifting back up into the clouds.

CHAPTER 33

NOR

HANDS CLAP from inside the carriage, and when I lean over, I see Halee poking her head out the window, her eyes on the sky. "Can we stop? Please? A friend wants to say hello."

My fear dissipates as Owen's worried voice spills out. "Friend? You sure, Halee?"

Her fingers eagerly grip the edge of the window as she nods. "Yes."

Silas ducks as a huge shadow passes overhead. The prazar screeches again, dipping back out of the clouds, its leathery wings blasting us with a gust of wind.

I grin as the Drakam guards form up, terrified eyes tracking the enormous beast, left hands raised, a few with weapons drawn, one aiming a nocked arrow at the circling prazar. Valsan claps his hands, pulling our team to a stop, and the carriage door flies open.

Silas barks with fear in his voice, "Don't stop! We need to move! Find shelter!"

I just shake my head as I climb down, thankful for the chance to stretch my legs. All the horses, including Silas' group are calm, some even dipping their heads to graze, Halee's magic keeping all the animals calm even in the presence of the great predator. Silas kicks his gelding, but the horse only cranes its neck to look at the captain with bored eyes. Miles laughs, patting Silas' horse on the rump as he follows Halee to the clearing off the side of the road. Silas yells after them, "Come back this instant! That prazar will tear us to pieces, your carriage too. We need to—"

Valsan's hand lands on Silas' horse's neck, stroking the gelding as Silas glares down at him. Valsan says, "Halee has everything in control. We met this particular prazar on our way to the Games. It's only polite to stop and say hello since she flew out to see us."

Silas and his guards remain mounted as the rest of us follow after a now jogging Halee. Dust kicks up, and I shield my eyes as the prazar flaps her vast wings, landing with surprising grace. She settles into the grass, tucking her wings to her back, bowing her head. Playful chirps trill from its sharp beak as Halee walks right up to the giant bird-like creature.

I flex my left hand, ready, just in case. Halee kneels then reaches up, and the prazar presses her beak to Halee's hand, her feathers ruffling, her long tail curling around her body. Halee slides her hand up, resting her forehead against the prazar's beak. "I'm happy to see you doing well. Your chicks are good? Healthy?"

More trilling chirps come from the giant bird as if

she's saying something. Her eyes turn up, and high in the sky, flashes of whitish-golden feathers break through the clouds. The prazar's body vibrates, and a growling purr-like sound comes from her chest. A few seconds later, two smaller prazar—these only the size of a horse—swoop low. Halee gasps, her brown eyes sparkling, her dark curls whipping in the wind as she watches the prazar chicks circle down to us. They land behind their mother, their heads cocking side to side as they chirp at Halee.

Halee turns to the mother, tears in her eyes. "They're beautiful. Thank you for trusting us."

The prazar warbles at Halee, and one of the chicks hops forward, sending vibrations through the ground. The young prazar chirps and bobs its head at Halee like it's telling her a story, and maybe it is. We all just stand and watch, close by, ready if needed, but all of us are in awe of Halee and her magic. But not just her magic, we are enraptured by her sweet nature, her kind soul.

Halee reaches back, holding out her hand, and Miles takes it, kneeling at her side as she says, "You remember Miles." The prazar dips her head with a little chirp, and the chick hops with a wild flutter of its wings, feathers still clinging to the leathery surface in its youth. Halee smiles up at Miles. "She is grateful, and the chicks say melons are their favorite."

Miles blushes, I'm sure from the love and adoration so evident in Halee's eyes. Lost in their moment, Miles traces a finger down her cheek, causing her face to tinge pink as well. His other hand slides to the ground, and vines curl up, flowers blooming. As the fruits start to grow and ripen, the young prazar hop and dance, their beaks spearing the mellons as soon as they turn bright yellow.

Halee laughs, and Miles presses a kiss to the top of her head, pulling her into his side as they watch the two chicks and their mother pick up the fat melons and crush them in their beaks. Valsan takes my hand, threading our fingers. Owen props his forearm on Aimee's shoulder, and we all just enjoy the moment.

Silas clears his throat, and I roll my eyes again as we turn to the Drakam captain. He keeps his eyes on the prazar as he says, "We need to move on if we're to make the next town on schedule. I'm expected back at my House in three days."

Owen wipes his hands on his thighs, turning towards our carriage, waving a hand over his shoulder. "Yes, yes, we all know. You're very important."

Silas sneers. "You'd know nothing of the responsibilities of being a captain of a House."

Owen shrugs, gripping the handle of the carriage door, but before he's able to say anything else snarky, Valsan cuts in. "Thank you for letting us take this small break. We appreciate your patience."

In the face of Valsan's calm gratitude, Silas remains quiet. Halee strokes the mother prazar's beak one last time, and as she stands, the chicks hop to her, one butting its head against Halee's chest. Halee laughs as she falls back, Miles catching her as she says, "I hope to see you again. Take care of yourself and your family."

The momma prazar dips her head, and as Halee and Miles rejoin us at the carriage, the enormous bird stands, shaking her body, spreading her wings, casting an intimidating shadow. The grass flutters, and the nearby trees sway as they all take flight, climbing until they catch the air currents then start to lazily circle. They follow us for a full hour as we continue south until they finally peel off heading towards the river further inland.

When we finally arrive in the next town, we find a single, slightly run-down inn. There is only one room available, so Silas and his guards opt to set up camp. Aimee settles on top of the carriage, her hands folded behind her head, her eyes on the sky. As the rest of us spill into the small room of the inn, I eye the narrow beds, my nose wrinkling at the smell of mold. Owen kicks off his boots and flops on the one near the tiny window, snores almost immediately sawing from his open mouth. Halee sighs, laying on top of the thin blanket, curling into a ball and closing her eyes. Miles takes the bed next to her, laying so he can see her. It's so packed in this room, there's hardly any space to walk between the beds as I make my way to one. Valsan gracefully lowers himself onto the one closest to the door.

When Valsan shakes me awake a few hours later, I groan, even more tired than when we arrived. I have to remind myself we have one more push, and we'll be at the Kapros border. We're all moving a bit slowly as we load up.

The carriage seat feels like it's getting stiffer and stiffer as the day goes on. We stop to rest and water the horses, and I take the chance to do a few laps around the carriage, stretching and swinging my arms. I stop next to Val, transfixed on his fingers as they move with practiced grace over one of the straps of the harness. The buckles clink softly as he cleans out some built-up dirt.

After only a few minutes, Silas saunters up to us, his horse in tow. "Break's over. Let's go."

Owen calls out from behind the carriage. "So eager to get rid of us?"

Silas' eye twitches, but other than that, he doesn't react. He swings onto his horse, and we all load up again. The rain held off yesterday, but as I look up at the sky and take in the approaching dark grey clouds, I don't think we'll be so lucky today. The wind picks up, and the trees of thickening jungle to our left sway and dance, fronds and branches crackling and swishing.

By the time the border crossing comes into view, heavy storm clouds blanket the sky. Valsan hails the border guards, while Silas approaches the Drakam guards stationed here. There is a short line waiting to cross, but as each approaches, they're turned back. Tensions on both sides seem high. Black-clad Kapros guards stand along their side of the border, wary looks darting to the green-clad Drakam guards on the other side. Left hands flex, and right hands hover over weapons.

Silas dismounts, exchanging hushed words with his guards. I don't trust that man. I don't like him, and I don't trust him.

Owen sees someone he knows—because of course he does—and steps out of the carriage with a laugh, hugging them tightly before they both erupt in animated conversation. A black-clad guard jogs over, saluting to Valsan. "Sir. We've been expecting you. Please, come right through."

Valsan drives the team into Kapros territory, leaving the still-scowling Silas and his guards behind, but then quickly pulls off to the side and stops again. He swings his broad body down to the ground and goes over to the Kapros border guards. I shift in my seat to watch as he speaks with each guard, giving them his full attention.

His life is so different from mine. He carries so much responsibility, but with seeming ease. Owen, Aimee, and Miles join him, the three catching up with their comrades.

A few of the border guards ask questions about the Games and what really happened at the Coliseum, and Owen is all too ready to tell the tale. I tune him out, but not before flashes of fire and exploding rock, screams of pain and blood, flood my mind.

Thankfully, I'm distracted from the horrific memories by the swaying of the carriage. Looking down, I see Halee's head of dark curls, her hand wrapped around the handle. I reach down and take her other hand, helping her onto the driver's seat beside me. She sighs, brushing her hair back. "It is nice up here."

"You're welcome to take a turn."

She looks around, a small smile on her face. "I'm fine inside."

I grin, holding back the urge to tease her. She looks so happy. Content. She scoots closer, and I wrap my hand around her shoulder, hugging her small body into my side. "I'm glad we did this ... together. Despite everything, I'm really glad I got the chance to really get to know you, Halee."

It might have been an odd thing to say since we both grew up on the tiny island of Oxtara, but she seems to understand because she nods. "Me too, Nor."

After nearly a full hour, Valsan and the others return to the carriage and we begin the last leg of our journey. We're still four days from the Kapros capital of Loudare, but now that we are actually in Kapros, it's beginning to feel real. I'm going to have to decide what I want to do. No. That's not right. *Valsan and I* will have to talk about what we both want and work from there. Flexing my fingers on my thigh, I glance over at Valsan, his attention on the road, the reins loose in his large hands.

He chuckles, startling me. "I can feel you thinking, Nor."

"Just working out some stuff."

"Hmmm."

My leg starts bouncing with nervous energy. "Maybe, when we stop tonight you and I can ... talk?"

His head swivels to face me, and I'm struck by his deep green eyes. A thick strand of dark hair falls over his forehead. He takes in my expression and dips his head. "Sure."

A single fat raindrop splats on my thigh. We both turn to face back forward. Another raindrop hits my cheek, but I ignore it. I have just a few hours to work through what I'm going to say to Valsan. What am I going to say? What do I want? What does *he* want? Sure, I can stay in Loudare for a time. My father has a place in the city. My crooked fingers twinge. No. I won't be darkening his door. But I have enough money to stay for ... about a month. But then what? Could I actually live in the capital? Gravity magic is fairly rare, so I'm sure I could find work. Would Valsan be able to get me a position in House Kapros? Even if he could, would I want to be *that* guy—the guy who got in because of his lover? I mean a win's a win, right?

The scattered rain picks up into a more consistent sprinkle as my mind spins. Around and around, it wonders and worries and creates far too many possible scenarios. I'm no closer to any kind of well-thought-out way to have this conversation with Val by the time we arrive in the first little town we come to.

After arranging rooms and meals for the others, Valsan grips my shoulder, pulling me to the side. "You were awfully quiet today. Did you get anywhere?"—he taps my temple—"up here?"

My lips tic up in a half smile. My mind quiets. Valsan

knows me. He sees me. He ... loves me. That, that is what I'm staying for. My smile grows. "Not until just now."

He returns my smile and takes my hand. "There's a small but really good restaurant here in this town." And with that, he leads me down a packed-dirt road, older but well-kept buildings lining the way, casting long shadows. As if Valsan planned it, the rain stops. The air is still heavy with humidity, but the breeze helps. Ahead, tables fill a small courtyard, almost all the seats taken. The wind carries the smell of fried plantain and spiced beans. Several people get up, smiles on their faces as Val and I enter. He shakes hands, greeting each person, asking after their families, and responding to their questions about what happened at the Games with polite but abbreviated answers.

We're given a table and told our meal would be on the house. Valsan tries to insist on paying, but the man laughs, hands on belly. "You leave so much as one coin I'll throttle ya." He holds out a meaty hand, and I take it, noting that he has Fire magic as he says, "Name's Elwin."

"Nor."

"Nice to meet ya, Nor. Nice to meet ya, indeed. The captain hasn't brought anyone here other than his guards. You must be someone special."

I blink at him as he drops my hand with a grin, walking off before I can respond. Looking at Valsan, he shrugs. "Well, you are."

Fuck. What was I so worried about?

Elwin proceeds to bring us a veritable feast. Every time I look down, there seems to be a new dish on the table. For almost two hours, Valsan and I eat and exchange idle conversation, each of us somehow knowing we're saving the heavy stuff for later. The courtyard slowly empties. Torches are lit, and the flickering light casts Val's face in beautiful relief. Before long, we're the only ones in the courtyard, and only a few stragglers remain inside.

A rumble of thunder shakes the ground as Elwin clears our table. He then sets down two glasses, filling them with deep red wine. Setting the bottle on the table, he pats Valsan's shoulder and walks off. Valsan picks up his glass, his large fingers gently gripping the stem as he swirls the wine. "So."

The glass is cool against my hand as I pick it up and take a swallow. I barely notice the good wine as it slides down my throat. "So."

There's a pause of silence, then we both speak at the same time, "How would you feel if—" "I'd like to ask you to—"

We smile at each other, some of the tension melting away. I take another sip of wine, this time to appreciate the cherry, oak, earth, and honey notes. I wave a hand at him. "Please, you go first."

He grins, his eyes following my glass as I bring it back to my lips. His look spreads heat across my body, and I almost don't catch his words. "I was going to ask you to move in with me."

My body goes numb, and I nearly drop my glass. I manage to set it on the table with shaking fingers. "Isn't that ... I mean are you sure? Isn't this ... too fast?"

He shrugs. "Fast. Slow. What does that matter? I know what I want." He tilts his head, the firelight dancing across his face as the torches flicker in the wind. "What were you going to say?"

A few fat raindrops splatter on the table, and one lands in my wine with a little plop. I take a deep breath and look into Valsan's eyes. "I was going to ask how you'd feel if I moved to Loudare. To be closer to you. But the fact that you just asked me to move in with you answers that."

His smile remains in place, but I see it starting to strain at the edges as one of his brows raises. "So?"

My dimple creases my cheek as I lean forward. "Yes."

"Good."

He reaches for me as I tip my lips towards his. But before our kiss connects, we both pause as a flock of birds swoop low overhead, their wings nearly brushing our heads, their squawking loud and angry. Something brushes against my ankle, and I sit back in my chair, lifting my boot just as a small army of rats scurry by. My gaze snaps up to Valsan, and I see my own worry mirrored in his eyes.

A primal roar rips through the air followed by a high-pitched scream that's abruptly cut off. We jump out of our seats just as the clouds unleash their heavy burden. Thick sheets of rain drench us in seconds, obscuring the road before us. Our boots splash through the quickly forming puddles in the dirt road. I flex my left hand, pulling on my magic, reveling in the tingling heat that spreads from my gut. I count the blocks as we sprint towards the silence that's hovering where the scream came from. It feels like it takes hours, the wind and rain pushing against us. Maybe it is. A gust of wind hits us so hard, my feet are ripped from under me, and my face slams into a puddle. I sputter and wipe my face as Valsan helps me up. We take off again, each step a battle against the storm.

I shout, "This feels like magic."

Val nods, digging his feet into the soggy ground, leaning into the wind, trying to move forward. My fingers wrap around the edge of a building to keep from being blown back, and I pull myself down the street.

I nearly face-plant again when the worst of the wind lets up, and the rain lightens. Valsan and I look at each other and take off at a sprint. We round a corner, and I skid in the mud to keep from stepping on the body on the ground.

Miles.

CHAPTER 34

KEIR

T HAEIA TUGS on my hair as I lick between her dripping folds. I tighten my grip on her thighs, wanting my imprint left on her flesh as I push her wider. Her ass flexes as she arches into my mouth, grinding into my face. I've learned she likes the abrasiveness of my short beard, so I curl my lips between my teeth and rub the bristles against her clit.

"Keir. Yes. Oh, fuck. Yes."

I smile against her writhing center as her legs shake. She keeps one hand in my hair, but the other one flies to the side, gripping the blanket, sending the tray containing our half-eaten lunch clattering to the floor. I love how uninhibited she is with me, and that I can reach that place with her as well—the place where all that matters is the person under you, over you, inside you, around you ...

Flicking her clit with the tip of my tongue, I draw a gasp from her as I then draw her sensitive bud into my

345

mouth and suck. My cock weeps at her cry of ecstasy, her release squirting all over my face, and I lick up every last drop. I'd much rather have Thaeia for lunch any day.

Her muscles relax, and she melts into the bed. I kiss my way up her body, nuzzling her breasts then nipping at her collarbone. She tilts her head back to allow me access to her neck, and I slick my tongue all the way up to her ear, biting on the lobe.

Thaeia's hands wrap around my back. Her cheek presses to mine as she whispers, "Inside me, please."

My dick pulses with the pleasure her words elicit, and I rub my length through her folds, needing that sweet friction. "You're not too sensitive?"

It's been almost five days since Valsan and Thaeia's friends left, and she has filled the void of missing them by reading, training, and fucking—and I'm all too willing to help her cope in any way she needs.

In answer to my question, she rolls her hips, pressing her pelvis into my cock, and I groan, "Fuck, Fox Slayer." Reaching between us, I grip my length, all too eager to slide into her heat, but when I press my head to her entrance, she grabs my wrist.

Bending her knees up towards her shoulders, she shakes her head, biting her lip before saying, "My ass, lordling."

It's like a current of lighting shoots through my body at her words. I swallow, blinking down at her. "Have you ever?"

"No, but ... I'm curious. I'd like to try. If you want t—"

"Yes."

She smiles, licking her lips, and my heart literally skips a beat. It's hard to catch my breath. Leaning over, my chest hair tickles her nipples, and a little squeak of surprised pleasure comes from her. Her legs fall to the side as I press my weight into her, kissing her lips, licking my way into her mouth. She tastes like the garlic spread and flatbread we had for lunch, as well as the cool, iced mint tea.

Propping myself on my forearms, framing her face, I stare into her golden eyes, seeing my bright blue ones reflected back at me. "I will take your tight ass, Fox Slayer, and my fingers will spear your eager pussy. You will be so full." My cock leaks precum onto her stomach, and I grind against her, rubbing it in. "See what the thought of stuffing my cock into your ass does to me?"

Her head presses into the mattress with a moan, her eyes rolling back, but I place my hands on either side of her head, holding her gaze to mine. "But not today." She blinks at me, her mouth falling open. I've never denied her, and I see the slow pull of disbelief creep across her face, and then it starts to morph into the pain of being rejected.

I kiss her nose before leaning over, stretching across the bed to reach into the drawer of the bedside table. She eyes the little bottle in my hand as I sit back on my heels, her legs relaxed on either side of my thighs. Thaeia's mouth falls open as a quiet pop resounds through the quaint library bedroom. I toss the cork aside and drizzle a little oil onto two of my fingers. Rubbing them together, I set the bottle aside and trace my slick finger from her clit all the way to her back hole. The oil glistens as I circle her ass, and she clenches beautifully. "We have to prepare you, Fox Slayer." I press one finger against her entrance, slowly pushing to the first knuckle. "We have to stretch you."

My dick is painfully hard, curved against my stomach,

aching to be inside her, so I stroke myself as I move my finger with tiny little thrusts, working my way deeper inside her ass. I'm almost to the second knuckle, and I groan. "So tight. You're doing so well, Fox Slayer."

Her stomach flexes, and her hands cup her breasts, pinching her nipples. "More, Keir."

I love the playful way she calls me lordling, but when she says my name, breathy and laced with desire … it's enough to make me come. I press my thumb under the head of my cock, denying myself the orgasm that's screaming for release.

"Play with your clit." Her hand dives for her nub, rubbing and circling. My second knuckle slips past her rim, and we both gasp. I curl my finger, teasing her as I continue to stroke myself. Her thighs squeeze my hips, and she pulls herself down on my finger until I bottom out. Her eyes go wide. "Oh!"

I release my dick to stroke down her leg to her hip and back to her knee. "You okay?"

She nods. "It's different. Even just your finger feels … full."

"Painful?"

Her hair fans across the blanket as she shakes her head, so I slowly draw my finger back, gripping my dick again. Her pussy clenches, and her ass tightens. Watching my finger slide in and out of her, I release my cock, slipping my thumb into her cunt. With fingers in both of her holes, I pump them, curling and twisting until she's panting, her little cries of pleasure teaching me what she likes.

I watch her face as a flush colors her cheeks. Her legs tense, and her mouth hangs open in a little 'O', and I know she's close.

"Give it to me, Fox Slayer. Give me another orgasm."

With the next thrust of my fingers, I curl them against the spot I've learned she loves. Her back arches as her entire body goes rigid. No sound comes from her open lips, and I stare at the place where my fingers are buried in her body as her walls flutter, gripping me. When I feel her start to come down, I slide out of her. Holding up my hands, I lick the thumb that was in her pussy. "So good, Thaeia."

She bites her lip, her eyes falling to my aching erection. A slow smile spreads across her face. Keeping her eyes on my cock, she says, "Well, since my ass is in training, why don't you use my mouth?"

I pause mid-lick, then my own smile lifts my cheeks. "My Fox Slayer is feeling naughty today."

Her tongue flicks over her lips. "I want you to use me, Keir. Fuck my mouth. Make me think of nothing else other than your dick sliding down my throat. Drown out the rest of the world, Keir."

My smile falls. We should probably talk about this. Thaeia is not coping well with everything that's happened to her, as well as the uncertainty of her future, the questions of her past, her Void ... And I tell myself we'll talk. Soon. But my cock is in charge right now.

I crawl up her body, her breasts pressing against my balls as I straddle her chest. Lifting to kneeling, I bend over, capturing her wrists in one hand, pinning them to the bed over her head.

"Since you won't be able to talk, you will pinch my finger if you want to stop." I shift my hand so I'm still holding her wrists, but my pointer finger rests in her palm, easy enough for her to curl her fingers around. "Show me." She does, giving my finger a tight pinch. I nod. "Good. Now. Open." Her mouth falls open, and I use my free hand to rub the tip of my dick over her lips. "Good girl." My praise has her eyes going soft, and she licks my cock.

That's all it takes. With a violent thrust of my hips, I shove into her mouth until I hit the back of her throat. She gags, and I pull back halfway, waiting for the pinch, but her hands are flexed wide open, and she squirms, pressing her thighs together. I thrust again, and she sucks.

"Fuck, yes, Thaeia."

Her nostrils flare as she tries to breathe around my cock, the wet slurping sounds getting louder as I slam farther down her throat. It feels so good. Spit leaks from the corners of her mouth, dripping down her chin, and I push harder, faster. I'm lost to the sensation of her wet mouth sucking and slurping and pulling at my cock. My hips pump, over and over, pressing my lower stomach against her nose, and I force myself to lift slightly so I don't suffocate her.

She writhes under me, her feet kicking against the blankets. The pulsing in my cock intensifies, and my balls draw up tight. I'm right there. Right on the edge. Liquid bliss starts to spread through my body as if euphoria has replaced my blood.

Thaeia's red, swollen lips close tight around my length, and her eyes meet mine. I'm lost in her golden depths as I slam harder against her mouth, causing her to gag again. Her eyes go wide. "That's right, Fox Slayer. Eyes on me. Watch me come in your mouth. Watch what you do to me. Watch me unravel." My hand grips her wrists even tighter as I thrust again and again. "Mine. Mine. Mine. And I'm yours, Thaeia. My Fox Slayer."

Her gold eyes sparkle, her breath wheezing from her nose as spit slicks down her chin. I come apart. That liquid bliss in my veins sparks and catches fire, and pleasure pulses through me in violent waves. My orgasm intensifies as Thaeia tries to swallow my cum, her throat constricting around my cock. I continue to shudder and spurt into her mouth until my cum starts to leak from the corners of her lips.

She's a beautiful mess. Mine.

Pulling back, I slide from her, and she stretches her mouth open before licking my cum from her lips. I loosen my grip on her wrists, massaging them as I bring her arms to rest at her sides. I'm still straddling her chest as I run a finger down her cheek, over her puffy lips, and down her neck.

"So beautiful." Even after what we just did, my words bring a flush to her face.

After we clean up and get dressed, I take her hand, threading our fingers. "Would you like to eat in our family dining hall?"

She blinks at me, then a slow smile lights her face. "Yes, please."

"If I can find my father, I'll convince him to join us, if that's okay with you."

She bites her lip, but nods. My free hand tucks her wild hair behind her ear, then I tug her towards the door. I feel her looking down the long carpeted hall, up at the ornately carved ceiling, and out the tall windows as we make our way through the family wing of the estate. A pair of doors stand open before us, and I lead her through. The room is empty except for one person. My grandmother sits alone at a table by the window, her cloudy eyes fixed on some distant place only she can see. But when she hears us enter, she turns, and a smile deepens her wrinkled face. "Ah, Keir, my favorite grandson. Who have you brought with you?"

Thaeia tries to pull from my grip, but I hold fast. Leaning down to kiss my grandmother on the cheek, I smell peppermint and clove. "This is Thaeia, Grandmother."

Her milky eyes travel down Thaeia's body and back up again. A grey brow rises as she waves a hand at the empty chairs. "I'm always alone in this dining hall, the family preferring to eat in the main hall. Too noisy for me. What's wrong with wanting a little peace and quiet with a meal?"

I smile. "Nothing, Grandmother.'"

As I pull out a chair for Thaeia then join her at the table, my grandmother huffs. "That's right, nothing. We are family. We should make the time to at least eat together. Keir, where's that son of mine?"

My smile grows to a grin. "I'm not sure, Grandmother. I was hoping you knew. I ... well, *we* need to speak with him."

She tsks as staff members push through a swinging door with trays of food and drink as if they were waiting for us—though I suspect it was Grandmother's doing. I glance at her thin wrist, her dark tattoo standing in stark relief against her pale skin spelling out the word for Insight. I smile as memories cascade through my mind of when I was a little boy. I couldn't even think of starting up any mischief before I was quickly shut down. My grandmother always knew when I was up to no good. And I'm pretty sure she knew, or at least suspected Thaeia and I were coming here today.

She waves her hand again, snapping me from my

thoughts. "It's just as well. I suspect he'll be along soon enough."

I just nod, trusting my grandmother's power, but Thaeia frowns as a plate of food is set before her. She darts a quick look at the staff, and when they quietly leave the room, Thaeia looks at my grandmother, staring at her wrist. "Your magic?"

She smiles, picking up her fork and spearing a roasted carrot. "No, my dear. It's oddly ... silent right now. But earlier ... I got a sense of what's coming." Thaeia shifts, as my grandmother looks to me. "It's nice to see you without those bright flames distracting from your handsome face. You have such pretty eyes, Keir." She turns to Thaeia. "Don't you think so?"

I feel my cheeks heating as Thaeia grins at me. "Yes, Keir's eyes are quite stunning, Lady Alopson."

My grandmother tsks again. "Now, none of that. My name is Fernola, but you just call me Fera."

Thaeia dips her head. "Fera, then. You, um, you don't seem surprised by, well ..."

"My magic being temporarily dormant?" My fork pauses halfway to my mouth, the seared duck dripping juices onto the table. My grandmother chuckles, "Close your mouth, Keir. You were taught better manners than that."

I set my fork down, and Thaeia drops her hands into her lap, the fingers of her left hand curling into her fist in the phantom motion of wanting to pull her sleeve over her naked wrist. I reach over, taking her hand, rubbing my thumb over her skin. Her hand trembles slightly, and she looks back at my grandmother who sighs, pushing her barely touched plate away. "I don't know what my son is going to reveal"—she rubs absently over her tattoo—"but

I sensed that long-lost pieces to an important puzzle are about to be found."

She smiles, her blue eyes faded with age turning towards the door. "Ah, here he is. Always so busy. Too busy for his own mother. How long has it been since my son kissed my cheek?"

My father crosses the room, a plate of steaming food in his hand, his presence imposing as always. Thaeia stiffens, pulling her hand from mine as my father leans over to press a kiss to his mother's cheek. "Three days, mother. Don't be so dramatic."

She winks at Thaeia. "But it makes my boring days so much brighter."

My father pulls out a chair, sits, but ignores his food. "I'm glad you've decided to venture out of the library. While it holds many wonders, House Alopson should be enjoyed in its entirety." Thaeia attempts to smile, but it doesn't quite work. My father notices. "But considering the circumstances, I understand your desire to ... play it safe."

A thread of anger pushes at my throat. "Father—"

He holds up a hand, jerking his head at the staff door then the main door in silent command. My chair scrapes loudly against the floor as I push back from the table and cross the room, locking both doors before returning.

My grandmother huffs a laugh. "Now who's being dramatic?"

My father drops his voice. "Mother."

She waves her hand, pulling her plate back towards her, poking her fork at the fragrant pile of rice. "Fine, fine. The old lady will just sit here and listen."

My father rolls his eyes. "Mother, that's not—"

"No, no. You have something of some seriousness to

discuss with my grandson and his ... lady friend. Go on, then."

Clearing his throat, my father faces me, then meets Thaeia's eyes. I have the sudden urge to pull her into my arms and hide her back away in the library as he says, "I owe you an apology, Thaeia. I've been avoiding you, hiding from you, from my past. I—"

A knock makes us all jump, all except my grandmother who keeps scraping her fork through her rice. I shake my head. "No. No more distractions. Finish what you were saying."

My father nods, but before he's able to say more, Daria's voice cuts through the room from the other side of the door. "Lord Alopson, I'm sorry to disturb you. It's an emergency."

Curling my hand into a fist, I shake my head again. "There's always an emergency." But my father gets up, crossing the room, and I say to his back, "Grandmother was right. Too busy for family."

Thaeia leans towards me, her hand resting on my arm. "Keir, it's okay, really."

My father pauses with his hand on the knob, turning back to face us, saying, "No, Thaeia, it's not. I've been delaying this for too long. Years." My brows scrunch. Years? "Let me just find out what Daria needs and send her away. I'll deal with whatever this is after we've talked."

We sit in silence as my father unlocks and opens the door, poking his head out. Whispered words pass between them, then my father's back goes rigid. His knuckles turn white where he still grips the doorknob. When he shifts, it makes room for me to see Daria. I push my chair back again. Whatever she just told my father, it's not good.

CHAPTER 35

NOR

THE HEALER PLACES his hands on Miles' ankle. Miles grimaces, slowly regaining consciousness as his foot realigns with an audible pop. I wiggle my foot in sympathy.

When we carried Miles back to the inn, he was unresponsive, hanging limp. Blood dripped from the back of his head, his right leg was bent at an odd angle, the fingers of his left hand were broken, some of the bones sticking out. His shallow breaths wheezed, and I suspected at least one of his lungs was punctured. We'd stumbled into the inn, Valsan barking orders for someone to fetch a Healer. Without breaking stride, he carried Miles to his room, laying him down. I helped Val strip Miles down, involuntary hisses leaving my lips at every newly discovered cut and bruise.

I shake myself out of the memory as I look out the window. The Healer has been working on Miles for almost an hour, taking care of the swelling in his brain and several places where he was bleeding internally. He didn't even think Miles would live. The Healer sits back, wiping his brow with shaking hands. Miles blinks, slowly sitting up, breathing through his pain. He's pale, and a few bruises still mark his face, but he's alive.

The Healer runs his hands over the remaining bruises on Miles' face. Owen passes Miles a glass of water, and he gulps it down then passes it back. He plants his hands on the bed, and tries to stand, but the Healer holds him down simply by pressing lightly against his chest, saying in a tired tone, "Don't move too much yet. There's still serious damage I need to Heal."

Miles grips the edge of the bed, violent eyes finding Valsan. "Halee."

I growl, "She's not in her room?"

Before Miles can answer, Aimee comes into the room. The dark hair on top of her head is windblown, and raindrops cling to the shaved sides. Her russet eyes hold barely contained rage as she says, "No sign of them."

I whip my head around. "Who?"

Miles says, "We have to go after them!"

The Healer struggles to keep Miles seated, and Valsan steps in, grabbing Miles' shoulder. "You're no good to anyone in this condition. Let the Healer work and tell us what happened."

Miles grinds his teeth, then says, "Gre—" Coughs fold him over, and he grabs his ribs. The Healer reaches for his waist, working to put Miles back together one piece at a time. "Grey-cloaks." Miles shakes his head, swinging his legs over the edge of the blood-stained bed.

"I didn't see them coming. Not in time. There were so many."

My nails dig into my palms. Does whoever is pulling the strings have an endless supply of pawns to wrap in cloaks and send after us? Fuck!

Tears well in Miles' eyes, and he drops his head, arms resting on his thighs. His voice goes distant, and I know he's reliving the horror of the attack. "Halee was hungry." My heart squeezes. "She was content to grab something downstairs here at the inn, but there's a place just a few blocks from here that I wanted to take her. I ... I shouldn't have ... I ... I'm sorry, captain, Nor."

I swallow around the warring fear and anger dueling it out in my chest, planting my feet to keep from storming outside to hunt for Halee. "Was she hurt?"

The Healer presses his hand against the two grotesquely bent fingers on Miles' left hand as Miles shakes his head. "Not badly at least. Not that I saw. She fought back. Dogs, cats, birds, mice, even a horse came running to defend her. It was mayhem. She was b-beautiful." His voice cracks, and he wipes at his downturned face.

Owen scowls from where he stands propped against the wall, arms crossed. "Did no one step in to help?"

Again, Miles shakes his head. "It happened so fast. There was a lot of magic flying around." The Healer releases Miles' hand, his fingers once more aligned, the bruising gone. Miles regrips the edge of the bed, the blanket bunching in his newly healed hand. "They knocked Halee out, and the animals scattered. I ... I think I blacked out for a bit. I remember clouds, then a face leaning over me. It was blurry. I think they had to repeat themselves a few times before I heard them."

Valsan places a hand on the Healer's shoulder. "Is there more?"

The Healer shakes his head. "All done, but there was a lot of damage. I'd recommend rest." His eyes sweep the room. "But I suspect that's an idle request."

Valsan smiles, but it's tight. "Thank you." Reaching into his pocket, Valsan pulls out some folded bills, counting out a few before handing them to the Healer—more money than I've ever spent on any one thing in my entire life. I never really thought about what a good Healer makes. Back home, we paid our Mender with food, or goods, or services.

"Easy, Miles." Owen reaches over to steady Miles who sways on his feet, pulling a fresh shirt over his head. He yanks on a pair of pants, and Aimee opens the door the Healer had closed behind him when he left. Miles stuffs one foot in a boot, and hops into the hall while putting on the other.

We all pour out of the room, following a jogging Miles down the stairs. Valsan grips his arm just as he pushes out into the rain. Miles tilts his head up at the skies, but Valsan pulls him away from the door of the inn and into the shadows of the overhang. We all huddle around like rats in an alley. The rain isn't cold, but my skin pebbles all the same.

Valsan leans down, getting in Miles' face, forcing him to look at him. "Miles, the person you saw leaning over you ... What did they say?"

Miles' dark blue eyes sparkle with the same rage that presses against my skin from the inside, begging to be let out. "That as long as Thaeia does as she's told, Halee will be fine."

I shift my weight to the balls of my feet. "So, what now?"

Miles pulls out of Valsan's grip, stepping into the center of the road, water splashing around his ankles. He looks up again, turning a slow circle, murmuring, "Come on, beautiful. You can do it. Wake up. Just long enough. You can do it. Tell me where you are."

Realization hits me, and I slosh through the puddles to stand at his side. Rain pelts my face as I look to the sky. *Come on, Halee.*

There's movement in my peripheral, but I ignore whatever it is, keeping my eyes on the sky. I blink the rain away, squinting, willing a sign to appear.

"There!" Miles points.

A dark shape breaks from the clouds, swooping low, water trailing off its leathery wings like ribbons. The prazar opens its beak and lets out a deep sound closer to a roar than anything a bird would make. She either lives fairly close, or stuck around. Either way, the giant prazar is here, she's agitated, and she's headed north.

Valsan's voice draws our attention. "I paid the innkeeper to send a bird to House Kapros to let Lady Kapros know we have been delayed ... that one of our own was attacked and taken." *One of his own.* Even through the fear and anger swirling in my blood, my heart warms. Aimee comes around the building, horses trailing behind her by their leads. Valsan takes one, tossing the reins to Miles. "Let's go."

The horse closest to Valsan shakes his head, spraying water everywhere. I want to ask where Aimee got the three new horses, but there's no time. Miles and Aimee swing onto their horses, and before I've even taken the reins that Valsan holds out to me, they are already galloping down the road. Owen gives chase as Valsan leans in. "You ride?"

I raise a brow with a little smirk, and he shakes his head. Pulling myself into the saddle, I gather the reins. "It's been a few years, but I'll manage."

He nods, gripping a handful of mane and swings onto his horse. He's galloping down the road before he even puts his feet in the stirrups. *Why is that so hot?*

It takes me a few seconds to find my seat, but the fear of losing Halee's trail clenches my thighs, and I lean over my horse's neck. Its mane whips my face, adding to the stinging pelts of the rain. The prazar shakes her head, her feathers flaring down her neck. We all slow as she slows then glides in a wide circle. We're in an open patch of field, a slight rise before us, the small town behind us, the jungle to our right. Normally, the chitter of insects, the scratch of palm fronds, and the rustle of animals would fill the air, but rain is the only sound pounding against my ears.

The prazar makes another circle before shaking her head again. She drifts down, angling east and into the forest.

Owen asks, "Do we follow?"

Miles is breathing hard, his hand tight on the reins. He shakes his head, then bows, closing his eyes. "I think the prazar lost the connection. Halee either passed back out, or they ..."

Owen's horse dances to the side, tossing its head, obviously not too happy to be out here in the downpour. "Maybe she'll come to again." He looks up and around. "Maybe if we just wait a—"

"I think I've got her."

We all look at Miles. His head's still bowed, his shoulders trembling slightly. When he looks at us, he nods. "The trees, the grass, the roots ... a large group of horses is moving north."

He can do that? How far is his reach?

Miles starts to slide to the right, but he catches himself. He's pushing too hard. He could pass out at any moment. He says, "They're moving fast. My magic is stretched thin ... I ... can't." He kicks his horse, and we all take off again.

My magic presses at my gut to the point I might be sick. I swallow it down. These grey-cloaks, whoever they are, followed us all the way from the desert. The next one I see will be crushed under the weight of my magic. There will be nothing left. Glancing at our group, a cruel smile lifts my mood. I suspect I'll be competing with Miles' Plant magic, Aimee's Petrification magic, Owen's Ice magic, and Valsan's Confusion magic. We all want a piece.

Miles pulls slightly ahead, his body hunched over the neck of his horse. Hooves pound into the wet ground. Thunder rumbles. Valsan's voice barks over the noise of the storm. "You still have them?"

Miles looks over his shoulder, shaking his head, frustration burning in his eyes. "They went beyond my reach. I'm trying. They're just too far away, but we're still going in the direction I last felt them."

Valsan barks, "Keep going. Keep trying. When we reach them, fan out." I appreciate his calm confidence, because my thoughts are pure chaos right now. "Miles, you focus on getting Halee away from the grey-cloaks. Owen, freeze anyone that tries to run. Aimee, defense. I'll Confuse them enough to immobilize them. Nor, protect the group."

I nod, though it's unnecessary. Valsan speaks as if he

expects his commands to be obeyed without question. And I will do as I'm told. I'll wrap each of us up in a Gravity shield so tight, nothing will get through.

But I swear to all the gods, if Halee is hurt ... or ... none of the grey-cloaks will escape me.

CHAPTER 36

THAEIA

I DON'T HEAR HALF of what Daria says. In fact, all I hear are the words, 'Halee was taken ... Severn has her ... Demanding I come ... Five days ...'

The clatter of my chair toppling over and hitting the floor sounds behind me as I race from the room. The door bangs open, and as I sprint down the hall, Keir and his father both shout, "Thaeia!"

I don't slow. My heartbeat is loud in my ears, drumming over and over, *Halee, Halee, Halee, Halee ... not Halee.* My vision blurs, and I blink. I hadn't realized I was crying, the mix of sheer terror and rage burning me from the inside. Dashing away the tears, I burst from the first door I find that leads outside. A red-clad guard gasps, stepping back as I sprint past. She flexes her left hand, then her head snaps up with shock, eyes tracking me. I don't care. Let her follow. Let her try to stop me.

My boots skid on the sandy path as I take a corner too fast. I windmill my arms, but keep going. There! The stables. Slowing just slightly so I don't startle the horses, I jog through the wide-open doors. A horse pokes its head over its stall door, nose reaching for me. Any other time, I'd stroke the velvet muzzle, but right now, I need …

A young girl with thick blond hair and warm brown eyes leans out a doorway about halfway down the stable. Upon seeing me, she steps out, a smile on her face. "Hi. I'm Arabell. Can I help you?"

I nod, curling my fingers into my palm, pulling on imaginary sleeves. "I need a horse. For an undetermined amount of time. I'll pay. I don't have much, but a friend of mine is in trouble and I really need—"

"Okay."

I blink at her, my fingers stilling in my palm. "Okay?"

She nods with a pretty smile. "You're Thaeia, right?" I just keep blinking at her like an idiot, but she turns, walking down the long aisle. Arabell lifts her left arm, waving her hand at me over her shoulder. "No magic. Easy guess. Lord Keir trusts you. You need a horse. You get a horse." My breath comes out shaky, and I look back. Keir. I just ran out. I should— "What level rider would you say you are?"

I turn back to face her just as she grabs a bridle off a hook. "Um, not quite beginner, but …"

She nods, passing two more stalls before she stops and unlatches one. I make my way towards her, my boots snapping sharply on the clean cobbled floor. Arabell comes out with a large bay gelding. "This is Sampson. He's gentle, responsive, but don't let that fool you. He's a fast one. He'll take good care of you."

She clips him to a hook, expertly and quickly saddling

him. I run a hand down his neck. "Hi, Sampson. Sorry to pull you away from your friends. I really need help."

He bobs his head as if he understands me, and it almost brings a smile to my face, but the pit of worry sits too heavy in my gut.

Arabell says, "Hop on up. I'll adjust the stirrups as needed."

She has a good eye, because once I've pulled myself onto Sampson's back, no adjustments are necessary. Taking the lead, she walks us out of the stables. She unclicks, but before I can nudge Sampson forward, Arabell holds up a hand. "Hold on." She jogs back into the stables, and I shift in the saddle, anxious to be on my way. To get to Halee. Arabell comes back out with a large bag. She passes it to me, and I nearly drop it, surprised at the weight. "Tie it down to the back of your saddle, there." She points at some long straps with buckles, and I twist to secure the bag as she says, "There's a blanket and some food I had left over. Nothing fancy, but will allow you to eat on the road." She gives Sampson a little pat on his rump. "Now this guy will push himself for you, but you make sure to let him rest. You'll need the rest too. Take care of him ... and yourself. Bring this guy back."

I nod on another shuddered breath. "Thank you, Arabell. I'll take good care of him. I promise."

Stepping back, she nods before striding back into the stables. I press my heels to Sampson's sides, and he moves into a relatively smooth trot—as smooth as a trot can be. Alopson guards watch as I move through the estate grounds, but none move to stop me. From the corner of my eye, I catch the ruby-red flames of one of Keir's Spirits, but I trot from sight quickly. As I pass through the main gates, another Spirit appears just beyond my Void. They make eye contact with me before puffing out. Keir is keeping tabs on me, but why didn't he follow me? I thought for sure ...

I shake my head, frustrated that I'm forced to keep our pace slow for now through the streets of the city. Keir has many responsibilities. He can't just up and run off with me, no matter how much I want him here.

That slimy Severn Drakam. And I'm sure his captain, Silas, is involved as well. Godsdamn it! My hands tighten on the reins, the leather creaking as I follow the road south. I turn to avoid taking a road leading west, but I'm forced to pull back on the reins, slowing Sampson to a walk. People fill the sidewalks, dipping in and out of stores and businesses. A line of carriages moves slowly in front of me, and a line just as congested comes up the other side of the road moving in the opposite direction.

Sampson snorts, feeling my frustration. I force my hands to relax, and settle into the saddle. It takes nearly half an hour to clear the city of Farcrest, but as soon as we hit open country, I move Sampson into a slow canter. I take a few minutes to learn his gait, his mannerisms, then I urge him to go a little faster. A little faster. Before long, we're moving at a near gallop. I know he won't be able to sustain this pace for long, but I need to move. I need to close the gap between Halee and myself.

Her name is like a chant my heart beats out. Is she okay? Was she hurt? Were any of my other friends hurt? I should have taken a moment to ask Daria for more information. Too late now.

I glance down, the wind blowing my hair back, the steady thrum of Sampson's hooves driving us south. My throwing knives sit in my thigh sheath, ready. The dagger

I swiped off that grey-cloak in the tent is strapped to my ankle.

As the greenery of the oasis falls behind me, and the arid landscape stretches before us, I slow Sampson to an easy canter. I can't keep from thinking about Halee ... sweet Halee, scared, alone ... I'll do whatever it takes. Whatever Severn wants I'll give him as long as he lets Halee go. And if he has hurt her, if she is ... I can only imagine the look on my face right now as I picture driving my dagger into Severn Drakam's neck. I can practically feel his hot blood dripping over my hand.

Sweat darkens Sampson's hide, so I slow him to a walk. If I recall the maps correctly, I should come to a small town in a few hours. I flex my left hand, turning my wrist, my lack of tattoo blatantly staring up at me. What does Lord Drakam want with me?

A strange mix of dread and excitement shivers down my spine. Whatever it is, I have a feeling he knows ... something about me, about my past, about my Void. He must, right? But all that is secondary. Halee comes first.

My eyes focus on the open road. *I'm coming, Halee.*

CHAPTER 37

NOR

WE'RE STILL MOVING NORTH. Miles hasn't been able to pick up the trail of the grey-cloaks, and Halee hasn't sent any obvious signs for us to follow. Miles slips his feet from his stirrups, stretching and flexing them with a wince. That must be where his magic sits. His face is clammy and paler than usual. When he lifts a hand to wipe his forehead, his fingers shake. I'd tell him to take a rest before he passes out, but I know he won't listen. I wouldn't.

I sit taller, twisting slightly one way then the other, trying to undo the knot in my stomach. I've never used my magic in this way. It's exhausting. My Gravity power spreads out as far as I can reach, a few miles by my guess, mostly to the north since that's the direction we lost them. I feel the push and resistance of trees, of the breeze, of birds passing through my magic—searching for a larger disturbance, a group, the group that has Halee. Nothing yet. Nothing for hours. My stomach cramps, and I almost double over, my vision darkening for a second before I'm able to breathe through the pain and sit up. I won't give up.

Owen presses a hand to his lower back. I hear the crack from here as he stretches. One-handed, he rubs his lower spine as he says, "I'm not even sure I'm doing this right." I shiver as my horse plods through a cloud of his misty ice vapor, the crystals clinging to my lashes for a second before melting. "I'm trying to search through the water vapor in the air, feeling for disturbances, but ..." He sighs, bringing his hand from his back to his head, running his fingers through his hair.

I try to speak, but I'm more drained than I thought, and my voice croaks. Coughing, I clear my throat and try again. "I'm trying the same. I've been able to keep track of Valsan and Aimee since they left, but nothing else that would suggest a large group."

Owen's smile is tired as he nods at me. Miles doesn't respond at all, just keeps his gaze ahead, sweat dripping down his temples. The three of us keep moving, keep searching, keep trying.

Valsan and Aimee moved ahead over an hour ago to scout, to see if they could pick up a visual trail of the greycloaks. I know Val is fine ... he's more than capable, but I'm unable to help myself. I decrease just a bit of the Gravity around where I feel Valsan several miles ahead. The physical space around him changes, and I can practically see his shape in my mind's eye. I picture him responding in one of two ways: that sexy half-smile of his lighting his eyes as he feels lighter, a little weightless; or he's frowning, shaking his head, wishing he could scold me for using my magic on him when I should be searching for Halee.

That thought steals the momentary lightness from my heart, and I refocus. I push my magic farther—reaching, searching, hoping. I'm so focused, I don't notice Miles start to slide to the left until it's too late. His horse stops and sidesteps as Miles thuds to the ground. I pull back on the reins and jump down at the same time as Owen. We rush to an unmoving Miles, turning him over. His eyes are closed and shadowed. His hair clings to his sweaty face as shallow breaths pant from his cracked lips. Owen rushes back to his horse, returning with some water. Holding it to Miles' lips, Owen tips a little bit of liquid down his throat. Miles swallows, but a second later, he starts shaking.

Quickly shifting, I position myself so his head rests on my thighs, and I hold him steady. I've only seen this happen once. It wasn't pretty. I jerk my head at Miles' legs. "Owen hold him. His body is shutting down. Too much magic."

Just as Owen presses his hands to Miles' thighs, Miles arches off the ground, his body shaking violently. We both hold him tighter as Owen shouts, "What do we do?"

I shake my head. We're in the middle of nowhere. No Healers or Menders to help. "He's gotta ride it out."

Miles' shaking becomes even more violent, so I squeeze his head between my thighs so I can use my hands to hold his arms down. His hands flex so hard into the ground, I hear a bone snap. Owen winces. "How do we stop this?"

I don't answer, because I don't know.

My own muscles begin to tire as Owen and I struggle to keep Miles from hurting himself too badly. It seems to go on forever, but eventually, his body goes lax. Owen and

I sit back, noticing the red marks on Miles' body where we restrained him.

Owen runs a hand through his hair. "Should we call them back?"

Before Valsan and Aimee left to scout, we set up a system for me to let them know we need them to return—two long squeezes of my Gravity magic around Valsan, like a long-distance hug. I look at Miles, at his pale skin. He's still clammy, but now there are bright red spots on his cheeks. Magic fever. He might be out for hours, or even days. "I think we should."

My knees ache, so I sit back, stretching my legs to either side of Miles' body, bracing my hands on the ground behind me. Feeling Valsan, caressing his shape with my magic, I increase the Gravity around him, holding it for a three count, release, and do it again. I do one last sweep, pushing even farther, hoping ... *Halee, come on. Where are you?*

Nothing.

Letting go of my power, my arms nearly buckle as sheer exhaustion slams into me. I blink. And blink again. Everything seems to be moving very slowly. Bringing my hand to my leg, I pinch my thigh, trying to keep myself awake, but I feel my head drooping.

Pain erupts across my face in time with a loud slap. I rub my cheek as Owen shakes out his hand. "Okay, now me."

I can't help but smile as I rear back. The crack resounds, startling a few birds from the nearby trees.

"Damn, man." Owen rubs at his face, my handprint red and clear against his brown skin.

We sit and wait, checking on Miles every so often until my horse nickers. An answering whinny turns our attention north as Valsan and Aimee approach at a slow canter. Both leap from their horses before they're even fully stopped. Aimee kneels at Miles' side, checking his pulse, drawing back his lids to check his pupils. Valsan drops to a knee next to me, his hand coming to my back. His strength and warmth seep into me, and I want nothing more than to curl up in his arms.

Valsan says, "Magic exhaustion?"

Owen and I nod, and Owen frowns. "It was pretty bad. Had a seizure."

At that, Aimee grabs Miles' chin, prying his mouth open, checking his tongue.

Valsan's fingers flex against my back. "You two okay?"

Aimee looks between us, a ghost of a smile teasing her lips. "Why do you both have palm prints on your faces?"

Owen chuckles tiredly. "Keeping each other conscious. But yes, captain, we're okay."

Valsan nods. "We'll rest. Here's as good as any. As soon as Miles wakes, we'll continue."

My gaze falls to Miles. The shadows under his eyes seem deeper. He wouldn't want to be wasting time like this, but we can't go on. Not like this.

I'm stretched out enough to tap Owen's knee with my boot. "We'll give him an hour, no more. If Miles doesn't wake before that, Ice him."

I feel Aimee's stare, but I keep my eyes on Owen. He sighs, glancing north before nodding. "Yeah, okay."

Hopefully, Miles will wake on his own, but if not, Owen's Ice should shock him awake.

Valsan grabs the water sitting on the ground next to Owen, holding it out to him. "Drink."

Owen takes it, and the water sloshes inside the container from his trembling. Seems Owen was close to his limit as well. He takes a few sips, then holds it out to me. I take it with both hands, not sure if the water will even stay down. I swallow a tiny bit, and my stomach revolts. Wrapping a hand around my middle, I hunch over, willing the pain to pass. Once it does, I sit up slightly, and Valsan takes the water, capping it and setting it aside.

The hour passes unbelievably quickly. It seems like I blinked once, and time was up. Miles hasn't stirred. Feeling a little stronger after the rest, I get to my knees, waving a hand at Miles. "Owen."

Owen's eyes find Valsan, who nods. Owen places his left hand on Miles' chest. Ice crystals form and spread down his fingers, blooming across Miles' shirt. Owen presses down, and crackling Ice punches into Miles. His body jerks, his eyes flying open, his mouth opening on a gasp. I'm in position to grab him as he bolts up, clutching his chest with a shout, "Halee!"

Owen dislodges his hand, crystals snapping and melting as he pulls away. My hand on Miles' shoulder keeps him seated as he tries to stand. I say, "Take it slow."

He shrugs me off, getting to his feet, his left hand flexing, and I know he's already sending his magic back out, searching as he asks, "How long?"

Aimee answers, "An hour."

Miles' left hand clenches, the veins standing out. He throws his head back with a cry, "Damn it!"

His scream echoes then falls silent. A heartbeat later, a high bark draws our attention. A wrasse trots from the trees, his skeletal body staying low to the ground, his long fluffy tail swaying behind him. His fangs extend past his lower jaw, his eyes on us. We all slowly stand, not turning our backs on the venomous fox-like creature. One careful step at a time, we back up. It's only when I reach my horse that I realize none of the horses are panicking. Usually they'd be ready to bolt with a wrasse so close. Watching the creature, I hold my breath, praying as it stalks towards us, its head low, but its ears perked. It barks again, and I can't help but jump at the sound. Where there's one wrasse, there's usually more. And if they wanted, they could attack and easily immobilize us with even a scrape of fangs on skin. Then we'd be dinner.

My gut clenches as I raise my left hand. Ice cracks as Owen prepares to defend, and Aimee braces her feet, her body taking on a rougher texture as she uses her Petrification magic to harden her skin against the bite of a wrasse.

Miles holds up a hand. "Wait."

He stares at the wrasse like the animal holds all his hopes and dreams. Maybe ...

The wrasse barks again, and it's answered by another, larger wrasse that slinks from the forest. This one lifts its snout, sniffing the air. It looks at us, then bolts, northwest. The first wrasse turns to follow, running a few paces, then stops. It looks back at us, runs back, then turns around. It stops again after a few paces and looks back at us again.

Miles pulls himself onto his horse. "Let's go!"

Putting our faith in these two murderous creatures, we all mount up, following an already cantering Miles. We abandon the road to follow the wrasse, tearing across the open land. Hope stirs. The longer we can avoid the press of the jungle or the rocky boulder fields, we can make good time, maybe even close the gap. I don't know how long Halee will be able to hold her magic this time, but I pray she'll have the strength to let us at least get closer. As our horses pound the ground, following the sprinting wrasse, my thoughts turn angry. Both Alopson and Drakam lie to the north, but I feel it, in my gut ... Drakam is behind all this. I disregard Saph's shadowy past with Alopson, and the fact that the grey-cloaks had Saph's weapons on them. I ignore the fact that Alopson is the wealthiest House and could easily fund a covert operation like this, and how such a powerful House would be threatened by someone like Thaeia. I disregard all that. This is Drakam. Why? I don't know, but I feel it with a certainty that boils my blood.

My horse picks up speed as my magic instinctually responds to my emotions. I reach out with my power, touching everyone until our weight is inconsequential on our horses' backs. Their hooves blur over the ground, practically flying. Tears stream from the corners of my eyes from the speed. The wrasse look back, barking as we come alongside them, easily keeping up with their pace. Wrasse can outrun almost every land animal, and they seem agitated at not being able to stay ahead of us. The larger wrasse hisses, flattening its ears, paws blurring as it picks up even more speed. The horses are blowing, and I'm nearly laid out over mine's neck as we race on.

CHAPTER 38

KEIR

My hand grips the doorknob, red flames dancing across my hand. Every muscle in my body tenses at my father's voice. I have to go after her. Who knows what Thaeia will be walking into when she reaches House Drakam ... *if* she reaches House Drakam. It's a four-day journey, three if you push, to get there. I doubt Thaeia will take the extra time it would require to go around the town and cities ...

"Keir, please."

I turn. My father's eyes plead, flicking to the empty chair across from him then back to me. Daria stands behind him to his right, her hand lightly resting on the hilt of her sword. With great reluctance, I cross the room, sitting on the edge of the seat, back straight. Gren flops down at my feet, and Hich sits at my side.

My father nods, then he does something very unlike him ... he begins tapping the table nervously. "I'm not keeping you from going without good reason, son. I ..."

He sighs, pausing his finger mid-tap. For a long moment, he stares at the table without really seeing it. My hand flexes on the arm of the chair, then I slowly force my fingers to relax. "Just spit it out."

His deep blue eyes meet mine. They hold such regret, it nearly steals my breath. "I'm ashamed. I was avoiding my mistakes, my past."

My brows pinch. What does Thaeia have to do with my father's past ... unless he's talking about Saph.

As if thinking of her loosened my father's tongue, he says, "The woman who raised Thaeia, Rhenara—well I guess Thaeia knew her as Saph—she worked for me many years ago. She worked for my father as well. A more talented mage I was hard-pressed to find."

I struggle to keep from fidgeting. I know all this already, but he doesn't know that I know. He doesn't know that Thaeia told me about Saph and her falling out with my father. What I don't know, is why. To settle myself, I run a hand through Hich's fire, wishing I could actually feel him, pet him. But we both gain a little comfort from the gesture.

My father continues, "I was new to my rule as Lord of Alopson. I wanted to prove myself. Ambition is all well and good until it blinds you to the hole you've dug yourself into. Rhenara had a connection at House Drakam." He tsks, shaking his head. "No, that's simplifying it. She had a lover who worked at House Drakam. I ..."

I lean forward, bracing my forearms on the table, letting the slight discomfort of the wood digging into my skin ground me. Gren shifts on the floor, resting his head on my feet. "What? Did you ask her to ask her lover for information, to spy?"

He seems to deflate as he sinks against the back of his chair, sliding down slightly as he rubs a hand over his face. "Worse, Keir. So much worse." His hand falls to the armrest, and he grips it tightly. "The look on her face. Rhenara truly hated me at that moment. I thought if she just had some time to calm down, to think it over, she'd see my side. I left it alone for a time, but I was a fool. I asked again." His head drops, chin to chest. "No, I commanded. She refused. The next day, she was gone."

I sit back, my leg bouncing in growing frustration, forcing Gren to roll to his other side. "And I take it you never found her? Or have you known where she was all these years? Did you know about Thaeia?"

"No. I never found Rhenara. I looked. I searched for so long. She was a friend. She was ..."

Something catches my eye, but I'm not sure I saw what I think I saw. But the raw emotion in his voice stalls my bouncing leg, and my mouth drops open when my father lifts his head. Tears swim in his eyes, one falling down his cheek, dripping from his chin. He doesn't bother to wipe it away. "I was such a fool. I drove her away—the one person who really ..."

I snap my mouth shut as I just sit and blink at him. Did he ... love Rhenara?

Finally, I find my voice. "Did you ask her lover where she was?"

"Fara? Yes. I suspect she knew where Rhenara was. She may be the only one who knew. I'm not sure if Fara still lives."

I tilt my head. "You haven't kept tabs on her?"

"No. I lost track of Fara many years ago." He sits up

straighter, eyes snapping with intensity. "Twenty-eight years ago."

Wait. Isn't that how old …

I shake my head. "I don't understand." Glancing at the door, my leg starts bouncing again. "I need to—"

"You *need* to know what I asked Rhenara to do. You need to know what I've suspected of House Drakam for all these years—what I think they have been hiding for generations. I have no proof. Nothing to back up my suspicions … other than Thaeia. Her existence could very well bring Sodoles to its knees."

It's a good thing I'm already sitting, because what my father tells me next would have buckled my knees. Even Daria, usually so stoic, has a horrified look on her face. My father's confession chills my blood. I'm out of my chair and sprinting towards the stables before my father finishes speaking. In my head, a chant repeats, getting louder, more urgent with every footfall. *Hurry. She doesn't know what she's walking into. Hurry. Hurry. Hurry.*

CHAPTER 39

THAEIA

I'M exhausted but practically vibrating with energy. The only reason I stopped at all the past three days was to let Sampson rest. Arabell was true to her word. Sampson has been the perfect horse—fast, steady, responsive, and willing to go as long as I asked. I chose to rest in open country, camping for short periods before moving on. The towns and cities I passed through were a blur, not giving anyone any time to recognize me or realize I was the cause of their temporary magic failure as Sampson quickly trotted through the streets. Sure, I got a few angry looks, and a few swears were thrown my way as people had to dodge out of the way, but I didn't have time to waste.

Now, House Drakam looms before me, and the anxious energy that's been driving me wavers. I wipe my hands on my pants for what feels like the dozenth time. It's early morning on the fourth day after I left House

Alopson, so the main thoroughfare leading to the gleaming gates of House Drakam is fairly empty. Only a few shop owners move about their businesses, some early risers out for a morning coffee or tea.

I swallow, rubbing my hands on my pants again. I would kill for some coffee right now. Shaking my head, I sit taller in the saddle. I press my lips together as the estate of House Drakam grows larger with every steady clop of Sampson's hooves. I can't help myself from looking over my shoulder like I've done obsessively for the past three days. Keir's still not there. He didn't come.

No matter. I force the press of sadness away, square my shoulders. Four green-clad guards flank the closed gates. One on the right shifts when he sees me. Leaning over, he says something to the guard next to him, and a second later, they fan out, stepping in front of the iron gates with iron dragons flying across the bars.

The guard calls out, "Gates open in an hour. Come back then."

Sampson keeps going, his hooves clopping loudly on the cobbled street. The moment my Void slips around them, I feel simultaneous twinges of power along my shoulders, my palms, my lower back, and my toes of all places. The guard on the far left gasps, but the one who spoke cocks his head at me. "You're the ..." He flexes his left hand. "You're her?"

I raise a brow. Obviously.

Without another word, the four guards step back. One grabs a lever and cranks it. The gates slide open silently. I keep my eyes on the estate as Sampson calmly walks past the guards. The morning shadows are long, but the sky is clearer than it has been in days, and the sun is warm.

But there's still a storm raging in my chest. All I can think about is Halee.

Unlike the smooth sandstone of House Alopson, House Drakam is constructed with hard tropical woods, some field stone, and some metal. It should be warm, but there's a starkness to it that makes me shiver. Or maybe it's the thought of my friend being held within those walls against her will.

No one stops us as Sampson walks right up to the base of the stairs before I pull him to a halt. Swinging down, I give him a pat, having learned over the last few days that even untethered, he won't wander far. But a guard appears, and I stiffen. He stumbles slightly when he crosses into my Void, but recovers fast enough, holding out his hand. "I'll take your horse."

I run my hand down Sampson's soft muzzle. His lips flutter, his warm breath puffing against my palm. If I'm being honest with myself, I may not come out of this alive. I have no idea what Severn Drakam wants with me, but I need to be realistic. Sampson has been good to me. I place the reins in the guard's hand, but don't let go, making sure he meets my eyes as I place a few coins in his other hand. "Make sure he's fed, watered, and rested. Then he needs to be returned to House Alopson." When he doesn't respond, I add, "Please."

He nods, closing his fist around the coins, and leads Sampson away. It's hard to swallow as a rush of melancholy hits me. He's just a horse, but for some reason, watching him being led away makes me want to break down and cry. I bite my lower lip, fist my hands, and start climbing the stairs. The iron and wood doors open, and two guards step aside without a word. The shadows of the interior engulf me slowly, and as the doors clang shut behind me, the warmth of the sun is cut off, leaving me in the cool, dim light of House Drakam.

Other than the guards standing at the door, there's not another soul in this receiving area or the hall beyond. I glance back, but when the guards ignore me, I shrug and stride forward. My footsteps echo down the empty, windowless hall. Reaching the end, I look right, left, then take a slow breath. Now what?

A door opens to my left, and a man steps out into the hall. I recognize him from the brief glance I got of Severn Drakam at the Games. This is a younger version of the Lord of Drakam, obviously one of his three sons. His brown skin appears almost black in the dim light of the hall, but his ochre eyes spear me with so much loathing, I nearly take a step back. What could I have possibly done to make this man hate me so much? Is my mere existence enough to warrant such rage?

Glaring at me, he nearly passes me without a word, but at the last second, mutters, "This way."

My brows rise indignantly. Down one long hall after another, I follow Severn's son, not seeing anyone else in the fifteen minutes it takes us to come to the solid iron doors now before us. The man places his hand on the door and pushes. Slowly, the room beyond is revealed. It's not a huge room, maybe forty paces square. The ceiling is low and painted a dull grey color. There are no windows, so a few flickering arsine torches provide the only light as I swivel my head, looking for Halee.

I spin as the door thuds shut behind me, and Severn's son smirks at me as he walks across the empty room, barking, "Stay."

Like I'm a dog? Oh, I don't think so.

I march after him, raising my hand, pointing angrily at him. "Look. I just want my friend. Where is—"

He's several paces ahead of me, and when he treads across a certain stone, it depresses. A soft click is all the warning I get as thick iron bars shoot out of the floor and slam into the ceiling. My hands wrap around the bars as Severn's son opens a door at the other end of the room. He dips his head inside, saying something before stepping aside.

The iron scrapes against my palms as Severn steps through the door. His eyes find me, hate spilling from their brown depths. But under that, he's afraid. Good. He should be. With slow strides, he moves closer, only stopping when the toes of his boots brush against the edge of a dark line on the floor. I'm a good judge of distance, I've had to be, and he's exactly twenty paces away—right outside my Void.

My knuckles go white, and the iron bites against my skin. "Where's Hal—"

He holds up a hand, nodding his head to his son who steps through the door, returning a moment later. He's not alone, and for a moment I think it's Halee, but this woman is older. Drakam's son practically drags the woman forward, shoving her to her knees at Severn's side. Our eyes meet. Her brown skin is a bit pale, her cheeks hollow. Her brown curls have wisps of grey running through them, and her wrinkled fingers curl into the folds of her dress. If I were to guess, she's about Saph's age ... if she were still alive.

The woman blinks at me with bright green eyes. She looks at me from head to toe and back again. Reading the tattoo on her wrist, I see she has Chromatic magic. That must be a beautiful power.

Severn's voice pulls my attention away from the kneeling woman. "Do you know her?"

My brows scrunch, and I shake my head.

Severn laughs, and the woman flinches as he says, "Go on, tell her your name." This time, when the woman lifts her head, there are tears in her eyes. Her voice is so low, I press my face to the bars, straining to hear her. Severn rolls his eyes. "Louder."

"Fara."

My breath stalls in my chest. *This* is Fara?

Severn's smile twists into something cruel. "So, the face doesn't mean anything, but the name does. Interesting." He turns from me, bending down to grip Fara's chin. "Right there, on the other side of those bars stands the evidence of your guilt. I'll deal with you later."

Severn's son hooks Fara under her arms, dragging her back through the door. Her watery eyes find me again, and just as the door starts to swing shut, she mouths, "I'm sorry."

Sorry? For what?

Doesn't matter. I step back from the bars, dropping my hands to my sides. "I don't know what all these theatrics are for. I'm just here for my friend. Where is Halee?"

Severn waves his hand, slowly walking along the edge of the line on the floor. "She's on her way. I just thought it would be good for us to have some one-on-one time before she arrives." I glare at him, but his smile grows into a knowing grin, the kind of grin that says he's delighted by something. He presses his palm to his chest with a mockery of sadness in his eyes. "After all, don't you want to get to know your father?"

CHAPTER 40

THAEIA

My hands tighten even more on the bars, and my head shakes slowly. No. That can't be true. I'm not ... he's not ...

"Ah, I see you really didn't know. Interesting." He waves his hand again with a dismissive gesture and I focus on his tattoo. ROMMAR. Channel. Four stars climb his light brown skin. He sees the direction of my gaze and smirks. "Ah, yes." Running a finger down his arm, he traces his tattoos. "My gift allows me to take on the power of anyone near me. That range has grown over the years, granting me access to so many different kinds of magic." His self-satisfied tone grates on my nerves. "But not only can I use their magic, I can amplify it, making it more, making it mine."

Keeping his head tilted down, he aims his look at me, eyes staring at me from under his lashes. "You are my antithesis." He drops his gaze again and resumes slowly pacing the edge of the line. "All the females of my line have your ... affliction. They have for generations. Every filthy female born of my seed, my father's seed, his father's seed, has possessed"—his narrowed eyes find me again, shimmering with hate—"the Void."

I release the bars, relaxing my hands at my sides, my left hand hovering over my thigh sheath. "You're lying. Why—"

"Generations ago, your kind were used to moderate, to constrain, to *punish*. And they were quite effective. Until you women got it in your head you were more powerful than the rest of us. It is a little-known fact"—he chuckles to himself, and my fingers graze one of my blades—"well, I guess it's not known anymore. Long ago, three sisters with the power of the Void staged a coup, taking Drakam from its previous ruler. So I guess I should be thankful for your wretched curse." He chuckles again and it sounds manic, the sharp tone echoing off the low ceiling. "It was a bloody affair, and all but one sister died. She held her position by swearing to leash her Void."

My body tenses at that. Leash the Void? How?

"She contained that disgusting nothingness within her, but when her youngest son came for her seat of power, she abandoned her vow ... but it was too late. Her son killed her and began what our family refers to as 'the cleansing.'"

Vomit burns in my throat, and I gulp it down, my eyes burning as my mind guesses where this story is going.

The toe of his boot taps the line as he smiles at me. "He saw the danger of your kind. And while he couldn't prevent his seed from creating female babies, he *could* control whether those babes lived or died."

My hand falls from the hilt of my knife. I stand in

stunned silence. Every female baby born to the Drakam line ...? For generations? Sweat breaks out on my forehead, and for a moment I'm dizzy. But I clear my throat before asking, "How have you kept this secret?"

He chuckles, turning to walk the line back the other way. "History is written by the victor. It took time to erase the records of your kind, and even longer for the memory of you to fade." He waves his hand yet again. "And it became well known that the Drakam line could not produce female children."

I think through what little knowledge I have of the Houses, specifically Drakam. All sons. No daughters. I shake my head. "All the bonded. *Your* bonded. She can't have agreed to this. Someone would have come forward. Someone would have stopped this" He's lying. He has to be lying. This can't ...

He throws back his head, barking a laugh. "They don't know. My bonded is beautiful, and too sweet for this world, but she's not the brightest. Stillborn. Every bonded knows that if the Drakam seed takes and produces a female, that child will be stillborn. They are warned, and to spare them the trauma of going through such an ordeal, they are drugged heavily for each birth. So you see, *daughter*, the lie is intact and easily upheld."

How many of my sisters has this monster killed? The image of Fara on her knees flashes through my mind. She must have gotten me out, gotten me to Saph. But why did she come back here? Why put herself back in the path of such danger? Why not hide with Saph? My hand shifts to hover over my blades again. "Why are you telling me all this?"

A sudden calmness falls over his face as he stops his slow progression along the line. "Because you should understand what is at stake for me, and what I'm capable of. I'm telling you so you are grateful for the opportunity I'm about to offer you."

I sneer. "Grateful?"

The door clicks behind Severn, and the same son from before comes in. My heart drops into my stomach with a thud. Halee lays in his arms, her hair swinging over his arm, her body limp. Severn sees the look on my face, and grins, waving that godsdamned hand again. "Don't worry. She's alive. We just couldn't have her furry little friends interfering."

My arms begin to shake from the rage that burns through me. Halee is alive because she's useful to Severn in some way.

"Let her go. She's not part of this, whatever *this* is. You have me. Let her go."

He tsks, taking a step back from the line. His son sets Halee down at Severn's feet, shooting me a look filled with loathing before leaving the room again. Severn moves to stand behind Halee. "When I saw you at the Games, I was sure you had come to kill me. To kill my sons."

"You blew up the Coliseum."

"I had to protect what is mine. But then I realized ... I might have been squandering something great. My ancestors were afraid of your kind, but with the right ... *management.*" He actually licks his lips. Gross. "Can you control it?"

I force my gaze up from Halee to blink at him. Control what?

He waves his hand at me, and I swear I'm going to cut it off. "Your power. Can you control it?" Should I lie and say yes? I didn't even know it was controllable. He hums at my silence. "Let's test it."

My eyes drop to Halee. *No.*

A single thread of his shirt unravels and drops to the floor. It snakes over the stone, then lifts into the air, stiffening. When the light of a torch hits it just right, it gleams with lethal sharpness. The point moves towards Halee.

My arm is a blur as I grab one of my knives and throw it at Severn's head. It hits an invisible barrier, clattering to the floor loudly. I stop myself from throwing another. I only have so many blades on me ... six more to be exact.

"Tell me what you want. Just let her go."

"That is up to you." He waves his hand, and I'm clutching another blade before I can think about it. I keep myself from throwing it, but it's a hard-won battle as he says, "Stop me, and she lives. She gets to go home."

Panic steals my breath. How? I search for some flaw in the barrier he has constructed between us, but I can't even tell where it begins or ends. I don't know what magic is available to him right now. How? Think.

He takes one step forward so his boot lands next to Halee's head, and the needle-sharp thread hovers over her neck. "Use your power to stop me. Take my magic, Thaeia."

That's the first time he's used my name, and it sounds dirty. I've never hated my name so much. In quick succession, I whip three blades at him ... face, chest, gut. Two hit his barrier and fall, the third stops mid-air right in front of his stomach. The knife turns slowly to face me, then flies forward. As soon as it hits my Void, it loses the momentum of the magic propelling it and clatters to the floor.

Severn growls. "Go on!" He cackles madly. "Stop me!"

The thread-turned-blade presses to Halee's skin, and a

bead of blood wells up. She stirs, moaning, moving her head, causing the thread to go deeper.

Shit! I look around frantically, another knife in my hand. I grip it so tight, the leather hilt creaks. My other hand comes to the bars, squeezing one tightly as I press my body against the cold iron. "Please."

He just raises a brow at me. I hold my breath and bear down, willing my Void to expand. Just a few inches. That's all I need. I plead with the gods, desperate. *Please, if anyone is listening, please.* I imagine pushing my Void outward. My lungs burn as I beg my Void to save Halee.

Opening my eyes, my breath wooshes out. Nothing. The thread still presses to Halee's throat, and now her eyes are open. Her confused gaze falls on me, and her voice cracks. "Thaeia?"

Severn drops his voice in warning. "Last chance."

Absolute terror and rage sharpen my vision onto my father. "I will kill you." Keeping my eyes on him, I shout, "Halee, use your magic, NOW!"

Severn sighs. "So disappointing."

Halee's eyes go wide, and her body arches as the thread slices deep.

"NO!" My blade falls from my hand, but I don't hear it hit the floor. Halee's blood pools around her, soaking into her dark curls. Her body jerks, her hands weakly reaching for her neck. Slowly, like the sun setting, her body goes still, her arms falling to her sides, her gaze emptying.

Severn tsks. "This is your fault, Thaeia. You could have sav—"

A force explodes out of me, and Severn takes several steps back, eyes wide with fear for the first time since he entered this room. *Yes. Let me see your terror,* Father. *Tremble before me.* The force pulses out of me again, stronger. My Void spreads like the shockwaves of an explosion. My entire body tingles as hundreds, then thousands of powers snuff out against my Void. The edges of my vision darken, and I grin at Severn who raises his left hand, arm trembling. His lips form my name, but I can't hear it. My gaze drops to the floor, to the bright red blood, to Halee's open, unseeing eyes.

My heart shatters into a million pieces. I'm torn apart. There's a ringing in my ears, and I realize I'm screaming. The next pulse that comes from me is so powerful, the bars shake. I grab them, my screams growing louder. My fingertips are black, like I dipped them in soot. With every pulse, the darkness spreads, crawling up my fingers, over my hands.

I have the vague thought that I should be worried, or panicked, or ... something, but I'm not. I'm just angry. So angry. As the black overtakes my wrists, a word circles my skin, created by the absence of the darkness spreading up my arms. I fully expect to see QUED, the word for Void, but instead I read, KURKODAM. Forsaken.

A laugh bubbles up through my despair. Of course.

Abandon all hope, those who enter my Void, for we are all Forsaken. The darkness creeps up my arms, tendrils curling around my biceps. Severn's eyes go wide, the whites standing out stark against his brown skin and the brown of his irises. He backs away, keeping his eyes on me as he leaves through the door.

I shout after him, my voice so filled with rage it doesn't sound like mine. "I will kill you! Severn Drakam! I WILL kill you!" My hands loosen on the bars, as I continue to yell, "I'll kill you! I'll kill you!"

My knees buckle, and the pulsing power slows then stops. I hit the floor, pain shooting up my legs. I don't care.

Halee's lifeless arm is splayed out from her body, as if reaching for me. I need to get to her. I ... She needs me ... My shoulder presses to the bars as I reach through. My blackened fingers stretch, and the iron digs into my chest. My body slides down parallel with the bars, and my cheek presses to the cold floor. My fingers scrape at the stone, reaching for Halee's outstretched hand.

"Come on Halee, wake up." My fist slaps the cold stone floor. "Come on. Come on!" She doesn't move. The blood around her is darker now. My hand falls flat. A sob tears from me. There's a crashing sound from somewhere, but I can't stop staring at Halee's blood, her life force. My body goes numb. I can't breathe. The darkness recedes down my arms, the script around my wrist disappearing. All I see is blood, so much blood—the consequences of the secrets kept from me my entire life.

My broken mind catches on those words, repeating over and over until I'm sure I've gone mad. *Blood and Secrets. Blood and Secrets. Blood and Secrets.*

ALSO BY T. B. WIESE

Scan the code below for links to my Amazon author page where you'll find all my other books - including the next book in this series.

You'll also find a link to my website for signed paperbacks & hardcovers as well as swag.

ACKNOWLEDGMENTS

A huge thank you to my readers. Without you, this crazy dream of being an author would not be possible.

To all my beta & ARC readers, thank you! Debbie, Mackenzie, Erica ... You had a big hand in making this novel what it is today. Thank you so very much for taking the time to help me polish this story.

Thank you to Marcelle for such wonderful edits. Your encouragement and insightful notes took this story to a whole other level.

And lastly, I want to thank all my friends and family for cheering me on and being as excited about my characters as I am—I love my tribe.

ABOUT THE AUTHOR

T. B. Wiese is a military spouse, dog mom, photographer, Disney nerd, and lover of spicy fantasy. She loves animals (She grew up with dogs and working with horses, including working at the Tri-Circle D Ranch at Disney World), so don't be surprised when you find yourself reading lovable animal characters in her novels.

If you'd like to keep up to date with future releases as well as new swag and sales, sign up for her newsletter via link in code below.

SCAN THE CODE WITH YOUR CAMERA APP FOR
HER SOCIAL LINKS